Prologue

Paris, 1 June 1944

Juliette Vernier lifted her apron to the glass door of the Café des Fleurs and rubbed at the condensation in a circular motion. Beyond the café's outside tables, with chairs leaning against them waiting for a new day to begin, was the broad boulevard of the Champs-Élysées and beyond further, the Arc de Triomphe. It was a view that had once exhilarated Juliette with the excitement of just being there, but now that she was older and thinner, and perhaps a little wiser, it invoked nothing, nothing at all.

The Café des Fleurs was a small, insignificant café and not one popular with soldiers. It had not been listed in the *Wichtig Für Soldaten* (the essential guide for German soldiers) but even so, a swastika insignia hung from a flag pole attached to the apartment above the café, which meant that even if she wanted to allow her imagination to drift beyond the realms of the occupation, there was no escaping the Nazis. However, this

1

particular swastika was beginning to look as tired and worn out as the people it presided over, and the soldiers too.

Wrapping a red shawl tightly around her shoulders (the tasselled type that spoke of brightly painted caravans and crystal balls), she stepped out of the café and began to set the chairs beneath the tables, shaking the night's rain off each one and wiping the tables down with a cloth. Juliette liked the rhythmic reliability of this action, even on the rainy days, when she would watch through the window for the clouds to part and dash out to complete her ritual. Today would likely be a busier day, the sunshine would bring them out – little else did, these days. She positioned the last chair neatly under a table, glanced down the tree-lined avenue and, raising a hand to shade the glare of the rising sun, felt a sense of wellbeing she had not experienced in quite some time. Even the sight of a German soldier emerging through beams of sunshine in the distance did not dampen her mood. She paused a moment to watch the polished boots approach, the officer's cap pulled low, his footsteps echoing down the avenue, an avenue designed for many things but not this kind of quietness. Stepping back into the café, she turned the sign from 'closed' to 'open', and even if the approaching uniform decided to pause a while and sit at one of her tables, today would be a good day. She was certain of it. She might even smile at him.

And he did take a seat at one of the tables, with his back to the window.

'There's a man at table seven,' said Louis, the owner, walking into the café from the back room, his hands covered in dough. He nodded towards the window, a curt kind of a nod. 'It's one of their lot. Top brass, by the looks of things.'

Juliette glanced at herself in the mirror that lined the wall behind the counter.

'Dreadful,' she said, attempting to tidy her hair.

'The hair or the soldier?' asked Louis.

'Both!' she replied.

Louis smiled and handed her a notepad and pencil.

'Don't be nice to him. We don't want his type here.' He placed the pencil behind her ear, leaving a trace of dough in her hair. He tightened the wrap around her shoulders. 'You're too thin. Have you eaten yet?'

'I'll eat with the children later.'

'Juliette …'

'I cannot eat while my orphans starve,' she said. 'And anyway, I'm not hungry.'

Louis took a deep breath and nodded. 'Looks like it might rain again,' he said, glancing outside.

'No,' she said, brightly. 'It's sunny now.' She kissed him on the cheek, skipped out into the street and readied herself for the faux show of civility she had become used to.

The officer was bent over, seemingly having trouble with his left boot.

'Bonjour, monsieur,' she said, with an appropriate but not offensive hint of gruffness.

'Pardon. Bonjour.' He began to straighten.

'Some coffee and a pastry, perhaps?' Juliette spoke in French, taking the pencil from behind her ear. 'I should tell you that we have no cream today …'

'No cream?' he repeated, sitting upright.

The answer was out before she could button it in, 'There is a war on, Monsieur.'

Regretting her foolish response, Juliette focused on the notebook rather than his face, a habit she had developed when serving the Nazis. But eventually, she had to look at the man, because he was staring straight at her, and when she finally saw his face, the light fell out of the day and the whole of Paris went black. And as she fell to the pavement she heard a name called out that she hadn't heard for quite some time ... 'Sophie!'

Chapter One

La Santé Prison, August, 1944

I always knew I would find myself here. I told Sophie as much. For some years I have held a healthy respect for the principle of karma. It is as if somehow, stored in that place of unconscious thought – that untapped place behind the mind where our ancestors left a wealth of information – lies the knowledge that, just as good deeds must be paid forward, so must bad ones be. Finding myself here in this place of dark depravity has, therefore, been of no surprise, because it was, ultimately, inevitable. As I have been running from karma for years, it is a relief to have been finally caught up with because running is exhausting, and I wonder, when the guard's key rattles in the lock for the final time, is that all that I will feel in the end? Relief?

The key rattles now.

I feel no relief.

Nor am I frightened. But that is only because I have heard no hammering of boots indicating the gathering of a squad in the courtyard above my cell, nor have I heard the dragging of wood on the dirt.

My cell is a squalid place of green/brown dripping walls and a bucket of unemptied excrement. I do have a wooden bunk, collapsed at one end, but my main complaint is that it is far too big for one man and his thoughts to inhabit alone. I would have preferred a smaller cell, I could have gathered my thoughts easier there, kept them penned in, controlled. But at least I am not tethered in chains and I have a little light. The light filters through a barred grate that sits too high in the wall for me to look through and yet awards a little air and an insight into the goings on 'up there' from day to day. Behind the grate is the prison's central courtyard, dusty at this time of year, and almost certainly as hot as hell. I am happiest when it is empty of marching boots, because marching boots are often followed by pleading – there is always pleading – followed by a round of gunshots, or the sharp slicing of a heavy sharpened blade cutting through bone and flesh.

The guillotine has returned to Paris. I fear it never left.

The key ends its rattling and the heavy door begins to open. I stand, although the beatings and insufficient rations render it a little painful. My jailor gave me water this morning, so I am at least lucid for my visitor.

A gas lantern enters the room first, followed by a cross – a Christian cross. It rests awkwardly at the end of a chain on the chest of a German army uniform, which in turns sits awkwardly on the body of the man wearing it – a Nazi chaplain, around my age, early forties, perhaps a little older. Like unicorns and mermaids, I doubted the existence of German chaplains as I have seen none since my arrival in Paris. In the last war there were many but now, hardly any at all. The SS don't have them, nor do the Luftwaffe – Göring forbade it. And yet one stands before me – Hitler must have kept a few for the army, perhaps to add legitimacy to his reign of terror. The swastika armband is loose around the man's arm. He is too thin. My father used to say, 'No man fills a uniform properly until he is at least twenty-eight' but these days, no man fills a uniform at all.

I sigh at the sight of him. Nazi or not, the chaplain has come, and like the unsettled caw of crows before a thunderstorm, they rarely herald good news.

He presses the backs of his fingers against his nose and takes a breath.

'It is the bucket,' I say. 'The guard does not empty it often.'

He nods to my jailor, indicating his wish to be alone, before glancing around in the dim light to find there is no stool for him to sit upon. I lean against the far wall, under the grate. He pushes spectacles further up his nose and as the door closes, he steps forward as if approaching a temperamental animal and says, 'Sascha?'

I sigh.

'I am not Sascha Braun,' I say.

He does not offer a strong reaction. 'Why did you not tell the authorities this?' he says.

'Because I would be tortured as a spy, rather than beaten as an undesirable. But as it is of no consequence now, you might as well know the truth … My name is Sebastian. Sascha is my twin brother. I probably know this already, but why have you come?'

He glances at his boots. 'To offer you absolution in your final days. And … to talk to you. To help you.'

'I'm sorry but you are wasting your time. Your religion means nothing to me, at least not when it is mixed in a foul concoction with that uniform. And the cross you wear will not loosen my tongue. You are nothing more than a stooge of the SS, of that I am sure.'

'I am a stooge for no one but the Lord,' he says, leaning his stick against the wall and taking out a handkerchief. He wipes the sweat from his brow and then coughs into it. He glances at the contents before swiftly folding the handkerchief away. There is a weariness to his voice. He retrieves the stick and leans more of his weight on it. 'I wish to hear your confession and attempt to save your soul,' he says. 'I have done so countless times for many other inmates and I assure you, it will help.'

I think of another pastor I once met, in another war. Such an occupation must surely warp a man.

Boots cross the courtyard. He glances towards the grate.

'How much time do we have, before …?'

'It is not confirmed,' he says. 'A few days?'

The next question has to be asked. 'Guillotine or firing squad?'

'I do not know,' is his answer, and I believe him.

'I would prefer the squad, if you can arrange it.'

He nods his acquiescence.

I lift a hand to my chin and rub. The sensation is not a familiar one. There is matted hair where I was once clean shaven, and my fingers are twisted where they were once straight. A few days … so that is all that is left for me. My mind's eye flashes to an image – a woman, an island, another time. How do I wish to spend these last days? In solitude, or in confiding (or confessing as he would put it) to this man of cloth? I briefly wonder what the difference is between the two words.

'What religion are you?' I ask.

'Roman Catholic.'

'And so the things I tell you within these walls ...'

'Are bound by confessional, yes.'

'I have nothing to confess ...' I hesitate for a moment because of course I have something to confess. We all do. I change tack. This man could possibly help. 'Look, if you allow me to tell you my story – my *whole* story – and prove to you my true identity, then afterwards, if you accept that I am who I say I am, will you make sure that my real name is written down ... on ... on whatever paperwork these monsters keep? I want to be recorded in my own name, my *own* name, you hear me, and in years to come, when they ask who was lost in this place, *my* name will be registered here. In itself, it matters not, but there may be one who looks for me ...' My voice begins to break '... and she will want to know to stop looking. If you agree to this – if you swear by that almighty God of yours to keep your side of the bargain – then I will allow you to hear my confession.'

He nods his agreement.

'And I will need sustenance,' I say. 'My confession must have the context of a story.' I smile, it is almost a forgotten sensation. 'And a story, even a short one, cannot be told on a stomach that knows only bile.'

He turns towards the door. 'Very well.'

'Also ... please. Could you ... could you bring me some other clothes? I do not wish to die in this uniform. I am not a Nazi.' He steps towards me to stand under the light of the grate and takes a good long look at my face, as if trying to solve all the riddles of the universe. His gaze is not disconcerting. This man has a gentle soul. His breathing slows. He is calmer now.

'This has not been a good war for you,' I say, for I have gazed at him as much as he has gazed at me.

He limps towards the door. I reach out to place a hand on his arm.

'Has your own soul not been corrupted too?' I whisper. 'Watching innocent men – and women – die horrible deaths for no reason?'

He steps away. 'I will return tomorrow,' he says, taking up his stick and heading for the door.

'Who sent you, really?' I ask. He hits the stick on the door but I continue. 'Prisoners are not usually allowed several days of pastoral care.'

'I'm here of my own doing,' he says, facing the door.

'Why?'

The door opens. He turns.

'I have my reasons.'

The chaplain disappears. I look by my feet. He has left me the lantern.

Chapter Two

The chaplain's name is Christoph Wagner and he is from Leipzig.

I know this because the next morning, when I say, 'What shall I call you? Chaplain? Padre?' he says, 'My name is Christoph Wagner, but please, call me Christoph.'

'Like the composer,' I joke. 'He was from Leipzig.'

'Like the composer,' he answers, dully.

True to his word he has brought food – bread and a little cheese – and water. And a stool.

'I didn't think you would do this, not really.' He unwraps a baguette from a cloth. 'Surely it is against prison rules to bring me extra food, even for a chaplain?'

He glances up. 'I have my ways.'

'Even though it is a waste as I am to be shot?'

'Even then. And it is not a waste.'

I try to keep the frustration from my voice when I say, 'I have told you, you remember, that I am not a Nazi officer. I am not Sascha Braun. I am a doctor, that is all I am.'

'But the guards do not know that,' he says, handing me half

of the bread with a wink. 'And they would never believe you even if you told them.'

'You believe me, though?' I ask, hopefully.

'I do,' he says. 'So for now … let us eat!'

If I devour the food quickly I will not only vomit but lose what little dignity remains. In a week's time I will be beyond hunger and have no worries about dignity – about anything – but for now, I am able to eat the food slowly, civilly, and pretend that I am breaking bread with a friend. He has brought herbs, too – lavender and some marjoram – and ordered the bucket to be removed and emptied. There is a quiet authority about the man, despite his soulful eyes. The guard senses it. He does not shrug with the chaplain as he does with other officers.

Christoph lights the lantern, hangs it on a hook on the cell wall close to me, then positions his stool so that it does not rock on the cobbled floor. He hands me the lavender after breaking off a sprig and attaching it to his lapel. Lavender on the lapel of a Nazi uniform? It gives me hope. And hope is what I must hold on to now, right until the last second before the blade drops or the shot is fired. I must never give up the fight to survive, but think of ways to keep my soul attached to this mortal body, this precious host. Sophie taught me that. 'Accept and give in,' she said, 'and the end will come. But keep planning, hoping, scheming, and there is always a chance, as slight as it may be, on changing the outcome.' I sniff the lavender and I am on the island again, in my garden, and despite my promise to keep believing, I feel great chokes of emotion building in my gullet. I love this earth, this planet. I love the seasons and the rise and fall of the sun and the moon. I love the swell of the waves against La Coupée after the storm has past, and I love the feel of a woman's hand in mine, her shoulder resting on mine, her lips touching mine.

I bow my head and fight back the building panic. When I look up, I am grateful for the dark.

'I am ready to hear your confession,' he says, wiping his mouth with a clean handkerchief. The man has eaten very little. His rasping breath worries me. His limp worries me, although he has good teeth, for all that. 'Where would you like to begin?'

I smell the lavender again and, smiling now at the thought of home, I turn my thoughts to where the foundations of this particular story found its roots, to a tiny island where time didn't so much stand still as simply fail to exist.

'We begin as we will end, with Sophie,' I say. 'And it is a story, not a confessional.'

**Sark
Channel Islands**

_____

June 1940

Chapter Three

The hand-written sign was unmissable, if suffering from a little weather damage, and stood tall as a church spire by the gate to Gardener's Cottage, my home on Sark. The sign, written in English rather than in the local Sercquiais, as my mastery of the dialect being sketchy at best, conveyed the following information:

Dr Sebastian Braun
Surgery hours 2p.m. until 3p.m. weekdays only
Stretcher cases to be taken directly to the potting shed
No malingerers

I was once, not so long ago, a strong, attractive man in possession of a full set of excellent teeth. It is my experience that a man in possession of strong, straight, clean white teeth has an easier time of things (being, for some reason, automatically regarded as honest and trustworthy) than a man who, for whatever reason (fighting or a fondness for cider, perhaps) has not been gifted with such dental blessings. And so, thanks to my teeth (and my bramble gin), the Sark islanders (six hundred of them in total, not including the animals to whom I also tended) accepted that they were allowed one hour per day to seek medical attention, which was all they needed as it happened, because on an island such as Sark, where everyone grows their own food and raises their own livestock and walks everywhere on account of the absence of roads and vehicles, the inhabitants were very rarely ill.

I arrived at the island fifteen years before, blown in on a warm, easterly summer breeze, a breeze laden with the evocative scents of French living, which for me had been wonderful but heady and overly stimulating. The food, the wine, the people of France – Paris, in particular – had been full of exotic exuberance, and I had loved it for a time, but suddenly found myself searching for a new kind of living – a slower kind of living – and so I set sail for an island that seemed to beckon me home. And when the island's doctor happened to fall ill and die on the very day I arrived, I took it as a sign to set myself up as doctor in residence, and never once did I look back.

At first there was plenty of talk about me. I am German and although I willingly threw off the shackles of nationality years ago, my nationality would not, it seemed, unshackle me. I was known locally as Herr Doktor, although I also heard myself referred to as the Good Doctor, which I preferred.

The question was raised now and again as to why I remained single, especially as a number of eligible women had glanced my way. There was also confusion regarding my passion for gardening, because on Sark, horticulture – when ornamental rather than agricultural – was regarded as being more suited to a man in his dotage than to a man who should be sowing his wild oats, both the literal and metaphorical kind, while he could.

After about five years of residency I began to be left alone to tend to my patients and my garden, which suited me perfectly, especially as I had been lucky enough to take up the tenancy of – and admittedly it is only my opinion but I do believe it is a correct one – the prettiest of all cottages on the island, which was nestled in the most delightful spot on Little Sark, where the sun, varying in intensity and colour depending on the time of year, cast a warming glow across the soft grey stone of the house, and where the shade of the apple orchard, just to the side of the cottage, allowed for an hour of hammock-induced slumber on a hot summer's afternoon. The fertile pasture at the rear, full south-facing and now established as a potager, played host – in perfectly ordered beds – to my passion for fruit, vegetable and cut flower growing, and of course, my roses. The whole plot was edged to perfection with a mixed hedgerow of hawthorn, hornbeam, sloe and elder, which I allowed to run rampant, providing a home to garden birds who repaid me by eating the slugs and snails. And all the while the bees that grew drunk on pollen slept the sleep of kings while resting on the soft bed of a sunflower heart. It was, frankly, perfection. But I doubt it still is.

June 1940 brought lovely weather; the type where a man can roll up his shirt sleeves, grab his garden fork and dig, which was exactly what I intended to do on the day my story begins. Nature had passed a threshold and the only way forward was growth and fecundity, warmth and contentment. The apple blossom had just gone over and with the next flush of rain, even more buds would appear on the roses and an abundance of little seedlings would break through to become bed mates for the faded tulips. And all was very much well with the world.

Having completed some heavy digging and thinking of my scented geranium cuttings which required some attention, I wandered into my wooden greenhouse – a dilapidated wood-framed construction that clung on, with rusty nails and fifteen coats of flaking olive-coloured paint, to the cottage's west facing wall. Absorbed in my pottering with the geraniums and enjoying Mozart on the radio, I heard the garden gate click open but did not glance at my watch. I sighed. The day had gotten away from me. It was two p.m. already and my first patient had arrived. Even so, I ignored the click of the gate because on every afternoon so far this week, some minor injury or another had conspired to keep me away from my garden and surely I deserved a little extra time now to potter. Also, the patient was Mrs Margery Picot, a thirty-seven-year-old woman with a very robust constitution who, until two years ago when she married a local man, kept house for me. I knew that she would happily let herself into my kitchen and tidy while she waited. And so I continued in my occupation of potting on a cutting in one of a selection of clay pots I purloined from Joseph Martin, who is the gardener at La Seigneurie, the house where the feudal dame lived – lives still, I hope. Joseph was in his mid-sixties with a few missing teeth but in excellent health for all that. I had lanced his bunion only last week. The pot was offered as payment and was gratefully received.

With the geranium cuttings firmly in place, I rubbed the leaf of the mother plant (lemon – delicious) before stepping out to quickly turn over the compost heap with my favourite garden fork, which was my mother's. The handle was repaired recently by the undertaker thanks to a spell of gout. I was just about to put down my fork (Margery would have brewed the tea by now) when I heard the gate click open a second time. It *could* be Joules Petard (haemorrhoids), or perhaps Jacob Jones (fungal nails) but either way, Margery would have tea and cake (hopefully lemon) on the table before their caps were removed and folded into a frayed pocket at the door.

When the gate clicked open for a third time, I decided that it really was time to rest my fork, dip under a honeysuckle archway and wash my hands and face at the water pump. Husbandry complete, I ducked under the door beam that leads directly into the kitchen and found Margery Picot smiling up at me, kettle in hand, while Joules, who had taken a seat at the table, was showing off his diseased fingernails to the admiring Jacob, who did not take up Margery on the offer of a chair but hovered by the mangle, on account of his haemorrhoids. Thankfully he did not return the compliment by showing off his own ailment too.

Polite conversation lasted for about an hour (Margery had not brought lemon cake but she offered up the last remnants of her infamous Christmas cake instead, which was a worthy substitute and still moist on account of her accidently spilling more brandy than strictly necessary into the mixture). We wandered out to take a look at my nursery beds, which had become a kind of 'pick your own' area for friends and neighbours. Margery helped herself to a rose cutting while Jacob and Joules tussled over a well-rooted hydrangea. A half hour later still, having returned to the kitchen for further repose, and after glancing purposefully at the kitchen clock and feeling that sufficient time had passed in neighbourliness, I cleared away the tea things and suggested that Margery follow me through to the surgery, which was the dining room before I arrived. She declined the opportunity of 'first dibs at the good doctor' (Jacob's words) and blushing a little, began to make a 'song and dance' (Joules' words) about the washing up of the tea things.

Sensing that Margery required more of me than a ten-minute appointment, I asked which of the gentlemen would like to see me first, and after ten minutes of wrangling, it was decided that Joules would, but they were, they confirmed, more than happy for me to conduct their consultations in the kitchen ('no secrets here, Doctor'), especially if 'Mrs Picot might be good enough to pop the kettle on again'. And she was. It was only when the garden gate clicked open for a fourth time to show that both Joules and Jacob, having decided to saunter home together and take a slight detour (to see if Jack Portreath's dahlias had survived the winter having been 'left out without a spot of mulch over them'), had definitely left the premises, that Margery finally stepped into the surgery for her consultation. I dropped formalities, gestured that my patient take a seat and began with, 'How have you been keeping, Margery?' ('How have you been keeping' was a turn of phrase I adopted shortly after arriving on Sark in order to sound a little more Anglo and a little less Teutonic, even though the phrase never sat comfortably with me in the context of a doctor's surgery. After all, if the answer is 'I'm keeping well, thank you,' then why on earth visit the doctor?)

'I am keeping well, thank you, Sebastian,' answered Margery, who was also quick to adopt our old Christian name informality. She glanced around the room, no doubt noticing the fine layer of dust that would have been absent in her day.

I tried another tack.

'That is very good to hear. But what is it that brings the doctor to your door today?'

Margery laughed. 'Ah, but you *haven't* come to my door,

Doctor. I have come to yours.' She smoothed down her tweed skirt. 'As you see!'

I laughed also, although it was a little forced, and I agreed that she had indeed 'got me there' while wondering why the people of Sark could never, not once, do me the favour of getting directly to the point. I placed my hands together and lifted my fingers to my nostrils – lemon balm. Margery's gaze drifted towards the window and wandered out into the orchard, where it stayed. The faraway look told me that I needed to grasp this nettle so I got directly to the point, which I could get away with on account of my nationality and accent, and said, 'Margery. Are you ill?'

Margery shuffled in her seat. 'Well, no, not really. But it's not easy to talk about such things … such womanly things, even with you.'

'What things?'

'Private things. Personal things. I suppose I've come to see you as much as a friend as a patient. After all, I did keep house for you for quite a number of …' She finally looked at me directly rather than out of the window. 'I mean to say … we are *friends*, aren't we, Doctor?'

I smiled and realised that I would be lucky to see my garden again before nightfall. 'Of course we are.'

She returned to the habit of smoothing down her skirt. 'But, as I say, it's a sensitive subject to talk about with a man – or a woman, come to that.'

I leant forward in my chair and raised a left eyebrow in a way that has never failed to hurry patients on. Suitably chivvied, Margery looked me straight in the eye and said, 'I need you to make my husband better.'

'Is he ill?' I asked.

'No.'

'Then how can I?'

'In bed,' she clarified. 'Better … in bed.'

I took a deep breath. After a moment's pause, I stood and gestured towards the door.

'In that case,' I said, 'I'm afraid we are going to need more tea.'

'Can we use the special teapot?' she asked, standing, her manner much improved.

I took a moment to consider this. 'Of course,' I said, before following Margery once more into the kitchen while wondering why on earth I persisted in trying to corral my patients into the surgery when they all – every single one of them that could still walk unaided (and even the ones who couldn't) – gravitated back to the kitchen after five minutes of consultation, that's if they ever left it in the first place.

———

Margery poured her cup first from my special teapot – it's called an assassin's teapot. To explain:

My assassin's teapot was given to me in the winter of 1920 by a Russian émigré – a count and a distant cousin – who had sought me out in Paris. He had fled the revolution three years before and thrown himself at my mother's mercy only to be sent on to me in Paris thanks to my father taking a dislike to him. The poor man subsequently fell ill with tuberculosis but in truth, he was already dying of a broken heart; heartbroken for his mother – not his real one, but Russia. On the eve of his death he gave me the teapot and explained its significance. It was an assassin's teapot, he said, which had been a family whimsy. Originating in China, it was a very old and very valuable teapot. Made of jade with a golden handle and in the shape of a dragon, it had two chambers, which could be filled with two different liquids. There was a small hole on the top of the teapot by the handle, and another underneath the handle itself. Place a finger discreetly over the top hole while pouring and one chamber would be emptied, place a finger over the other hole and liquid would pour from the second chamber. Place a finger over neither, and both would empty simultaneously. It is all to do with air pressure and it is called the assassin's teapot because it can be used to kill. The person in receipt of the tea watches his adversary drink first, unaware that his own cup has been poured from the second chamber. The adversary then sips up his poison willingly, believing it to be safe.

Margery *loved* this teapot!

She placed her finger over the hole by the handle on the top of the pot, and tea appeared. Moments later, she placed a finger over the hole at the bottom of the teapot and whisky poured out into the same cup. She beamed up at me.

'It never fails to amaze me,' she said, her eyes beaming. 'And to think, this very teapot may have actually been used to assassinate someone – more than one person – all those years ago.' She put the cup to her lips and paused before drinking. 'Do you think there might be traces of arsenic in it?'

'I should think any poisonous traces have long since disappeared,' I said. 'And we have drunk from it many times before.'

She smiles and sips on her concoction before laughing. 'You wouldn't want to get your holes mixed up though, would you?' she said. 'You'd end up killing yourself, not the other fellow!'

'Indeed you wouldn't,' I said, glancing at the clock. 'Now then, do carry on with our discussion …'

'You see ... I wouldn't have known that we weren't doing it properly if it wasn't for another man I once knew.' She hesitated a moment and blushed. 'Called ... Matthew.'

Now, living on an island three miles long and under two miles wide, where everyone travels by foot or by horse and cart, there was inevitably a lot of chatter as people passed by each other's houses and fields, and as a result I knew that there was no Matthew, and that the man in question was in reality a plumber called Tom, who arrived on a clipper out of Plymouth three years ago having been sent for by the Seigneur of Sark (Dame Sibyl) to attend to her 'monumental problem' at La Seigneurie (her house), that being acres of corroding pipework running rampage around the house and also a somewhat temperamental boiler. But the middle-aged Lothario otherwise known as Tom spent more time working his magic on the only amenable spinster on the island (Margery) than on the plumbing, and it was common knowledge that she had been led 'right royally down the garden path' (Joules' words) by a chancer who, two months after arriving, had jumped on board another clipper bound for Brittany in the dead of night, leaving both Dame Sibyl and her dodgy boiler, and the newly pregnant and unmarried Margery, 'up shit creek without any kind of paddle' (Joules again). Rescue had come in the form of Harold Picot, the butcher of the island and a bachelor, who had immediately stepped in to save Margery's blushes 'and to have the best cook and bottle washer on the island tend to his home' (that from Joseph). Margery had subsequently miscarried on her wedding night, leaving her, as always it seems in matters of the heart, much worse off than when the whole sorry saga began.

'I think you mean Tom,' I said, while pouring Margery her second tot of brandy, the first having been necked back immediately. The cup paused in front of Margery's mouth. 'It is always best to tell the truth, Margery,' I added, taking a sip from my own cup. 'We have known each other for a long time and the truth saves much ...' I paused to search for the correct word in English.

'Bother?' offered Margery.

'Exakt!' (I often returned to my native tongue when moments arose that required exclamation). 'Yes, there is no doubt that the truth saves bother – in the long run.'

'Then the truth is, Sebastian, that I would like to divorce my husband, but I cannot.'

'Why?'

'There is no divorce on Sark. Dame Sibyl does not allow it.'

I put a hand to my forehead. Feudalism! I was about to enter into my diagnosis of the problem, the problem being her husband's 'want of passion' as Margery eventually worded it, or more precisely, Harold's inability to pleasure his wife in a manner she would like him to pleasure her due to his being a shy, fifty-five year-old toothless man (see!) – previously a virgin – who was no doubt experiencing intermittent erectile disfunction, probably brought on by a combination of age, diet, alcohol consumption and the stress of trying to please a much younger wife, and suggest a programme of treatment, when the garden gate clicked open and Joseph Martin, the gardener from the big house, rushed in.

'I'm sent to tell you there's an emergency, Doctor.' He panted out the words while leaning with both hands on the kitchen table.

'Is it Dame Sibyl?' I was already heading to the surgery to

grab my doctor's bag. Joseph took a seat while I paused at the door. 'Or is Poppy about to whelp?'

'It's not the dame, and it's not the dog, neither, although she can't be long before she's dropping those pups. Got titties swinging around like udders, she has. No, it's the new lassie who needs you.'

New lassie?

'What new lassie?'

'Niece of Dame Sibyl. Sophie somebody. Come over from France to escape the ...' Joseph floundered and looked towards Margery for help, but Margery was finding the back of her hand rather interesting suddenly.

'Nazis?' I finished for him.

'Well, yes. The Nazis. She's American! What do you think about that? *And* a divorcee!'

'I heard that, too!' said Margery.

'It's true,' said Joseph. '*She* divorced *him*! But then she's from America so what do you expect.'

'An American, then?' repeated Margery, somewhat unnecessarily.

'Sort of.'

'How can you be 'sort of' American?' asked Margery.

'I'm only repeating what I was told,' he said, a little haughtily. 'She's some kind of government official for the Brits now, that's how she ended up living in Paris – she's been living there, you see – but then she jumped ship to here, what with the Germans being on their way.'

'It all sounds very complicated,' surmised Margery, quite correctly for once. 'Does she have an American accent?'

Joseph shook his head. 'Yes and no. It's more ... neutral. Her mother was French and her father was American and ...'

'I do not need her life history,' I said, trying to grab a hold of the madness. 'Just a reason why I am beckoned to attend.'

Joseph shrugged. 'She's gone lame all of a sudden …'

'Lame? The lassie or the dog?'

'The lassie. Although, she's a bit long in the tooth to be calling her a lassie.'

This pricked up Margery's ears.

'*How* long in the tooth?' she asked.

Joseph shrugged. 'Not sure. Thirties? Looks good on it though.'

Margery's lips formed a thin line.

'Dame Sibyl wants you to have a look at her ankle.'

'How did she damage it?' I asked.

He pointed with his thumb in the direction of La Seigneurie. 'There's a fallen tree across yon brook. Sophie – she's quite the live wire – was using it as some kind of balancing pole. She used to be one of them gymnasts, when she was a nipper.'

'But not a very good one, it seems. Is she screaming out in agony?'

Joseph noted my tone and replied with, 'No, Doctor.'

'And are broken bones protruding through the skin?'

'Not that I could tell, Sir, no. It's just that her ankle is swollen, but only if looked at from a certain angle.'

I put my bag on the table. Being kept from my garden by Margery due to her desperate desire to experience passion was one thing, but to be beckoned by a bit of a girl (all right, a grown woman) at such a key time in a gardener's year could not be tolerated.

'Please advise Miss …?'

'Hathaway – same as the mistress. Related on the master's side.'

'Hathaway, that my next surgery will be held here tomorrow, at two p.m. If the symptoms persist she can visit me then.'

'But she's lame, Doctor.'

'Then she can ride on Dame Sibyl's donkey.'

'Dame Sibyl's donkey won't cross La Coupée.'

This infernal island!

'Nevertheless, I'm afraid I already have a patient in attendance right now, as you can see, so if you wouldn't mind ...'

Joseph stood and fidgeted with his cap. 'But Dame Sibyl ... she never does like to have her orders disobeyed.'

I disappeared into my glasshouse and returned a moment later with a set of crutches I had been using to prop up a wobbly shelf. They were a very handy addition and would be sorely missed.

'These will help the niece,' I said. 'And as for Dame Sibyl, I may be her tenant and she my feudal mistress, but I am a free man and will not be "ordered" as you say to attend to a patient when I am sure the lady will be able to skip over La Coupée by teatime tomorrow. Now, if you don't mind ...' I glanced at a clock above the door. 'Surgery hours are over and I really should be getting on.'

Joseph rested the crutches against the table, put on his cap, nodded, tucked a crutch under each armpit and used them to make a swift exit into the garden. Once alone, Margery stood to leave; her expression was one of intense distress.

'What shall I do, Sebastian? About my husband's ... problem? Is it serious?'

I looked at the poor woman and noted her expression was full of lost opportunity and regret. I wanted to say, 'Margery, the Nazis are marching on Paris, your husband's problem is of no significance' but instead I rested a hand on her shoulder and said, 'It is nothing to be worried about. Unless, of course, it is an indication of a more serious underlying problem.'

Margery's eyes flashed with the first glimmers of what could only be described as … hope?

'Serious? How serious?' she asked, standing.

'It's impossible to say without examination. Ask him to come and see me.' I rushed out a hand. 'No hurry.'

Taking my doctor's bag from the table, I turned towards the surgery but paused a moment at the door. I had told Margery that the best thing was always to tell the truth, on account of it saving bother, so …

'Margery,' I began, 'please understand that there is a difference between love and passion. What you experienced with Tom the plumber was carnal lust, pure and simple.' Margery, who was by now clearing away the tea things, blushed the colour of my deepest red pelargonium. 'He was a trickster who made you feel good about yourself. When he was here you bloomed better than *Madam Chevalier*.' (One of my best roses.) 'But I want you to understand that really, one man's touch is much the same as another, and it is the actions and thoughts and feelings of the woman in her own head that determine how her partner responds to her in bed – in a way, a man dances to the woman's tune. If you want passion with your husband, perhaps make believe that your husband is your lover. Do you understand what roleplay is?' The blush went deeper still but she nodded. 'Good. But you should know that having spoken with many – many – of my patients over the years on such matters, I believe that it is impossible to sustain passionate sexual relations in a marriage – which is a more mature thing altogether. Marriage is about so much more than sex, which trust me, you only desire because you crave the hormone it releases into your bloodstream because you are still of an age to produce children. So, I retract my last comment and suggest that it is perhaps impossible for your lover to be your husband and your husband to be your lover, especially once the novelty has worn off.'

'But his teeth, Sebastian!'

'Are unfortunate, I agree, but the good news is that pretty soon, your ovaries will be wizened, your appetite for passion will be minimal and you will be relieved to be married to a man who is not demanding in the bedroom.'

I disappeared into the surgery to deposit my bag.

'But what should I do in the meantime?' shouted Margery through the open doorway. 'You know, while my hormones are raging?'

'The only thing there is to do,' I shouted through the doorway while having a quick tidy of my desk. I had mislaid a pruning knife after using it to lance a boil, and it was my best blade. 'Accept your lot in life or find yourself a lover.' I reappeared at the door, knife in hand and with a smile on my face expecting to find another satisfied patient.

'A lover?!' exclaimed Margery. 'And you, a Christian man!'

Why did they always presume this?

'After the events of the last war, Margery, I do not hold with any religion. However, I do try to follow the commandments, where I can, it being as good a blueprint for a moral kind of life as any, although on this occasion, with the situation so dire, perhaps you could … overlook one or two of them?'

'The commandments?'

'Jack Johnston should do you quite nicely. Healthy specimen. Firm jaw. Strong hands. Not a bad set of teeth …'

'Jack Johnston?!'

But there was no time to go into why I had chosen the widower, Jack Johnston, blacksmith and brewer of as fine a beer I have ever tasted, to act as Margery's lover, because Joseph Martin had returned and was standing at the door waiting to speak. He winked at Margery who, drenched in shame, fell into a chair at the table and put her head in her hands.

'Sorry to disturb again, Doctor,' he said, 'but I just remembered another thing I was supposed to tell you.'

'And what is that?' My tone was a little hard, but the man could at least have coughed.

'It's just that they've found you a Juliet.'

'A willing one?' asked Margery, looking up.

That was harsh.

Joseph shrugged.

(I had been persuaded to play Romeo as a guest appearance for the Sark Dramatic Society – the lady who ran it having threatened to withhold the sweet pea seeds she provided me with each year if I didn't reprise my Romeo. I was hoping to find the performance cancelled due to the lack of a Juliet.)

'Who is it?' asked Margery.

'Sophie.'

'The lame niece?' I asked.

'That's the one.'

I held back an eye roll while Margery breathed in deeply through her nose and seemed to bristle slightly. I intended to interrogate further for Margery's sake (women are interested in such things) but Joseph added another titbit to the pot.

'Oh, and the Nazis are on their way,' he said. 'We're not sure when, but definitely before your main crop of potatoes are ready.'

Margery's face reflected my own emotions – pure despair. I

placed a hand to her shoulder, but the bad news didn't end there.

'The French are sabotaging the fuel reserves in St Malo because they're expecting an attack any day now. Big black bellows of smoke can be seen quite clearly from the harbour if you nip down for a look.'

'But ... surely ... we'll be all right?' asked Margery, looking up at me for reassurance. 'We're under the protection of the British, after all, and—'

'They're leaving,' announced Joseph.

'Leaving?' I repeated.

'The whole lot of 'em. Churchill doesn't think we're worth defending, apparently. That's what the officer in charge told Dame Sibyl, anyhow.' Joseph sniffed and turned to leave. 'She thought you'd want to know, what with you being a ...'

'German,' stated Margery.

'Mark my words, Doctor, Jack boots will be marching over La Coupée and knocking on this very door before you've time to pick your first dahlia.' Joseph gave the door a firm rat-a-tat to complete the roleplay. 'There's an emergency meeting tonight at the hall, but Dame Sibyl is having a meeting of the island's big nobs beforehand ...'

'I think you mean the Chief Pleas?' I corrected, trying to recover some form of formality.

Joseph simply shrugged. 'Whoever. And you're asked to attend,' he said. 'Shall I say you're coming?'

I was not sure I had the stomach for it. Having been listening to the radio, on and off (more off than on) and fooling myself otherwise, I was hopeful that France would not fall. Just the previous month, Dame Sibyl had been encouraging tourism to continue on the island, stating that the war would be a storm in a tea cup – something that happened elsewhere –

and that the English should continue to holiday in Sark – to get away from it all – until the rest of the world came to their senses. But that was the thing with war, no one ever did come to their senses until millions of people were dead and the natural world was left in chaos and confusion. A thousand, long-buried emotions sparked deep within my keenly private soul, but as I did not want any of them to be witnessed, and subsequently talked about, I said, 'Tell Dame Sibyl I'll be there.'

Joseph tapped his cap in acknowledgement and turned to leave. He halted at the door once more.

'Shall I tell the mistress you'll be taking a look at Sophie, then, too? Only she'll need her foot fixed if she's to get up the scaffolding for the balcony scene. We could walk there together, maybe.' He was already taking off his cap and pulling out a chair. 'Only, I want to talk to you about my greenfly problem … no hurry. I'll wait for you. Any more tea in that fancy pot of yours, Margery?'

I placed the knife on the table. With an air of resignation, I pulled out a chair in order to break further bread with my neighbours, but knew very well that when I returned home later, I would have slept my last restful night in that house. The night terrors were bound to return.

Chapter Four

La Santé Prison, August 1944

C hristoph glances up.
  'Night terrors?'

'They were worse when I was younger. In my twenties. I knew trauma in my teens.'

'The last war?' he asks.

'The last war,' I confirm.

We sit in silence. He is waiting to see if I want to speak on. Chaplains are good at that – not probing but simply waiting to follow in the direction of the speaker. I often wanted to try this approach as a doctor, but with my patients on Sark, if I had not probed, I would never have come to discover their malady. Nevertheless, I have always respected men of cloth for their reserve and quiet patience and as he sits and waits, I wonder how (and if) I want to move the conversation on. Should I simply return to my story – there is still oil in the lamp and I have barely even begun – or shall I pause a moment to discuss with this man where in truth it all really began – in 1915 with a woman called Edith Cavell, and in a courtyard, not dissimilar to the one above the grate. If this man of God is to truly believe that I am who I say I am then I must tell my story honestly and without censure. I decide to tell him the story of how Sascha and I were once two kinds of brother – real brothers and brothers in arms. During the last war we served as soldiers directly for our father who was the Kommandant at the Tir national, a military training camp and shooting range, in Belgium. My brother's name was put forward by our father to be part of a firing squadron – we were eighteen at the time. To cut to the point, my brother hadn't the heart or, perhaps, the ability to go ahead with the shot and asked me as his twin to secretly take his place. And that is why I once stood in front of a young woman in a courtyard such as the one above me now, took aim without flinching, and fired a single shot, which entered Miss Cavell's forehead, just above the glabella, and slightly to the left. And that is why I know that my long-held belief in karma is not a foolish one.

'You and your brother are identical,' he says.

'Yes. The only difference was that I was born three minutes earlier.' I smile. 'Sascha always hated that.'

'There are perhaps scars now – physical scars – injuries from your adult years, that would tell you apart?'

'Perhaps,' I say. 'But I neither know nor care.'

'Is that really true? Even though he is your brother. Your twin?'

I wonder if offence is meant. But no, he speaks without judgement, I'm sure of that.

'Brotherhood cannot be bought purely by blood,' I say. 'It is earned over time, or else it is nothing but a commonality of genes. I adored my brother when we were younger, but we lost touch which was foolish, and then more recently I have discovered that we have chosen very different paths. It has become clear that Sascha is more like my father in his beliefs … beliefs I could never condone.'

'Your father was a harsh man,' he says.

'He was brutal. Dead now, of course.'

'And your brother? You do not know if he is alive or dead either?'

I look to my shoeless feet, blackened by grime and blood. 'I do not. Not for certain. But it is likely that he is alive.' I shake my head and laugh a ridiculous laugh of a mad man. 'And now I am to die in his place, which is so very typical of Sascha.'

He smiles rather than consoles me. 'Then perhaps we should return to Sark while there is oil in the lantern … I am enjoying your story greatly.'

I nod my agreement. 'So am I,' I say, surprising myself. 'So am I.'

Chapter Five

It is exactly one and three-quarter miles (Joseph measured it) from my cottage on Little Sark to Dame Sibyl's impressive feudal house – La Seigneurie – on Sark proper. Little Sark is not an island in its own right but is joined to the main island by a narrow ridge that is nine feet wide and three hundred feet long. It has a low barrier erected to prevent wanderers from falling two hundred and sixty feet directly into the sea on either side below. This walkway, an unusual geographical feature known as an isthmus, is just wide enough for a (very) brave donkey to pull a cart along and is known as La Coupée – it is delicious in its perilousness! A place of folklore and fairy tales, it is where giants or pixies or phantoms – depending on the teller and how much ale they have drunk – will happily, I am told, drag a hapless wanderer off the path and down to an agonising death below. Treacherous in high winds, many refuse to cross it, although my patients were forced to cast off their doubts and trip-trap across the ridge if they wished to be seen by Herr Doktor. (In fairness, I have been known to meet those genuinely anxious on the far side and guide them across, or even treat them in situ, depending on the malady.)

I adored the majesty of La Coupée and that feeling of living in the complete serenity that the isolation of Little Sark afforded me. I sometimes allowed my mind to wander in the direction of considering if my happy state was because I enjoyed the freedom of living the life of a single man in an isolated fortress. There was always the very definite sensation that, if the need arose, a non-existent draw bridge could be raised at La Coupée to keep intruders out, and whatever madness might break out across the world, it would be of absolutely no consequence to me. Life on Little Sark would go on as it always had done – tranquilly. Nothing, however, would stop the Nazis.

Joseph, having been skipping across La Coupée carrying messages and errands to the residents of Little Sark since he was a child, did not blink an eye when crossing, although as we walked together to La Seigneurie, he abandoned the crutches at my suggestion and elected to carry them instead. It remained a lovely day, late-afternoon by now, and with much to see and talk about – the encouragement of invertebrates into the ecosystem to tackle the greenfly problem being the main order of the day – the walk lasted a good half hour longer than it should, which meant that the meeting of the Chief Pleas, the island's council, was already underway when we arrived at La Seigneurie. I stepped through open French windows carrying a tray of young plants intended as an offering for my neighbours. Joseph, not being party to the group, happily scuttled away to his greenhouse. Lucky man.

Dame Sibyl, dressed in one of many twill suits – this one olive green – was standing by a chalk board, chalk in one hand, gavel in another, while the assembled guests, thirteen of them, sat on ballroom chairs in a circle. Her husband, Mr Hathaway, the American she had met during her free, younger days, sat quietly by her side as ever and threw me a wink as I arrived. There was one empty chair. I sat on it and smiled around at the group. The usual crowd were in attendance, most being descendants of the original settlers on the island, including the harbour master Alex Vibert (nasal congestion), farmer Jerome Le Brocq (heartburn), and the renowned botanist John Hamon (hayfever). There was just one other that I did not recognise, a woman in her thirties with dark, glossy, shoulder-length hair and olive skin. She had one foot resting on a pouffe and was wearing a combination of trousers, a checked shirt and the loveliest of smiles.

Sophie.

My Juliet.

I nodded and smiled in her direction and gave a cheery wave of my doctor's bag by way of saying, 'Hello, I acknowledge that you are new here and that you need my attention – and that you are also to be Juliet to my Romeo. I will attend you shortly.' I hoped my smile didn't convey any other emotion, because surely, this woman was pure loveliness.

She replied by winking at me. It must be a family trait. Her head was tipped to one side – a little provocatively, I thought – as she appraised me. I looked away to find Dame Sibyl also appraising me over her spectacles while Major Jenkins, who had served at Ypres, murmured to the woman on his left (Nicole Dupré, irritable bowel), 'Let's hope all Germans are equally as tardy, eh?'

'Apologies,' I said, addressing the assembled group, who had a collective look of haggardness and dread about them. 'A medical emergency …' I offered no more.

I was given a very quick recap by the secretary, John

Hamon, and discovered that the purpose of the meeting was twofold: firstly, we were to decide how to break the news to the islanders about the imminent German invasion (and the fact that the British were leaving and not intending to protect them). They had agreed that it need be done in a way that did not instigate panic. I did not believe such a way was possible.

Secondly, we were to decide what to do about the invasion itself. Both questions did not, I felt, require a whole meeting to ponder upon, and when asked my opinion I gave it.

To cover the first question, I proposed that the Chief Pleas simply tell the islanders what was expected to happen regarding the retreat of the British, both at the full meeting later this evening and door-to-door for those who could not – or would not – attend. And secondly, regarding the invasion itself, we should (could) do nothing except either evacuate all or some residents – the children and the weak, for example – to England (as the British had suggested) or attempt to fight. The latter would prove to be a fruitless loss of life.

A vein in the major's left temple pulsed while Dame Sibyl took off her spectacles to make sure she had heard me correctly.

I glanced around for support but realised that the collective look of dread/fear/anger on the faces of the assembled group suggested that I had reached my conclusion far too quickly, and that the purpose of the meeting, after all, was for frightened people to get together to hash the thing out in order to feel that they could hold onto some kind of control. They could not, of course, but I quickly realised my folly and began to back-pedal.

'Of course, when I said that you have two options,' I began, 'I should have said that you have three.'

There was a collective letting out of breath.

'Which are?' asked Dame Sibyl.

'Leave, surrender or fight.'

Excited by this, the major jumped up. The vein was still pumping.

'The charter granted by Queen Elizabeth I,' he began, with the solemnity of a statesman, 'states that the dame must keep forty men on the island – at least – and each is to be armed with a musket!' He turned to Dame Sibyl. 'Ma'am, I demand to be issued with my musket!'

Everyone looked at Dame Sibyl, presumably because she had failed in her duty to provide them with muskets, too. Dame Sibyl rolled her eyes and glanced at her husband. 'Do we have any muskets, Robert dear?'

Mr Hathaway shrugged. 'I think there's a couple on the wall in the study? I could give them a dust off, if you like?'

'Good! Then I say we fight!' shouted the major, his fist in the air, his tirade not yet complete. 'I'd rather die a free man than surrender to the Hun! What do you say?' He looked around. No one said anything, so he sat down.

'Fight?' I repeated gently, trying to hide any hint of a derogatory tone from my voice. I did not, I fear, disguise a sigh. 'A couple of mounted donkeys and a handful of muskets will not suffice.'

The major turned on his audience like a politician at the husting.

'What weapons will we use, the German asks? Ha!' He turned to me. 'Farm tools,' he shouted, jabbing an arm forward like a swordsman. 'While riding on horseback. The tools will be used as jousting poles.' The men stared at him in bewilderment while Nicole Dupré did not even try to hide her contempt.

'Jousting on horseback?' she said. 'You get your manure

from Joseph Martin to feed your roses. You have no horse, man!'

The major shrugged. 'Then I shall adapt and overcome! I shall mount Dame Sibyl's donkey if necessary? That's how the last war was won, Madam – by adaptation and ingenuity – and with no surrender!' The major glanced around again for support but with none forthcoming, he sat down whilst nodding towards me and adding, 'Not that your kind would know anything about that sort of thing – not surrendering.'

I was impervious to insult, but not to stupidity.

'I speak as I find,' I said. 'And the truth of the matter is that you may stay on the island and surrender, or you may evacuate and run, or you may fight. If you choose the latter then most certainly, you will die.'

I regretted my statement immediately, because there was, perhaps, something about the fact that this statement had been made in English and not the local patois, by a German man who, when necessary, could alter his voice to make the devil himself sit up and take note. I sobered the party to the extent that Mary Rhoe the postmistress (absolutely no illness whatever – ever!) began to cry. And why shouldn't she? I too wanted to cry. Life as we knew it – yes, isolated and somewhat feudal and not suited to all, but heavenly for all that – was about to change. Forever, maybe.

A quiet voice eked out into the silence. It was John Hamon, the botanist. 'Perhaps … in that case … we should all just … leave?'

Dame Sibyl banged her gavel and the hem of her silk blouse, which was previously tucked into her skirt tightly, edged out. The dishevelled look really did suit her.

'Leave?!' she exclaimed, taking over from the major in his

hustings role. 'So, you would abandon our island into the hands of strangers, would you?'

The poor, red-faced John Hamon shrunk into his chair. I considered grabbing my bag as his blood pressure would no doubt be at boiling point by now, but Dame Sibyl, a terrier with a rabbit in her teeth, had more.

'You would gift our island to strangers who would not care a jot for it, would you? Who would not tend the land, would not protect the wildlife and the way of life – *our* way of life?!'

John looked directly at me for support, which I was about to give – either that or medical assistance – but the major stepped in to steal the attention. I offered John a friendly smile.

'Finally, a fellow fighter!' said the major, looking flushed but remaining seated at least. 'We shall pull up the draw bridge and fight them from battlements and ...' But he was cut short.

'We shall *not* fight them, you silly man,' interrupted Dame Sibyl, taking a moment to put down her gavel and tuck in her blouse. 'But neither shall we leave.'

There were gasps at this, mainly from Mary Rhoe who whispered. 'Not leave?'

'That is correct.' Dame Sibyl, ears like a hawk, was becoming deeper in voice and stronger with every syllable. 'I believe that not one of us – island-born, at least – should step foot off this island and abandon our way of life.'

'Well, see here ...' began Jerome Le Brocq, but Dame Sibyl cut him off.

'I am the Seigneur of this island and whether we stay or leave is my decision to make. My family have been governing Sark since 1852!'

'Since the privateer John Allaire *stole* it, you mean!' said

Alex Vibert, the harbour master and a man of strong opinion (and a fine set of teeth).

'Stole? Stole?' Dame Sibyl raised her gavel in his direction. I did not expect him to back down but I did wish someone would hand him a handkerchief to blow his nose. Mr Hathaway gently retrieved the gavel from his wife.

'Yes, stole,' he shouted. 'And I will not be *ordered* to stay by anyone. If I choose to remain it will be by my own free will!'

There was a bit of a clap and a spontaneous murmur of 'Here, here,' which was not received well by the dame.

I considered intervening and throwing water on the fire, but decided to let the argument progress. These petty squabbles will insist on being aired. I thought they might as well get the thing over and done with now.

Alex stood. His face was as red as his prize beetroot, the prize having been handed to him by Dame Sibyl only last summer, when there had been smiles all round. So is life. One minute friends, the next enemies.

'You are a tinpot dictator, Madam,' he said, his tirade, now released from the jar, spilling out uncontrollably. Mary gasped and the gavel, snatched back from her husband, hovered, but Dame Sibyl, to my everlasting surprise, eventually laughed.

'A dictator?' she scoffed, looking around for support. None came. Eyes fell to the floor.

'Yes, dictator,' he insisted. 'Demanding your feudal tithes – taking *my* grain, *my* cider, *my* chickens! Your father – a benevolent man – did not insist on the payment of tithes. We are the last bastion of feudalism in the whole of Europe! See here, when a property is sold, you take a cut. You take a chicken for every chimney a tenant has stuck on the side of his house. All flotsam and jetsam is yours, even though it would be mightily useful to all of us.' He then glanced at Poppy, the poodle. It seemed even the dog was to know his wrath. 'For God's sake, you are even the only person allowed to own an un-spayed dog! You do not even allow us a vehicle! Poor Jerome still ploughs with a horse!'

'But I quite like …'

Jerome was silenced.

'You revel in your power, Madam. A power only granted to you by the fortune of birth. It pains me to say this,' (it didn't) 'but we all know that you once lived in Germany. For all we know you are a sympathiser – a Fifth Columnist – and are actually looking forward to the arrival of jack boots!'

Mr Hathaway laughed. It took him some time to compose himself.

'Now see here … steady on …' interjected the major, somewhat unsuccessfully.

I glanced across the room and noted that Sophie was buttoning in a smile.

'The payment of tithes is for your own good,' said the dame, throwing in a dismissive wave of the hand, having clearly decided that, rather than attempt to shout him down, she would simply downplay him with a superior yet benevolent manner. She was particularly good at it. 'And anyhow, the tithe is merely a token gift to me – my household – as a gesture to acknowledge my tireless work in the community.'

'A gift,' scoffed Alex, sitting down.

'Yes, a gift. Do I complain when you always give me your skinniest chicken? I do not.' There was a gasp at this. 'And as for refusing to allow vehicles on the island … there is nowhere on Sark that you cannot reach easily very quickly by foot. Mark my words, motor vehicles will pollute the earth and scorch the soul. The day will come when the whole world will regret the introduction of the motorcar. If you cannot see that then I must protect you from yourselves.'

'Perhaps we are not your children to protect?' stated Nicole Dupré, who owns her own house and is far too wealthy to worry about offending the dame. The support bolstered Alex's resolve.

'My point exactly!' he said, before taking out a handkerchief and finally blowing his nose. I was surprised he had completed his tirade without having brought up the subject of pigeons.

'And tell me this,' he added. 'Why are you the only person to be allowed to keep pigeons?'

There it was.

'I'll tell you why,' he began, just as Dame Sibyl opened her mouth. 'To preserve the place as a museum for your own benefit!' Dame Sibyl's expression showed that she was impervious to insult also. 'Yes, for your own benefit. To encourage the tourists to come and line your pockets, no doubt, and to give your well-to-do friends from England and America a smorgasbord of "old England in France"!'

'Are you finished?' asked Dame Sibyl, throwing water on the fire.

Alex glanced around the room and on receiving no encouragement to continue, he nodded.

'Then I shall explain – again. If I do not insist on the payment of the tithe from my tenants then the relationship we islanders have with the land will disappear. We will move away from the basic requirement of growing our own food, of raising our own livestock, of brewing our own ale. We have all of these things *because* of the tithe, because you *have* to do it. We are a remote island and we need to uphold our self-sufficiency. Can you not see how beneficial our way of life will be when the Germans arrive? You will thank me, one day, I'm sure, when your family do not starve because I always insisted that you provide for yourself and for others. But we have diverted from the purpose of our meeting. The facts of the matter are this. The British soldiers are leaving – packing their kitbags as I speak. The French are burning fuel in St Malo and meanwhile, Paris – the whole of France – is about to fall. I have word confirmed today that the British have offered to evacuate us, beginning with the children.'

There were several relieved sighs at this.

'However,' Dame Sibyl went on to say, 'at the meeting of the Balliwick this evening I shall inform everyone that my husband and I intend to remain.' Mr Hathaway took his wife's hand. 'As some of you are aware I returned from a visit to Guernsey yesterday and I tell you this: the chaos and panic at St Peter Port, where hundreds are scrambling to leave their homeland, was heart-breaking. There are queues at all the shops, the banks are overrun and the air is thick with an over-riding sense of doom and disaster. Pets are being put to sleep …' She paused then. Her voice faltered and she glanced across at her beloved poodle, whose pregnancy could have been timed better. 'Nevertheless, those who wish to leave the island may do so. We will arrange for a crossing to Guernsey where they may board ships for England. However, it is my *firm* belief that if the Germans do come, they will not bother us so very much and will not remain here for long. We are self-sufficient, are we not?' She threw a pointed nod in the direction of Alex. 'And I fully intend to explain to the officer in charge, who will almost certainly be a German aristocrat who, I'm sure, will treat me – us – with dignity, that there is absolutely no reason for anything on the island to change. I give you my word that if we all stick together on this – as we always have done – we may know hunger, we may know sacrifice, but we *will* survive. Also, we have to be realistic. The Allies may not prevail in this. England may indeed be invaded, and those who go there will, I'm sure, be worse off than if they had stayed put. What is better than living where a small amount of people can look after each other? We need not worry about losing electric power as we have none. We need not worry about a shortage of fuel as we need none. All we need is food and water, and we can supply that for ourselves from the sea and the land. We have pigs and sheep and rabbits and fish. To abandon this island would be the beginning of the end of our way of life, which should be preserved at all costs. As I say, at the meeting tonight I shall ask everyone to stay. Those who wish to leave may do so, but I fear they will be making a mistake.'

At this, all nodded their agreement and the major gave a standing ovation. Alex remained unconvinced.

'And when you are proven wrong,' he said, 'and the Germans – Nazis – eat my crops and kill my chickens and drink my ale … then what?'

Dame Sibyl took a moment before answering. I noticed a look of uncertainty. She glanced at her husband. He squeezed her hand. Here was a moment when the great Dame of the Seigneury did not have all the answers and was not completely certain. She looked at me too, perhaps for reassurance. They all followed her gaze, except for Sophie, who was stroking the dog.

'I am as blind as you in this,' I said.

'But they are your countrymen,' said the postmistress. 'What is your instinct? How will they behave?'

'My instinct?' I repeated. 'You want me to second guess the actions of soldiers?'

She nodded.

I tried to force an image away but could not, for suddenly in front of me was a woman I once faced in a courtyard, her head bowed, her eyes blindfolded, a weapon in my hand. Then I remembered what happened later … other trenches, other shells, other bloodshed. I was so tired of it all: war, peace, war, peace, war, peace. I had nothing left to give. The thought of wearing uniform again, of fighting again, of even touching a weapon again, of knowing that feeling of fear, of smelling the stench of rotting flesh … my heart began to race, my hands were clammy. I took hold of the chair to steady myself.

'My countrymen? Can you not see that my countrymen are here, all around me? My countrymen are you. My countrymen are the whole of humanity.' I realised that I was beginning to wander down sanctimonious street but could not prevent myself from airing my frustration. 'I am not defined by my place of birth,' I concluded.

'But you must have an idea, surely.'

They were all staring at me with much hope in their eyes, and so it was no use. I was going to have to give them an answer.

'Although I have not resided in Germany for many years, my country – as you declare Germany to be – is not the country I once fought for.' The major grumped at this. I moved on. 'Therefore, my opinion is of no consequence regarding the possible morality of the soldiers they send here. This is the army of an aggressor I do not know. We on Sark have been ambivalent observers of a war that has been declared but does not seem to have begun properly, and yet we hear that Paris is soon likely to fall and it will not take long for German boots to march this way. We must grasp the nettle in the manner I have suggested to you – surrender, fight or leave. Which path each of you chooses to follow is a purely personal matter but as a man who put down his weapon for the last time in 1918, I will never again support warfare and the unnecessary loss of life fighting a battle not one side can ever truly win,' I glanced at the major with a smile, 'however brave and noble the soldier.'

There was a moment's silence until a stranger's voice, a calm, gentle voice offering shelter in a choppy sea, said, 'What about the children?'

My heart shattered. The children. Why must we always create such disharmony for the children? Cannot we love them more?

'They can leave if the parents so wish,' said Dame Sibyl, re-establishing authority and finding her confidence and her voice. 'But at least one parent should accompany their child. I do not relish the thought of our children travelling to an unknown destination alone.'

John Hamon coughed to indicate he wished to speak. I was pleased to see by his pallor that his blood pressure had dropped from its peak, although perhaps a little too much. I made a mental note to check him before he walked home.

'And will you choose to leave, Herr Doktor,' he asked, 'when the British send their ships to evacuate us?'

I considered this only momentarily. 'I will not,' I said, and for some reason after noticing the confused expression on Sophie's face, I felt the need to repeat the words: 'I absolutely will not.'

Chapter Six

La Santé Prison, August 1944

'And yet you are here, in Paris,' says Christoph, breaking into my thoughts.

'And yet I am here,' I repeat. 'But we are not always masters of our own fate.'

Christoph glances around the cell and then up at the grate. He takes a deep breath and closes his eyes as if it is he who will live out his few remaining days in this place, not I.

'It is cloudy today, I think.' I cannot quite see the sky through my grate, but the light on a cloudy day is different from a sunny one. In some ways I prefer it.

Christoph takes a fresh handkerchief from the pocket of his uniform jodhpurs. Cloudy or not, it is hellish hot in here. He unfolds the cloth, which seems too clean to be allowed into such a place, and dabs his face and eyes.

'It is cloudy,' he says. 'But I doubt we shall see rain. You miss your island.' It is a statement not a question. 'You are most animated when you speak of it – when you speak of your patients, your friends.'

'It was a wonderful life, I am lucky to have had it.' But in the silence that follows – as I have very quickly become used to now with Christoph – I wonder if I was, in fact, lucky to have had it, and if luck comes into things at all. Karma, yes, somehow. But luck? Surely every single thing that happens to us is created, crafted – narrated – by ourselves?

'You said that after you put down your weapon in 1918, you vowed you would never fight again. The fact that you are wearing uniform shows that not to be true, but we shall come to that, no doubt. You were, at one time, a pacifist, then?'

'Of sorts,' I admit. 'Although I recall that I said I would not support the futile loss of life, not that I was a pacifist.'

'Unnecessary,' he says, correcting me. 'You said, *unnecessary* loss of life.'

'Very well, unnecessary, in fighting battles no one ever really wins.'

'And yet you are sitting opposite me wearing the uniform of a German Brigadier.'

'I am. But as I said yesterday, this uniform does not represent me. I am not Sascha. It is complicated.'

He smiles a little, and I know it is to show me that this is not a trial, but that he is merely intrigued. I have asked him to listen to my story, have I not?

'Shall I go on?' I ask. 'With my story?'

He pushes his glasses up his nose in preparation. 'Do. But first, may I ask … you refer to your countrymen as "the Germans" when you speak, as if you are no longer German yourself. Are you ashamed to be German now?'

I wonder for a moment if I am being tricked by this man and if his soft, kind manner isn't simply a ruse for me to take him into my trust. But no. There is something about the way he poses his questions that shows he already has the measure of me. I wonder if in me, he sees himself a little.

'I am not ashamed to be German,' I say. 'A man can be German and not a Nazi. It is more that, over the years, I have come to see myself without nationality. In truth I have been unable to sit comfortably inside any one nation – they all use propaganda. They all wish to pigeonhole.'

'Except on your island,' he says.

I laugh. 'Yes, except on my island, which is ironic given that it is the last place with feudalism in Europe.'

'I think I would like this island of yours,' he says. 'Perhaps you would take me back to it now?'

It is a genuine request. So, I do.

Chapter Seven

Considering the explosive nature of the meeting at La Seigneurie and the number of bright-red or deathly-pale faces in the room, it was perhaps for the best that I was there with my doctor's bag in hand to attend to them (although it was usually the folk whose backs I noticed disappearing out of the door before I had the chance to speak to them that I worried about the most).

A line began to form in front of my chair after the meeting, but Dame Sibyl would not allow her guests to loiter in the living room. Instead, she ushered the group into the kitchen where they were instructed to wait their turn for the doctor and to not 'meander about the place'. She had 'matters of great import' to discuss with me first, apparently. I assumed that such matters concerned the imminent arrival of the German army, rather than the fact that she had found a willing, or more likely, unwilling, Juliet. She closed the heavy door as the last of the attendees were shooed away.

'Now then,' she began. 'About this blasted play!'

It is worth noting that Dame Sibyl was, and I hope still is, a force of nature. She lived in

Germany after the First War – in Cologne. Her first husband died of Spanish flu in 1918. She was pregnant when he died but her father, the last Seigneur of Sark, had not approved of the marriage and as punishment would not support her financially or emotionally. Unperturbed, the dame taught herself German and subsequently lived in Germany eking out a living. According to Dame Sibyl, she loved it there, and she spent an undisclosed amount of time raising prize cattle. It was with this background that she found herself keen usually to speak to me in my native tongue. Today was no exception.

She gestured towards two sofas positioned opposite each other in front of the fireplace. We each took one.

'I was wondering,' I began, 'if we oughtn't cancel the play when there is so much to be done, so much to consider, before the arrival of the Germans?' (Yes, it was possible that I wished subconsciously to ingratiate myself even with the islanders and create a distance (a vast chasm) between myself and my country of birth even then.)

'Cancel?' said Dame Sybil, who went on to say that this was exactly the time when Shakespeare was needed the most. If one thing was certain, she said, it was that we needed to carry on as if absolutely nothing had changed, because it hadn't (yet). When the Germans arrived, as they surely would, they would see that she was the upholder of a certain way of life that they would approve of – a feudal way of life – then they would most probably decide to leave the island to its own devices and even, perhaps, learn to adapt to our way of life.

She truly believed this. I wondered how to explain.

'I do not think that Hitler is expecting his soldiers to bend to another authority's will,' I said.

'Yes, of course, you are quite right,' she agreed. I sensed the inevitable 'however' was about to follow. 'However …'

There it was.

'German boots may not even bother to step a toe on this soil, and if they do, like the British, they may feel that occupation is simply not worth the effort.'

I tried to interject.

'But if they *do* come,' she added, 'then we will have the advantage over our fellow Channel Islanders.'

'How so?' I asked.

'Well, Sark is the last remaining feudal state in western Europe and I – the Dame of Sark – am listed in the Almanac de Gotha!' She said this with a bat of the hand as if she was the Queen of Sheba discussing her provenance. 'The officer in charge will almost certainly be of an aristocratic bent and …'

'Why would you assume that?' I asked.

'Because the occupation of this island will be seen as an easy billet, and I should imagine that there remains a sufficient amount of old school sway within the ranks of the German army to ensure that men of a certain background will choose the postings they regard as safe. I have made many noble friends there, you know, in Germany, over the years, and no doubt such friends will all be officers in the army by now. The commanding officer and I will have acquaintances in common, I'm sure, and I fully intend to see to it that the German contingent, should it arrive, sings to our tune, not the other way around.'

I would have laughed at this if Dame Sibyl were not being perfectly serious. Also, somewhere deep in my heart, I was convinced that if anyone could tame the German army, it was her.

'Nevertheless—'

'Which is why,' she added, cutting me off, 'as I said in the meeting and shall explain at the larger meeting later, the best course of action is for everyone to remain calm and not abandon the island, which brings me back to the play. Can you not see, Herr Braun,' – Dame Sibyl was still speaking to me in German. I believe she was practising for when 'the Germans' arrived – 'if we, the elders of the island, continue to behave in as unruffled a manner as possible and retain command of our emotions, then there will not arise a state of panic, such as I saw in Guernsey yesterday.' She returned to English to add, 'Poor souls. Dreadful situation.'

I saw her point, although I did not regard myself as an 'elder' of the island, being quite young still. In my prime, really…

'Nevertheless—'

'The German officers who are sent here will respect my position. The British have abandoned

us and so what choice do we have – we can neither work with them nor against them. I shall merely do everything in my power to protect the people and our way of life. I am determined that we will illustrate a firm dignity of sorts and show that we can take it all in our stride, or at least give the impression that we can. Which brings me back to the play … I appreciate that we may have to look for another Romeo …'

'Another Romeo?' I repeated, surprised to find myself disappointed. 'I meant for the whole play to be cancelled, not for me to be thrown out.'

Her smile faded. She stood and walked to an occasional table where she opened a drawer and took out a photograph.

She handed it to me and I saw a moustachioed man in a British army uniform.

'My first husband,' she said. At first I was uncertain as to the direction of her train of thought, until she added, 'You fought in the last war, did you not?'

Ah, in that direction. I must turn this train around.

'I did.'

'And you are a pacifist now?'

'If refusing to take part in another war makes me so, then yes.'

I handed the photograph back. It had no bearing as to why I should or should not continue in the part of Romeo.

She returned the photograph to the drawer and joined me on my sofa, perching on the edge, her back an iron rod, her knee almost touching mine.

'You say that you intend to stay on the island when your fellow countrymen arrive ...'

I was tempted to reply with a simple, 'Yes,' but she wanted more and I felt obliged to give it.

'If the people of Sark remain here,' I began, 'and I assume that most of them will as that is what you are encouraging them to do, then I have a duty to remain here also.'

'Why?'

What a question. This was obvious to me.

'I am their doctor, and I feel a sense of duty – as do you – to look after them. I cannot leave my patients.'

She laughed. 'Really? Your patients are the bane of your life, you have said as much yourself, many times.'

This was true. 'A father can be irritated by his children. It does not follow that he would abandon them should life become difficult.'

'But they are not your children, Sebastian.' She touched me

on the arm, leading me to look down at her hand to see the skin of a woman who did not mind chores. 'What do you see happening when the Germans arrive?' she asked. 'How do you think they will treat you, when they discover your nationality – when they know that you are one of their own?'

This, I admit, had been the question I had already asked myself often since the war began, because I had no clue how to answer it, and yet if I was honest with myself, truly honest, any variant of the answer was an unsatisfactory one. I began with a bold statement.

'I do not hold with boundaries of nationality,' I said, my hackles rising. 'And I am not, I assure you, "one of their own". I do not hold with the notion that my place of birth – an uncontrolled irrelevance – should dictate how I behave and where I belong. I am simply a living creature on this earth choosing to live a peaceable life.'

'Fine talk, very noble,' she said, just as her poodle Poppy interrupted her flow by pressing her nose against the glass of the French doors. Dame Sibyl swiftly walked to the door to let the dog in. I was grateful to see that she returned to the sofa opposite me, where Poppy lay down by her feet and crossed her paws. 'Sebastian, can't you see that the soldiers who arrive here will not care two hoots about your principles? In the meeting earlier you said that we islanders have three options: go, remain or fight.'

'That is correct,' I said.

'You, I fear, have only two, and I believe you know this yourself, deep down. You may leave or you may fight, but you cannot stay. As soon as they arrive, an inventory of islanders will be made and cross-checked. I have heard that they are hunting out Jews, amongst other people, and I do not use the word 'hunting' lightly. In the process of doing so they will find that they have a doctor living here and that he is German. I'm certain you will be instructed to enlist.'

'And I shall refuse to do so.' The words came out of my mouth with feigned ignorance. I knew what she was saying was correct so why did I continue to fight it? I was forcing her to verbalise the things I could not even allow myself to think, because I simply did not want to leave my island. How could I live and breathe without my garden, my daily walk, the high cliffs and the rolling pastures, the gentle-natured Guernsey cows glancing over hedgerows, their soft brown eyes taking in my every step as I sauntered down the lane, mesmerised by the primroses and wild hyacinths, sea-pinks, bluebells and pansies? And that was merely a scant collection of the wild flowers and only covered the spring; the other seasons brought their own beauty and wonder to every pasture, every clifftop, every wooded valley.

'You have never really spoken of your family,' she said, changing tack. 'I believe that you are from an aristocratic background?'

'I am,' was the only answer I was prepared to offer.

'You have a brother – a twin.'

'I do.' I had no idea how she knew this.

'Who is in the SS.'

'I have not been in contact with Sascha since long before the war began,' I said. 'Not since I heard word that my father had died. And forgive me, Dame Sibyl, but how do you know all of this when, as you say, I have never discussed my family?'

She glanced away to pat the dog. 'Oh, it was some years ago, when you first arrived. I asked some questions of friends in Germany when we appointed you as the island's doctor, and of course, when the war began, there may have been some discussion regarding your … connections …'

She looked up, her eyes challenging. 'Are you offended?' she asked.

'I am not,' I said, and it was true.

She joined her hands with a satisfied clap, leaving them in a prayer position.

'I should tell you, then, that my sources report your brother to be in quite a high position. Can we assume that he will protect you?'

'Protect me?'

'Surely, if you send word to request to remain here, as our doctor, he will arrange it? I can easily speak to the commanding officer when he arrives and explain the situation ...'

The thought was kindly meant but she had no understanding of German High Command. I indulged Dame Sibyl with a smile, but my heart entered into a cocktail of emotions that always began to surface when I allowed Sascha – my whole family – into my thoughts. Dear Sascha. He was not truly suited to the army. All he ever sought to do was to please Father. What a conflicted path he was forced to walk along.

'I could try,' I said. 'But he is unlikely to have significant sway.'

'And if not, you insist on staying here?' she asked.

I could have screamed.

'Tell me, in my position, what would you do?'

She snorted out her answer. 'I would leave in a heartbeat. I only stay because this is my home, Sebastian. My birth right. I am the Dame of Sark, after all.'

Home? But was it not my home too, and was I not equally as entitled to stand fast there, even if I was not born there? What was birth right after all, other than an excuse to exclude others from seeking out a better life?

I leant forward in my seat.

'Being born in one place,' I began, 'does not preclude a person from belonging wholeheartedly in another, and nor does it give any one person more of a right to feel that they have ownership of a place. I may not have been born on this island, but I love it as well as any man. When a person has tended the earth and walked the lanes and slept under the stars in a place as I have here, then they develop a connection – a bond – and it is as unbreakable as if they were born there, more so perhaps, especially if they have known unhappiness elsewhere.' I stood. 'I am sorry. I do not wish to preach and I have patients who have waited for my attention for far too long.' I bowed slightly and turned for the door. Dame Sibyl followed on behind, rushing to place her hand on the door knob ahead of me. The dog, having followed her, looked up in bemusement by her feet.

'You and I are used to speaking plainly,' she began. 'And the plain truth is that you will be of no use to us if you stay because if you refuse to bend to their will within days of their arrival they will send you away to a prison camp, or worse, shoot you as an objector. They will not tolerate one of their own—'

'I am not one of their own.'

'You are, Sebastian. Your papers declare it so and that is that. Did you know that a yacht pulled into the harbour yesterday, crewed by ten men who stole it in Normandy? They were attempting to sail to Spain but were poor sailors and were very lucky to have landed safely with us. I tell you this because they spoke of the horrors of the occupation in Europe.'

'But earlier you said ...'

'I said that I expected our occupation to be a benevolent one, and I stand by that, but that is because I have deduced that there is no one here of any particular religion, or persuasion, or nationality that they may feel the need to … flush out. No one except, perhaps …'

'Me.'

'If there were more men like you – and I wish there were – Hitler would be nothing more than a lunatic that no one listened to. But there are not many men with your conviction. Just promise me that you will return to your cottage and consider all of this?' She turned the handle on the door and opened it slightly. 'Please, Sebastian.'

My eyes must have betrayed my confusion and disappointment, and even my belligerence, because she added, 'Remember that I am your landlord, and if I have to evict you from Sark to save your life, I will.'

'And who will play your Romeo if I leave?' I asked with a smile, aware that, some short moments ago, I'd suggested that the play be cancelled.

Dame Sibyl threw her head back and laughed. 'If you insist upon staying,' she said, 'then no one shall play him but you, although I fear you shall meet the same sticky ending if you do stay, which is why I shall do anything, however underhand, to persuade you to leave.'

An hour went by while I conducted my doctorly duties in the kitchen. The conversation varied between the imminent arrival of 'the Germans' and what best to do about blackspot on roses. (Nothing, was my answer to the first, and feed the soil with well-rotted manure and compost to strengthen the plant was my answer to the second). Eventually, I looked up to see the newly arrived Sophie Hathaway, Dame Sibyl's niece, standing in front of me.

She took a seat while a small number of the other patients who had chosen to stay looked on with interest from their seats around the table. I dropped my stethoscope on the floor. Sophie picked it up.

'Hello, Doctor,' she said, the woman of the wink. There was a definite trace of the American about her, in accent and manner, but there was a tinge of France in there too. Confidence. That was it. She had that devil-may-care confidence many of them have. Unnerving. 'It's wonderful to meet you. I'm afraid my aunt insisted upon my seeing you, but there really is no need. I've suffered no more than a sprain that will no doubt heal itself in a few days with rest. But perhaps you could pretend to give it a once over for my aunt's benefit.' She glanced around at the assembled onlookers. 'We all seem to have taken up too much of your time already.'

No one agreed.

'Are you trained in medicine?' I asked, slipping off my chair and dropping to a knee.

She shook her head. 'No.'

I smiled up at her. 'Then perhaps, *I* should be the one to decide if there is a need for medical attention.'

She nodded and the hint of a smile appeared. I lifted her left foot gently to remove the shoe; she was wearing a silk stocking.

'Ah, I wonder, could you ...'

I glanced away while Sophie rolled up her trouser leg to remove the stocking and noticed that Nicole Dupré, who was sitting next to Sophie, was finding the business of my impromptu surgery much more interesting than the life-changing meeting she had just attended.

'Are you proposing or examining, Doctor?' scoffed Nicole. Damn woman.

Nicole leant in for a better look as I rested Sophie's foot on my knee and examined the ankle gently. There was no swelling and no bones were broken. I noted that she had a slender ankle, an athletic calf and her skin was beautifully soft, if a little pale.

'You have good bones, young lady,' said Nicole as I lowered the foot and rested it gently on the floor. 'Beautiful skin, too,' she added. 'Do you bathe in milk?'

Sophie snorted out laughter while slipping on her shoe, leaving the stocking rolled in a ball on the table.

'I've never had the pleasure of bathing in milk, I'm afraid,' she said. 'But I'd happily try it. Do you bathe in milk, Madam?'

Nicole shrugged in a way that betrayed her French ancestry. 'Milk is expensive,' she said. 'I don't like waste.'

I knew something of this subject and, taking to my chair, stepped in.

'Now here's an interesting thing,' I began. 'It is a proven fact that Queen Cleopatra bathed in *sour* milk because she found it improved the texture of her skin.'

'*Sour* milk?' repeated Madam Dupré.

'Yes,' I confirmed, 'and remember it *has* to be sour.'

A hand travelled to her heavily lined forehead and then to her throat. 'And it works?' she asked.

'Yes, indeed. There is scientific proof that such an activity may work … to improve the look of … wrinkles, yes?' I glanced from woman to woman to assess their interest. I sometimes found that when I entered into scientific discussion with women, they soon took on the impassive expression of the disinterested, or as my English brethren would say, they 'glazed over'. Sophie had not glazed over, although Madam Dupré was examining her fingernails.

'I suppose sour milk contains acid,' said Sophie. 'And so it must work as a kind of peeling agent.'

'Peeling agent?' repeated Nicole, who had taken on the role of providing an intermittent echo to the conversation.

'Yes,' answered Sophie.

Nicole's expression turned as sour as the hypothetical milk.

'The Greeks and Romans used other agents such as limestone for the same purpose,' I added, catching Sophie's eye. 'Although I would not recommend it, clearly.'

'Clearly,' said Sophie, amused.

'And the ankle?' asked Madam Dupré, forcing me back to the moment.

'The ankle is fine,' I said. 'There is perhaps a little bruising …' (There wasn't.) 'A day of rest is all that you need.' (She didn't.)

'And her other ankle?' asked Madam Dupré, looking at me with, if I was not mistaken, something of a challenge in her eyes.

'Her other ankle?' It was my turn to take on the role of echo.

'Goodness, Doctor! You never asked the girl which one was the injured ankle. I specifically thought so at the time and said to myself, "He hasn't asked her which ankle is the injured one". For all you know she could have twisted the right one. You simply assumed it was the left.'

Was this correct, I wondered.

Good God, it was!

I was the essence of mortification. For the first time in my entire career I had not asked the patient which was the injured ankle/leg/arm/collar bone before examination. I dropped to my knees to remove the other shoe.

Sophie glanced down and rested a hand on my shoulder.

'I believe Madam Dupré is joking,' she said. 'It is indeed my left ankle that is injured. Joseph must have told you when he came to your house earlier.'

I glanced at Nicole Dupré, who did not in the least look like she was joking.

'That is quite correct, yes,' I said, standing, my voice deeper suddenly. 'Now that I remember, he was quite specific as to which was the offending appendage. I must have remembered subconsciously.' I began to tidy my bag as Sophie stuffed the stocking in her pocket. She grabbed the crutches and attempted to stand.

'Well, thank you for these,' she said, standing and edging away from the table. 'And I'm very grateful to you for taking up your precious time, Doctor … it's Doctor Brown, isn't it?'

'Braun, yes.' I remembered my manners and held out my hand while quickly adding, 'But do, please, call me Sebastian …'

At this, two men who were loud-whispering to each other about the best places to hide their treasures from the Nazis (the cave in the cliffs, apparently) threw a knowing glance at each other before carrying on with their conversation. Madam Dupré also raised an eyebrow in my direction. I felt a blush coming on. In all my years on Sark, I never once allowed my patients to refer to me by my Christian name, feeling that the formality of surnames provided the appropriate separation a doctor requires from his patients. (This excluded Margery, of course, but even then, she only referred to me as 'Sebastian' in private.)

Sophie glanced around the table at the plethora of overly

interested faces and I noted took an air of devilish defiance. She took a deep breath, awkwardly manoeuvred the crutches to enable the holding out of her hand and said, 'And I'm Sophie Hathaway.' (Truly, her skin was pure Jersey milk). 'And I'm very pleased to meet you, Sebastian, or should I say, Romeo? Did Aunt Sibyl tell you that I'm to be your Juliet?'

All ears perked up like attentive rabbits.

'Yes, yes, she did. Wonderful news!' I was such a transparent fool. 'You are staying here for a while, then?' I asked.

'A little while, yes. I'll probably leave immediately after the performance. I *should* leave before, but I have some business to attend to.'

'The show must go on and all that, as the English say.' I sounded exactly like the sort of man who made my teeth itch – or the major. I seemed unable to prevent myself from playing the blundering fool.

'And what would *you* say?' she asked, with more kindness than playfulness in her eyes. 'Is there a translatable phrase in German, or does the German language not hold stock with such phrases?'

I looked at her to decipher her agenda, but she seemed genuinely interested, as if making a point that being born in Germany did not a Nazi make. The whole room quietened for my answer.

'Yes, the German language has many such phrases, and this one is almost directly translatable and used in the same manner. We say, "die show muss weitergehen".'

'Die show muss weitergehen,' she repeated softly. 'We're not so dissimilar then, after all.'

I shook my head. 'We are not.'

As statements go it was not a profound one, and yet there

was an instant silence to the room, which Sophie crashed straight into.

'Right!' she exclaimed, making Nicole Dupré jump. 'I'd better skedaddle to learn my lines. Only a couple of weeks or so until curtain up, as I understand it?'

'I believe so,' I said.

She shrugged playfully before nodding her goodbyes to the assembled crowd, and with an air of playfulness and yet great decorum, which was difficult to achieve at the best of times let alone on crutches, Sophie hobbled out of the kitchen. But something nibbled at my subconscious as I watched her leave, and as Madam Dupré and I tilted our heads to watch her departure, Madam Dupré said, 'I told you it was the other leg.' And she was quite correct; it was indeed the right ankle Sophie had injured, after all.

Chapter Eight

A few short days later, I took Shakespeare for a jaunt along the cliffs above La Coupée. I watched a host of early butterflies as they bounced between a patchwork of sea pinks, ragged robin and sea campion that carpeted the cliffs at that time of year. It was, in fact, the perfect day for whiling away in the garden, which was exactly the reason why I was *not* in the garden, having closed the gate on it regretfully an hour before. I had lines to learn. But with the warm sunshine on my back and the gentle southerly breeze nudging along wisps of clouds overhead, it was impossible to concentrate. I watched one particular cloud for several minutes, noting changes in the colour of the sea and fields as it passed overhead, at once dark and, moments later, light again. I wondered why it is that we always feel lifted by brightness? Why a twinkling turquoise sea is more pleasing to the soul than a deep grey one? Is it our association with the light? Does not every living thing prefer to feel the sun on its back than to sense a dark cloud above it?

And yet a dark cloud had covered our island since yesterday – Paris had fallen. I could not comprehend such a thing could happen in the modern world but it had. It all seemed so unconscionable, the fact that I was now living in dread and fear of the arrival of my own countrymen – men that I once studied with, played sport with, fought with. My old compatriots were now my enemy, and my old enemy – the British – my allies. Did this not show how ridiculous war was? I could not believe that my countrymen had not laughed in the face of Hitler, had not shaken their heads with disgust at his crazed desire to expand on this idea of an Aryan master race … The last war had much to answer for. I both commended the French for their decision to capitulate and despised them in equal parts. The latter emotion was excessively hypocritical, given that I personally refused to fight – on any side – but there it was: I was a much-flawed man.

So yes, Paris had fallen, which meant that France had all but fallen too – or capitulated – yet Dame Sibyl would insist that *die show muss weitergehen*. But I could not settle into learning my lines, and as I looked east across the sea towards France – a mere blink away – I saw the smouldering remains from the burning of the oil depositories and I knew that the blue sky above me was nothing more than an illusion, and that the blackest of all storms was a mere blink away. If I averted my gaze and turned to the west I could look upon our neighbouring island of Guernsey, a place where fear had overtaken reason, and where a whole population of children were at this very moment being torn from their mothers and shipped away to safety. But how could children be safe without their mothers by their side to protect and guide them? I understood Dame Sibyl's desire to maintain a sense of calm and normality on our own island, but really, how could 'die show weitergehen', when it was simply impossible to concentrate? I should have gone to my greenhouse that afternoon, closed the door on the world and listened to the radio, or read a little Goethe – that was, after all, what I would usually do – but the radio ceased to offer a sense of calm reflection anymore, while Goethe's relevance became staggeringly more profound. As for my garden – my oasis – which had already reached its first peak of loveliness, it was becoming a stranger to me. I stood within it as a man who has gorged on a bed of Arabian sweets and yet has lost his sense of taste and can only see the desert around him. What once brought so much joy, peace and a sense of completeness, was lost to me, perhaps because I knew – oh how I knew – that my little place of paradise would be lost to me soon, and that one way or another, my freedom and my absolute sense of being home would be gone.

Rough digging, that's what I needed to do. I would create a new bed in the meadow. Just thinking on the physical labour and the idea of expanding the garden brightened me immensely. I took up my book and stood to leave, but with a sudden spurt of enthusiasm for the play, looked out to the west and shouted, 'See, how she leans a cheek upon her hand, O, that I were a glove upon that hand, That I might touch that cheek!'

'Ay, me,' shouted Juliet. It was a distant voice but a voice nonetheless.

'She speaks?'

I turned to the direction of the voice and saw Juliet (or Sophie, depending on where I was with my suspension of disbelief) sitting atop a braying donkey on the other side of La Coupée, at the point where the broader island meets the narrow spine. She was squeezing her knees, trying to edge the donkey onto the ledge while shouting 'cush!'. This would not, I feared, end well. Firstly, only cows respond to 'cush' and even then only occasionally, and secondly, if that was Dame Sibyl's donkey she was riding, she would never persuade the beast to cross La Coupée because not one single soul ever had.

I slid down from my clifftop perch, dashed across La Coupée and halted in front of Mabel, the donkey, while trying not to appear breathless. Sophie ran the back of a hand across her forehead and blew hard upwards to push strands of her (somewhat flyaway, it must be said) hair from her eyes. This would prove fruitless. The persistent south-westerly breeze would simply blow the strands back again.

It did.

She offered me the reins, which I took. I was about to enter into polite greeting when she threw her right leg over the rear of the donkey and dismounted, landing on her left foot, I noted, confirming Nicole Dupré's diagnosis.

'I was on my way to see you,' she began, 'but old Mabel here decided it was time for a rest. I don't think she likes me.'

'All is good?' I asked, wondering if Sophie had been dispatched to alert me of some kind of medical emergency (to be sure, that was usually the only reason anyone from Great Sark crossed the precipice to see me).

'Yes, perfectly,' she answered, turning her attention to the donkey rather than catching my eye.

'I doubt that she holds any animosity towards you,' I said, 'it is simply that Mabel has never been persuaded to cross La Coupée by anyone, including the Dame. Did Joseph not explain this? Also,' I added quickly, 'for your future safety, it is best not to remain on horseback or in a carriage while crossing the ledge, but to lead the beast across … not that Mabel would have allowed herself to be led, so it is immaterial on this occasion.'

Sophie scratched the donkey's ear.

'Then it is me who is the irresponsible ass,' she said, 'not the donkey. I'm afraid I put the bridle on myself and led her out without telling anyone – my ankle isn't quite up to the walk yet, you see.' Sophie ceased to scratch and began to nuzzle. 'I wonder what it is that frightens her so?'

'Perhaps the severe drop into the sea below?' I offered.

She laughed. 'Yes, I should think that's about it.'

I considered if this was a good moment to tell her one of the many stories of ghosts, ghouls and fairies that are said to haunt La Coupée. It had long been thought by Joseph that Mabel was more sensitive – psychic, even – than most donkeys. I could also tell her of the headless horseman said to attack late night visitors, or perhaps I could recall the story of Tchico, the black dog the size of a calf who belonged to a witch ... but she would think me silly, would she not?

'And if you ever see Tchico,' I concluded, having decided to lighten the mood with my storytelling after all, 'then be on your guard! For he is nothing less than the harbinger of death!'

Sophie threw back her head and laughed, and so did the braying donkey, which made Sophie laugh all the harder.

'And have you ever seen the black dog, Sebastian?' she asked, lowering herself onto a grassy knoll, her eyes bright with happy tears.

My lips twitched a little. 'Well, I cannot say that I have and I cannot say that I haven't. All I know is that I have dug up many fairy pipes in my garden ...'

'Fairy pipes?'

'Indeed. Tiny clay pipes that are far too small for human use. The islanders believe that they belong to the little people ...'

I paused, feeling foolish, but Sophie was looking up at me,

enthralled, rubbing her ankle and waiting for further explanation.

'Aaand, such fairies are believed to live in the many burial mounds and standing stones you may have seen about the place. You are in pain,' I said. 'Your ankle.'

Sophie shrugged. 'Just a little.'

I dropped once more to my knees to assess the injury. This time, she took my hand and without any words of teasing, simply guided me to the correct ankle.

'It is definitely swollen,' I said, standing. 'You have not rested sufficiently, I think …'

'I have not rested at all,' she said, holding out her hands, which I took before gently lifting her to her feet. She looked up at me, at once apologetic and challenging. I wanted to lean in. I wanted to touch her face. I wanted to …

'I hear you have a very interesting teapot!' she said, stepping back slightly and interrupting my runaway thoughts. 'I thought, perhaps we could have tea – so long as you don't wish to poison me of course – only there's something that I'd like to …'

But I wasn't listening. I was too excited. It was too late to try to hide my keenness to spend time together. Mother once said that my eyes were my weakness – they were far too expressive. In which case Sophie would know exactly what thoughts were racing through my mind – although not *exactly* what thoughts, hopefully – and so I might as well declare my hand now. Live a little!

'Yes, do come for tea!' I said. 'And if you have the time … perhaps we could rehearse the play? Let us tether Mabel to the post and we can …'

But she took the reins and cut me short. 'Gee, I'm sorry Sebastian, but the truth is – and this is a bit awkward – but the thing is, and I couldn't really explain yesterday, in front of everyone, but I'm from a government office that is focusing on Germans who are living in British territories. That's why I have come to see you – the main reason I'm here on Sark, in fact, but not the only reason ...'

My face was a picture of confusion and, almost certainly, disappointment.

Sophie patted a satchel hanging from Mabel's saddle. 'I have paperwork that you are required to complete, and I need to interview you too. I thought we could have tea and—'

'Interview me? Why?'

'Because you are German and we are at war with Germany and we have to make sure that you are not ... well, let's say, aligned, that way. It's nothing to worry about, and quite straightforward.'

'Aligned,' I repeated softly. 'But what if I was, as you say, aligned that way?'

'Then I would have no choice but to escort you back to England where you would be interned.' She placed a hand on my arm. 'It's just a formality, Sebastian,' she said. 'Truly.'

It was taking longer than it should for me to process what was quite a simple conversation, but why on earth had Dame Sibyl put forward this woman to play Juliet and more importantly why had she not told me after the meeting the truth about her niece?

'Forgive me,' I began, 'but I am confused.'

Sophie was nudged by Mabel, who had turned around and was trying to pull away from the ledge. I loosened the reins and allowed the donkey to wander a short distance away to where she felt safe. I followed on, fearing there was nowhere on the island far enough away anymore for me to walk in order to feel the same sense of safety. I continued to walk until

Mabel began to graze on a nice patch of long grass next to the pathway. I offered Sophie the reins and took a deep breath. If she wanted to know about me, then I would tell her, but on my terms, and now.

A ran a hand through my hair. 'So here is who I am,' I began. '*What* I am,' I corrected. '*Why* I am. My name is Sebastian Braun (or "Brown" depending on my audience). I am a German doctor who stands at six feet tall exactly and am blessed with a head of thick blonde hair and decent teeth; Hitler would adore me. I have made a life for myself on the small island of Sark, which sits neatly in the English Channel (or *La Manche* as the French, not wishing to concede ownership, refer to it). Sark is an island that, thanks to a quirk of history (and some rough and tumble between the British and the French) sits in the sea only a stone's throw from France yet comes under the patronage and protection of the British. The carving up of the planet into boundaries of ownership has been an odd and complicated thing, but nevertheless, the British once took this island for their own – probably after a bloody altercation – which is why you, rather than a Frenchman, are standing in front of me now.'

'Sebastian, please. You don't—'

'I have never married, although time spent in Paris during my twenties brought me close to matrimony, but I found that, on balance, I am happier without a wife, but then as I have never had one, how can I tell? Perhaps it would be better to say that I have simply never fallen deeply in love, or my idea of love, at least, which I think would be an all-encompassing thing that would ultimately lead to nothing but a confusion of thought and a troubled mind. As I require clarity of thought for my work, I am most probably better off alone.'

'Please, you …'

'I say that I am German because it seems convention dictates – the British Empire dictates, and I say "empire" sardonically – that I *must* be defined by the country of my birth, even if I do not wish to be. I am also defined by my name, my age, my language, my profession and marital status. All of which provide a stereotype of a man that, make no mistake, I actively portray myself to be to my patients, even though I know that none of these attributes are really the things that make me "me". I believe that our lives – our personalities – are fluid things of our own creation, and for me, that creation comes in the form of my garden – my very own Eden – although that may not be the best analogy to reach for because as far as I remember things did not end so well in Mesopotamia. Speaking of the bible, one of the proverbs states that a man is known by his actions – an evil man lives an evil life; a good man lives a godly life – and although I only give a glancing nod towards religion, I really must think that statement out sometime because if it is true, then I am surely an evil man, for I have seen and done many unspeakable things. And yet I see myself these days as a good man and so I ask myself, can a man of evil deeds ever wash himself clean or are his future actions forever to be tarnished with the sins of the past? Shakespeare surely knew my mind better than I know it myself – *Out! Out! Damn spot! Ach! So!*

'You want me to answer the questions that wait for me in your satchel, Miss Hathaway, but really, there are no answers, only questions, questions, questions. And it is exactly this kind of question – whether or not I am a good man or a good doctor – that I sit and ponder upon, alone in my glasshouse, or garden, or kitchen, for far too much of the day. I do not – and this is the most important part – sit and contemplate how best I can serve a poor excuse of a man with a ridiculous moustache who would call himself my leader if I gave him half the chance.'

Sophie opened her mouth again but I was already speaking.

'Additionally, you should know that no one can persuade Mabel to cross La Coupée.' I tried and failed to keep my voice void of emotion. 'And nor should anyone try. She is a frightened animal and it would be terribly unfair to force her to do something she has no appetite to do, so I'm afraid you will have to take her home.'

Sophie nodded her agreement. I must confess that her eyes knew nothing but kindness. That is not correct. They also knew sadness.

'Now, if you will excuse me, I must return home as I am expecting patients ...' I glanced at my watch. 'Very soon.'

Sophie bit her lip. It was Saturday and she must have known that I was not expecting any calls, especially as I had offered to rehearse our scenes not five minutes before.

'Very well, Sebastian,' she said. 'Perhaps I will catch you another time and see the teapot then.'

'Please inform Dame Sibyl that she will need to find someone else to play Romeo. I have no taste for romance anymore.'

Sophie tugged at Mabel's leash and I watched as the two of them, their heads hung low, sauntered away down the path. I wanted to shout out, 'Sophie! Wait!' I felt an overwhelming sense of disappointment that this stranger, this woman with the kind, loving (if a little mischievous) eyes, was not now to come to my cottage to while away the afternoon. I had allowed my imagination to run wilder than Sophie's unkempt hair. While regaling her with stories of Sark's ghouls and ghosts, I had visualised us sitting together in my kitchen, drinking tea, laughing, teasing, joking. But this was ridiculous. We had only just met. I was no foolish teenager. And yet, hadn't Sophie's presence turned me into one from the very first? I too turned for home, across the draw bridge, across the cavernous void. Sophie was not now to be my Juliet, and I hoped more than anything that unlike Romeo, I was not just another fortune's fool.

Chapter Nine

La Santé Prison, August 1944

'Have you ever been in love, Christoph?' I ask, watching the last remaining flicker of the lantern as it dances in the dark.

Christoph removes his spectacles and rubs his eyes. When he looks up, I see that he has the look of a man who has definitely known love, even passion, although the cross on his chest is perhaps an indication that this love may not have ended well, although who am I to dictate what the definition of 'ending well' is?

'I have known it,' he says. He glances down at his cross and smiles.

'But have you never missed that side of life?' I push. 'Ever yearned for it – forgive me, I do not seek to question your faith. It is a mere curiosity.'

He shrugs good naturedly. *'The sight of lovers feedeth those in love ...'* he says.

'Ha! Then you are also an admirer of the bard, but from

which play do you quote? No, don't tell me ... *A Midsummer Night's Dream*! Ha, I am correct, am I not?'

Christoph smiles again. I like his smile. It is always just enough to convey the merest amount of emotion and yet says so much more than a full grin.

'You are not correct,' he says.

'Blast. Which one, then?'

'*As You Like It*.'

'Really? Are you certain?'

'Perfectly.'

I bow my chest to acknowledge defeat. It is not a comfortable thing to do with healing ribs.

'And when you met the person you loved, were you every bit the immature fool that I was with Sophie?'

He slides his spectacles back up his nose. 'More so, I suspect. But, *Whoever loved that loved not at first sight ...*'

'*As You Like it* again?' I ask.

'Correct answer.'

'Good old Shakespeare. He knew a thing or two about love.'

'He did. But I was young and youth makes fools of us all.'

I wonder. 'Perhaps it is love that makes fools of us?' I suggest. 'I was hardly in my youth when I met Sophie.'

But Christoph shakes his head. 'Never fools. It is love that makes *humans* of us all.'

Our silence returns. It is pleasant, but I am becoming more and more distressed that my time on this blessed earth is limited. If we fill the space – the time – with talk, I do not have to think about what is to come, or more precisely, what is *not* to come. I say this to Christoph, and how grateful I am of his company. He has been sent from heaven, I say.

'Sometimes, it is more restful – more soothing – to allow the space in to have its moment,' he says.

'Forgive me,' I say, pointedly. 'But you speak not as a man with a bullet to his head.'

'True, but …' He sits forward, animated at the thought of what he wants to say. 'Take the gaps in a Japanese-style painting, for example, or in a piece of music. They are every bit as important as the composition. The space adds meaning to the picture, or the music … or in this case the conversation.'

I think of Cornwall and a part of my story he has not heard yet. 'Ah, the Japanese concept of Ma, you mean. I have a Buddhist friend who taught me ikebana.' I glance up to see if he is familiar with the word. He is not. 'Ikebana is a Japanese style of arranging flowers,' I explain. 'It began when floral offerings were made at altars in China. The idea bled into Japan with Buddhism, becoming an important part of the tea ceremonies there. When I took tea with my friend …' I feel my eyes begin to swell. I swallow down the emotion. 'That is to say, we would prepare branches from the garden in vases, taking great care with shape and form. It was a wonderful thing to do, and yes, the space between them – the branches – was just as important as the composition.'

'You must have enjoyed taking tea with your friend,' he says, reading my emotion.

'I did, but then I had a very special teapot from which to pour it.'

'Really? Tell me.'

And so I tell him more about my assassin's teapot before eventually concluding with, '… and so you see, my time in Cornwall, which I shall come to in turn, was a peaceful time – spiritual, you might say. Are you interested in Buddhism, at all, Christoph?'

'Very,' he says.

I nod towards his chest. His cross glistens in the lamp light. 'Really? Despite that chain around your neck?' I ask.

'Quite so,' he answers.

Space.

'You know,' I begin eventually, 'I always thought that I would be at complete peace and have reached a state of calm acceptance when my moment came to leave my life. I thought that I would be so at peace with myself that I would be able to throw out forgiveness as one who has suddenly discovered the real purpose of the universe and has nothing left to discover ... but alas, that is not the case, and I am screaming inside with fear and the disappointment of being taken away too soon.'

Christoph does not comment. He stands awkwardly and grabs his stick. The damp in this place does not serve him well.

'You have time yet to find a little peace,' he says, putting on his officer's hat. 'Settle into the spaces and breath. Your breaths are the spaces. They will help you, I'm certain.'

He bangs on the door. 'I will return tomorrow to continue with your story,' he says.

'There is more to tell you about the teapot,' I say, trying so desperately to appear enthusiastic, normal, even.

He smiles. 'I don't doubt it.'

And as the door closes, I see that he has not only left the lantern behind, but the stool and the cushion also.

Chapter Ten

The note delivered by Joseph was from Dame Sibyl and was brusque to say the least.

Dear Sebastian,

I understand that you are disgruntled about Sophie's requirement to interview you. Why? You have nothing to hide and you are behaving childishly. Also, I would have mentioned it but I was preoccupied with my greater concern of trying to persuade you to leave. Make no mistake: if I thought that interning you would lead you to safety then I would instruct Sophie to slap you in chains and march you over to England tomorrow. Having said that, I would be left without my Romeo, so internment can wait.

Robert (who knows the strange workings of a man's mind) says it's understandable that you are cross, something about pride and truth and honesty, but please see sense. When Sophie arrived, I told her that you are no more a Nazi than I am, but she would insist on harnessing up Mabel and trotting over to ask you to fill out that damn paperwork. (I wonder why? No matter. From what I hear you messed up that little liaison quite nicely!) I also hear that you have

pulled yourself from the play and I think that this would be a damn
foolish thing to do and refuse to accept it. Therefore, in anticipation
that you will come to your senses, I will expect to see you at
rehearsal tomorrow – ten a.m. sharp. I hope you know your lines!

Yours, etc.

Sibyl.

I attended the rehearsal, which did not go well. I spent my
time either off stage sitting with my head in my hands and
watching through a gap in my fingers or on stage botching my
lines completely and appearing like an amateur in front of
Sophie, who was a little wooden in her performance but at
least she knew all of her lines. I was surprised to find that my
memory of the play had diminished substantially since my
teenage recital of Romeo in 1913.

So be it, I thought. We had greater issues to concern
ourselves with, although you would not have believed so had
you heard the row about iambic pentameter that ensued
between Jacob Jones and Margery Picot (whose erratic
behaviour I put down to a mixture of anxiety about the war
and sexual frustration).

The fine weather held, however, and I had the rest of the
afternoon ahead of me to tend to my garden. Possible
occupation would not prevent me from sowing fresh seeds or
planning for the future; after all, if no man ever planted a tree
he perhaps would not be around to witness mature – where
would mankind be then? Without trees in our gardens,
presumably.

When I stepped out of the dark of the hall and into the light
of the day I saw Sophie standing on the track talking to Mary
Rhoe, the postmistress, who was sitting in her cart. It is
perhaps ungentlemanly of me to say so, but Sophie was

wearing a floral patterned dress that did a great deal for her figure. Her thick hair was tied loosely in a bow. On her feet were plimsolls. I decided to glance away. Nothing good could come of appreciating Sophie's form. She was the deceptive Eve to my Adam, the conniving Cleopatra to my Anthony, Delilah to my Samson, Lady Macbeth to my ...

'Doctor! Doctor Brown. Over here, if you please.'

It was Mary Rhoe, beckoning me over. I removed my Panama hat. 'Good afternoon, Miss Rhoe,' I said. The snub on Sophie was obvious, and perhaps beneath me, but entirely justified, I felt. 'How may I be of assistance?'

'Tell me. How old are you now, Doctor Brown?' she asked.

There was a pause while we all considered the directness of the question. I would have thought it rude had it not come from Mary's lips. (Mary Rhoe is a gentle but frank person known to be without malice or gossip or devilment of any kind.)

'I am forty-three,' I said.

Mary nodded slowly. 'Hmm, forty-three.' She took a moment to consider this, although what she was considering, I could not say. 'It *sounds* old,' she said, turning to Sophie, 'but that is still a very young age for a man of Sebastian's energy and virility.'

She assessed my hair. 'And not a spit of grey. Yes, there's time for you to have children yet, although not so much time as to not get on with it.' She glanced at Sophie who, as usual when in my company, was stifling a laugh. Despite my determination not to allow myself to give Sophie much more than the time of day – she was the enemy at the gate, after all – I was pleased to see the light return to her eyes.

'Thank you for the advice, Madam,' I said, putting on my hat, 'but really, I ...'

Mary interrupted by holding out her hand in a manner that suggested she required help to step off her cart. I offered my hand but she handed me the reins.

'Miss Hathaway would very much like to see the island today,' she said, stepping off the cart without assistance. 'I would offer to drive her around myself – she can't walk as she's sprained her ankle, poor thing – but my dog, by coincidence, also has a sprain on an ankle and I must get back to him.'

'Which one?' I asked, my eyes narrowing.

'The back right one,' she answered without a pause. (I meant which dog had the sprain as she has two miniature Schnauzers but I let the answer stand). 'Also, on stage,' she went on, 'you're both very wooden together, yes, definitely very wooden. Well, you are, Sebastian, Sophie wasn't too bad, but no one will ever believe that the two of you are in love if you carry on that way. So, if you have nothing else to do this afternoon, I think you should get to know each other better ...'

She waited for me to answer but I had no idea what I was expected to say. Sophie stepped in to explain.

'What Mary is suggesting, Sebastian, is that you drive me around the island for an hour or so in her carriage to show me the sights. I was just explaining that Aunt Sibyl has instructed me to become more familiar with the island and all of its idiosyncrasies before ...'

'Before the Germans arrive?' offered Mary Rhoe.

'Before I leave,' corrected Sophie.

Mary elbowed me in the ribs.

'Right. Well. Of course. If that is what is called for then ...'

But Sophie began to excuse herself. 'I'm sure Doctor Brown has much more urgent calls upon his time than to while away the afternoon gallivanting around the island with me, Miss Rhoe. I can easily ask Uncle Robert to show me around.'

The elbow hit my ribs a second time.

'It is no trouble,' I said, finally looking at Sophie directly, and finding, of course, that I meant it.

'But don't you have patients to attend to?' she asked, her face an image of innocence. (I noted that she already had one toe on the foot plate.)

Mary answered on my behalf. 'On a Sunday?' she exclaimed. 'You're lucky to get an appointment with this one during the working week, let alone on Sunday!'

'Shall we?' I offered my hand, half hopeful, half resigned.

'I'd love to!' she said, holding out her hand. She climbed into the cart taking the weight on her right foot, I noticed, which was pleasing.

'No need to hurry back with the cart,' said Mary as I took the reins. 'Take your time. Oh, but just wait there a moment … I need to grab something from inside the hall.'

The smiles were awkward between us while we waited, at least, mine was awkward, but there had returned something of a sparkle to Sophie's eyes that suggested amusement. A full five minutes later, Mary returned with a small parcel wrapped in a gingham cloth. 'A late lunch for Romeo and Juliet,' she said, handing the parcel directly to Sophie.

'But … this is too generous. Who arranged this?' I asked.

'Sibyl, obviously,' said Mary with a shrug. 'Make the most of these days while we can, you two. Who knows what the future has in store!'

I offered my thanks to Mary, nodded my respects to the assembled onlookers of which there were many, flicked the reins and off the donkey trotted; my garden would be nothing but a jungle by the time I returned home.

We toured Sark for two hours without much of a break and I admit, I enjoyed myself. We took in such highlights as the stone circle, the Gouliot caves, the window in the rock and the island's prison. (It is a surprisingly fascinating place.) I explained that touring Sark by cart wasn't so much a matter of going from this place to that, while peering over the banks and verges to grab a quick glance of a landmark before moving on, but instead it was better to meander wherever the donkey chose to take us and enjoy the beauty along the way, both rugged in parts and achingly gentle in others, depending how the mood took us (or the donkey, rather). Luckily, our donkey chose to travel via many interesting parts, and so the conversation flowed well – too well. I tried to educate and enlighten Sophie regarding the ethos and mood of the place (the fact that there were no cars, no airstrip and no electricity did not seem to bother her in the least). During a brief stroll through Dixcart woods while Mabel took a rest, I told of the flowers in springtime – the banks of primroses and wild hyacinths, the sheets of bluebells and wild pansies – and she looked me in the eye and declared with the sort of excessive exuberance typical of an unrestrained person of American influence that she had *fallen in love*! (I wished her Juliet persona were so free and loose on the stage, but perhaps that would come). 'But truly,' she went on, 'what is there not to love about this island? I defy any person to visit Sark and not to fall in love!'

She held my gaze.

I held hers.

Margery would call it, 'a moment'.

And so to the picnic. The donkey chose a delightful spot in

the middle of a large patch of yellow gorse on the cliffs above the lighthouse for our afternoon tea.

'Did you know that Aunt Sibyl has brought the Sark Derby forward?' Sophie was munching her way through a roast chicken sandwich. 'It's on Wednesday, this week.'

This week? I thought, with an appropriate amount of consternation. It really did seem that Dame Sibyl was determined to keep the home fires burning (and the populace entertained) for as long as possible.

'Do you usually enter the race?' she asked.

I shook my head. 'I am usually waiting at the finish line to tend to any medical emergencies.'

'Really? And are you usually busy? With your medical emergencies, I mean.'

'It depends upon how much cider Joseph Martin and his friends have drunk beforehand, or if Alex Vibert is involved.'

Sophie laughed. 'Why?'

'Let's just say his horse is best described as … unpredictable, and Alex likes to have a few drinks. The race is usually in September, the week after the flower show.'

'Oh, I've heard all about the infamous flower show. You're quite the man to beat – the competition. Or so I hear.'

Me? Competitive? And at a flower show? I felt frumpish. Old before my time. I did not wish Sophie to think of me as an old man who only grew flowers, like Joseph, and suddenly had a hankering to own a horse, just so I could gallop over the horizon like the hero in an Austen novel and appear a little more … mannish. It was a ridiculous thought, and yet I visualised myself wearing tight jodhpurs and carrying a whip … Why was I having these thoughts, these doubts about my lifestyle, I wondered. Was I really so easily swayed as to have my foundations rocked just because this firebolt had catapulted itself into my life and fired up certain feelings, certain reactions that, make no mistake, as a person of medicine I knew were simply a man's natural responses to spending time with an attractive woman?

But to answer the question: yes. I was.

Even so, why now? Why Sophie? I had lived on the island for years, easily turning the other cheek to a number of lovely women who passed by my door, and slowly, bit by bit, I had grown older, not in age, but in spirit, in conversation, in attitude. Then, in walked Sophie, stage right, and bang! Thunderbolt!

'I confess, I do take my roses – in particular – quite seriously,' I said, simply confirming my conclusion that I am nothing more than an old, boring man. 'I am nothing like my alter ego, I'm afraid …'

I leant across to pick a stem of gorse. It was tough and I struggled to snap it off.

'Your alter ego?' she asked.

'Romeo. Compared to him, I am really quite dull.'

I offered her the stem, which she took.

'For what it's worth, I was expecting a toothless old man to attend to me at Aunt Sibyl's the other day, but when you showed up … well, let's say it was a nice surprise. I don't think you're dull at all. Quite the opp—'

I held up my hand. I wanted her to stop, but then I absolutely did *not* want her to stop! 'Forgive me,' I said. 'I was not fishing for a compliment.' (I was.) 'I suppose I am merely trying to explain that I lead a very simple life. I tend to my fruit, my flowers and vegetables and I tend to the sick.' I tittered to myself. 'And most people here would say that I do so in that order.'

Sophie put down a bottle of apple juice, looked out to sea,

stretched both arms above her head and lay herself down on the grass, resting on her elbows. I tried not to look, but God help me, I couldn't help it. After a few moments she turned onto her side to face me. This helped, but only marginally. The curve of her hip under the dress ... the line of her neck ... the moisture of the juice on her lips ...

'It sounds like a marvellous life to me,' she said. 'But are you never lonely?'

I considered this. Was I lonely? I had been asked this before, not often, but it had been asked of me, and I usually answered with an immediate and expressive, 'Nein!'. But perhaps with Sophie, a transient stranger who – let us not forget – was there to assess and analyse me, I might as well be truthful. Was that what she was doing now, I wondered. Analysing me? Did the British government care if I was lonely? I doubted it.

'Now and again,' I said, 'in the evenings, but only in winter. There is usually someone to call upon – either as a doctor or as a friend – and so I do not remain lonely for long. You have probably worked out by now that men as a species are really quite straightforward beings. I cannot speak for such creatures as Hitler or Atilla the Hun, or even great minds like Aristotle or Goethe, but I can definitely say, having spoken to many men in my surgery,' (kitchen) 'that most people of our sex really only desire a straightforward, easy kind of existence.'

She narrowed her eyes playfully and her lips twitched. 'I think what you're really saying is that life for a man is straightforward right up until the point they fall in love.'

'Well, I ...'

'I also hear that your potager garden is the best on the island ... you even put the roses at La Seigneurie to shame. Joseph says so.'

I was secretly pleased with this.

'No, no …' I stammered, shaking my head and pulling up tufts of grass. 'Joseph exaggerates, which is good of him. My modest plot cannot compete – although I do think my chances of success in this year's show are quite …' I paused and glanced across the water towards France.

'What is it?'

What is it? Two things. The first, there would be no flower show this year, of that I was certain. The second … here I was, immersed in my garden like an old widow. I used to be such a vibrant, confident man – a man's man. But after the last war, I turned away from the overt masculinity of the young. After all, it was a whole tribe of men's men that had led us across the fields of Europe to hell and back, and I had been one of them – raised by my father to be a fearless soldier, smug at my own attractiveness with women, successful in my profession (there was talk of becoming a surgeon at one time) but then I woke up one day in a Parisian bedroom and I felt numb. I felt nothing. I felt empty. The images of the battlefields, the courtyards of firing squadrons, the burial of the dead, it was all still there, on constant replay. And so I came to Sark and buried myself in nature, and it worked, I became content. I found peace. But here was this woman lying next to me and suddenly I knew that I had found peace at the cost of something else: youthful fun.

'I was just thinking that it is unlikely that there will be a show this year,' I said. I looked down at her and shrugged. 'There will be other years, I'm sure.'

She sat up then, shuffled her bottom towards me and rested her shoulder against mine. We sat for a while – letting the space in – staring across to France, hidden inside our own minds and yet connected.

'Did I mention that Victor Hugo was a keen visitor to the island?' I asked, eventually.

'No, you didn't.' She adjusted her scarf in an attempt to keep her hair from blowing across her face. I edged towards her a little to act as a block to the breeze.

'When he visited the Channel Islands he wrote about his time on Sark, and let me see … ah, yes, that is it, he said, "I gorge myself on flowers and dew … the beauty is absurd". What would you say to that summation?'

'I would say that I have to agree with him,' she said, glancing around.

'And he was not the only man of literature to appreciate it. A few years later, Swinburne …' I paused to see if she recognised the name.

'The poet?'

'Yes. He referred to Sark as, "the loveliest and wonderfullest thing I have ever seen", so he was a man of good taste, I think.'

She rested a hand on my arm. 'That's how you feel, isn't it?'

I looked down at her hand. She removed it. I had not intended for her to do so.

'Yes, but who could not? Did you know that the island has been inhabited, one way or another, since 2000 BC?'

'I did not,' answered Sophie, her eyes dancing again. I felt I must keep them dancing.

'Then you are probably also unaware that religion arrived on the island via Saint Magloire who was riding on the back of a sea monster!'

'A sea monster!' she exclaimed. 'He sounds like quite the man of the hour. A super-saint!'

'Indeed he was. In the thirteenth century, the Crown – the English Crown, of course – took ownership of Sark, if that is the correct term, but the island was practically deserted for a while and it was only used as a stopping off place.'

'A stopping off place? For whom?'

I suddenly felt an urge to cover an eye, grab a branch as a makeshift sword, take Sophie by the hand and dance around the cliffs pretending to be pirates. I buttoned in the urge.

'Oh, the usual crew – pirates and murderers, I should imagine. But then in 1565, Queen Elizabeth granted a charter for a well-connected Jersey man to set up a fiefdom here, insisting that he brought forty families with him.'

'And did he?'

'Yes. Most of the families came from Jersey and their descendants remain here still. He offered each family a parcel of land, and that is where the Chief Pleas originates. This is the last feudal state in Europe, although some of the privileges of La Seigneurie are perhaps in need of review …'

'Hmm,' murmured Sophie. 'I noticed that tempers became a little frayed in the meeting.' She bit into an apple. A little of the juice slid down her chin. She wiped it with her sleeve. This was a woman who would not mind getting her hands dirty, I thought – I hoped. 'Although Aunt Sibyl did seem to be able to justify most of them – these privileges.'

'Most, but not all.'

'Such as?' she asked, taking another bite.

'The one that allows La Seigneurie to sleep with any bride on her wedding night is perhaps a little outdated.'

'No!' Sophie rolled onto her back and laughed, so much so that she began to choke on the apple.

A slap on the back did not dislodge the offending morsel, leaving me no option but to stand, manoeuvre my arms under her ribs from behind and thrust upwards. Her breath returned after a second thrust, but even so, neither of us moved, my arms remained around her ribs, holding her closely to me, keeping her safe, feeling her breath slowly returning. Sophie's body tucked into mine felt warm, it felt secure, it felt … right. And I knew it then as I know it now – the two of us, we fit.

If she turns around to face me, I said to myself, *then damn it all, I shall kiss her.* But the scarf was loosened during the tussle and began floating away in the strengthening wind. Reluctantly, I released Sophie and chased after it. The silk smelled of lavender, I remember.

Having retrieved the scarf and after a few moments of assurance – laughter, jokes about how good it was to have a doctor present – we began to pack away the picnic. Our time together was coming to an end.

'You're an excellent tour guide,' she said as we walked back to the cart. She wrapped her scarf around her wrist, having given up on trying to control her medusa hair. 'Very …. informative.'

I thought she would wink when I glanced at her – I had perhaps been a little thorough in my offer of historical information – but there was not one trace of irony across her face. Sophie had been a keen and engaging companion the whole afternoon.

I will tell her this! I thought. She would think it a compliment.

Her response as I helped her onto the cart showed how unprepared I was for discourse with women.

'Really? You think it unlikely that my sex will be interested in history, or nature, or science, perhaps?'

'No, I …'

I passed up the picnic basket which she placed by her feet.

'Perhaps in your discussions with other women,' she

added, 'when they became disinterested in your conversation, were you addressing them as patients, or as friends?'

In truth I had no female friends, except perhaps Margery, and she had definitely glazed over on several occasions.

'Patients, mainly,' I confirmed.

She laughed. 'Then, forgive me, but I think that anyone would seem disinterested if you were explaining the fascinating science behind the fact that the small lump in a breast was something called a tumour and that she will be dead before her family could bring in the corn.'

Tumour? Corn? 'I have no such patient ...' I said. My temples were beginning to throb.

'It's an analogy,' she explained. 'You know what an analogy is?'

'Of course!'

'Well, the lady concerned would no doubt simply want to leave your company as quickly as possible so that she could go home and ...

'Sob.' I said, now up to speed with the scenario.

'No, not initially. The poor thing wouldn't have the time. All she would be able to think of is how her family would ever cope without her, and all the measures she must put into place in order to ensure that they did. Perhaps, Sebastian, women are too busy to have the time to listen to a complicated explanation. Often it's best to just offer the facts so that they can move on to deal with the thousand other things they have to do that day while their husbands potter in the garden.'

'You are teasing me,' I said. 'And I deserve it.'

'Only a little.' She squeezed my hand, smiling.

I untied the donkey from a fence post. I had intended, the next time we spoke, to ask Sophie about her job and about the true nature of her enquiries into my life ... but right now, I was happy to see that I was not, as the English say although I have no idea why, 'in the bad books' and I did not want to spoil the afternoon.

'Tell me,' I began as we trundled down the road and I ruminated. 'From where do you think the English expression, "in the bad books" originates? Was it used in America?'

And then she laughed spontaneously, as if I had just told the best joke in the world. And when she laughed, the world was perfect.

Chapter Eleven

The last of the British army contingent left Sark on the morning of 20th June. I watched as the boat disappeared around the headland. I had not made a special trip to Creux harbour to wave them off, but was attending to an elderly gentleman who lived alone in a cottage above the harbour. He was a previous harbour master and on retirement chose to continue to live 'above the shop'. Watching the British leave, he said, was the straw that broke the camel's back (another odd English term that I ought to have examined for its genealogy). The worry of being abandoned by the British brought on palpitations, and given that he already had a heart condition, the situation was not ideal. It did not help, of course, that he had been sitting at his window for the past week, watching on as the last bastion of hope gradually sailed away, and sailed away without so much as a backward glance, either. As was the case for all Channel Islanders – we now felt a sense of vulnerability and fear, the type of which not one of us would have thought could ever come to pass, and some of my patients began to compare their anxious states to a variety of

English phrases about animals, such as … sitting ducks, lambs to slaughter and going to the dogs. None of this helped to alleviate the fears of my vulnerable patients. I did my best to soothe them, but my German accent, I feared, did not help the issue. Nevertheless, die show muss weitergehen, as they say, although I wished to your almighty God that it didn't.

The Sark Players continued to meet each evening at the hall for an agonising three hours of rehearsal. None of our hearts or minds were committed to the creation of a half-decent performance and none of us had a chance of remembering our lines. I half-hoped that 'the Germans' would arrive early, simply to save us the embarrassment of an agonisingly poor performance. The only person who was effective in the whole company was the prompt – Margery – to whom I had prescribed honey and brandy because her voice was hoarse from all of the talking she was having to do. She remained in fairly fine spirits, which might have had something to do with the fact that I caught her giving the eye to the butcher. It seemed she had taken my advice and had begun to encourage the attentions of the most suitable mate on the island. (I regretted afterwards encouraging such immoral activity, but do remember that 'the Germans' were coming!)

In the afternoon I found myself on the wrong side of La Coupée once again – the right side being the sanctuary of Little Sark and my garden – but it was of no matter as I was taking the opportunity to call on Dame Sibyl, or rather her pregnant dog, Poppy, who had been suffering from malaise. I took Penstemon cuttings – for Dame Sibyl, not the dog. Dame Sibyl, unlike Poppy, was still in the 'dog house' with me a little (another phrase I did not understand the background of), but that was no reason to abandon neighbourly generosity, and anyway, Joseph had asked for some.

I was shown to the living room and examined the dog. She was strong as an ox.

I then examined Dame Sibyl. Ditto.

We took tea in the garden and I glanced around as we sat in companiable silence.

'You spent yesterday afternoon with Sophie, I heard?' Of course she had. 'Which must mean that you have recovered from your bout of churlishness. Has she actually gotten around to doing that blasted Home Office interview with you yet?'

'No.'

'Bright little spark,' she said. 'Very clever girl. Incredible pianist, did you know?'

'I did not.'

'Lonely, though. It shows in her playing. Bad divorce, too, a while back'

Could I ask? Would it be obvious? I bit on a scone and said, 'Divorce?'

'Married an American oaf to please her father, but she always missed Paris. She grew up there, for part of the time, at least. You should ask her about it sometime.'

This was clearly all the information I would receive on that score. But …

'And her job? You mentioned the Home Office. Is she some kind of elaborate spy hunter who travels the world seeking out enemies of the state?'

Dame Sibyl laughed. 'Well that's the point of spies, I suppose. They're always the types of people you don't suspect. No, I asked her about her job when she arrived and she was quite woolly about it so I knew better than to pry. I know she has a role in the Home Office and that's all I know – loose lips sink ships and all that, old chap.'

And that was the conversation strand over.

'And what will you do if this interview of hers proves me to be an enemy of the British?' I put down the scone and picked up the tea cup. 'You will have lost your doctor *and* your Romeo.'

'Enemy of the British?' she scoffed. 'You? I'd more likely suspect the major. Anyhow, I filled in the form for you already. Did it when Sophie arrived on the island.'

'You did what?'

'Filled it out for you. I wasn't for one second going to let you trip yourself up, with all your honesty and over-thinking of things and whatnot. You'll be happy to know that I more than amply proved that you are a fit citizen for Sark – even though you are German.'

'But Sophie. She came …?'

'To interview you anyway. I can't imagine why.'

And then she threw me a complicated look that said … well, I am not sure exactly what the look said because reading complicated expressions has never been one of my strengths. I always wished that my fellow human beings would simply vocalise what they were thinking rather than throw out glances and hints. I often said so to my patients. My opinion being that if something is worth saying, say it. If not, then say nothing at all, but do not throw out glances that are prone to misinterpretation.

'I have been making enquiries as to where we could send you to live in England,' she said, pouring more tea.

Ah.

I threw her an eye roll while appreciating my hypocrisy on the facial gestures issue.

'We have discussed this,' I began. 'And I will not leave my patients.'

'So you say. But at least hear me out on a possible

104

contingency plan that would be viable should you ultimately choose to leave ...' She glanced at me over her glasses. 'It is always sensible to consider our options, is it not, Doctor?'

'Quite so. But by what means would I live? The English would not, I think, wish to be cared for by a German doctor ...'

'You could sell that fancy teapot of yours ...' she suggested.

'Hmm,' was my response.

'I have a cousin,' she said, 'in Cornwall, near Penzance. We have spoken on the telephone. I explained your situation and she would be happy to take you in – my cousin is what is often referred to as Bohemian, or an elderly eccentric. But to me she is simply marvellous – and an obsessive gardener, so you should rub along quite nicely.'

I really was far too old for my time!

'I should warn you though ... German nationals living in Britain are not being treated with a great deal of kindness at present. You've heard of Fifth Columnists?'

I had and I said so.

'It seems the British government has taken paranoia to the next level and suspect every German in Britain of lenience towards the Fifth Column. Churchill has given orders to "collar the lot".'

'Collar?'

'Intern them, dear chap.' She picked up a ball and threw it for Poppy, who was far too advanced in her pregnancy to be bothered to chase it. 'Round them up and shut them away; that's their motto. All of which means that when you leave here – I beg your pardon, *if* you leave here – there may be an issue of jumping out of the frying pan and into the fire, although perhaps it would be the other way around in this scenario. The basic fact is, as a German citizen who is unwilling to fight, there is nowhere for you to belong in Europe – neither side wants you.'

She patted my arm. 'But I should throw your lot in with the Brits if I were you. Maybe even allow Sophie to take you home with her. Internment in Blighty would surely be better than being forced into being a Nazi. Although, Fortune – my cousin in Cornwall – would do her best to ensure that you were kept safe. She's a *very* well connected woman.' Dame Sibyl turned in her chair to assess me. 'Out of interest, do you think you could pass yourself off as a Scot?'

'No.'

I drank my tea and considered how to change the conversation. The weather, perhaps? Too bland. The play? We were unlikely to agree. Sophie? Absolutely not.

'Your roses are looking well,' I said, turning to nod in the direction of the rose garden. 'I thought *Madam Le Carrier* was looking particularly healthy when Joseph showed her off to me last week. He did the right thing with that harsh prune in February, I think.'

Dame Sibyl shook her head and smiled.

'Sebastian, please. Do be sensible and think clearly about your fate ...'

I put down my cup. She was a dog with a new bone.

'The Germans may not come,' I said. 'But if they do, then I think they will allow me to remain here as your doctor. Perhaps you were correct when you said that I could ask my brother to offer assistance.' I selected a second scone. Best to make the most of baked goods now before the soldiers arrived. 'We have not been in touch for some time, but ... perhaps this would be a good moment to correct that. It has been too long and I am beginning to see that now.'

'Why?'

I paused mid-bite. 'I'm sorry?'

'Why have you not been in touch for some time?'

I shrugged before biting. 'It's a complicated family matter.'

She smiled a sweet smile, which sat oddly on Sibyl. 'These things usually are. Families are always messy. Do yourself a favour and uncomplicate it, if only to make a middle-aged woman happy?'

I scratched my head and sighed. Where to start? With my mother? No. With the First War? No. With Father? Yes.

'I have a twin brother as you know – Sascha. We were very close, but Father joked – to both of us – that I got all the best bits while we were in the womb. Strength, looks, brains, daring spirit, charm … yes, you might look surprised, but I was not always the mild-mannered gardener I have established myself to be on Sark. Before the war – the first one – I was smug, showy, a crack shot. Father – a devout military man, if one can use the words devout and military in the same context – would …' I paused, this was still not easy to speak of.

'Your father would?'

'Beat Sascha – if he couldn't keep up with me. Try to make more of a man of him.'

'Beat him? You mean, hit him?'

'Exakt. There is lots more to tell but let's just say that the war changed us both. Sascha stayed on in Belgium with Father during the war as a soldier on Father's regiment, constantly trying to prove himself. I escaped by volunteering for the front. After the war I went home and found that Father was still being cruel to Sascha and also, as a new development although perhaps I simply hadn't noticed before, to my mother. When I knew for sure that he hit her, I hit him back. I beat him till he was nearly dead – there was so much anger in me then. I asked Sascha and Mother to leave with me, but they wouldn't. They seemed angry that I had defended them, although Mother never remained angry for long. I wrote to say that I was living in Paris, and then later from Sark. I received letters from Mother initially and then Sascha wrote not long after I arrived on Sark to say that Mother had died, which broke me, not just because Mother was dead but because Sascha wrote only three words. *Mother is dead.*

'I'm sorry,' said Dame Sibyl.

'So you see, I do not know if my brother will be of any assistance and he may still be under the influence of Father, but make no mistake, if the Germans try to recruit me as a doctor in the SS. I shall refuse.'

It was time to change the subject again. Sophie it was. I asked her whereabouts, feigning some requirement to discuss the play.

'Oh, she's gone for a cycle – and before you ask, her ankle seems better now, thank you.' She returned to her indecipherable look. 'I heard mention that she was going to head over to your neck of the woods. *And* ... she took Shakespeare with her.'

Dame Sibyl stood and shouted for Poppy, who had taken to foraging around one of the herbaceous borders like a snuffling pig. 'Perhaps you should catch up with her. I hear you could do with a little thespian practice?'

I laughed. 'I certainly could! But with regret, I have patients to see ...' I glanced towards the gate.

'And are any of them seriously ill?' she asked.

'No.'

Poppy arrived for a pat.

'In that case ...' She paused to ruffle the dog's ears, 'I suggest you make the most of your freedom whilst you have it and skip off and find Sophie.'

'Skip?' I mocked. 'Since when did I skip, Madam?'

She grasped my hand, tucked my arm into hers and we began walking along the driveway.

'You never have,' she said. 'But isn't it time that you did?'

I thought of Sophie riding her bike, probably flying across La Coupée at this very moment, even though it is not really safe to do so. But no, the Germans were coming. This was no time for skipping. And also, who on earth was Sophie Hathaway? Who was this impetuous woman who could make my breath catch just by glancing my way? Old man I might be, but I had been a contented man for many years and surely it was best to keep it that way. After all, as Sophie said, men are generally very contented until a woman comes along – until love comes along – to ruffle things up. But wouldn't that be wonderful, just for a while? To ruffle things up? I imagined us kissing on the beach.

Good God man, find some self-discipline and attend to your patients!

'I shall look out for her,' I said.

And I did.

With my doctor's bag swinging away in my right hand (it was as close to a skip as I could muster) I walked out of La Seigneurie and headed, not in the direction of my patient who lived half a mile to the north (Noel Hotton – gout), but south, towards Little Sark, and if I happened to bump into Sophie in the process, so be it. Obviously I would not look out for her with any deliberate intent. We were barely friends, after all, and it would be inappropriate to seek her out, but two hours later, having wandered the paths and byways of Little Sark twice and with the sun much lower in the sky and my doctor's bag no longer swinging quite so merrily, I arrived home to find Sophie sitting in a wheelbarrow in my front garden – her bicycle was abandoned in the lane. She was reciting Shakespeare. I detected only a marginal improvement.

I coughed.

She put a finger in the air to suggest I held my tongue.

'*Oh happy dagger!*' she exclaimed. '*This is thy sheath; there rust and let me die. O, O … O?*'

I decided to help her out. '*I am slain!*'

'Thank you. *O, I am slain!*' she repeated while jumping out of the wheelbarrow with the swift motion of a gymnast. She rolled up her script and thrust both her hands and Shakespeare deep into the pockets of her dungarees. The headscarf was a different colour today: pale blue. It suited her. Good God, it was great to see her. I was just about to say, 'Hello,' and offer some kind of beverage when she said, 'I'm afraid some ass has damaged your sign.'

Striding past me, she gestured towards my doctor's surgery notice. I followed to the front of the gate and saw that someone had crossed out 'Danke' and written, "Go home Boche!"'

Ah.

'It is my accent,' was my response.

'It's horseshit!' was Sophie's. 'I thought we'd rehearse our closing scene,' she said, turning towards the house. 'The big suicide one. That way we'll knock 'em all dead at the rehearsal this evening.'

I glanced around. My house stood alone, but still, I considered the possibility that someone may have wandered past and seen Sophie there, whiling away the hours in my wheelbarrow.

'Unless, of course, you're worried I might tarnish your reputation with my ill-gotten Gallic- slash-Yankee ways?'

I feigned repudiation. 'Not at all. I thought I heard a cuckoo, that is all.' I gestured towards the door. 'Please, do, go into the kitchen.'

And as Sophie stepped under the rose-covered arch (*Alfred Carrier*) and wandered wide-eyed into the kitchen, I realised that she was the first woman other than Margery to enter my house in quite some time (ever) who was not Dame Sibyl or a patient.

'Say, why don't we start by putting the kettle on and you can tell me all about this interesting teapot of yours,' she said, stepping into the kitchen. She batted her eyes somewhat. Was she flirting, or was it grit from the wheelbarrow? 'Perhaps you could even … show it to me?' She wiggled her left shoulder and raised her eyebrows. Flirting. Definitely flirting.

'Perhaps I could!' was my (somewhat coquettish, I thought) response.

Chapter Twelve

La Santé Prison, August 1944

'It has been quite the conversation starter, my little teapot, over the years ...' Nostalgia drips off every word.

Christoph has returned, and with more trinkets.

Having positioned his stool next to my bunk, he takes a metal cylinder out of his army-issue knapsack and I watch while he twists the top off the cylinder and pulls out a field-stove. Even under the light of the lantern the stove looks immaculate, and highly sophisticated.

'I thought Hitler had run out of money,' I say, edging forward to take a closer look. 'Is he issuing new equipment in the hope of improving morale? It seems odd to issue such equipment just as the Allies approach the gates of the citadel?'

Christoph unfolds three metal legs from underneath the gas cannister. 'This is a Coleman stove,' he says. 'Only recently issued.'

'To whom?'

He glances up and smiles. 'To the US army,' he says.

I let out a long whistle through broken teeth. 'And I thought chaplains were the innocent slaves of the Lord! Where on earth did you get it?'

'It is a long story,' he says. 'Maybe another time.' He realises the folly of what he has said and adds, 'Later. I will tell you later. But look! It has spare parts contained within this tube … clever, no?'

Indeed it was clever, I agreed, and we spent the next ten minutes taking it apart to assess the quality of the engineering before putting it back together again.

'But I think the leather seal on the primer will wear too quickly,' he says, starting to prime the gas. 'But it will suit our purpose today quite nicely.'

I'm not exactly sure what our purpose is, but I recline on my bunk and watch him prepare the stove, grateful of yesterday's cushion. He turns a knob on the cannister and we hear the hiss of releasing gas – with a match the burner beneath the stove is lit. He then takes several further items out of his knapsack: a mess tin, a flask of water, two cups, a small muslin drawstring bag, a candle, a vase, some birch twigs of all things and, even more incredibly, a teapot, wrapped in silk. The cups have no handles. I shake my head.

'A Japanese tea ceremony!' I exclaim. 'It is as though you know my story ahead of me telling it to you!'

Christoph sniffs back the compliment and shakes his head. 'We are very similar, I think, you and I.' He pours water into the mess tin and places it on the stove. 'Now, be silent while I prepare for the ceremony.' He sets the twigs in a cup artfully and places his hands together. 'I could not source matcha and we cannot carry out the full process, but we can improvise, can we not? After our little ceremony we will drink our tea while you continue with your story. Would you like that?'

I drop my head. A lump of fond memories builds in my throat. 'I can think of nothing better,' I say, and I mean it.

Chapter Thirteen

Sophie sat down at my kitchen table at four p.m.

I made tea, secretly pouring water infused with leaves in one chamber and the milk in the other. To her great amusement, I poured the tea, and then the milk.

'And from the very same pot!' she declared. 'It's like magic! But how does it work?'

I explained the science behind it.

'And the whole point of the design is to enable a person to poison his enemy?' she said, picking up the teapot and pouring from each section herself. 'What a wonderful – theatrical – way to do it! I love it!' Her eyes were wide open, her smile contagious. 'Have you ever … you know …' She sent her eyebrows skyward.

'I'm afraid not. Are you disappointed?'

'A little,' she joked. (At least, I hoped she was joking). 'But there's always time! Shakespeare should have given such a teapot to Juliet. The outcome would have been much happier if he had …'

'So long as she remembered to cover the correct hole and not poison herself,' I said. 'But knowing Romeo and Juliet, they would have poured it the wrong way round.'

She laughed. 'Yes, you're quite right. The human element is always the flaw in the plan. I'm sure if I was about to poison someone I'd go and put my finger over the wrong hole and darn well poison myself! Say, that lid isn't *real* gold, is it?'

I nodded that it was.

'And the diamonds around the rim?'

'Entirely authentic.'

Sophie whistled, which brought our discussion of the teapot to a close.

By five p.m. we had not even turned to the first page of our manuscripts, but our lively conversation had run down many interesting rabbit holes as we ruminated over a variety of abstract ideas and concepts, including an attempt to go so far as to define what an abstract idea actually was. We decided that an abstract idea or thought was something removed from human senses in that it could not be tasted, touched or smelled – like democracy, government, world peace, good and bad. I also offered 'freedom' while Sophie offered 'love'.

At around six p.m. Sophie sat back in her chair, kicked off her plimsolls and declared this to be the 'driest pub on Sark!' at which I dashed off to the potting shed to fetch a bottle of last year's elderflower wine, which had become more potent with age but was all the better for it. (Margery called it 'Doctor's Ruin').

We sat happier still while I told of the legend of the elderflower – of how witches congregate in late summer under the branches when full of fruit – and how one must always ask permission of the elder before cutting, while chanting a song to the mother of the elder. If not, I stressed while also grabbing her arm for added effect, terrible – shocking, even – things would befall the person who did the cutting.

'And have you ever cut an elder without asking its permission, Sebastian?' she asked.

'Never!' I knocked back my wine and opened a second bottle.

We moved on to discuss the principle of Occam's Razor, or the law of parsimony in problem solving, which I often advocate, that being (I quoted to Sophie, although I could not remember to whom I should credit the quote) that 'entities should not be multiplied beyond necessity' and that when faced with some form of question, it was best to go for the hypothesis that made the fewest assumptions. To which Sophie said, 'So basically, what you're saying is, that we shouldn't overcomplicate things and that we should always go for the most straightforward answer to any question.'

I replied that this was an inadequate summation to which she laughed (properly laughed, a from the stomach kind of a bellow) and said that it was ironic that the one time you could not apply Occam's Razor was when discussing Occam's Razor, to which I had no answer and became instantly sure that I would never apply it again.

After this topic we briefly suggested that perhaps we ought to rehearse the play, and opted for the suicide scene, which led to further discussion by pondering over the psychology behind Romeo and Juliet's thoughts at the time of their death, but only briefly, because we both agreed that we would never commit suicide just because a lover – even a 'star-crossed' one – had died, and so that put an end to that thread of conversation very quickly. There was some discussion as to whether the play would have been quite so successful if it had been titled Juliet and Romeo, and again we decided that this line of debate was unnecessary as Shakespeare knew what he was doing and it was a simple fact that some names of couples flow better one way than the other and let that be an end to it. (I took a private moment to consider which way would be best if the two of us were in a relationship – would we be Sophie and Sebastian or Sebastian and Sophie?) I did not have time to reach a conclusion as we quickly moved on to discuss the cottage and the garden, resulting in my promising to show her the garden another time, hopefully in the early-morning light, when the flowers were at their best. A second bottle of elderflower wine had been drunk by eight, which was when, with the summer sun finally beginning to dip, I stood with a slight wobble to light the oil lamp on the windowsill and was delighted to see Sophie's flushed happy face illuminated in the soft light. Moments later, however, I noticed to my horror that her happy face had contorted into one of consternation when she noticed the time. I was reminded of Cinderella at midnight. She nodded towards the clock – we were half an hour late for rehearsal.

'Do you have a bicycle?' she asked, jumping up but then quickly sitting down again. She followed on with a loud burp and placed a hand over her mouth.

'Goodness! Sorry, Sebastian!' She picked up the empty bottle and waved it to show that it was quite empty. 'But if you will entice a woman with alcohol!' Then the laughter began and Sophie was soon laughing so hard that she rocked back on her chair and promptly tipped over. As I peeled her off the floor it hit me that perhaps my constitution was better suited to alcohol than Sophie's.

Nevertheless, I did have a bicycle and despite pleading as

we left the cottage that we were both far too inebriated to cycle, she jumped on her own machine borrowed from Joseph and began to race the mile and a half distance to the island hall. I had no option but to drag my own bicycle out of the shed and follow on behind. I never used the thing, but as the bicycle also acted as my emergency vehicle should someone on the far side of the island require urgent assistance, the tyres were always pumped up and the brakes checked and ready. I shouted after Sophie as she careered down the lane – 'Don't forget to dismount and walk across La Coupée, Sophie!' – my words were but muted echoes on deaf ears.

Within only a minute, I reached the brow of the rise that looks down on La Coupée and saw Sophie freewheeling at speed down the hill. I knew for certain as she lifted her feet off the pedals and straightened out her legs that she was, to coin a term, 'going for it'. Absolutely no islander has ever been known to 'go for it' on La Coupée and live to tell the tale, not on a breezy day, and certainly not inebriated. I considered shouting after her to slow down, but she was too committed on her run by now and the shout might be the distraction that caused a fall because, make no mistake, if Sophie should wobble, or if her wheel hit a stone, she would career three hundred feet off the ledge and die a horrible death on the beach below. I couldn't watch. And yet I had to. Moments later she was on the other side of La Coupée waving up at me, having skidded her bicycle to a halt like a cowboy dismounting after a rodeo.

Who on earth was this woman, I wondered.

She *was* a wonder, certainly. But was such recklessness the pathological habit of the unhinged madwoman or the result of four (or maybe five) glasses of elderflower wine? One thing I *was* sure of as she waved violently at me from across La

Coupée and encouraged me through mime to ride across the ridge, was that she was a most unlikely Juliet, but then, perhaps I was no Romeo, either. I jumped on my bike and cycled over the ridge. Sophie was becoming a very bad influence!

Chapter Fourteen

Three days on from the elderflower wine episode found me edgy because of two things:

Firstly, the rehearsal did not go well and for a number of reasons. On arrival at the hall it was clear to everyone present that Sophie was a little tipsy. I did not show my inebriation so easily, although there were a couple of raised eyebrows when I stumbled off the stage. Sophie laughed her way through the suicide scene and despite her attempt during the afternoon while sitting in my wheelbarrow to remember her lines, cometh the hour, faileth the man – miserably. Things became even more chaotic at the point where Romeo (me) was lying dead and she (Juliet) wakes up, sees him dead and says, '*I will kiss thy lips, Haply some poison yet doth hang on them … Thy lips are warm,*' and so on. I had been anticipating this moment in our rehearsal schedule for some time, and had imagined that it might be a notable moment of romance (within the parameters of the play, of course) but Sophie sniggered while lowering herself down to kiss me and whispered, 'Pucker up, Buttercup,

I'm coming in!' as only a French woman infiltrated with Anglo/American influences would do.

And that's when we started to laugh so hard we were ordered out of the hall.

We began to walk, while still laughing, in the direction of La Seigneurie. I should have allowed the space in, I have learned that lesson now, but I was a nervous fool and began to babble and so expressed my concern that her performance might be a little wooden.

'Wooden?' she shouted (I think she was still drunk). 'Wooden? If anyone is wooden in this partnership, Sebastian Braun, then it is you, not me, I assure you! Why do you have to return to being so serious all of the goddam time!?'

Truly, she became more American with each passing day.

'Serious? But I ...'

'It's my nose, isn't it?' She pushed her face towards mine, stating that she had noticed me staring at her nose for some time now.

I hadn't. I had been staring at her beautiful face. I did not say this.

Also, for my information, all she was trying to do in her 'wooden performance' was put me at ease for the kissing scene because I was an uptight German who probably didn't even know how to kiss!

This was hurtful. My response as we walked along the road, began with, 'Firstly, I *can* kiss.' She rolled her eyes. 'And secondly, I do not have issue with your nose. Not at all.' I was quite emphatic. 'It is really quite pretty and ...'

But I wasn't allowed to finish because she said, '*Quite* pretty?'

I tried to rescue the situation by saying, 'All I am trying to say Sophie is that, as yet, I do not feel that you are completely in love with me—'

Sophie's eyes widened.

'Romeo! I mean, in love with Romeo, not me, obviously. That would be ridiculous.'

A flash of something I could not interpret crossed her expression (I had not improved on this inadequacy in the days since my similar confusion with Dame Sibyl) and I was just about to apologise and blame my bluntness and opinionated nature on my German ancestry when we arrived at her front door, which closed on my face with a slam.

Drunk. She was definitely, really quite drunk.

Second on my list of woes was the undeniable fact that 'the Germans' were edging ever closer across France. Perhaps my ordering of the severity of what ailed me was a little skewed but nevertheless it was now Derby Day and it had begun to rain, which was not ideal. I did not like to see the ponies slip and slide around the track, which was a four mile route around the island taking in cliff top paths and woodland streams. What happened to the riders was their own affair, but I did hate to see the butcher called in to deal with a fallen horse. Nonetheless, I grabbed my doctor's bag once more and headed across La Coupée, having heard that Sophie would be riding one of Dame Sibyl's ponies. All I could hope was that she was not as wild in the saddle of a horse as she was in the saddle of a bicycle.

I need not have worried. On arrival at La Seigneurie I discovered that the derby was cancelled.

'Because of the rain?' I asked, addressing the major, who

had just returned from putting out word of the 'postponement' (as the Dame insisted he refer to it).

'No, it bloody well isn't!' I realised that I had caught him at what the English call a 'bad time'.

'It's because of your lot!' He caught himself then, but there was scorn to his words and venom in his eyes. I neither corrected nor reprimanded him. He was frightened, tired and desperately unhappy. 'I'm sorry, Sebastian,' he said, placing a hand on my arm. 'That was unfair of me.' It was the first time the major had called me Sebastian or been particularly pleasant – ever. He fought in the First War and I could well understand the bruises he carried and the utter desolation at the thought of it all happening again. I felt his pain. 'I meant the Nazis,' he confirmed. 'No offence taken, old chap?'

His eyes had the watery film of a tired older man. I smiled.

'None whatever.'

He took out a pristine handkerchief, unfolded it and blew his nose. 'Thing is, Dame Sibyl heard word this morning that they've reached St Malo – the Nazis.' St Malo was just across the water from us, which of course meant that 'the Germans' were mere moments away. 'Did you know that there's an emergency boat coming from England ...' He glanced at his watch. 'Around about now. It's taking away those who are leaving, and the children, if they want to go. I've just been putting the word around.'

'And does anyone intend to leave?' I asked.

'The English are going, mainly. None of the true islanders seem to want to go.'

'And what about the children?'

The major dabbed his eyes. 'Dame Sibyl says that if a child goes then at least one parent must go too. To be perfectly honest, I have no idea who is going to leave.' He shook his head. 'It's a terrible, terrible day.'

'And what about you, Major? What do you intend to do?'

The major was an English incomer. Like me, he came to Sark on holiday, found sanctuary and never left. It struck me that the major and I had a great deal in common and perhaps could have been true friends had our individual prejudices not got in the way. He couldn't see beyond my Germanic background and I couldn't see beyond his adopted nomenclature of 'The Major'. His real name was Peter Jenkins. I could have been good friends with Peter Jenkins.

'I suppose I'll stay.' He spoke in a steady tone that dropped all previous bravado and yet managed to convey much more truth and emotion than his usual posturing for all that. 'There's no one left for me back in Blighty anymore, you see. And you?'

'I will stay, also,' I said, and then smiled. 'There is no one left for me in Germany, either. Also, the island needs a doctor, and this is my home. I know no other.'

He nodded his complete understanding. 'Will you fight for them, if they try to recruit you?' He rushed out a hand. 'Please, don't feel you have to answer. There is no hidden agenda to my words.'

It was my turn to rest a hand on his arm. 'I will not fight, not again. I think you of all people will probably understand why.'

'You were in the trenches,' he said.

'Yes. To return to uniform after having fought in the war to end all wars would seem barbaric.'

He surprised me then by shaking my hand. We then saluted each other simultaneously, as if a wonderful, silent armistice had just arrived – a new understanding and respect between two old combatants, who were now comrades.

I watched as the major – Peter, I decided to call him Peter from then on – walked away down the lane. His shoulders were rounded, as if he carried with him all the worries of the world. How desperately frustrating it was that the overbearing presence of a physically powerful force – as yet unseen – could destroy a community like this. Just like that slippery devil, Death, the spectre of the Nazi arrival in Sark hovered over us providing an ever-present sense of terrible unease. It was as if we could hear Nazi boots as they marched across France, becoming louder and louder until they drowned out our own thoughts, our own freedoms, our own will. I had not agreed with Dame Sibyl before today, not about the derby, or about her stance at the meeting to persuade people to stay on and uphold our way of life, and not about the nonsense of blundering on with the play. But I found, suddenly, that I agreed with her completely.

Die show muss weitergehen, I murmured to myself.

Feeling a sense of renewal, of wanting to live in hope and not fear, I turned towards the front entrance of La Seigneurie and gave a sharp knock on the door. There was someone inside to whom I must make reparation before it was too late, for she would surely be leaving on the boat today and I wanted so much to tell her … well, I wanted to tell her …

'Sorry, Sir, but Miss Hathaway has given instruction that she's not taking calls today. She's retired to her bedroom to read and reflect, at least, I think that's what she said.' This was from the maid, a feather duster in her hand. It was a tableau straight from Victorian England.

'Is she ill?'

'No, Sir. She's in the best of health, thank you for asking. But then she has American blood in her and most Americans usually are.'

But this was nonsense. Not taking calls? Since when had Sophie – wild and free and uncomplicated Sophie, who burped when she drank wine and sniffed her dripping nose onto her sleeve – started acting out the role of lady of the house? I wondered what she would do if it was I that was not 'at home' to callers. I knew exactly what she would do: she would sit in a wheelbarrow reading Shakespeare until I came out!

The large, white-painted door closed on me. I stepped back on the driveway to look up at the first floor windows. La Seigneurie was a beautiful place. Built of granite in the French-style, it was symmetrical when looked at from the front, with several tall windows to each side of the door and matching windows above. But which window was Sophie behind today? I recalled visiting a house guest at La Seigneurie who had developed a fever some years back and decided that Sophie's room was probably the oft-used guest room and was as good as any to begin my quest for an audience. I would re-enact the balcony scene! That would surely make Sophie laugh and show the light-hearted side to my personality and that I was absolutely not serious in spirit 'all the goddam time …'

It took a little while to find stones light enough to damage neither frame nor window pane, but eventually with a near perfect shot, my stone tinkled across the guest room window while I limbered up and tried to fall into character.

'I am Romeo,' I said to myself. 'And I shall woo the lady out of her room!' I tried to remember my lines while I waited, although I did not have to wait for long because the window – a heavy sash type – was being lifted up.

'*But soft!*' I began, my right arm raised up towards the window. The rain was a little lighter now but was dripping down my upturned face. '*What light through yonder window breaks? It is the east and Juliet is the sun.*'

'Light?' I heard echoed, but the voice was not Sophie's. 'What on earth are you playing at down there? Is that you, Sebastian?'

It was Dame Sibyl. She looked at first annoyed and then, surprisingly, amused. I was about to fashion an answer when a second window opened in the adjacent room and Sophie's head appeared.

'Sebastian?' She glanced to her right to see her aunt mirroring her movements.

My moment had passed. The joviality had been missed. To carry on with the charade would have me appear ridiculous.

'I think Sebastian is serenading us, Sophie dear,' said Dame Sibyl. 'Carry on, my good man. Let us hear your lines.'

In truth, I had only one line worth saying and it was my own – *Oh, sweet earth, open thy soul and bury me now!*

'No need. No need,' I said, feigning laughter. 'It is the funniest thing. I, er, I was just practising for the play and was hoping to find Sophie at home, and I thought the authenticity might improve upon my performance.'

'Why? Is it a little wooden?' asked Sophie.

I deserved that.

'In that case, I'll leave you to it,' said Dame Sibyl, stepping back from the window and beginning to close it. 'But for goodness' sake, Sebastian, try knocking on the door next time!'

I stepped sideways to stand under the correct window and raised my right arm again. What was that absurd English phrase often used … in for a penny, in for a pound? I returned to my lines.

'*Arise, fair sun, and kill the envious moon, who is already sick and pale with grief, that thou … that thou …*'

I searched my mind, but the words did not come.

'… her maid,' offered Sophie as a nudge, her voice shot through with boredom.

'Ach, so. "*Her maid, art far more fair than she.*" That is correct, I think?' I continued to glance up at Sophie, my arm outstretched. (All credit to Romeo; looking upwards permanently is quite straining.)

'What are you doing here, Sebastian?' she asked.

Ah.

'I wanted to apologise for my behaviour at the last rehearsal,' I said. 'It was unconscionable and I am an ignorant ass! I was nervous – for the kissing scene, you see. And a little inebriated, given the wine. Also, I am anxious that you might be leaving and I won't ever see you again. Are you … leaving?'

She waited for a moment, as if only now making her decision. 'I am not,' she said.

This was excellent news.

'In that case, forgive me, fair Juliet? Can I tempt you down from your ivory tower to take a stroll or a ride out with me on this fair …' I wiped my rain-soaked face with my hand. 'Day?'

Sophie paused for a moment, her face contorted into consideration. Then she smiled and it was one of her most wonderful, thousand-watt smiles.

'Yes, let's!' she declared. 'I'm bored now anyhow. This "retiring to one's room" is deadly dull!' She nodded towards the sky behind me. 'The sun is trying to break through beyond the trees over there, look.' I turned around and when I looked back again the window was empty but I could hear her shouting from within the room. 'Wait for me, fair Romeo! I'll be down in a jiffy!'

Chapter Fifteen

O ur joviality did not last for long. Inevitably we were drawn to the harbour to watch as the first tranche of those who had chosen to leave the island waited by the walls. They had only a few, basic belongings with them in small suitcases. They all waited in relative silence for the boat from Guernsey to arrive, their coats shining from being caught in the rain. Sophie and I sat side by side on the footpath above the harbour and watched on in silence, observing as if witnessing another world entirely, where our newfound friendship – our laughter, our teasing of each other – did not seem to belong.

'It crossed my mind that you might choose to go with them?' I said, breaking the silence. 'Especially now the Germans have reached St Malo. You must be anxious to leave.'

She nudged my arm with her elbow. 'And miss my chance to play Juliet? You're not that lucky!'

Another silence.

'I *should* leave,' she continued. 'Aunt Sibyl wants me to go – and maybe I will.' She began to pull at tufts of grass. 'I just thought I'd wait a little while longer … to see what happens.'

'And where is your permanent home?' I asked.

She shrugged. 'I don't really have one right now. I'm in lodgings in London. You might say I've been living the life of a traveller for a while ... since my marriage ended.'

'What about your work for the government?' I edged in, aware that I was finally crossing the line between acquaintance and closer friend. 'Don't you need to get back and hand in your report about the Fifth Columnist doctor living on Sark who is going to bring about an end to the British Empire singlehandedly using only a musket?'

Sophie turned to me and laughed. 'I knew you were a traitor! I shall have to change my report and drag you back to England with me! Would that be so bad?'

I replied with the first quip I could think of. 'And have me miss the flower show? Never!'

There was a return to silence as we watched the harbour. It was as if we both felt guilty to laugh when there was so much pain around us. I wondered if I could edge into her private life again, just a little more. After all, she hadn't ever answered my questions about her work. But *why* did I want to know, that was the question.

Oh, come on Sebastian! Stop being a child. The room lights up for you the second she appears and did from the first moment. The war seems insignificant whenever she calls your name. You want to know about her because, well because ...

'Joseph mentioned a little of what he knew of you ... of your previous life, your marriage and so on, when he asked me to come to La Seigneurie to attend your ankle. I assure you, I did not ask.'

'Ah, Joseph told you.' She was looking – and I could easily have been mistaken – a little disappointed. 'Have you not been even a little curious to ask a few questions about me for yourself?' She looked directly at me for an answer.

Had I been curious? I'd been desperate for information. But the greater part of me wanted to keep our developing friendship exactly as it was, with no complications of other lives, other histories, other … people.

I flailed around for an answer. 'Well, I suppose …'

Sophie helped me out by resting her hand on mine. 'You don't need to answer. As dear Aunt Sibyl said just yesterday, you have kept the world away for nigh on fifteen years. I can see – and understand, truly – that you like to keep people at arm's length.'

Had I really kept the world away from me for fifteen years? Yes, I had.

I remembered what I said to Margery several days ago about honesty and frankness usually being the best solution. I really must start taking my own medicine.

'*Although*,' I began, 'there is no doubt that you *are* an interesting mystery to me, Miss Hathaway.'

This pleased her. The light returned to her eyes.

'How so?' she asked.

'Well, I am simply Doctor Braun, resident physician of Sark and a man who whiles away his time either in the garden or roaming the island admiring nature. I am, there is no doubt, dull. But you … '

'I?' she prompted.

'You … are the mysterious woman who limped into my life one day. But who is Sophie Hathaway, I ask myself? Who is this enigmatic beautiful Juliet who has stolen Romeo's heart?' I held up my hand, quickly. 'In fact, do not answer that.'

'Why?'

'Because if you prove to be an exotic, wild and interesting

creature with a dangerous past and start to open up and share your dreams with me for an adventurous future, then I shall only feel inadequate and you will realise that I am far too old and far too boring to be your ... friend. And to be perfectly honest, that is why I have not asked you any questions until now – about your own circumstances, at least. Because I have become a dull man, and you are not a dull woman.'

Her mouth opened in what appeared to be complete surprise at my words.

'But you're not *any* old doctor, Sebastian Braun!' She edged towards me a little closer. 'And you are in no way dull! Ask anyone on the island – they all love you!'

'Except the person who wrote, "Go home Boche",' I said.

'Well, yes, but there's always one bad apple. No, there's a kind of light that follows you around. I see it. You share that light wherever you go.'

I was not sure how to respond. But her words did bring me immense happiness.

'It is very kind of you to say so. But I notice you have stepped away from my question ... who is Sophie Hathaway?'

'Ah, yes. Who is Sophie Hathaway?' Sophie looked up to the sky, thinking. 'I suppose we could start with the basic detail that I'm a thirty-five-year-old woman who was born in France to an English mother and American father – he was ambassador there. I moved to Long Island in America when I was a teenager which is where I met my husband – I married very young. I didn't do all the things that well-to-do young women who live in Long Island usually do because I was either practising gymnastics, playing the piano or riding my pony. I married a wealthy business associate of my father's because I thought he was magnificent. Turned out he was actually quite dull – which is how I know that you are not at all dull, by the way – and also, he couldn't provide me with children which caused a great deal of hoo-ha because he comes from the type of American family who wants an heir. He put the public blame for lack of children at my door so I asked him to divorce me and he did.'

'I'm sorry,' I said.

'Thank you. Although don't be sorry about the marriage ending. I was nineteen when I married him which was a crazy thing to do.'

'And the fact that you haven't had children, yet?'

'It's not a path I would have chosen,' she answered.

It was impossible to know what was best to say in this moment, so I went with the only response I knew – 'You have time still.'

Space was allowed in, but only until I broke it by asking, 'What happened after the marriage ended?'

'I moved right away, to England for a change of scenery. I stayed with an aunt from my mother's side, got a job in a government office, worked my way up and eventually found work at an embassy in Berlin.'

'Berlin? Goodness me.'

'Anyhow, once we saw that the way things were going with Hitler was becoming irreversible, I got out of Germany, moved to the Paris office and worked there for a year or so, and then … the war broke out. Once it was obvious that Hitler had designs on France, I moved back to London and have been working in a department dealing with "alien immigration" ever since.'

'Hunting out Germans,' I said.

'I'm sorry. I wrote to Aunt Sibyl asking about you – I'm afraid someone on the island wrote in to inform us.'

'It was probably the same person who wrote on my sign,' I suggested.

'Yes, it probably was. And before I knew it, my supervisor approved for me to come and interview you, and Aunt Sibyl was more than happy for me to stay at La Seigneurie – which also meant she could make sure (by stealing the paperwork from my satchel) that you weren't interned.'

'She is a very good woman,' I said.

'She certainly is.'

'And now what? Aren't you tempted to throw in your job and run back to your family in America and see out the war there? You'd be safe, at least.'

She shook her head.

'Not a chance. I want to do my bit. I'd hate it if I didn't contribute to the war effort somehow. What did Queen Elizabeth say? *I may have the body of a weak and feeble woman ... but I have the heart and stomach of a king*, etc. No, I need to help the cause.' She bit her lip, thinking. 'With all that in mind, I suppose I should be standing in that queue down there and hotfooting it back to Blighty, but there will be other boats later in the week, and I would so like to finish what we've started here ... I mean to say, with the play and all.'

We both considered her words while watching new events unfold at the harbour. A fishing boat pulled alongside and a commotion started. There was a pause while I pondered on the fact that Sophie's words left me feeling a little odd, like I was on the brink of a sadness, a loneliness I had never experienced before. I considered telling her this – I *was* the new, more dynamic version of myself today, after all – but she interrupted my thoughts by saying,

'Aunt Sibyl told me you're a pacifist.'

This question put the new Sebastian quite firmly back into

his box. I visualised a lid being put on the box and screwed down tightly.

'I do not like to have labels attached to me,' I said. I tried to explain this away by adding, 'Labels are too definite. Too unmoving.'

'You would refuse to fight, though? If you were asked?'

I turned to her. 'On which side would you have me fight?' I was trying very hard to keep an edge from my voice, and yet I knew my words were defensive.

'Isn't there only one side? If you fought for Germany you would be supporting Hitler…'

'Which I cannot do.'

'Or you could side with the Allies, but then you would be fighting against your own countrymen, which would be odd.'

'Which would be very odd indeed, considering the fact that I fought *with* them for four long years not so very long ago. This is why I see war as an utterly futile event, Sophie, and one that I could not possibly be part of again. Those of us that were very young when fighting in the last war and are still young enough to fight in this one must all, surely, see the futility of it. If one is expected to fight for one's country, surely having done that once already is enough? This idea of 'fighting for' something, against other countries, is truly nonsensical. One moment you are enemies and twenty years later the best of friends. With wars such as the last one and, I suspect what this one will become, it would be simpler to shoot half the male population, destroy the landscape, kill all the wildlife, exhaust all the economies and then agree to call it a draw.'

'But this one is different, surely. Hitler won't stop until he's conquered the whole of Europe – or the world, I think. It is, I know, so unfortunate that our generation is bearing witness to such awful, awful bloodshed again. But surely we all have to stand up to him, Sebastian. We *have* to.'

'You think less of me, because I will not fight.'

She glanced away, towards the boats.

'What I think is that there is more to Sebastian Braun than he is allowing me to see,' she said. She tucked her arm through mine and rested her head on my shoulder. We took a moment to watch the harbour.

'Have you heard of a nurse called Edith Cavell?' I asked, after a while.

She lifted her head. 'Wasn't she the British nurse who was shot by the Germans as a spy, or something, in the last war?'

'Yes. On the night before her death, she spoke to her pastor and said, "Patriotism is not enough. I must have no hatred and bitterness towards anyone." And she made that declaration knowing that she would face the firing squadron the very next morning. The reason I mention it is because that is how I wish to live my life now. I became a doctor to save lives, Sophie, not to end them. To take up arms again would be impossible for me.'

'Even to stop Hitler?' she asked.

'One man alone cannot stop him. This island, these people … they are my life.'

Sophie began to pick daisies.

'Still, you think I should fight,' I said.

She paused with a few daisies in her hand. 'What I think is that we ought to change the subject …'

I tried to not appear dismayed.

'Actually, I've got another question for you, if you don't mind?' she said.

'Go on?'

'If the war didn't exist, would you ever consider leaving Sark and, you know, broadening your horizons ... just a little?'

I gestured out to sea. 'I doubt many men have such a broad horizonal view as this.'

'You know I meant metaphorical horizons. Come on, Sebastian. What about a desire for adventure? A need to break out?'

We fell silent again while I considered. I then felt the need to fill the silence with some kind of profound comment.

'The thing is,' I began, 'I have long believed that the most contented of men have all they need close by ... how to put it best? Perhaps to say that, I simply do not want to be the main character in the story of my life. It's so much easier to have a minor part.'

'Because there are fewer lines to learn?' she joked.

'Exakt! And you know how poor I am at learning my lines. What about you? Do you crave for new adventures?' I half-dreaded her response.

'Yes, always – and then again, no. I'm beginning to see that there might be a certain comfort to being settled, but I do love Paris! Oh, how I do love Paris! If I'm drawn anywhere, it is always back to there.'

'Ah, Paris,' I said. 'A true city – a passionate city. I lived there myself for some time. It is a special place, I admit.'

'Really?' She glanced up at me, and it was a very definite coquettish glance. 'And did you ... you know, have a wild affair while living in your passionate city? Did the city of love deliver its promise?'

She is teasing me, and yet ...

'Oh, you would be surprised. I had my moments,' I say, offering only enough to allow me, I hope, to seem très interéssant! 'And you? Have you also had your moment in Paris?'

Please let her say no!

Sophie screwed up her face. 'Nah. I never found anyone who I was crazy about enough to allow them to sweep me off my feet – I'd *love* to be swept off my feet. Truth is, I'm not really attracted to the French.'

'Right. That is probably a good thing, I think. There are many Romeos in Paris.' I screw my courage to the sticking place. 'So, if not the French … then, to whom are you attracted, Sophie Hathaway?'

A shoulder flew up in a shrug as she fixed her glance out to sea. 'Oh, gee, I don't know … Germans, maybe?'

She smiled up at me just as a cry rang out from the harbour below. I looked down to see Peter waving frantically. 'Doctor! Sebastian!' he shouted. 'Come down here! Quickly, man!'

Sophie removed her hand. I stood but paused to look down at her, not wishing to leave our conversation – not wishing to leave Sophie at all – without a proper ending. But I was not reckoning on the practicality of Sophie. She smiled up at me and shouted,

'Go!'

The fishing boat was from a little harbour south of St Malo. That in itself was not unusual as a number of boats had arrived using our island as a first port of call before heading off to England or Spain in an attempt to escape the Nazis, but this one was different. It carried three highly malnourished emigres who, Peter quickly appraised me, spoke not one word of 'any language I can damn well understand!' but they were almost certainly wearing prisoner-style uniforms. 'Be on your guard,' he murmured, patting my back.

I was shepherded onto the boat to attend to a man who was slipping in and out of consciousness. He was lying on the deck with his head propped against a lobster creel. There was a pool of vomit to one side. One of the conscious men cowered as I approached, but the other beckoned me over and lifted an oilskin coat covering the injured man's arms and torso. A make-shift tourniquet was wrapped around his left leg and it was soaked through with congealed blood. He mimed firing a pistol towards the man's leg. I nodded my understanding. I turned to ask Peter to arrange a stretcher party and found Dame Sibyl standing behind me, looking on.

'Jerome Dupont and his herdsman are coming along now with a stretcher,' she said, raising a hand to her forehead. 'I shall tell them to take him straight to La Seigneurie. You can work on him there.'

'Does anyone have a bicycle?' I shouted out with urgency, looking towards the intrigued crowd of onlookers. 'I need to go home to collect the necessary tools.'

John Hamon's booming voice echoed from the far end of the jetty. 'Alex Vibert's best mare is tethered to the gate post on the path up yonder, there …'

I looked up the hillside beyond the harbour master's house and saw the mare, but hesitated before answering, in the hope that someone else would shout out that they had a bicycle at my disposal. That particular horse was a feisty beast and I was not the most gifted of horsemen. I glanced towards the injured man; his narrow face of nothing more than bones and skin was contorted with pain.

'Very well. I will meet you at La Seigneurie.' I jumped off the boat and began running to the top of the hill, where Sophie was waiting for me, atop the horse. Smiling down, she gathered the reins with her right hand and reached her left one down towards me.

'I thought you might need a driver,' she said. I hauled myself onto the beast and nestled firmly on the saddle behind her.

'How fast do we need to go?' she asked, settling the horse down, who had begun to prance a little.

'Very.'

'And are you happy to gallop across La Coupée this time?' She turned to face me. Her face was so alive it was utterly contagious.

'Yes!' (And I was surprised to find that I actually meant it.)

'In that case, hold on to your hat!'

The wild mare, like Sophie, required no additional encouragement. And with a rear from the mare that was straight out of a Wild West picture book, we headed out across the fields for what I was certain would be the ride of my life ... and do you know, it was!

Chapter Sixteen

La Santé Prison, August 1944

Christoph has returned today with a second cushion – and a teapot.

'That's quite something,' I say, watching on as Christoph pours from a small clay pot.

'It is a Zisha teapot – Chinese, like yours,' he explains. 'Crafted from a very special clay.'

The cup he hands to me has no handles and it takes me straight back to another time, not so long ago, when I was in a warm kitchen eating a buttered English muffin sitting across from an elderly lady with flowers in her hair.

'A special clay?'

'Yes, from the mountains of the Yixing region of China. The tea infuses in the clay pot to create a much-improved experience. Zisha teapots are at the core of Gong Fu Cha.'

'Ah, Gong Fu Cha – the art of making tea with great skill. You are an expert, then?'

'Not an expert, but I do appreciate the meditative qualities of the process.' He lets out a laugh of irony. 'Our situation here is not, perhaps, the most conducive environment for the ceremony, but we shall make best with what we have.'

I hold the cup to my nostrils and take a deep, breath. 'You are good. This tea is wonderful,' I say.

He takes a sip of his own. 'Hold your judgement until you have tasted it,' he says. 'But you're right, it is. I brought spring water – the minerals will give you a boost.'

'A boost? For what?' It is a quip that I regret a moment later.

'For whatever comes,' is his answer.

We break bread and eat it with a little cured ham. What with the company, the tea, a lit candle and greenery in the form of small branches he has brought once again, along with the herbs and the food, I am feeling very definitely human. I could almost forget that I am sitting on a broken bench in a dank cell that reeks of my own faeces.

'Now then,' he says, resting his cup on a knee. 'Shall we return to Sark and happier times?'

'I'd like that,' I say, 'but before I begin …' I place my cup on the cobbles, lean forward and grasp Christoph's hand. 'I want to say, thank you, my friend. Thank you from the very depths of my heart, for being here.'

'It is my pleasure,' he says. And I do believe he means it.

Chapter Seventeen

The men on the boat were escaped Polish prisoners. They had fled across Europe, one step ahead of Hitler, until the land eventually gave way to the sea and there was nowhere left to run. With the arrival of the German army at the port of St Malo, the men hid in a sewer until the opportunity arose for them to steal away (literally) in a boat, but not without taking last minute flak from gunfire as they flashed up the engine at dead of night. None were experienced mariners and considering their poor health, with ailments ranging from dysentery to infected, punched-in teeth and, of course, the gunshot wound, it was only through the miracle of decent weather and the fact that Sark is visible from France that they managed to land here at all. The mood on Sark had changed now. There could be no more denial about what being 'occupied' by the Germans really meant, because the Polish men had told the truth about the Nazi occupation of Europe, and how my countrymen were going about their work more than diligently in their effort to create the so-called Aryan race. I was heartily ashamed.

The Poles were called Antoni, Alek and Fabian, and were brothers in their twenties of varying ages. Fabian spoke a little English and was prepared to converse with Sophie, who acted as my nurse and go-between for two days straight. I spoke only in English when in their presence, at Sophie's suggestion, her assumption being that they would no doubt cower at my touch if they were to become aware that I was German. She used the analogy of how a beaten dog will forever cower from any man who tries to touch it (it is always a man who does the beating, she said) and I am sad for myself and for my country that something as simple as my native language, once deemed noble, could bring about such a sense of fear and despair in others.

Dame Sibyl joined me at the bedside as I cleansed and dressed the wound – the retrieved bullet having already been handed to one of the healthier brothers as a macabre souvenir. She watched on, asking at one point if I enjoyed this kind of work. I said that I had indeed enjoyed it, explaining that, while *very* content to be the island's doctor, the islanders were in such good health that it was a rare day I was able to get my hands dirty with some 'proper doctoring' (her words, not mine). The conversation was cut short with the arrival of Sophie who was holding a bedpan. Dame Sibyl leant towards me and whispered, 'But I bet you wouldn't have enjoyed yourself half as much if you hadn't had the company of such an attractive nurse!'

I made a hasty retreat.

Later, at home, I sat in my kitchen with my head in my hands and pondered over the events of the past couple of days. I thought of Sophie and her question – would I fight to beat the Nazis? I wanted so much for Sophie to not be disappointed in me. Wanted her to understand that choosing not to fight was not an act of cowardice, but of principle. I must have seemed so weak to her. The only person I knew for certain that would understand my principle was Peter. But even so, I felt the embryo of a change growing within me. Sophie's desperate desire to 'do her bit' challenged my perspective – my long-held beliefs about war. Frankly, her strength made me feel weak. But then, she had not fought the way I had and had not seen the things I had seen. Stepping through to the surgery, I opened the top drawer of my bureau and took out two letters that I hadn't read in years. I put the letters on the table and thought of the Polish brothers, who had also shaken my resolve. What had happened to my country in the years I had been gone? What did they mean exactly about this hunting out of undesirable people? Perhaps this war was, after all, very different.

I picked up the first letter and decided it was time to refresh my memory – to remind myself as to the real reason why I once vowed never to fight again. But then the gate clicked open. I tucked the letters into my pocket, ran a hand through my hair and took a quick look at my appearance in a small mirror that sat on a shelf above the sink. Joseph Martin appeared at the door, removed his cap and stroked a few strands of what remained of his pure white hair back into place.

I gestured towards a chair and took a seat opposite at the table, adopted my doctor's face, rather than my disappointed one, and asked,

'How might I be of assistance today?'

'A glass of ale would be nice.' He glanced around as if to look for the small brewery he believed I hid in the kitchen.

'Ale?'

'I don't mind if I do.' He nodded towards the clock. 'I know how partial you are yourself to a little snifter in the afternoon, Doctor.' A wink was thrown in before he added, 'A splash of last year's homebrew would be just the ticket if you've got any left over?'

I stood and patted him on the back. He would not be the first man to require a little of Herr Doktor's home-brew to loosen the lips sufficiently to reveal his ailments.

'So,' I began again, handing him a bottle filled with my finest amber brew. 'How may I help?'

He popped open the swing top lid, looked on with admiration at the bottle, took a good long drink, and subsequently held the bottle out in front of him, looking on still with admiration and delight while wiping his mouth with the back of his hand. I allowed him a moment to enjoy the refreshment.

'I've been sent to tell you that the play is off,' he said.

'Off?' I released the stopper from my own bottle.

'Off,' he echoed, taking another drink. 'Dame Sibyl said to say that she's very sorry but this is no time for Shakespeare, what with the Germans hovering on the doorstep.'

I fought to keep my expression impassive and resisted the urge to say anything reproachful about his beloved employer's apparent about turn.

'She said that I was to rush up here and tell you first – straight away – as you'd be the most, what was the word she used … disappointed.'

Disappointed?

Me?

Yes, I suppose I was.

But was I not the man who said – from the very beginning – that this was no time for Shakespeare (Sibyl, after all, had simply repeated my words back to me)?

But this was irrational. *Romeo and Juliet* was, after all, my least favourite Shakespearean play. Did Romeo not irk me greatly with his lovestruck, foppish ways? The answer to that was a very definite yes. And yet, there was no denying that I was indeed, most definitely, disappointed.

I took another sip, thinking of Sophie. 'Disappointment' was one of the abstract concepts we'd discussed just last week when, sitting exactly where Joseph was sitting now, she sipped away merrily at my elderflower wine and said that disappointment was a kind of abstract feeling that began at the back of her head and passed to the front of her eyes, before trotting back again to travel down her spine and land, like a lead weight, in her gut, where it hid, trying to disguise itself. She went on to say that, like any other strong emotion, it took on the form of a wave that passed through the body in a pulse. At first the wave was a powerful tsunami of emotion, and then – like all energy – it eventually petered out and settled down into a gentle ebb and flow that ultimately calmed itself into a still pool of acceptance. I smiled thinking of her analogy. Sophie had an analogy for just about everything … what was it she said the other day about love …?

'Doctor?'

'Yes?'

'What shall I say to the Dame, about the play being cancelled?'

Another wave of disappointment washed over me and landed – Sophie was quite correct – in my gut.

'Tell her that I agree that it is the best course of action.' I threw in an exaggerated shrug of nonchalance. 'Now then,' I said, feigning brightness, grabbing my bottle and gesturing like a character from a Gilbert and Sullivan musical. 'Take up your ale if you will and follow me into the garden. I would very much appreciate your opinion on a strange parasite I have found on my cabbages. You will be quite perplexed, I am sure. It is black with yellow spots and I have not the first idea what it might be. Come!'

Joseph did not know the name of the parasite but agreed that it was newly introduced to the island and must at all costs be destroyed before it destroyed us, or our plants, at least, which was ultimately the same thing. The garden tour was a diversion of sorts but as I sat on the cliffs and watched Joseph wander his way home across La Coupée, I realised that my old friend Disappointment was not only lingering in my gut but seemed to have invited Fear and Uncertainty to join him, all of whom struck a new friendship with my heart, who was drawn into the conversation – that conversation being a mixture of the cancellation of the play, the imminent arrival of the German army and ultimately how on earth my life was likely to play out over the coming weeks. My head, it seemed, was not invited to the party. All I knew was that there had been a role reversal between myself and the Dame. It was I now, who wished the islanders to carry on as if nothing had (or was about to) change. But why was this? Why the sudden desire in me to throw off responsibility, push all thoughts of the future as far away from my mind as possible, throw off my doctor's coat, turn off my radio, run out of the house and run wild along the cliffs and gambol over fields and frolic in the heather while pretending to be Romeo with …

'Sophie?'

She had come, and on foot this time and was waving madly from the other side of La Coupée. I wondered at first if she was trying to catch my attention on behalf of a patient? Perhaps the injured man had taken a turn? No, she was smiling and her demeanour was relaxed, as was her attire – dungarees again and stout shoes, while the familiar scarf was still trying – and failing – to hold back her hair. I stood while running a hand through my own unruly mop (I'd noticed just that morning that a little grey had begun to creep in at the sides) and walked – casually, of course – towards her, across the precipice. The minute or so that it took me to meet her in the middle of La Coupée awarded me a little time to consider why my heart was racing … no, leaping, and why I suddenly felt so very, *very* happy? It seemed that my heart was no longer lingering in my gut, hanging around with Disappointment, but that an interloper to these parts – Joy – had pitched up and joined in on all the fun.

'Hello,' she said. She was holding a sprig of wild mint. 'A button hole for you.' She placed the sprig artistically into my shirt pocket. 'It's my favourite scent of all the herbs. So fresh.'

I rubbed a leaf and lifted my fingers to smell them before gesturing to my side of La Coupée. I did not need to ask why she had come. More can be said in one sprig of mint than in a thousand unnecessary words, which was why we walked in companiable silence to my cottage, our shoulders almost touching, our hands occasionally brushing, both abandoned to our own thoughts as we meandered down the leafy lane towards the place I called home.

Chapter Eighteen

I have two rattan chairs in my glasshouse. At least, I did. I doubt they are there now. They faced each other with a small table in-between. The chair opposite mine was usually empty and it always seemed to be waiting for someone. It was – Sophie.

The mid-afternoon sun highlighted the copper tints in her hair while she listened to Liszt on the radio and waited for me to reappear with two glasses of elderflower wine. I did consider taking a safer route and offering cordial this time, but then remembered that I was, after all, the new Sebastian – the more relaxed Sebastian – who was a devil-may-care kind of a man who ran in tune with the wind and rode with the devil on his back. (Well, perhaps not the devil, but certainly a fun-loving nymph seemed to be encouraging me on.) I glanced at the mirror quickly and ran a hand over my chin. There was more stubble than I would have liked, but stubble or no, I filled two glasses to the brim with wine, opened the door with my elbow, and humming a jaunty tune, sauntered in.

'What do you say we have another go at our last scene?'

she said. Sophie was pulling a battered script out of her dungarees pocket like a kangaroo removing the debris its baby left behind. Before I could answer she took a glass from me and said, 'Here's mud in your eye!' and the glasses clinked. 'So ... last scene?' she repeated, taking a seat opposite. 'I think it is our weakest.' She sat back in the chair.

I put my glass down on the table and scratched my neck. Was it possible that Dame Sibyl had omitted to inform Sophie of her decision to postpone the play?

'Have you seen Dame Sibyl today?' I asked, taking up my glass again.

Sophie shook her head. 'Only at breakfast. I've been with the Polish brothers. We're trying to figure out a way to get them to England. And then I spent a while helping the major dig up his roses ...'

I almost spat out my wine.

'Dig up his roses?! Surely not. They are some of the best on the island!'

Sophie shrugged. 'I know. But he's clearing out his garden to give himself space to plant crops that he can eat, which is sad, but very sensible, I suppose.'

I took a long look out of the glasshouse to survey my own garden. Yet another wave of disappointment crashed down unexpectedly. Had I the heart to destroy all these years of love, sweat and toil?

No.

Forget that. Yes, I had. Of course I had.

'So, would you like to?' she asked, breaking my thoughts. Retracing my steps conversationally, I realised she was talking about the play. The play that had been postponed. The play that I was loath to be part of and yet felt utter remorse that it had been taken away. The play that, just an hour ago, I would have given anything to be able to rehearse just one more time …

'I'm afraid it has been postponed,' I said, 'or more likely, cancelled. Joseph brought word earlier. Dame Sibyl feels the time is not right for Shakespeare.'

Sophie shook her head, her eyes bright. 'Then, you've not heard?'

I said that I had not. Hope swelled in my belly.

'The other players protested at it being shut down. They said that it wasn't Aunt Sibyl's decision to make. Then – and you'll never guess in a million years …' She paused and I confirmed that I wouldn't. 'Well, Gilbert Jones' wife stormed up to La Seigneurie, threw the script on the hall floor and said that she hadn't brought the cattle in and shut the chickens away for him for six nights out of seven for weeks now, only to find that it was all for nothing. So, it was generally agreed – and the main protest led by the major, by the way – that die show muss weitergehen. And so it is – going on, I mean. But they've decided to bring it forward to the twenty-eighth. Which means that we probably really did ought to rehearse.'

My heart swelled to the size of a balloon. A really big balloon. An airship, in fact. I stood to fetch my script but Sophie stretched out to place a hand on my arm.

'How do you fancy some fun?' she said, knocking back her wine, her eyes twinkling.

I was at once nervous and excited.

Don't ask what kind of fun, just say yes, man. Just say yes!

'What kind of fun?' I asked.

She stood and laughed. 'The fun kind of fun, silly. What other kind is there?'

Sophie held out her hands. I took them and she pulled me to standing.

'Do you have bathers?'

'Bathers?'

She started heading to the door without awarding me time to answer. 'It doesn't matter if you haven't. I haven't either. We'll just have to improvise …'

'But wait! Sophie!' My shouts fell on deaf ears as she skipped out of the door. 'Where are we going? What about your wine and the play?'

'It can wait!' she shouted back. 'Come on! We're off to the harbour!'

I followed her down the garden path. 'Harbour? Why would we go to the harbour?'

She turned around to face me while walking backwards. Her eyes flashed with excitement.

'Why else? To take a running jump! The children who have stayed behind are all jumping off the harbour walls into the sea, and as I sat down, I suddenly thought … that's what we should be doing right now. I mean, why the hell not?'

I paused for a moment, thinking of bathing suits and towels, but then realised that this was it. It was finally my time to be young again. I grabbed Sophie's hand and we began running together, across La Coupée and down towards the harbour.

Why the hell not indeed?

Sophie had been holding out on me. Not only was she wearing her bathing suit beneath her dungarees, but she was also an excellent diver and swimmer – I was not the least bit surprised. I had lived on Sark for all of those years, but not once had I jumped off the harbour wall, or splashed around in the evening sunlight in the sea. It was exhilarating; it was magical; it was real to goodness living. I no longer felt old before my time, but like a strong young man again, because that is exactly what I was, a strong (youngish) man. And it had taken the contagious spirit and energy of Sophie to make me see that.

We came home to a light supper and, with Sophie's hair almost dry, we returned to the place we had left off – to the glasshouse with a refreshing glass of elderflower wine and Shakespeare.

'Actually, we've got all evening,' began Sophie as I lowered myself in the chair holding the script. 'Might I see your beautiful garden first, before we lose the light? I have heard so much about it from Joseph, after all.'

'But you have seen it before, have you not?'

'Yes, but only the area around the garden gate.'

'From the viewing platform of my wheelbarrow,' I reminded her.

'Gosh, yes. That was the second, no, third time we met.' I was pleased to see little red blotches appeared on her cheeks. 'Anyhow,' she went on quickly. 'It's best to see it now, isn't it?' She pulled herself out of the chair. 'Just in case … you know. You lose it?'

I did know. And it broke my heart.

We sipped on wine as we sauntered through the first of many gates that sat within the first of many hedgerows that divided the garden. At first we walked in silence, although my thoughts wandered in the direction of considering if showing Sophie this side of my character was a bad idea, after all, Sebastian – the generous gardener – was the old me (literally). I shook my head at the folly of my own thoughts. *There is no fool like an old fool*, I whispered to myself.

'I'm afraid I have not tended the space quite so diligently of late.' I noticed a patch of groundsel emerging from within a bed of pinks. I kneeled to pull some up. 'Although, I have never wished it to be too neat a garden,' I added quickly. 'I prefer only to have a gentle hand on the tiller, and allow nature to establish herself as she would like to, not according to my greater … plan, I suppose.'

'Not like God, then?' She bent down to pick a strawberry and popped it in her mouth. 'Or Hitler.'

I laughed and shook my head. 'No, definitely not like Hitler!'

'Here's a question …' she began, after swallowing the strawberry. 'Do you think Hitler would have been quite so successful if his surname had been something else? You know, like … Smith? Or …'

'Hathaway?' I offered. 'You mean, would a rose by any other name smell so sweet, or sour, in this case?'

'Exactly. That's exactly what I mean. Hitler as a combination of letters has such a menacing ring to it. It's like God knew that he would become an evil tyrant and gave him an appropriate name … or maybe Lucifer did.'

'Now there's a thought,' I said. 'Although I do believe Hitler is derived from Hiedler, which sounds much nicer. The Hiedl is a river. It may also be a variation of Hüttler …'

'And what does that mean?'

'One who lives in a hut,' I said, flatly.

Well, we started to laugh, and we simply could not stop laughing for five minutes straight.

'From now on,' began Sophie as we wandered on through the orchard, ducked under rose arches, dawdled past the vegetable patch and waded through the cutting garden, 'I am only ever going to refer to that vile man as Hüttler – he is much less frightening when thought of that way!'

The garden tour continued. Sophie took great delight in touching every tree, every flower, every shrub, every gnarled bit of fence post, asking questions about what variety of fruit and vegetables I had chosen to grow. She delighted in hearing about the superstitions associated with the keeping of bees and laughed out loud when she caught sight of my disastrous attempt at a scarecrow, who, she decided, bore an uncanny resemblance to her Uncle Jeremy, whoever he was.

Our arrival at the rose garden completed the tour. I admit, I kept the best until last. It was a private area, surrounded on all sides by a high ewe hedge and separated into six dedicated areas, with grass paths in-between. Despite my neglect of late, and sharp showers to damage the petals, the roses did not disappoint. Sophie stood underneath the entrance archway which was covered in a pale yellow climbing rose – *Lady Banksia*. She placed her hands on her face and looked around.

'Oh, Sebastian,' she cried. 'It's …' She squeezed my hand. 'Well, it's sublime. It really is sublime.'

I gestured for her to step forward and enter the garden properly. She floated from rose to rose as I followed on behind, pausing as she buried her nose in the petals now and again. I explained, as far as I knew them, the name and history of each rose, such as the pale pink *Souvenir de la Malmaison* which was grown in Josephine Bonaparte's garden, and was also a favourite of Catherine the Great who filled the Imperial Gardens in St Petersburg with it. Sophie nodded while I chattered away but I became aware that my enthusiasm may have become, like the scent, a little overpowering, so I took a moment to remove faded heads from a white China rose (the name of which eluded both myself and Joseph to our great annoyance). Sophie continued to work her way through the roses until she arrived at the end of the garden, at an iron bench. There was an arbour over the bench. A rose of a pretty pale pink was trained up each side of the arbour and across the top. The main stems were thick and a little gnarled with age. I planted both of them when I arrived.

'The arbour is beautiful,' she said, cupping a bloom in her hand. 'Has the rose a name?'

'*The Generous Gardener*,' I explained, looking on, I admit, with pride.

She smiled up at me. 'Just like you, then …'

I shrugged. 'All true gardeners are generous.'

Sophie sat on the bench, closed her eyes and took in the scent before looking across at a bed planted up with many of the same type of rose. Of all the beautiful plants in my garden, this rose was the most important to me.

Please let her like it, I thought.

'Why so many repeats of the same rose?' she asked.

'Because it is my favourite,' I answered, simply. 'I believe that it is the oldest known rose in existence.' Delving for the penknife in my pocket, I snipped a bloom and handed it to her. 'It's called *Rosa gallica officinals*. I think it the most fragrant of all of my roses. In olden times it was known as—'

'The Apothecary's Rose,' she said, bringing the bloom to her nose.

'You know it?'

'I admired it at La Seigneurie. I asked Joseph what it was called. He told me you had given him several cuttings. It has herbal qualities, I believe?'

'Yes, the Benedictine monks used it as a cure-all, and it makes a very nice rose tea, too.'

'Ah, do you whip up potions to cure your patients?'

I laughed. 'Sometimes, yes. But do not tell them.'

'Is that why you have so much of it?'

I thought on my answer before I gave it, eventually explaining that it was my mother's favourite rose, and that she gave me a cutting when I left Germany – the family home – for the final time. She said that whenever I needed her to be with me all I had to do was to smell the rose and she would be there, and the same for her, too. If she needed to feel me close to her, she would smell it, and I would be there.

'You were fond of your mother?' she asked.

'I adored her.' I took off my sunhat.

'Did you see her often, after you left home?'

'No. My father cast me off after the last war and I was not allowed to return to the house.'

'Why?'

'Simply because when I returned from the war, I had changed and was no longer of a mind to accept the way he treated my family. Inevitably, he beat my brother and my mother, as he always had, and so I beat him – badly. I am not proud.'

'You fought for what is right.'

'I fought aggression with aggression. It left me feeling empty.'

'You must have been very sad.'

'I was. I am still. Mother had money of her own. When I left she gave it to me to study medicine. I owe my mother a great deal.'

'It must have broken her heart … when your father sent you away.'

'It did. And mine, too.'

'And that's why you have so many of her roses.'

'I propagate new ones each year and keep them tended to in the glasshouse, just in case the old ones don't make it through the winter, or are hit by disease.'

'That way you will always have your mother with you,' she said.

I agreed that I would. 'And it is also why nearly every garden in Sark has at least one – I propagate far too many.'

We allowed the space in.

I thought of the letters in my pocket.

'Sophie.'

'Yes?'

'When you would not answer my question, about whether or not I should fight … I thought of these.' I took the letters out of my pocket.

'Please, Sebastian, I would rather …'

'No, just hear me out. I'd like you to read them. They were written some years ago. The first is my letter to a pastor, which he returned with my reply. I'd like you to read them, please. It's important to me that you understand why I will not fight.'

Reluctantly, she began to read.

Chapter Nineteen

15 January 1921
For the attention of M. Le Seur, Pastor
C/O Tir national
Brussels

Sir,

    Please excuse this unannounced correspondence.

    My name is Sebastian Braun and I am writing in relation to the death of the British nurse, Edith Louisa Cavell, who was killed by firing squadron at the Tir national firing range in Brussels in 1915. I understand that you are the pastor who attended in her final hours at Saint-Gilles prison, and also accompanied Miss Cavell during the drive to the Tir national and stood by her in the last moments. I hope you can allow an intrusion into your memories because for years I have pondered on the circumstances of her death and I am certain that only you can assist me with finding the answers to my questions. My particular interest in this matter arises from the fact that I was eighteen years old and an infantryman at the time of her execution, and it was my bullet that entered Miss Cavell's forehead, just above the glabella, and slightly to the left.

If you were to look in the records of her death and check the list of names of personnel on the firing squadron, you would find the name Sascha Braun, rather than Sebastian Braun. Sascha is my twin brother but it was I who took the shot. Our father was the commandant of the camp and was a tyrant of a man. He would never have accepted Sascha's unwillingness to shoot, and so I stepped into his place, thinking myself to be a stronger man. I took the shot, but I was not stronger. He, at least, refused to shoot. As proof that it was I who attended the execution and not my brother, I shall describe to you Miss Cavell's final moments as I remember them.

When you and Miss Cavell arrived by car at the Tir national there was a company of two hundred and fifty soldiers waiting for her – as was the protocol of the time – along with a handful of officials, my own father being one of them. You were dressed in the uniform of a German army pastor and you led Miss Cavell to where a squadron of sixteen armed men waited – eight for Miss Cavell, and eight for another gentleman, a Belgian national called M. Baucq. We stood waiting to fire at a range of six paces from two wooden poles. Just before the sentence was read aloud, M. Baucq shouted out words of comradeship but was quickly silenced. You spoke briefly to Miss Cavell and a second clergyman spoke with M. Baucq. The Catholic priest took longer speaking with his charge than you did with yours, and I couldn't help thinking that your brevity was better. I could not hear what you said in those last moments, but I know that she responded. You led her to a pole and a bandage was placed over her eyes. The command was then given and the shots were taken – no soldier refused to fire. Having been taught to shoot from an early age, I had already decided to aim for the forehead as I felt that a clean shot awarding immediate death was the most honourable course of action. Miss Cavell dropped down and forward and what happened next remains a mystery to me, even though I am now a medical man. She jolted upwards three times with her hands raised to the heavens. This was, no doubt, some form of reflex movement, but all the same, it was both chilling and extraordinary. A very short while later, the coffins were lowered and you prayed over Miss Cavell's grave.

I hope that you will now accept my validity and I take the liberty to ask my questions. Firstly, what were the final words you offered to her and what was her reply? Was she accepting or was she frightened? I have no right to ask – to intrude on such intimacy – and yet the question stands. In the years since her death, much has been publicised about her final hours. Is it true that she was not afraid of death? Did she also say that she had no hatred towards anyone and that patriotism was futile? Additionally, I wonder if you can help me to understand why not one man on the firing squad refused to fire? Although deeply regretful now, I do understand my own motives at the time and I am ashamed of them, but Pastor, why is a man prepared to act as a savage, rather than speak out and dare to take a kinder path? In whatever guise, why do we not question and why do we kill?

I am certain that my face was the last thing she saw before her eyes were covered and I know this because she looked at me directly and her gaze was still, although her eyes were clearly awash with tears. She offered me a look of something that I find impossible to define and this, perhaps, is the route of my torment. That look, fleeting as it was, had within it a certain kindness, a forgiveness, a deep sorrow and so much more. Truly, if I could only freeze that moment, I think that I could reach out and understand every answer to every question ever posed on humanity. It was as if she suddenly understood everything that is worth understanding in the world, and in that moment she shared the secret with me. Those collections of thoughts that crossed through her mind in that final moment are a cloud I grasp for but cannot hold. If there was some kind of meaning behind her death – some enlightenment at the end – did you feel it too?

Finally, and this is the most personal question of all, but can you tell me how she was feeling during her final days? I ask this not through any kind of macabre interest, but because I want to believe that when you came for her she was able to take her thoughts to the happiest of places, her happiest of times. I want to believe that she was able to transcend into a place of great beauty and peace – that is certainly what I would want to do. I think I would go to a paradise of perfect peace and natural harmony, and take myself on an early morning walk, probably in April, when the dew is at its heaviest and I would watch that perfect moment when the sun has not quite broken the horizon but there is, to the east, a relief emerging, a light seeping into the dark blackness – a taste of the sunlight to come. That is where I would go, to that place between night and day, when the heartbeat of the Earth is at its most relaxed pace, and while the men raise their weapons I would watch the stars disappear, one by one.

Please know that in reparation for my act of extreme cruelty at the Tir national, I have tried since then to be a good man and a good doctor, and truly, as God is my witness, I shall never fight or take a life again.

I am, Sir, your grateful servant.

Sebastian Braun

---

15 February, 1921
Sebastian Braun
Gardener's Cottage
Sark

Dear, M. Braun

Thank you for your correspondence, the details of which I have considered. I have entered into prayer in the hope of receiving guidance on how to reply, but in the end, I have decided to answer your questions (in so much as any mortal can) honestly but also with brevity, as I find that it does not generally help to dwell on the past unless it can assist with the present. Perhaps, however, on this occasion, it can.

On the evening of Miss Cavell's death I took some moments to sit and write a memoir of the day, and so I can answer your question as to the nature of our final words without the need for imagined embellishments. But perhaps, to consider whether or not she was frightened, I must return to the evening before when I informed her that her execution was to be carried out the following day. Her cheeks flushed at the news and she displayed a calm emotional response but was always gathered. I sensed that, as a German in uniform, I would not be her favoured choice of clergyman at this time, and offered to find an Anglican chaplain (I knew of one, a pious Irishman) to offer her the sacrament. She accepted this willingly but asked that I, not he, accompany her to the Tir national as she felt that the Anglican chaplain would not be used to such things. I was not used to such things either, but confirmed that I would stand with her to the end. I offered to collect her personally from the prison, rather than wait for her at the Tir. The offer was gratefully received and accepted. And so I drove with Edith to the Tir national and stood by her side for the execution, but it was Mr Gahan who offered the sacrament on the previous day and therefore it is to Mr Gahan that you may wish, perhaps, to direct your questions. All I can say with certainty is that he told me later that, as she stood on the verge of eternity, she said that patriotism was not the highest thing, and that one should never hate, but love all.

You asked, was she accepting? Was she frightened? I would say, probably both, but in a measured way. When I went to her cell to collect her she was kneeling at the table with a gas flame flickering for light. She had packed her belongings with great care into a handbag and was ready to leave. As she passed by the guards, she returned their greetings with a polite nod but was silent and composed. We travelled in silence to the Tir national and from there you know the rest. In our brief exchange after sentencing, I said, 'The Grace of our Lord Jesus Christ and the love of God and the Communion of the Holy Ghost be with you forever. Amen'. After pressing my hand she said, 'Ask Mr Gahan to tell my loved ones that my soul, as I believe, is safe, and that I am glad to die for my country.' That was the sum of our exchange. You asked if she turned her thoughts to a memory of better times to help soothe her soul during her final journey. My answer is that I do not believe she needed to. She had seen death so often as a nurse that it held no fear for her and I do believe she held with this to the end. This is all I can tell you. Anything else considering her emotional state would be pure conjecture.

You asked, why did no man refuse to shoot? To be sure, this is always how wars are fought and lost and won, this acceptance to be part of a camaraderie of men who are prepared to carry out the wishes of others without thought or consequence. I can offer you no more on this without hours of intense reflection and I feel that such questions have to be answered within ourselves, not via the thoughts of others. As to why any man kills? Again, I could not do justice on a single sheet of paper written under a low light with failing eyes. As for wondering if, as she stood in the shadow of death, she became enlightened and attempted to pass that enlightenment onto you … all I can say is that I have witnessed the final moments of many, many people, and there is a noble reverence at the end of life, often it is nothing more than acceptance and peace. This, perhaps, is what you saw in her eyes, and it was almost certainly Edith's ultimate gift to you – acceptance and peace. Please remember, Sebastian, with

events such as these, there is not one victim, but many, and you, I
fear, are one of them. Rest easy and enjoy your life in freedom and
hope. Edith hated no one and loved all – including you. It is time to
close this chapter and begin again.

The Grace of our Lord Jesus Christ and the love of God and the
Communion of the Holy Ghost be with you forever.

M. Le Seur

Placing the letters on the bench between us, Sophie stared out at the garden and took a very deep breath.

'How dreadful. You were so young. Such a waste. Such a terrible waste. But surely, you cannot blame yourself, Sebastian. You were so very young at the time and you wanted to protect your brother … could you not find a way to forgive yourself and, I know it sounds glib, but as the pastor says, move on?'

I shake my head.

'You think I do not wish to?' I ask gently. 'Every time I blink I see her face, or if not her face, the trenches. My nights are only recently my own. When one has experienced horror, true horror, over and over again, it stays with you. It haunts you at night and terrorises you in sleep. My mind wants me to forget, but my heart won't let me. I tell you all this, because I … I don't want you to see me as a coward, or that I do not care, or that I secretly support the German cause. But nor would I have you pity me, either. I simply cannot face picking up a weapon again. It is impossible to fully explain the reality of war to those who have not lived the experience, which is why wars keep happening, because new generations have not known the true horror of it. Perhaps … I hope … you will understand now.'

Sophie took a deep breath.

'I can,' she said. 'Truly. But we must agree to disagree that we should all lay down our weapons and allow one party to force their will over another rather than to fight, whatever the consequences. I can see that for a man who has been through so much already, to be asked to do it again would be woefully unfair. And so, do I judge you? I do not. I suppose if anything I—'

I put up a hand to silence her. 'Please. Don't say you pity me,' I said quickly. 'I can take anything but pity.'

She folded the letters and handed them back. 'Then I won't.'

After some moments, she turned to face me on the bench and took my hands in hers.

'Close your eyes with me,' she said. 'Let's forget about everything and just close our eyes and take it all in – the perfume, the sunshine, the freedom. These are the moments we shall remember – when the days ahead become dark – these are the moments that will keep us strong.'

And so we sat hand in hand for a moment, our eyes closed and our senses heightened. I matched Sophie's breathing and her serenity. The scent that swaddled us was a familiar old friend – musky but there was a sweetness too. I knew the scent of every rose in that garden. I knew when the first bloom would open and the last petal would fall. What would happen to my garden, I wondered, my eyes closed, my hands in Sophie's, if I was ever forced to leave. Who would tend to my patients? Would my mother's rose survive? A panic swelled within me. An image of a woman flashed across my mind, her eyes blindfolded, her body shaking. Then I was lying in a stinking trench, with water to my waist and the bodies of men strewn around me. Sophie squeezed my hands gently. She was telling me to calm my mind, and I knew that I *must* calm it. I matched my breath to hers, dropped my shoulders and began to feel the anxiety wane. I must empty my mind of all that had been before and all that may come in the future and focus only on this moment, this scent, this touch of my hands in hers. I must, whatever happened, remember this moment.

Chapter Twenty

La Santé Prison, August 1944

'You would prefer brevity from me, I think,' says Christoph. 'When the time comes.'

'I would.'

Christoph is silent. He is holding his breath, I think. When he starts to breathe again his breath is faster, shallower. He is not a well enough man to carry out this task.

'You took Sascha's place to save him from your father's wrath,' he says.

'I did. The foolish man had volunteered to be part of it.'

'Why?'

'To please Father. He was constantly trying to please Father, who thought him weak, you see. Lesser. Cowardly, perhaps. Sascha seemed a little … different, sometimes. Softer. Which was why Father insisted he spend his teenage years being taught how to be braver than he felt, tougher that he felt – stronger. It was not pleasant to watch.'

'What was he like?'

'Sascha?'

'Your father.'

'Vile.'

I pause to drink tea. This is too fine a brew to tarnish with such miserable talk. It feels like I am finally entering the confession that Christoph originally thought I should have.

'I always thought that it was almost as hard on the pastor as on Miss Cavell,' I say. 'But now that I am in the same situation, I think not.' I look at him over my cup. 'No offence, of course.'

'None taken. But tell me … did you feel that the pastor's response in the letter satisfied your desire to find peace?'

I breathe in the aroma of the tea and consider this. 'Yes … and no.'

'Perhaps there are some questions that are only for each individual soul to answer for themselves,' he offers.

'True. Although I thought I would know all the answers to my questions by the time of my death. I am a self-important fool, you must see that by now.'

'What kind of questions?' he asks.

'Oh, the weightier questions life throws at you, I suppose? But in the end, I see that it doesn't really matter what the answers are, it is merely important to have spent a little while considering them, perhaps.'

'Consideration … it is what makes us human, is it not?' he says.

I laugh. 'You said that it is love that makes us human.'

He allows laughter to escape too. 'Ha! That too.'

We let the space in as the candle flickers. And I spend a while wondering why it flickers when there is no breeze.

Chapter Twenty-One

We did not, in the end, rehearse the play that night. My evening with Sophie was brought to a premature conclusion shortly after we left the garden, with the arrival of Joseph, who was sent to ask that I attend La Seigneurie at once because Antoni, the wounded escapee, had taken a dramatic turn for the worse. Disappointment sank deep into my gut once more with a wicked vengeance.

On arrival at La Seigneurie I found Antoni to be in a delirious state with a raging temperature. On inspection of the leg I saw that despite regular cleaning of the wound and the application of fresh dressings, the leg had become so hideously infected that the only hope of saving the man's life was amputation. I had witnessed a small number of such procedures during the early years of my work, but during the fifteen years I lived on Sark, never once had I been required to saw off a limb – until now. I sent for morphine, my surgical saws, needles and threads, and asked that the butcher assist me as he was a stout, strong man who would not shy away from such work. He would also have the strength to hold down the patient when he fought back – as he inevitably would. At midnight I began the procedure but not ten minutes had passed before poor Antoni was dead, either from internal bleeding or heart failure – or both. I washed down my instruments, refused the offer of a stiff drink and hurried my way home, wondering how on earth I had failed the poor man so desperately. Sophie ran after me on the lane and grabbed my arm. She asked that we might go for a walk later, after we had both slept, feeling the fresh air would probably 'do us both the world of good'. I removed her hand from mine and – God forgive me – said the first thought that came to mind, which wasn't my own thought at all, but Shakespeare's.

I said, 'These times of woe afford no time to woo.' I shall never forget the look on her face afterwards. It wasn't anger, just the purest form of one person being so utterly hurt and disappointed in another. It would be ungentlemanly to try to justify my response. It was cruel despite the fact that Sophie was the last person on earth I would ever wish to be cruel to, but I felt impotent and ashamed. Antoni was a man who had ultimately offered his life in the fight against fascism, and here was I, a man who wanted to save lives, not take them, and I hadn't even managed to do that. As I had stepped out of the house, Sophie's words of disappointment that I wouldn't fight were ringing around my head. She had chased after me and offered kindness. I did not deserve kindness and lashed out, as one does when they are tired and frustrated. I regretted it instantly, and yet offered no apology.

Once at home I sat in my glasshouse with only the sound of summer rain bouncing off the windows for company. The chair opposite was once again empty and I deserved no more. With my eyes closed, my thoughts drifted across the memories of time spent with Sophie. I smiled thinking of her – her bright and spirited effervescence, her kindness, her openness of being. Our moment in the garden yesterday seemed like a lifetime away. Indeed, it was as if another man – a carefree and kind man with no past to be guilty of and no uncertain future to worry about – stepped into my shoes for a few short hours and took control of my life. He was a very happy man.

Why must I always be pulled back into the darkness? What on earth must she think of me now, I wondered.

The gate clicked. I glanced at my watch to find that it was already two p.m. Surgery hours. I stood like an automaton and headed for the door. The first of my patients had arrived. And so the world kept on turning.

The next two days brought many people to my door, so much so that I took down the sign dictating limited surgery hours. In fact, I lit a bonfire and burned the thing, not just because of the graffiti, but because such pedantism seemed more than a little unnecessary now. Perhaps it always was.

Not all my visitors were patients. Peter arrived with a 'Dig for Victory' flyer painted superbly in watercolours by himself. The man holding the spade looked remarkably like me. After a glass or two of rose tea (with a little extra something tippled into his glass for good measure) he agreed that he had perhaps been a little rash in digging up his rose garden and that yes, indeed, we must approach Dame Sibyl for an acre or two of sheltered pasture that could be cultivated for vegetable crops rather than destroy our own gardens after what, for both of us, had been many years of dedicated work. After all, he said, he was told on good authority (Joseph) that she (Dame Sibyl) had no intention of ripping out her own flower beds and so why should we?

'So that we have enough to eat?' I said. 'Perhaps you were right in the first instance.'

'Hmm,' murmured Peter.

Peter's swift departure with the intent to rehydrate and replant his torn-out rose bushes left the gate wide open for the arrival of a whole stream of islanders who seemed suddenly to require general health checks. One particular islander who had rarely passed through my door – Jennifer Green – even stopped by. Jennifer was the choir mistress and a sturdy woman in her middle years of great voice and personality. She had been a little withdrawn lately but I did not concern myself with this because – to be frank – 'the Germans' were coming (or we thought they were and the fear of a thing is sometimes worse than the thing itself) and I would have been more concerned if she had *not* been reacting in a down in the mouth kind of way. But it seemed that Jennifer had had an extra burden of worry on her mind in the form of a large lump that had appeared just under the surface of her left breast. She was shaking as she showed me, both with fear, I think, and embarrassment. But there was no need. I explained that in the human body there were 'lumps' and there were '*lumps*', my eyes protruding to show the nature of the latter. She asked me which category hers came under and I smiled and said, 'lumps'.

The drainage procedure I performed was swift if a little uncomfortable, but I offered her a batch of rose tea afterwards (my mother's rose for this one) and suggested she prepare chicken broth which is truly the ultimate cure-all. I told her to come back to me in two weeks for a check-up.

'But surely you will not be on the island by then …' She buttoned up her blouse.

When I asked why she would think this, she explained that as the Germans were in St Malo, it was generally expected that they would arrive in the coming week or two and that I was intending to leave before they arrived. 'That's what Dame Sibyl is telling everyone,' she said. 'And that we should all come for a check-up before you go. That new friend of yours is leaving too.'

'Friend?'

'Sophie Hathaway. Believe it or not, she's some kind of British government official – a spy, some say. They kept that quiet, didn't they? Quite high up too. She was supposed to leave on the boat with the English but decided to stay.'

'First of all,' I began, 'I think that if she was a spy, she would not admit it, and secondly, why?'

'Why?'

'Why did she not leave?'

'I heard say she'd fallen in love.'

'In love? With whom?'

'Not with *whom* …'

'Pardon. My English …'

'No, I mean, with *what* has she fallen in love …'

I was confused and my expression betrayed it.

'She's fallen in love with the *island*, what else? Anyhow, a telegram came yesterday to say she's got to go home sharpish. Some say she's in trouble for staying too long. AWOL apparently. Didn't you know all of this?'

'I did not,' I say. 'I did not.'

I approached La Seigneurie wearing my best clothes and carrying a large bouquet of flowers cut fresh from my garden. Joseph once showed me a secret entrance through a door covered over by an overly enthusiastic laurel hedge and I was feeling anxious enough to use it. Truth was – and it had taken me far too many days to come to face the reality of it – I adored Sophie. Adored her. I had told Sophie that Swinburne the poet said that Sark was the wonderfullest thing he had ever seen, and I used to agree with him, but not anymore. That prize went to Sophie Hathaway – my Juliet. But would she grant me any kind of audience today? She was a kind-hearted soul, yes, but I was unforgivably rude when we last spoke, and yet here I was, about to ask for forgiveness.

The doors to the lounge were open. Pausing at the door, I heard Sophie and Dame Sibyl discussing something – someone. They seemed to be in disagreement. I waited at the door for a sufficient pause in conversation to facilitate a cough, but to my disappointment found that they were discussing me, and there was no doubting this as I heard my name spoken twice and there was only one Sebastian on the island. May God forgive me, I stepped out of view and listened. The conversation went like this:

Dame Sibyl: *Need I remind you that you were sent here with the express intention of either recruiting him for the service, or interning him, Sophie!*

Sophie: *You need not, but clearly I need to remind you that I was only given this task because it was you who indirectly told the office about Sebastian and his oh so interesting twin brother at a dinner party in my flat last year, and that's why I was instructed to come here. It was your loose lips that got us into this pickle in the first place. I was to monitor Sebastian and decide if he was likely to be a Nazi sympathiser. If not, I was to befriend him and attempt to recruit him into the British Secret Service. It would have been morally wrong to intern him, Sibyl. You said yourself that he's no more a traitor than you or I. You were against his internment initially.*

Dame Sibyl: *That was before I knew that the damn foolish man was determined to stay. He needs to be sent away to safety.*

Sophie (sotto voce): *And I've been trying my best to find a good moment to broach the whole thing ... but it's not been easy.*

Dame Sibyl: *Well then, you have not tried hard enough! There is no way on earth the German army will allow one of their own to be a pacifist – especially not a doctor. Also, if his brother finds out ...'*

Sophie: *His brother. His brother. I am sick of hearing about his brother. Everyone at the office is obsessed with him even though he's not seen him in years and the guy isn't even that high up!*

Dame Sibyl: *If Sebastian refuses to wear the uniform he will be a disgrace to the family. I know these people – these kinds of people, at least – and the safest place for Sebastian is in England.*

Sophie: *Where he would be bullied into acting as an operative? Because you and I both know him well enough to know that he'll never fight, never. The treatment of Germans in England is shocking just now. Shocking! The authorities will not care to listen to his sensibilities, and if he refuses to work for them then they will not allow the brother of a senior German officer to roam free in Britain.*

Dame Sibyl: *That may be so, but you have done him a disservice by befriending him, Sophie. You were only supposed to get to know him and – one way or another – take him away to safety. You were not supposed to behave like a schoolgirl around him and—*

Sophie (interrupting): *But you were the one who forced us into doing the play. You were the one who forced me into playing the lovestruck Juliet to his damn ridiculous Romeo! You were the one who kept hinting at more than a friendship!*

Dame Sibyl (dryly): *I thought it would assist you in persuading him to leave. A broken heart never hurt anyone in the long run. To be perfectly honest, in my mind you were supposed to fall in love – for real – and persuade him to go with you that way. There's no fool like an old fool, I suppose.*

Sophie (coldly): *Love? Don't be ridiculous. Sebastian is not a toy to be played with. And anyway, times of woe afford no time to woo, Aunt Sibyl. You of all people should know that!*

There was a pause in conversation but I was too stunned to cough. Sophie sensed my presence and turned around. I am not a person who holds stock with listening unseen at doorways and yet I was all the better for knowing the details. Sophie reached out an arm. Dame Sibyl turned also, but Dame Sibyl's expression, which for once I could read, knew no embarrassment.

I lay the flowers on the carpet, retraced my steps across the garden and with wide and fast strides, headed for home.

Chapter Twenty-Two

La Santé Prison, August 1944

'Y ou behaved rashly,' says Christoph. 'Why did you not just seize the moment and tell her how you felt about her – you had plenty of opportunity, especially when sitting in your rose garden. That moment would have been perfect. It's clearly what she was hoping you would do and that's why she asked to see your garden – to put you in the place where you felt most at ease.'

'You think so?'

'I know so. I suppose now you are going to tell me that you could not forgive her treachery, or some such nonsense.' He takes off his glasses. I am beginning to see a pattern regarding the removing of the glasses. He usually does this when he is somewhat frustrated with my story.

'I did not tell her in the garden,' I explain, keeping my voice calm, 'because the conversation had turned to past trauma. It would have been inappropriate.'

'Pah!'

'No, hear me out. At the same time, I was uncertain. One does not sit down one day and think to oneself, *I have met a woman and I have fallen in love today and I shall tell her and expect her to feel the same way and spend the rest of her life with me.* Blossoming love is ...' I glance around the cell. The candle is still burning, the green branches are in the vase, the empty cup is in my hands. 'Well, it is like a tea ceremony, is it not?'

Christoph expression is awash with sarcasm. 'A tea ceremony?'

I hand him my cup. 'It must be nurtured, Christoph. Savoured ... cherished. Not rushed. Never rushed. All I knew was that I was thrilled to be in her company and when she wasn't there, I felt ...'

'Empty,' he says, looking into the cup. When he glances up, I see in his eyes that he is a man who has known that emptiness.

'Our lives at the time, remember, were most uncertain, especially mine. Would it not have been excessively selfish of me to declare my undying love to a woman only to dash off on the next boat a moment later?'

Christoph frowned. 'But that is exactly when you should declare your love! And also, next boat? You said you had no intention of leaving ...'

I pat his knee. 'You are frustrated with me, I think.'

He lets out a breath and his shoulders relax. 'No, it is merely that you remind me of someone else I once knew. It is that which is frustrating.'

Christoph replaces his spectacles. He wishes me to move on. I look at the cross on his chest and I wonder ... did he ever really let go of his first physical love, before he grabbed onto his second, a spiritual one?

'I'm sorry if I frustrate you,' I say. 'Believe me, I frustrate myself sometimes.'

He pushes his spectacles up his nose. 'I am merely trying to understand you, that is all. If I understand you more then perhaps I will understand someone who is very much like you. And also …'

'Also?' I repeat gently.

'Love is a gift, Sebastian. And I feel frustrated that you did not fully embrace the gift you were given every single moment that you had it.'

I lean forward to pick up the Coleman stove and begin to prime the gas. 'You and I both, my friend. You and I both.'

Chapter Twenty-Three

I t was twenty minutes at the most before Sophie appeared at my garden gate, but the brisk walk home allowed me the time to consider, although there wasn't much to consider. It seemed that my friendship with Sophie had been a façade. Yes, I was being melodramatic, but these were intense times – they always are when people are living on the brink of things.

I left Sophie on the other side of the garden gate. She could speak to me across it briefly if she wished as there could, after all, be very little to say. She was holding my mother's roses close to her chest.

'Sebastian.' Her face was not quite as angst-ridden as I would have expected. 'I am truly sorry that you overheard our conversation.' I nodded curtly to accept her apology. 'But I'm not sorry that you're now aware of the situation. We've had such a wonderful time together and I guess I just didn't want to ruin it.'

This held no store with me. If a person wanted to say something to another person then it was not difficult to just step out and say exactly what it was that needed to be said. (As usual I was aware of my hypocrisy and excused myself for it.)

'Thank you for the apology,' I said, smiling. (It was a false smile, I'll admit.) 'Consider it accepted and think on it no more. I have no wish to quarrel.'

'But don't you want to talk about it? Don't you want me to explain?'

'There is no need,' I said, turning to walk away. 'Honestly, do not concern yourself. I understand.'

She opened the gate after a fiddle (I made a mental note to fix the thing) and followed on. I knew she would.

'If you would just stop and listen to me for a second, you might actually feel a whole lot better about it.'

'Better? How, when I do not feel badly in the first place?'

I ducked under *Jacques Cartier* who was rambling over an archway and looking rather tatty. We disappeared into the orchard. She stayed on my tail like an ace pilot in a dog fight. I talked while walking.

'I have just discovered that you befriended me in order to categorise and recruit me as means of gaining information about me – my politics – and my brother.'

'Yes, initially. But not after a while. And you knew that already.'

I continued to walk. 'Not the part about my brother. You should tell your superiors that they are barking up the wrong tree. As you said to Dame Sibyl, I haven't seen Sascha in years and you clearly know more about him than I do. It's sounds as though you believe him to be Hitler's right hand man, but I tell you now, that is most unlikely.'

'I know, I know, but …'

I stopped and turned to face her.

'No, you don't know. You know nothing about it.' I began to walk again.

'Please, Sebastian … I was simply doing my job.'

'Your job? Ah, now there is a subject to ponder on. No one actually knows what your real job is. Who is the real Sophie Hathaway, that's what I ask myself. Does she even exist?'

I felt a hand grab my arm to halt me. '*Please* believe me when I say that I do, so very much, want to be your friend. Honestly, Sebastian, I don't understand why you're so cross. Once I got to know you better there was no way I was going to try to recruit you for the Allies … you must know that, surely. You must also know how angry I am that a wonderful, kind man who wants and knows only peace, who would never hurt a soul, is forced to choose either one awful situation or the other, and so please Sebastian, don't look for subterfuge where none exists, well, not anymore. I just don't understand why you're so cross with me …'

We reached the rose garden – a dead end. My emotion, like the path, had run out of steam. There was nothing to be gained by arguing with Sophie and I was suddenly overcome with such an exhaustion I hadn't the strength to argue. I had been here before, with these impossible moral dilemmas. Why was I upset, really? Was it because in my heart I knew that our time together on Sark was over, just when I thought my life might be beginning again? *This is why it is best to remain closed up*, I thought. *This is why I am better off alone*. I sat down on the bench, all I could think about were Sophie's last words to Sibyl – *Love? Don't be ridiculous*.

That was why I was cross.

I fixed my gaze on the roses. 'Are you leaving?' I asked.

'I'm taking the lifeboat to Guernsey with the Polish

brothers and then either flying or sailing to England with the final tranche of refugees.'

'When?'

'Tomorrow evening, after the play. I have to get back to my department, before the Ger ...' Her voice followed my gaze into the roses. 'Well, you know, just in case.'

'Will you be reprimanded for not taking me with you?'

She shrugged. 'I suppose I will, yes.'

'I know we shall see each other tomorrow at the play,' she said, 'but do let us say goodbye properly now, as we always should have.'

She stood and held out her hand, but I was so confused and conflicted, I did not take it.

'The play?' I repeated. 'But surely, now ...'

She smiled. 'As you always said, Sebastian ... die show muss weitergehen.'

I looked at her then. It was a group of words that so aptly surmised our brief moments of time together. I also noticed that although her smile was there, it was a watery imitation of that contagious and enigmatic expression of joy that I had grown to know and love.

'Can we say goodbye now, then?' she asked.

'I will see you at the play,' I said.

'Yes, but I want to say it as Sophie and Sebastian, not Romeo and Juliet. I would so hate to say goodbye as two hapless characters who suffer a terribly unhappy ending. I would hate ... I would *so* hate for that to happen to us. And truly, about what I said to my aunt, before ...'

She floundered but I took too long to throw her a rope, nor did I reach and take the hand that had fallen away. Sophie leant forward to kiss me on the cheek and I felt a wetness on my face as she lingered with the kiss. Laying the roses she had carried the whole time on the bench next to me, she turned on her heel and very quickly walked away. Disappointment slid down my spine once again to bury itself deep inside my belly. So, I had finally found my true affinity with Romeo. For never was, and never would there be, such a fortune's fool as I.

Chapter Twenty-Four

But let us move forward to the night of the play.

I was on stage in Dame Sibyl's garden and we were several acts in. It couldn't be regarded as Sark Theatre Society's most successful performance. Audience numbers were high – the whole of the island was there, or those of us that were left, at least – but the atmosphere, like the performance, was wanting. Dame Sibyl was sitting in the front row, willing us on with what could only be described as a painted smile, and the prompt – Margery – had spoken more lines of verse than all the players put together.

Going ahead with the performance was supposed to prove that life goes on, that the islanders of Sark would not bow down under tyranny – a tyranny every bit as powerful as we sat in its shadow as it would be in actuality. German jack boots may not as yet have stepped as much as a toe on that tiny rock in the sea, but their heavy footsteps already echoed down every street and across every field. It is said that humans have lost the ability to sense imminent danger … that was not the case tonight. The air was charged with nervous energy and every soul in the audience could feel it. Nevertheless, we must finish what we had begun – *die show muss weitergehen*.

'*Did my heart love till now?*' I asked aloud. I was supposed to engage the audience at this point but I caught the eye of Sophie who was waiting in the wings. She glanced away. Every time I tried to approach her off stage when out of character, she offered only a weak smile and turned away. As Juliet, however, she was electric. No more was she the jovial, happy-go-lucky (slightly wooden) Sophie, pretending to be Juliet. There was only Juliet, and I was humbled by her performance. '*Forswear it, sight!*' I went on, acutely aware that my accent sounded harsh against the beauty of the words, especially while shouting against the noise of the poplar trees that were swaying in the strengthening breeze. '*For I ne'er saw true beauty till this night.*'

And thus the show stumbled on: from scene to scene, act to act, with poor Margery becoming increasingly hoarse, until finally – finally – I found myself looking down on a shroud-covered Sophie lying on a crypt. We were performing the scene that never was – the death scene – and suddenly there was no audience, there was only Romeo and Juliet, Sebastian and Sophie. My heart was an echo chamber and my words of love and regret utterly real and brutally honest.

Oh, my love, my wife, it is time to join you in all eternity.

Somewhere in the distance a phone rang and yet I did not lose the moment. I *would not* lose the moment. I pulled back the shroud. Sophie lay there as still as death. I took her hand and lifted it to my face.

Eyes, look your last. Arms, take your last embrace. And lips, the doors of breath be forever sealed with a righteous kiss.

I lay myself down next to Juliet, leant over her lifeless body and as our lips brushed, I rested my forehead on hers, threw caution to the wind and behaved like the man I was born to be. There would never be another moment like this, and I absolutely did not care that the whole of the island was watching, which is why I whispered, 'I have been a fool, Sophie Hathaway, but only because I love you'. To my great surprise and delight, even though she was supposed to be dead, Sophie kissed me and whispered, 'I know'.

And so we kissed. It was the sweetest, most longed-for kiss a man could have, and for longer than perhaps we ought to have. I pulled away but I had more to say and frankly cared not if the whole of the audience could hear me. 'One day, Sophie Hathaway,' I said, 'I intend to kiss you like no woman has ever been kissed before.' I kissed her tenderly again. 'When all of this is over, will you permit me to behave like a grown up man rather than a lovestruck fool and … what is the word in English … court you? Properly?'

Sophie was about to answer, but with a cough from Margery there was no time because I took up a vial of poison and shouted …

'Oh, true apothecary thy drugs are quick!'

At which point Sophie was supposed to open her eyes and sit up. But Dame Sibyl's maid who had no part to play, ran on the stage and gave the greatest performance of the night. Only it wasn't a performance, it was absolutely real.

'They're here!' she shouted, an arm flying out pointing towards the west. 'The Germans! They're bombing Guernsey! I just heard … on the phone … the man said they're gunning people down on the street. On the street, Ma'am!'

Dame Sibyl stood but none of us had time to respond because an arrow of darkness flashed overhead accompanied by the unmistakable drone of Nazi aggression, and within moments we heard a sound that placed me directly back inside my nightmares and I was no longer in Renaissance Italy, nor was I even in the garden of La Seigneurie in 1940. No, it was twenty-four years before and I was wading through the trenches of the Somme, with my hands over my ears to cover the sound of the guns, praying to a God I do not believe in that if one good thing could come out of it all it would be that this would be the war to end all wars. But I was not on that battlefield anymore and my wish had not come true. This was a different war and a different time entirely, and this was not the end of it, but only the beginning.

Chapter Twenty-Five

La Santé Prison, August 1944

'Are you not proud of me, Christoph?' I say.

I watch as he pours boiled water (slightly off-boiled to be precise as he is quite the pedant) on fresh leaves in the pot.

He does not look up. 'Proud of you?'

'Of course! Proud that I seized my moment!' I shout my words and they echo uncomfortably around the cell. 'That I grasped the nettle, as the English say. You doubted I had it in me. Go on, admit it, you said as much yourself!'

Christoph sniffs. 'I would not say "proud" exactly. You have reached a point in your story where the Germans – yes, you note that I refer to my own countrymen as you do now – are shortly to arrive on the island. By the fact that you are sitting here with me, and not cuddled up with Sophie in England, tells me that the outcome was not necessarily a good one. This makes me sad.'

He stops talking but this time it is not so much a gap of silence he is leaving, as a chasm.

'You had known for some time that they would come, that your time was limited.' He swirls the water in the pot. 'You knew that they were in St Malo and that you loved her. You knew that you would most likely have to leave the island and yet it took until the very last moment for you to, as you say, grasp the nettle. I will never understand why you are simply unable to seize the moment, Sascha!'

The elephant that has been cowering in the corner of the room since our first conversation seems to have woken up.

'Forgive me, my friend,' I begin, 'but you seem to be speaking as a lover rather than a chaplain. And my name is not Sascha, it's Sebastian.' I leant forward to touch his arm. 'Isn't it time you told me a little of your own story?'

Space again.

'There is not the time,' he says eventually, starting to pour, although I do feel that he must be distracted because no true tea connoisseur would ever allow the leaves to steep for such a small amount of time.

Chapter Twenty-Six

The Luftwaffe attacked Sark harbour on 28th June. A week later I was captain of a small dinghy crossing the Channel heading for England. Despite my best efforts to steer north using nothing but the position of the sun and a broken compass, I feared we may have drifted west into the depths (and dangers) of the Atlantic Ocean. I thought that if we were very lucky we might catch a glimpse of the Cornish coast, or find a friendly vessel to assist us before nightfall, but most likely we would find no landfall and see no vessel at all.

By day three of sailing we had a little bread still, some apples and three bottles of ale, although my traveling companions and I were in dire need of the most important commodity of all – hope. If we were to die out here, then better that we simply lie with our backs against the hull, fall asleep in the sunshine and never wake up, except that I did so very much want to wake up, because I had never in my life felt as alive as I felt at that moment, or more desperate to cling onto the thin stream of reality that was hidden within the raging sea of this futile war. For the first time in my life, I was in love: wholly, completely and honestly in love.

My timing could have been better.

I once read the memoir of a writer who said that it takes fifty thousand words before a reader is convinced that two of his characters have fallen in love. For me it took just one – 'Hello.' I could say that I didn't realise it at the time, of course, and that it was only now, with hour upon hour of reflection behind me, that I had seen the truth, but that would not be true. I knew the moment she limped away on those crutches while carrying the wrong ankle. I rested my head on the hull and tried to come to terms with the turn of events forced upon me during the past few days. It had all been so very, very strange.

The attack on the harbour was short and relatively ineffective. The idea within German High Command must have been to hit the islanders with a first blast of shock and awe – to show us who was unquestionably in charge now, and to illustrate that it would be futile to consider fighting back. That being so, I was ashamed of my country and abhorred their unnecessary tactics. The British government sent out a clear notice to Hitler that the Channel Islands had been left undefended and that no British troops remained there, so why the aggression? Poor Guernsey was attacked with much greater vigour than Sark, causing considerable destruction and unnecessary deaths. The islanders were gunned down on the streets of St Peter Port, their houses and their boats sunk, and for what? A show of force? A declaration that Germany had taken British land and British people? Probably.

But then we heard no more because the telephone line to Guernsey – the only line out of the island – was cut the day after the attack and Sark was left entirely in the dark. Our fishermen dared not venture out. The message of the attack on our harbour and boats was loud and clear: *stay put; do not defend yourselves; we are on our way.*

When they came they arrived without aggression and in the form of a small troop of men on the Guernsey lifeboat, which had been requisitioned by their commanding officer, Major Maass. Dame Sibyl sent out word that they were not to be greeted on arrival at the harbour but we were to stay close to our homes, ignore them and leave the rest to her. For myself, I had no choice but to carry on as normal. In the absence of a veterinary surgeon on the island, I was required to help my closest neighbour with the delivery of a breech calf, but even so, I do not believe I have ever been so impressed by a person's grace and fortitude in the face of peril as I was with Dame Sibyl.

As requested, no one greeted the German troop when it arrived at the harbour, which meant that the commanding officer and his deputy were forced to walk to La Seigneurie to find the 'man in charge' only to be led by the maid to Dame Sibyl's study where, I am told, the dame sat with her husband in calm splendour and forced the men to approach her desk and introduce themselves. It was a risky strategy, but it seemed that she assessed the situation with the guile, insight and precision of a great military leader. As she suspected, the commanding officer was indeed from German nobility and offered Dame Sibyl the respect her rank deserved. (The fact that she addressed them in German can only have helped). After a short meeting it was declared that island life was to carry on as normal, apart from the minor fact of course that all civil liberties had been revoked and the island was, effectively, under house arrest. For me, the situation was not so straightforward.

Major Maass was already aware of my presence on the island and when he could not operate the latch on my garden gate, his adjutant simply kicked it open. I was pleased that I had not taken the time to fix it. The knock on the door when it came was unmistakable in its forcefulness. My reaction when I saw the familiar uniform standing on my doorstep – the uniform of my youth – surprised me. It was all I could do not to vomit on the man's highly polished boots. Major Maass explained that he had received orders from within the Oberkommando der Wermacht (from my brother, no less) that I was to be escorted to Berlin where I was to take up the position of senior physician within the Waffen SS – my uniform would be fitted on arrival. It was a great honour, apparently.

He went on to explain that I would be leaving on the Guernsey lifeboat the following week, and that I should spend that time putting any outstanding business in order. With my hackles now raised and nausea abated, I asked if Sascha (I used his Christian name on purpose) had said what the consequences would be if I simply refused to leave Sark. His expression was impassive when he answered. 'You will be shot as a traitor, like anyone else who refuses to serve the Reich.'

'And those were my brother's actual words?' I asked, dumbfounded.

'Would you like me to show you the memorandum?'

'No,' I answered. 'I would not.'

Not more than two hours later another knock, thankfully a softer one, sounded at the door. Sophie and Dame Sibyl's husband, Robert Hathaway, were standing there. I had not seen Sophie since our moment on the stage, when she was Juliet and I her Romeo, when the world for just a moment was perfection. My heart leapt to find her standing on my doorstep, leading me to consider momentarily how powerful – dangerous – this thing we call love really is. I should have been wracked with despair and worry about my immediate future, and yet at the sight of her face I felt nothing but joy. What fools we are to be so out of control of our emotions as a consequence of one brief kiss, and yet how wonderful, is it not?

Robert stepped past me and asked Sophie to close the door behind her. We quickly got down to business. Maass had explained to Dame Sibyl that the island's doctor would be leaving Sark in the near future and that another doctor – from the German military – would arrive soon after. When Dame Sibyl asked why this was necessary, after all, they already had a doctor on the island, it was explained that Herr Braun was expected to take up the rank, position and responsibility that his status and connections demanded.

But that was not why they were here, Sophie explained, her breath quick. They were here to help concoct a plan of escape for me because I must leave tonight at the latest as surely they would not suspect so soon that I had gone.

'Let's say, hypothetically, if you *were* to go to Berlin, Sebastian, would your brother not look after you?' asked Sophie. 'Couldn't you explain that you don't want to be part of it, that you want to be left alone to live here. You already – more than amply – did your duty for Germany during the last war. Surely your brother wouldn't allow anything bad to happen to you … would he?'

Two sets of eyes glanced up at me.

'According to Major Maass my brother has ordered me back to Germany. Yes, we have lost touch and I was disappointed in his response when I left home and further disappointed with his brief correspondence when Mother died, but to manipulate events to insist that I return to Germany seems entirely out of character. Perhaps he holds his own bitterness too, that I have not been in touch with him, either. He may still be under the influence of our father, in fact, I would wager heavily that he is.'

'Your father?' repeated Sophie. 'But I was under the impression that he was ...'

'Dead? No. Old, yes. A tyrant still? I should think so. Families can be such tricky courses to navigate. But all that is of no matter. Sascha will not protect me now, it seems. Perhaps he has slowly become the man my father always wanted him to be – an image of himself.'

And so, finally accepting that what Dame Sibyl had insisted for weeks would happen had actually come true, I took control and devised a plan. Despite curfew, Robert said that, yes, he could arrange for a clipper to be left on the beach below La Coupée that night. There would be only a thin sliver of moon to navigate by but it would allow me to silently drift away and I was to take the Polish brothers, Alek and Fabian, with me. Provisions for several days of travel would be left in the boat, along with a letter of introduction from Dame Sibyl to Fortune Findlay-Jones, her cousin in Cornwall – they had already spoken on the phone, of course. Robert had heard stories of Dutch prisoners of war escaping Europe by rowing singlehandedly to England. If the Dutch could row to England from the Netherlands to escape the Nazis, he said, then we could damn well sail to Cornwall, but only if we had a fair sou'westerly behind us, and we would.

'And I'm coming too,' said Sophie, her eyes bright with excitement.

'With me? Nein!' I looked to Robert, but he simply nodded his agreement and explained how, on landing in Cornwall, we should work our way towards Penzance and knock on the door of the house at Godolphin where Sibyl's cousin lived. It was thought best if I passed myself off as the third Polish brother – the man whose life I'd failed to save. Sophie would then travel to London by the next available train.

I took Sophie's hand. 'This is the real thing now. If they see us sailing away then I am certain that they will not hesitate to shoot. I have no choice to leave Sark if I am to stay out of the SS, but you do, Sophie. I cannot guarantee that we will ever reach England and, my love, I could not bear it if …'

Sophie and Robert glanced at each other.

'Tell him, Sophie,' said Robert.

I glanced from one to the other. 'What? Tell me what?'

'Only that I am not as fresh behind the ears as you think. I'm more than merely the woman who seeks out Fifth Columnists. My trip to Sark to find you was only a small part of the reason I was here. Let's just say, it might be more dangerous for me to stay here. I have a great deal of information regarding our intelligence agencies held in my head, and I would not wish to be deported to France in order to have that information beaten out of me. Women are every bit a part of the fight too … just not necessarily in a traditional way.'

There was a noise outside. We sat in silence listening before deciding that it must be my neighbour's cat, or something equally benign.

'Then you must come,' I said. 'We will set sail from the west side of La Coupée this evening and be out of sight before daylight. You are a proficient enough sailor, are you not?'

Sophie saluted. 'I am, Capitan!'

'Good. Major Maass most likely won't visit me again for a couple of days, by which time we will be long gone.'

'Is that it, then?' asked Robert, standing. The man looked wrung out.

Sophie nodded. 'I think so,' she said.

'Then tell the Poles that we will travel light. Warm clothes and rations is all that we need.' I jumped up, thinking of something. Moments later I returned with an intricately carved wooden box. I handed it to Robert. 'It is most valuable,' I said. 'Perhaps you could find a hiding place … It is my insurance policy, for when all of this is behind us.' I turned to Sophie and saw nothing but absolute confidence on her face. It was contagious. I took her hand. 'We can do this!' I said.

'You're damn right we can!' was her answer.

But when at midnight, carrying a knapsack over my shoulder, I slid down the embankment and onto the beach at La Coupée, I could make out only two shadows standing by a small boat.

'Where is Sophie?' I asked, speaking in a whisper in my native tongue.

'She chose to stay.' Alek took an envelope out of his jacket pocket. 'For you,' he said.

'No, but this is not acceptable!'

Fabian was already pulling the dinghy into the water. He beckoned me on but I did not move.

'Herr Doktor,' whispered Alek, grabbing my arm as I tried to grasp a hold of the situation in the darkness. 'Please. Come. If we are found, we will be shot – and so will you.'

There was just enough ambient light to see the silhouette of La Coupée above me. I saw an image of a carefree Sophie riding across the ridge and I felt the touch of her lips, her hand on my face, the vibrance of her smile.

Another hand pulled on my arm. 'Please. Sir. We will die without you … and we will be killed if we stay.'

I looked towards the ocean and saw the shadow of Fabian standing in the water. He was holding the boat awkwardly as it bobbed on the rolling tide. I had no option but to jump aboard, turn my back on my island and sail away.

And that is why I found myself on a small dinghy that had both a broken daggerboard and a flimsy sail. We were constantly on the lookout for other seagoers, be it friend or foe, and yet incredibly for two days we saw not one vessel. I took out the letter Alek had pressed into my hand for what was probably the hundredth time since our voyage began. My eyes stung with fatigue and salt spray but her words were all the lifeline I needed:

Dear Sebastian,

I must be quick. It wasn't possible to sail the clipper around the coast to La Coupée without being seen because they have already set up a checkpoint at the harbour. I remembered seeing a decent-looking dinghy on a beach near La Seigneurie and so I stole it and sailed it around to La Coupée this evening. There isn't enough room in the dinghy for all of us, in fact there isn't really enough room for two, let alone three, but you stand a significantly increased chance of success without me on board, and so we – the Hathaways and I – decided that I should stay behind. Do remember that I have dual citizenship, and the American passport will, I think, hold sway with our occupiers to keep me safe, but make no mistake, I shall return to England soon.

There is a parcel of food in a barrel tied to the mast. You will also find a small parcel wrapped in hessian in the footwell – it is a plant. I asked Joseph to dig up the rose cutting you gave him recently – the one of your mother's rose – because I thought you might want to have it with you when you start a new garden again, where ever that might be. We have also wrapped your teapot (very safely) into a package and tied it to the mast having decided that you may need it sooner than you think, and for some reason I feel strongly that it might bring you luck. Don't ask me why, I just know you should have it with you.

*I must go now, but I think (I hope) that there is a great deal left unsaid between us, and that one day we will have the opportunity to say it. I have faith that you will make it to England, Sebastian, because I **see** you there – in Cornwall – and when I close my eyes and think of you, I see an image of a walled garden and you're in it, and you're happy. You'll like Cornwall, I think. From what I've heard, its gentle wildness will suit you.*

We both have a very long way to go before we find each other again, but I promise you that when I make it off this island I'll find my way straight to Godolphin, and there you will be, in the garden, with your roses. On the night of the play you promised to kiss me one day as no woman has been kissed before – I will hold you to that.

S

Chapter Twenty-Seven

La Santé Prison, August 1944

'D o you think you would have been persuaded to leave earlier if not for your developing friendship with Sophie?' asks Christoph.

I shake my head. 'No. I was determined to stay.'

'And do you think she would have left earlier if she hadn't fallen in love with you?'

I know this to be the case, and it torments me.

'Yes.'

'You were both very naïve,' he says. 'But I have yet to meet anyone who is rational when falling in love. It is not your fault, Sebastian.'

'Maybe so. But I was stubborn,' I say. 'And angry. I did not want to move on. Mine was an easy existence on Sark.'

'Perhaps life is not meant to be too easy for too long,' he says.

I grunt at this. 'By whose say so? God's?'

'You have always been closer to God than you think.'

'Pah!'

'You are a gardener, Ipso facto you have been "with God".'

'My friend. I told you. I would love to have been a believer …' I glance around. 'Especially now, but it simply hasn't happened for me. I have never – and I apologise for the tone of my voice – but I have never "found God". He seems to have wished to remain hidden from me.'

Space.

I notice the flicker of the candle is becoming agitated. That non-existent breeze again.

'I don't believe he was hidden when you spent time in your garden – your Eden. You even referred to it as such yourself.'

'It was merely a turn of phrase, I assure you.'

'Was it?' he asks, flatly. 'Was he not also with you in that little dinghy. When the other men lost hope, you said that you had not? The Lord was with you then also, I think?'

'If he was, he was very quiet, and he certainly wasn't there on the fourth day when we watched a bank of black clouds approach from the west and all three of us fumbled with the sail to try to outrun the storm, which, of course, was impossible.'

'Tell me.'

'What can I say? The rhythm of the little boat increased at pace as the first drops of rain arrived, but they were a mere trickle compared to the torrent that followed. The nose of the dinghy rose up and crashed down, over and over. With all the food and water now gone, an atmosphere of grave inevitability overwhelmed us. Truly, your Lord was not with us then. Like three little tinned sardines, we lowered the sail, put our arms around each other, hunkered down and yes, I'll admit it, we prayed. Alek and Fabian prayed for the saving of their souls and a swift exit to heaven, and I to be dead before I hit the water, a conscious drowning being low on the list of ways in which I would like to meet my maker.

'At the peak of the storm the little boat began to rock so violently that I knew we must be only a matter of minutes – seconds, even – before one of the waves had us over. We remained huddled, but then an even darker shadow crept over the boat like a reaper's shroud. When I heard the sound of our little boat rubbing up against the hull of another, I forced myself to look up and, like angels from heaven – and I use that purely as a phrase, you understand – I saw two men in oilskin coats, their faces dripping with water, their hands blue with cold as they hauled a coil of rope over the side of their clipper and the life line was lowered, inch by inch. With my arms raised up like a baby crying to its mother, I grabbed the rope, secured it to a ring on the bow, and with my arms wrapped tightly once again around my unlikely brothers, very slowly, we were towed to shore.

'And all right, I'll admit it. I did wonder, as we came alongside at Porthleven if we hadn't been witness to a miracle, especially as we were just four miles away from Godolphin House. But in the cold light of day, I realised that there are no miracles, only happy coincidences and damn good luck! We said thank you to the crew, and they set back out to sea to catch the next day's haul.'

Christoph packs up his things and turns out the lamp.

'Perhaps,' he says, 'by the end of our time together, I may have persuaded you to believe in miracles.'

'You are a good man,' I say, 'but I don't believe any one man can persuade another of such things. If we are to believe, perhaps we must arrive at that destination by ourselves.'

He grabs his stick and I watch him limp – more severely than previously – to the door.

'Auf wiedersehen, Sebastian,' he says, with a click of the heels.

'Auf wiedersehen, Christoph.'

And when he is gone I see that he has left me the stove, the tea and the pot.

Miracles? No. But angels? Maybe.

Chapter Twenty-Eight

La Santé Prison, August 1944

L ast night I heard the dragging of heavy equipment as it was positioned in the courtyard. I stood on the stool and tried to peer through the grate, which was a mistake. A senior officer gave directions as a heavy wooden frame was placed into position in the centre of the yard. The young men who did his bidding were at least sombre. Their uniforms hang loosely now, like old skins that are about to be shed. This morning the blade was fitted and I confess that I wept. I should not have looked. I was better placed without the stool. I wanted, so much, to find peace before my time came – to have the courage to behave as calmly as the woman who faced me across the courtyard once did – find within me her grace, her kindness, her forgiveness. But I cannot. I am screaming inside and afraid, and do I not, in the end, deserve this fear? Do I not deserve this punishment – a life for a life? It hurts to think that it is due to my brother that I am here. I fled Sark because he ordered me back to Germany, and perhaps I am here, facing the courtyard now, not only because of the karma brought on by him all those years ago but by his lifestyle choices that I am being punished for. That is unfair. Every man should be free to live how he so chooses, and the truth of what I must face now – and what I have needed to face for years – is that when Sascha backed away, I took the shot. Even though I knew it was wrong, I took the shot, I killed a woman and I said absolutely nothing about it.

Perhaps it is the case that every embryo has good and evil in it. In recent times I would have said that when ours split then I became the good and Sascha the bad, which is a convenient way for me to look at things. But there is good and evil in all of us. It is more likely that I have striven to be good because I have witnessed evil on the battlefield and I have seen that good men can do bad things – I was such a man. We are all of us only a moment away from choosing to dance with the devil, and if I have striven for anything in life it has been to keep the unpleasant man that I am aware I could become, at bay.

———

I hear footsteps on the cobbles outside the cell door. It is Christoph, I recognise the beat of his laboured walk. The timber door opens slowly, as is its way. I rush to him.

'Is it me?' I grab onto his lapels. 'Is it me today?'

He looks up at me, for Christoph is not a tall man.

'Settle yourself, Sebastian,' he says, dropping his stick and taking me firmly by the arms. 'Settle yourself. You have time yet, dear man.' He forces me to look him in the eye. He smiles. 'You have time yet!'

Godolphin
Cornwall

Chapter Twenty-Nine

There was a commotion when we came ashore at the harbour village of Porthleven, with many questions asked and suspicious brows furrowed. Who were these washed-up men with unrecognisable accents wearing peasants' clothes? I elected to take Dame Sybil's advice and assume the identity of the brother of my shipmates, but kept my own Christian name, stating in broken English that I spoke only a little of the language and that my brothers spoke none. We were Polish emigres, I explained, chased across Europe by the Nazis, leading to our most recent escape from Sark. I thrust the letter of introduction from Dame Sibyl into a policeman's hand while repeating the word 'Godolphin', over and over again.

It brought me no pleasure to deceive good people, but Dame Sibyl was insistent that I would be interned by the British and at that moment, looking at my bedraggled comrades, all I wanted was a hearty meal for us all and warm beds to sleep in. I would have said just about anything to secure it. We slept the sleep of kings that night in rooms at the pub. It should have been wonderful to feel so safe, but having left Sark without Sophie, nothing would ever be wonderful again.

The winding lane that led out of Porthleven the following morning followed a slow incline away from the sea and worked its way upward past villages and farmsteads towards the hamlet of Godolphin Cross, where four lanes met and the road reached its highest point. The hamlet was surrounded by dense thickets of woodland, giving the place the damp feel of a fairy glen. Alek, Fabian and I made the journey squeezed into the back of a car belonging to a guest who had also stayed at the inn. He was a kindly, if naturally inquisitive, older man on a driving tour of Cornwall. He offered to 'give the good fellows a lift'. The constable rode shotgun.

Godolphin was not quite the establishment I had envisaged it to be. The high iron gates flanking the entrance hung lopsided from broken hinges. The driveway itself, although bearing the length associated with a house of grandeur, had the overgrown look of a deserted castle about it, as did the house itself, which we approached over an area that was more weed than gravel. Nevertheless, the house was like nothing I had ever seen before, impressive in its untouched grandeur. The front was styled with a doff of the cap to neoclassical Italianate grandeur, with Tuscan columns and a double-loggia layout. Attached wings headed off at right angles behind the house, and an enormous barn with a dovecot sat to the right. The whole establishment echoed with the ghosts of medieval England. It was at once eerie, yet strangely familiar and welcoming for all that.

When Fortune Findlay-Jones (tall, wiry, fit-looking for a woman in her seventies, strong ankles, decent enough teeth) opened the door wearing a full-bodied apron and found a policeman and three washed-up refugees on her doorstep, not for one moment did she take on the expression of someone who was either annoyed or confused. On the contrary, after quickly reading the letter of introduction penned by her cousin, she ushered us into the house while shouting up the stairs for the attention of someone called Bunny who, she turned to explain, was her companion, and who would happily make us some tea and a hearty breakfast.

The constable was waved off with Fortune arguing jovially that they were perfectly safe and that she would, 'take it from here, Constable'. Just minutes later we were sat at the kitchen table, our clothes having been dried by the fire at the inn, watching Bunny (a more anxious type than Fortune and almost certainly suffering from cataracts) flit around the kitchen before placing watery but wonderfully hot vegetable broth in front of us. When our two hosts eventually took seats across the table (each with a cup of tea in their hands and eager to watch us eat) I saw that this was as good a time as any to begin with our story. I turned to Alek and Fabian now and again, who were dipping thick chunks of bread in their soup and looking happy and at ease, to explain what I was saying. I asked Fortune if she minded my speaking to them in German, to which, looking on at me as one who could read all the secrets of the soul, she said, 'Natürlich! Whatever gets the job done, old chap. Whatever gets the job done.'

Within the hour I concluded both my story and the fact that Fortune was the kind of woman who had second sight and a good grasp of witchcraft. The house so far (and I had only ventured through the grand hallway to the – significantly less grand – back kitchen) was speckled with spiritual objets d'art that whispered of European (if not worldly) travel. She also had a black cat and a whole apothecary of herbs, which could only serve to confirm my deduction, could it not? This was a woman after my own heart, I thought, and as time went on we spent many an evening discussing the half-forgotten healing properties of herbs. Nevertheless, on that first day, I felt I owed this remarkable woman who had opened her door to three strange men based on nothing more than a phone call and a letter of introduction from a distant cousin, the absolute truth of my circumstances in the assumption that she would not judge a book by its cover, or a man by his nationality.

She did not. Indeed, she appreciated my honesty, but said it would be best, perhaps, if the broader community believed that I was Polish – 'loose lips sink ships and all that'. I offered her a gift of the cutting of my mother's rose, and after blinking back what looked like a dampening of the eyes, she handed it over to Bunny who dashed out to the potting shed and set about giving the poor dried up thing a new home in fresh compost. As we cleared away the dishes and were shown to our billets it seemed to me that although Godolphin could not be regarded as a long-term solution for the three of us (Fortune and Bunny could not possibly feed and house three men indefinitely), for the first time in quite a while, I could allow my shoulders to drop, my jaw to unclench and my lungs to breathe. We were safe. And yet a void lingered – an emptiness, a longing. And the longing was not for Sark, it was not for anything tangible, or anything flesh and blood and bone. It was for that feeling of being whole again, of being completed by another, of being happy. It was for that nebulous thing that one feels when in the presence of the person you love. Sophie. Was there anything to cause the heart to ache more deeply than to be forced to leave the person with whom you have only just fallen in love? None that I could think of.

Four short weeks after our arrival at Godolphin, a very excited Alek and Fabian set out on foot to Penzance with travel warrants tucked into their pockets. It had been arranged for them to join the Royal Air Force. Both were desperate to get back into the battle. As with many a man I have known before, despite their experience in France at the hands of the enemy, Alek and Fabian held an idealised, romantic notion of what being enlisted into the British armed forces would entail, especially as they were entering into the vestiges of the glamorous RAF. They could not speak much more than a smattering of English, but what was this to stop them? I felt sick to my stomach as I stood on the doorstep with Fortune and Bunny, and waved them off to what I knew would be a true awakening to the reality of warfare. I hoped and even prayed to that same God I kept turning to while denying His existence, that they would not see the things that I once saw, or be called upon to do the things that I had done. And yet … grains of guilt were beginning to catch between my toes. And something else: new guilt. The guilt of a healthy man that was not rushing off to enlist, to 'do his bit'. But to which side would I pledge my allegiance? My country or my conscience? I was beginning to ponder, too, on my pacifism, my refusal to fight, my desperate need to follow Edith Cavell's words: *Patriotism is not enough, I must have no hatred or bitterness towards anyone.* I felt that she was right, and yet in a way, she *had* fought, by nursing all soldiers, whatever their nationality. I am also a person of medical training. Does the war effort not require doctors? Are there not ways to assist the effort without the necessity of holding a gun? Why am I really here, in Cornwall and not headed down the lane with the boys? I had to conclude as I watched them walk away that it was not, after all, pacifism that held me back, but trauma. Year after year of trauma brought upon by war. It was a trauma that, no matter how long I had hidden from the outside world on Sark, I had never managed to outrun completely. I could not heal others now, not on the battlegrounds of this new war, not until I had healed myself.

Fortune placed a hand on my shoulder as we watched Alek and Fabian disappear down the lane. We walked back into the house and closed the door behind us.

One question lingered in the halls of the old house, and followed our footsteps down the stone-flagged hallway as we returned to the kitchen: what to do with Sebastian? It was a question vocalized by the rightly concerned Bunny to Fortune, while I helped to run their departed guests' bedding sheets through the mangle. Fortune was sitting on a bench casting an eye over the obituary page of the local newspaper.

'What do you mean, "what are we going to do with Sebastian?" asked Fortune, her tone dismissive. 'We'll treat him in the same way that we've treated all the other stray dogs that have passed our way: he's going to stay here, with us.'

'Keep him?' repeated Bunny, who, despite speaking about me as if I was not in their company, offered an apologetic smile. 'But dearest ...' – Bunny often referred to Fortune as 'dearest' when she was uncertain (or when trying to win an argument) – 'with rationing as it is – and I'm so sorry to say this Sebastian because I do love you dearly – but we can barely—'

'Barely feed ourselves. Yes, I know,' interrupted Fortune,

sighing. 'I'm all too aware of that, *dearest*.' She closed the newspaper with a slap. 'But sometimes you simply have to speculate to accumulate!'

Bunny and I exchange confused glances.

Fortune tapped a finger on the newspaper. 'This damn rag is full of the names of dead men.'

'The *world* is full of dead men,' said Bunny.

'But we, the lucky things that we are, have a man who is very much alive and right here in our midst. He's handy with a hammer (no craftsman, but he's handy) *and* he's a gardener, which is bally helpful given the state of the place. Add to that the fact that he's a doctor and we're sitting on a gold mine. Mark my words, Bunny, if we're going to get through this war then we're going to have to get back to basics – grow our own food, rear our own livestock, that kind of thing. Cousin Sibyl and I were only talking about this on the telephone a month or so ago when she rang with her monthly state of the nation address …'

'Poor Sibyl,' said Bunny. 'Fancy having to bow down to the blasted Nazis like that!'

'Firstly, don't swear, Bunny, and secondly, Sibyl will be fine. We must believe that, or we're all done for!' Fortune picked up the paper again and flicked it out. 'Sibyl has the perfect constitution for such a challenge. No, I want the walled garden to return to its former glory days and I can't possibly do that all by myself, and you're no use to me with your arthritis, Bunny …' (I was surprised at this comment as I had noticed no traces of this affliction in Bunny, who was nothing short of a workhorse). 'I hate to admit it,' Fortune went on, 'but a strong, reliable man comes in jolly handy for such things. I only rue the day we had to let the last of the staff go.' She turned to me. 'Family money is gone – bad investments made back in the day by my dear pappa paid to all that. He was a silly old fool but we loved him.' She turned her attention back to Bunny, the newspaper acting as nothing more than a prop. 'And let's not forget that this poor chap,' – a flick of the paper in my direction – 'is a German alien living in England pretending to be Polish with fake papers belonging to a dead man and no money. But despite all that, in the end you'll find that it's not us that is doing Sebastian a favour, but rather it is he that is doing one for us ... You should start seeing him as he really is.'

Bunny threw a wry smile in my direction. 'Which is?'

'The newly arrived prince to our fairy tale plight.'

Bunny scoffed. 'We're hardly princesses! And I thought you didn't agree with the systematic labelling of the sexes into socially constructed stereotypes?'

Fortune glanced over the top of the newspaper. It was her turn to throw me a cheeky wink.

'That is correct. I don't. But nor will I look a gift horse in the mouth. Ergo, he's staying put.' She glanced me up and down. 'And he can wear Daddy's old clothes, so get them down for him, will you?'

I put a hand up to speak. 'Perhaps, ladies, I could offer you something even better than my labour in return for your kindness?'

Both looked on with bewildered expressions as I left the kitchen and dashed upstairs, returning with an item wrapped in a silk scarf. I placed the item on the table and unwrapped it.

'This little thing stowed away with me,' I said, turning to take in their expressions, which were a mixture of confusion and delight. 'It is a strange kind of teapot,' I explained. 'Very old and worth a great deal of money – perhaps not as much now, with the war, but still very significant. Thousands, perhaps. It is my gift to you, as payment ...'

I took up the teapot and tried to hand it to Bunny. She shied away. Fortune stood and placed a hand on my arm.

'It is kind of you, Sebastian, and we are grateful. But you must keep it, really.' I glanced at Bunny. She nodded her agreement quite vehemently. 'One day, when this chaos is over, you will want to start again, and you'll need money to do so … Take care of that teapot, Sebastian, and one day it will take care of you.'

She walked over to Bunny and put an arm around her shoulders. 'And anyway, we have every treasure we could ever need right here at Godolphin … don't we, old fruit.'

Bunny rested her head on Fortune's shoulder and her face filled with love.

'I suppose we do, now you come to mention it.'

And so I stayed on at Godolphin.

For a while, at least.

Chapter Thirty

The latch on the gate to the walled garden was much looser by the time my first full summer at Godolphin came around, and by the time my second summer came, not only had the gate been rebuilt to its former glory but my mother's rose had grown three feet up an arch that covered a path leading from the back of the house towards the old piggery. By November that year, 1942, my old life on Sark was nothing but a mere shimmer to me, so ensconced had I become in everyday life at Godolphin, a most individual property, where the name 'Godolphin' did not simply provide a name for a grand house, but more a statement for a way of life – a gentle, somewhat bohemian way of life, where allcomers were welcome and alternative ways of thinking encouraged. Sophie once asked if I would consider broadening my horizons. I had thought myself very clever and grown up when I replied that the most contented of men have all that they need close by. All the horizon could bring me, I said, would be a perpetual search for something that already existed in the heart. I still held by that sentiment, and yet I couldn't help but wonder if there was more to it. Could I be wrong? After all, my life was becoming enriched beyond measure at Godolphin. Fortune called me her 'right-hand man' while Bunny, despite her early misgivings, adopted me as the son she never had. She referred to me as 'our saviour' which was perhaps a little excessive, although the improvements I made to the place were, I'll admit, significant.

I came to realise that Fortune and Godolphin were basically one and the same thing. They mirrored each other. The house had a pillared front – a folly – while directly to the rear was an open courtyard, flanked on two sides by the wings of the extended house. The open side of the courtyard was further enclosed by a large barn and other stone outbuildings, and so despite its grand façade, Godolphin had the feel of a welcoming medieval farmstead about it, which was exactly like Fortune herself who, despite her aging years, her upper-class accent and posture of a grand dame, was the most human, loving, thoughtful woman a person could ever hope to meet. She taught me so very much: a different way to garden; a different way to approach illness; a different way to approach life, and even a different way to approach death – I must remember that now. And it all started one afternoon in late September 1940, when I tried to open a wooden door set within a far wall of the garden and found it to be locked.

'That's Fortune's private space,' explained Bunny, her glasses steaming up as she hovered over a bowl. 'But I'm sure she'll take you in there and show you … when she's ready, of course.' Bunny was in the back kitchen spooning bramble jam into a line of Mason jars on the table.

'When I'm ready for what?' asked Fortune, crashing through the door and kicking off her wellingtons. Bunny put down the spoon to tidy away the boots. 'Ah, there you are

Charlie. Do remember that you are *my* dog, you mangy hound, not Sebastian's!' She threw a wink my way. Charlie was a black and white border collie dog, young and spritely but calm for all that. He'd become my shadow since Fortune adopted him last year. I adored him. He rushed to Fortune to nuzzle in, as if understanding every word, which he probably did. She sat down and began rubbing bunions through darned woollen socks.

'Your shed,' answered Bunny, not deviating from her preserves production line. 'You know, behind the back gate.'

Fortune stopped rubbing. I knew from her expression (I was learning) that the next comment would require an exclamation mark. 'Shed?! I presume you mean my sanctuary – my sacred space. My tea house.'

Bunny glanced up.

'You built it out of the remnants of that old wooden lean-to round the back of the pig sties and stole the windows from the Victorian glass houses that were on the back wall.' She nodded in my direction. 'Which is a shame because Sebastian could have made good use of those.'

I could, she was quite correct,

'Firstly, I didn't steal, I reclaimed, and secondly, you are making light of my craft Bunny.'

'Craft? Drinking tea? I do it every day.'

'Dearest!' It was Fortune's turn to use the word. 'My tea house took a whole year to build – to me it is a work of art.' She turned to address me directly. 'I will speak to you Sebastian as Bunny is a Neanderthal … but the study of the craft of the tea ceremony – rooted in Chinese Zen philosophy – has taken many years of study to master. Philosophy, calligraphy, not to mention studying the actual preparation of the tea – the details of which are meticulous …' (she directed the last part to Bunny) 'are the stuff of life. Of a meditative life, I should say, removed from the ramifications of piffle-paffle nonsense.'

Bunny continued to spoon the jam. 'It certainly is ramifications of nonsense,' she scoffed.

'You're just too much of a home counties girl to appreciate it, that's all,' said Fortune, throwing a conspiratorial eye roll in my direction. 'But you know, now that I come to think about it, maybe the time has come to expand Sebastian's horizons beyond the wall ...' Fortune began to drum her chin.

Bunny paused. 'Wall? You make him sound like a prisoner!' She offered me a spoonful of jam while placing a hand underneath the spoon to catch spills. I opened my mouth as a chick to its mother.

'Yes, wall. And isn't a prisoner exactly what he really is?!'

I had taken a seat at the table by now as this kind of conversation – the kind that developed from nowhere while we were gathered in the kitchen, mainly about me – could lead down all sorts of rabbit holes.

Fortune turned to me. 'What do you know about ikebana, Sebastian?'

I had no idea what she was talking about. I said so.

'How about chanoyu?'

'Bless you,' said Bunny, thinking Fortune had sneezed.

'You mean, The Way of Tea?' I said, once my laughter had stopped.

Her face came alight. 'Yes! So you practise it too? I knew there was something of the Zen master about you!'

I laughed again. 'Zen master? Do not be mistaken. Beyond having heard of chanoyu, I know nothing.'

Fortune's shoulders dropped. 'Nothing? But you have that

wonderful teapot! Surely you must have used it for its proper purpose?'

'To assassinate someone?' I joked.

Fortune's face scrunched into disdain. 'To make tea, foolish man.' She slapped her hands on her knees and stood. 'In that case, we'd better crack on!' She gathered her wellingtons from where Bunny had placed them neatly behind the door, took a big iron key from the key hooks and put it in her apron pocket. 'Put the kettle on, Bunny,' she said. 'We're going to have a ceremony!'

'What? Now?' asked Bunny. 'But I'm just about to boil up my next batch of jam!'

'Now!' repeated Fortune. She turned to me. 'Go to the gate in the wall in an hour, I have much to prepare!'

'Might I help?' I asked, standing.

'Well, that depends. Tell me: have you studied the craft of chanoyu for at least five years?'

'I have not.'

'Then no, you may not help.'

And that was how it came to be that Fortune versed me in the Japanese Way of Tea, while sitting on a rattan mat in her shed, hidden inside a secret garden, behind a locked gate in Cornwall. Bunny was right, it was more of a shed-cum-greenhouse than a classical tea house, but it was beautiful for all of its tumbling down appearance.

Our first few sessions concerned themselves entirely with teaching me the Way of Tea. No two sessions are ever exactly the same, because its beauty partially lies in unique experience. Fortune's steps always follow the same process, nonetheless:

Having been greeted at the gate in the wall, I was led through the garden to the hut. In the months I had been at Godolphin by now I had never noticed the moments when

Fortune must have retired to her tea garden to tend it – a space of green simplicity and serenity. I was instructed to wash my hands, a cleansing process by means of leaving the outside world behind me. The door into the hut was low and purposefully so, ensuring the requirement to bow. I was then instructed to kneel on a cushion while Fortune cleaned her instruments in water from a kettle on a sunken stove. She would then remove a silk cloth from her sash (she always wore a kimono and sash), inspect it, fold it and unfold it, and then use it to handle the hot iron kettle. All of her movements were graceful – purposeful. Water and matcha were then combined in a bowl and stirred with a bamboo whisk. I rotated the bowl through 180 degrees before drinking, then wiped the bowl and passed it back. Fortune would then serve something sweet made by Bunny to work with the bitterness of the tea (this was not strictly the Japanese way, she said, and added that there was a war on and I should accept that she had to work with the limited materials she'd got!). I knew I was headed in the right direction when I was allowed to help with preparations. This was when calligraphy and the ikebana art of flower arranging were introduced, and ultimately, when we began to talk.

Chapter Thirty-One

La Santé Prison, August 1944

'Ikebana,' repeats Christoph. 'This interests me. As does the lady ... Fortune. She has been on this earth before, I think, many times.'

I smile. 'Tell me, why would a Buddhist monk hide behind the cross of Christianity?' I nod to his chest. 'There's more Zen in you than Zion, I think.'

He laughs. 'And you have the sound of Dickens about you! Well, perhaps there is. We are all connected. It is all one whole. You were saying about ikebana? It helped you, somehow, I think.'

'It did ... and it's odd, you know, that flower arranging rather than gardening, which I had done for years, would have achieved that. Of course, when I say flower arranging, what Fortune taught me was a philosophy – the Way of the Flowers. Ikebana is not simply the process of prettily placing a few buds in a vase, and I cannot do it justice in describing it to you in a few short sentences – one has to study ikebana to understand it. Let us simply say that it is a study of nature in a vase, an expression of creativity while following certain rules about line and form and so on. One does not aim for symmetry because this is not how nature grows, necessarily. It is about the branch as well as the bloom, which I had not considered so much in my own garden. Balance is found in the imbalance ...' I shake my head. 'You see how I flounder? This is why it is impossible to explain. Let us just say that during my time in Cornwall, while sitting on a hard floor in a pretty little shed in a secret garden drinking tea and arranging flowers with a wonderful older lady, I visited my trauma, not just from the war but my family, too, and in representing that trauma in art form, then moving on to represent it in a more positive way, I could become a man I used to be ... one with much more ...'

'Fight?' asks Christoph.

'Yes, I suppose so. But I was going to say, understanding. I thought I had found peace for all those years within my beautifully constructed garden on Sark, but it was *too* well constructed. Despite all of those wonderful blooms, I had not, as Fortune showed me, found the Way of the Flowers.' I glance upwards towards the grate leading to the courtyard. 'Of course, one might say that it was ironic that although Fortune helped me to move away from a stuck way of thought, it also, ironically, led me here. Tea and flowers brought me life, but they have also, it seems, brought me death.' I smile. 'Fortune would have thought that symbolic – a circle of connection – although she would not wish to find me here as a result, for sure.'

'You came here because of Fortune?' asks Christoph.

'I doubt I would have had the strength of mind to come to Paris without her teachings. But there was another, too, who helped.'

'Bunny?'

'No. A man called Elijah. We shall come to him presently, I'm sure.'

Christoph picks up his cup.

'Then let us have a toast,' he says. 'To tea and flowers, and all the joy that they have brought us.'

I pick up my cup. Fortune would have liked that.

Chapter Thirty-Two

I loved that little place – Fortune's tea shed – and I loved it because it's where I began to see myself differently – not as an old man who was marooned at sea, but someone who had found an engine and a rudder and could begin to steer a new path, rather than bob along with the tides.

I was treated as if I'd been part of that small community of the house and, in time, the surrounding hamlets for all of my life and yet, despite everything, I missed having my own home. But if a man is to be marooned somewhere then Godolphin was about as good a place as it could get, and not so different to Sark, really. I was given the task of regenerating the medieval walled garden – a task I grasped with relish – and Fortune (selling off for a pittance what little remained of the family's art collection) bought pigs, chickens, goats and a few cows, which I was happy to preside over as stockman. Having spent the past fifteen years living on an island that is only three miles long by two miles wide, I was used to finding contentment in living in a restricted place; in fact, it suited me. I was able to see the sea by walking to the top of Godolphin

Hill, always with Charlie the collie in tow. We had little of anything but as yet we had not gone hungry and with the garden vegetable plot up and running again we were able to assist our neighbours, too. I was grateful and content, except for the fact that each day I woke with a nagging heaviness in my heart that weighed down like an anchor I could not coil in, a heaviness that would lead me to rush from the garden to the house if Charlie alerted us to the arrival of a guest, in the hope that one very special person might have somehow found her way to Godolphin. That special person, of course, was Sophie, the woman who could fill a dark room with light just by stepping through the doorway. The woman who had somehow visualised me in that very garden and who had sacrificed her own escape in order that I might know freedom. How could I ever know true contentment – tea ceremony or not – until I knew that she was safe? The fact remained that I had received no letter, no phone call, no news, no visit, which could lead me to only one conclusion: Sophie was either trapped on Sark, or worse, deported to Europe. Above all of this, of course, was the lingering memory of our time together, because as brief as it was, it was perfect and I missed her. The heaviness of heart was further weighed down by a stirring in me that it was time to consider further options too – options as to how I might, perhaps, help the war effort. It was time. And yet, I did not want to leave Cornwall, not merely because I had no wish to be interned, but because this was where Sophie would come if she ever set out to find me. And so the question lingered like a whisper in the wind: should I wait for Sophie, or join the war?

Chapter Thirty-Three

I was sitting in my potting shed whittling a length of ash, which would eventually become the shaft and handle of Bunny's favourite border fork, when there was a cough, rather than a knock, at the door. To be accurate it was more of a clearing of the throat rather than anything more biologically sinister. I glanced up to see a gentleman that I would guess at being in his early sixties who was dressed in clothes only a couple of stages improved from the attire of a beggar. I did not know this man. He had most likely wandered in off the road, looking for food.

'You're making a proper job of that,' he said, his accent that of a local man.

I rested the wood and knife on the workbench. 'Thank you,' I said, standing.

'Rewarding work, whittling.'

'It is. It is.' We stood a moment. 'May I help you? Are you looking for the lady of the house, perhaps?'

He glanced around the shed.

'You've tidied up a bit,' he said with a sniff. 'But then, the whole place looks a lot better than it did in the old days.'

We stepped into the garden. My shed was tucked away in the corner of what once would have been the ornamental parterre and was now beds of winter vegetables and fruit trees. Rusty Victorian cloches covered the more tender crops.

There was a hoe leaning on the side of the shed. It had been there for more days than I cared to admit. He began to clean the blade with the cuff of his coat. I allowed him a moment of silence with the tool. One thing I learned living in Cornwall was that, just like Sark, there was really never any reason to hurry into chatter.

He nodded across the garden. 'I planted that quince,' he said, 'the one beyond the low yew hedge over there. And the Bramley ... nice cooker that. Aye, those were the days.' He returned to the hoe. 'Good times.'

He took out a packet of Woodbine cigarettes. His hands had a gnarled, earth-stained beauty about them. With the shading of a bark-coloured moth, they seemed to have been specifically designed to camouflage themselves within a natural landscape. He twisted a cigarette into the corner of his mouth where it hung as if on a sucker.

'Smoke?' He offered me the packet.

I shook my head.

He fiddled around in his coat pockets before eventually coming across a box of matches. His hand shook striking a match against the box. He placed his spare hand over the active one to prevent a shudder. With the cigarette lit, he took a long draw and the hands slowly ceased to shake.

'You're the new gardener I've been hearing about, then?' He shook the match and buried it into the soil in a plant pot.

'Of sorts.'

'Polish, I heard.'

He took another long draw while taking a while to look me over, then turned his head slightly as he exhaled. 'Polish my arse,' he said. 'I know a Kraut when I see one. You're as German as Hitler, no mistake.'

'Hitler is Austrian,' I said, throwing caution, not just to the wind, but directly into the eye of the raging storm.

The man laughed and returned to his cigarette. I leant my back against the wooden slats of the shed.

'You're a doctor, they say.'

'I am.'

'A man of many talents!'

'It would seem so.'

He turned to me. 'Do you think you could look at my feet?'

I laughed. 'Now?'

'Good a time as any.'

'In that case …' I gestured towards the shed door. 'Please step into my surgery, Mr …?'

He looked at me once again as if processing some in-depth analysis of my character. I must have passed the test because he said, 'Elijah.'

'Then step into my surgery, Elijah.'

And he did.

'They called it the WWGC …' he explained, pulling on boots that were far too small, far too old, and far too hole ridden for human use, which was part of the problem with the feet. I had soaked them in a salt bath and then dealt with the bunions and the overgrown toenails. The gout would have to be eased via improved diet, but looking at Elijah, it was clear that the man would be grateful to eat anything he could get hold of, or forage. We stepped outside and I led him towards a bench with my flask and my lunch, which had been lovingly placed inside a tin tea caddy we used to house my daily bread and cheese, put together by Bunny that morning.

'The WWGC?'

'The Walking Wounded Gardening Club. The woman who lives here …' He paused, presumably trying to hook onto a name. 'Hardy type. The sort that likes wearing men's clothes …'

'I think you mean Miss Findlay-Brown,' I suggested.

'Who?'

'Fortune …'

A light bulb went on. 'That's the one! Decent kind of a woman. Odd, but decent enough. Anyway, she set up this kind of … I suppose you could call it a club, for ex-soldiers, after the last bust-up.'

'A club?'

'Club. Soup kitchen. Legion-type thing. The idea was that we could all get together and … well, garden. I think she thought it would help us get over what we'd seen in the trenches, either that or we were free labour, but I never did like the name of it …'

'Why?'

He reaches for his cigarettes again. 'Think about it – the *Walking* Wounded Gardening Club … some of those poor beggars *couldn't* walk! No legs left. Bill Portreath used to hobble around on crutches with a bandage hanging off his stump! Half of them were deaf, one blind too – mustard gas, you know?'

I nodded. 'Yes. I do. And when was this?'

'Let's see … it would have been the summer and winter of '19 and '20.'

'And did it help?' I asked.

Elijah crinkled his mouth.

'Well, I wouldn't say it did, and I wouldn't say it didn't. Too sceptical for my own good back then. Never goes away, you see … the thought of it all. Never goes away. What age are you?'

I knew where he was heading with this.

'I am forty-three.'

He nodded. 'Then maybe you missed it?'

He knows I am German. I will not deny this man the truth.

'I did not. I was seventeen when I enlisted.'

'Conscription?' he asked.

'In a way. My father insisted we join.'

'We?'

'My brother and I?'

'Your brother's dead?'

I shook my head. 'I believe not.'

'Where were you?' he asked.

'I started at the Somme in '16, and it all went downhill from there. Gallipoli was tough.'

He patted my leg. 'You were very young.'

'I was,' I agreed.

He began to laugh. It was a big, hearty, full-bellied laugh. And then I laughed, too, and I'm not sure either one of us knew why, except the laughter could easily have turned into tears.

'What a total bloody waste of time that was,' he said, trying to light a match. I took the matches out of his fumbling hands, lit the match and held it gently to the cigarette in his mouth. He took a drag and sat back on the bench. It was a cold, cold day, and yet this man's company was very warming. 'Here we are,' he went on, 'sitting in a garden in Cornwall, chewing the fat together, and not so long ago we were throwing every kind of hell at each other. What for, in the end?'

'I have contemplated those thoughts for many years,' I said, 'and I have never reached a satisfactory conclusion.'

'And now we've got this new mess going on.'

'Exakt,' I say. 'Exakt.'

'Did they expect you to fight this time?' he asked.

'They did – they do. I said no.'

'And that's why you're here, pretending to be Polish.'

My silence was the only answer he needed.

'Then let me shake your hand,' he said, turning to face me on the bench. He placed the cigarette on the arm of the bench. There were tears in his eyes, I noted. 'Yes, indeed. Let me shake your hand, my man. Let me shake your hand.'

'Will you break bread with me?' I asked, removing a crusty chunk of bread from my lunch tin. I offered half. He paused, as a dog who is unsure as to whether he should accept a treat will pause. He took the bread.

'Thank you,' he said. I turned away to pour soup out of a flask into two tin mugs.

'Now then,' I said, as we began our feast together. 'Tell me about this gardening club of yours …'

Chapter Thirty-Four

I t was almost dark outside by the time I stepped barefoot into the kitchen. Charlie followed on behind and jumped onto Fortune's chair. The windows dripped with condensation thanks to wet clothes drying on the pulley airer hoisted up above the stove. Bunny, wearing many layers of jumpers under her apron, looked up from her occupation of peeling potatoes at the table. She noticed my feet. We were not people who took off our stockings when entering the house, the floors were too cold for that. Her response was predictable.

'Sebastian Brown! Where on earth are your socks and shoes? Your feet are filthy!'

I had the good grace to look contrite, but not contrite enough to prevent me from helping myself to a piece of shortbread from a tin on the table.

'A man in greater need wandered into the garden looking for help,' I said. 'I gave them to him.'

There was a moment while this registered. She placed the knife on the table and poured me some tea, which I drank with relish. Even in the kitchen we drank tea in an abbreviated Japanese way, from small bowls with no handles, and with gratitude. Fortune always said that by having to place two hands around the bowl to lift it to the mouth, it made for a more mindful, more grateful, more satisfying experience. I had never thought of this before I arrived at Godolphin, but I soon learned that she was absolutely right, and I would never by choice drink tea from a standard cup again.

'So let me get this right,' began Bunny. 'You gave Fortune's late father's best boots away to a complete stranger?'

'He wasn't a *complete* stranger. He knows Fortune. He's an old soldier who deserves better than the worn leather he had, and also they were not her father's best boots, I do not wear those in the garden, they were a very average pair. I'll be happy wearing galoshes, or I'll find another old pair in the attic.'

'And what was his name, this man who took your boots?'

'Elijah.'

'Elijah who?' asked Fortune, wandering into the kitchen.

'I do not know his surname,' I said. 'He wanted to be known only as Elijah. He used to come here after the last war. Something to do with a wounded soldiers' gardening club?'

Fortune, who was wearing a kaftan over a pair of her father's plus fours and two woollen jumpers, looked up to the ceiling to consider this. Her memory required help. I offered it.

'He said he planted the quince, the one by my shed…'

More thought occurred while Bunny and I waited for the lightbulb to come on.

'Ah, yes!' She turned to Bunny. 'He's the chap who called me an ass for asking them all to hold hands and sing.'

Bunny shook her head while wielding a knife towards some frightened vegetables.

'Oh, you remember him Bunny. Shrapnel ... attitude dripping off every pore ...'

Fortune took a jug of cider out of the pantry and grabbed three glasses from the shelf of the dresser. 'He was always a bit aloof, you know, suspicious. Thought I was only using them for free labour.'

'And weren't you, a little?' asked Bunny, not looking up.

'Absolutely not! Anyhow, he said that gardening couldn't possibly help them all to cope with acclimatising to normal life again. Silly man. He stopped coming along to the group. Although to be fair to the poor thing, I think he felt guilty.'

'Guilty?'

'Because some of the men had significantly worse injuries.'

'I see.' And I did. I totally understood.

Fortune handed out the filled glasses. 'Here's mud in your eye,' she said, and Bunny added, 'Slange!' They both knocked back the whole glass in one.

I dearly loved those two women.

'So, Elijah has decided to come back to the old homestead, then?' said Fortune, shooing Charlie off her chair by the range and sitting down. Bunny quickly crossed the room to rub Fortune's feet. 'Looking for work, is he? Because he's the best hedge-layer in the county, that man.'

'I don't think so. He'd heard that you have a new gardener who is also a doctor, so he came to ask that I might look at his feet. Oh, he guessed that I am German, also.'

Bunny gasped.

Fortune rolled her eyes.

'And did you?' asked Fortune.

'Did I?'

'Look at his feet?'

'Of course.' I abandoned my tea (spiritually nourishing or not) and took a good drink of cider.

'Good man.'

'You should have told him to leave,' said Bunny, who had dropped Fortune's foot and returned to the peeling of the potatoes. 'And what do you mean, he knows you're German? How?'

'He guessed.'

'And you didn't tell him he was wrong?' asked Bunny. The knife was put down again – firmly.

I shook my head. 'But nor did I tell him he was right!'

'Well, that's all right, then.' (I felt there was more than a tinge of sarcasm to Bunny those days.)

'Don't worry, old thing,' said Fortune, stroking the cat who had jumped on her knee. 'Sebastian is old news now. And everyone in the hamlet believes that he's Polish.'

'Except Elijah,' corrected Bunny.

'Well, yes. But Elijah won't cause a fuss. He's probably moved on by now at any rate. Did he say where he was headed to, Sebastian?'

I shook my head. 'He said he'd found a temporary billet nearby which is why I said that he would be welcome in the garden at any time. He thanked me for the boots and said he would see me again tomorrow. He is going to help me to turn the compost heap – as payment for the boots. I think it brings him peace just to be here. "Just like the old days," he said.'

'Peace is one thing,' said Bunny, 'but boots and your lunch, which you shared with him, no doubt, is another!'

Fortune frowned at her companion, who had finished with the vegetables and was filling a pan with water. 'You're getting awfully bourgeois in your old age, Bunny,' she said. 'No, I think Elijah has appeared just at the right time, I really do. Let's call it a kind of karmic reminder of our responsibilities.'

Bunny and I remained silent because the noise of the cogs turning in Fortune's mind was deafening. Eventually, Fortune said, 'It's time for action. I do believe we should consider reinstating the … oh, what did I call it, again?'

'The Walking Wounded Gardening Club,' I said.

'Oh, Fortune, not that again,' moaned Bunny.

Fortune gave Bunny a hard stare. 'Yes … that again! Just look at how Sebastian has relaxed since he's been here. No more night sweats – yes, I know you have them. No more drifting off into a chasm of despair …'

'A chasm of despair?' repeated Bunny and I at the same time.

'Oh, you would drift off into one now and again, believe me,' said Fortune, 'which is perfectly understandable, given what you experienced in the last almighty bust-up!' Fortune took a great gulp of air. 'No,' she began, letting out the air slowly. 'You've much improved, and that's all down to spending contemplative time in the garden. The plants are our teachers, Sebastian, and it's because they are the ultimate communicators – they've had to be, to evolve. And just as a bright flower will attract an insect or a bird, it will attract us too.' She turned towards Bunny. I felt a lecture coming on. 'For *five thousand* years humans have been picking flowers for no other reason than to feel good. I tell you this: Beauty and love are intertwined in nature, both creating a sense of calm from within.' Bunny harrumphed leading Fortune to turn her attention back on me. 'Why do you always insist on growing flowers, Sebastian? Why are you obsessed with tending your roses, do you think?'

'Well, I should think it's because—'

'I'll tell you why … it's because flowers are the best medicine of all. And don't even get me started on scent. It's one of the most powerful and, after all, primitive sensors that we have. It unlocks *emotion*, Sebastian. Emotion! Just think about that for a moment … I'll say it again; it unlocks *emotion*.'

I thought of Sophie. Every single time I crushed mint in my fingers, my heart filled with love and longing.

'Lavender, rosemary, and yes, most delicious of all, your roses, they all invoke a lingering calm, and don't even get me started on nature's colours. It must be a kind of genetic response to it all. What response does the colour green give us if it is not calming – is that not why nature is swathed in it? Flowers are the greatest gift that nature gave to us, and the greatest gift we give to each other. Hand someone a flower and you will in return receive a true, spontaneous smile. When we started the gardening club the last time, guess what all the soldiers wanted to grow?'

Bunny jumped straight in with, 'Turnips?'

'You're just being a silly old fool, Bunny Williams, because you know jolly well that it was flowers.' Fortune turned to me. 'Did you know that British soldiers even asked for seeds for the front, Sebastian?'

I shook my head. As much as I adored Fortune, 'the front' for someone who wasn't there, was not the same thing as for someone who was. Even though they know it was a shocking place, they will simply imagine a line of trenches and between them no man's land, and the whole experience was considerably more nuanced than that. Personally, I cannot imagine my German comrades asking for seeds to plant – food to eat and cigarettes to smoke, yes, but seeds for flowers? Perhaps it was different for the British, but I doubted it.

Fortune broke into my thoughts by reaching a summary.

'No, mark my words, flowers – any plants really – invoke nothing but joy in the giver and the receiver. They are not a luxury item at all. They are a necessity. Of course, you subconsciously know all of this already, Sebastian, which is why you are a gardener – and a doctor. I bet there are lots of wounded soldiers out there who are in desperate need of our help. We've got two wars' worth of wounded to round up now, and I really do believe that contemplative time spent thinking of nothing but the tender care of a garden while watching it flourish, is exactly what they all need. The best thing one can do when the chips are down is focus on helping someone else – or some*thing* else. It wards off melancholy.'

'And will you put boots on all of their feet and food in all of their bellies?' asked Bunny (I sipped on my cider wondering what on earth I had started).

'If I can, yes.' Fortune turned to me. 'What do you think, Sebastian? Am I a fool to open my home and garden to any waif and stray that might wander in?'

I was not sure what to say, except, 'Given that I was such a stray, I can hardly object to it, although I do believe you might need to think of another title than the Walking Wounded Gardening Club …'

'Why?' asked Bunny.

'Because some may not have the requisite number of limbs required to necessitate "walking" at all.'

Chapter Thirty-Five

La Santé Prison, August 1944

'There is a great light in your eyes when you speak of these women,' says Christoph, setting up the stove. 'Even in the darkness of the cell, it shines out of you.'

I have no time to respond to his compliment as I hear movement in the courtyard. There are boots, many boots. I glance up to the grate. Christoph continues to talk, only louder.

'I have brought you a treat today!' he says.

'You bring me treats every day.' My answer, I realise, is flat and so I quickly add, 'and I am beyond grateful.'

The flame on the stove flashes orange, then blue. Christoph places the stove on the floor and reaches into his backpack. A flask appears.

'Soup!' he proclaims. 'And not just any soup; it is your favourite, I think?'

'Leek and potato?' I feel a great excitement at the prospect of warm soup.

Christoph pauses in the opening of the flask. He frowns.

'Leek and potato? No. You said chicken broth was your favourite – I am certain of it. You said it was a cure-all.'

Poor Christoph. 'It is! It is!' I say. 'And, of course, chicken broth is my *real* favourite, but not for one moment did I think there were any chickens left in Paris to put into such a broth ...'

'Oh, I have my ways,' he says with a wink, returning to the opening of the flask. 'You are aware that Parisians have been hoarding for some time ...?'

'Of course, but it would be rather difficult to hoard a chicken ... they don't seem to take well to wearing a disguise!'

We laugh then, really laugh. Christoph hands me a cup of broth. It is mainly warm water and I doubt there is anything but the merest memory of a chicken in there, but I am beyond grateful. Yes, I am beyond grateful, although I do have the sensation of a man being fattened for slaughter. I do not say this to my genteel companion while trying to blot out further noises echoing from the courtyard above.

'I wanted to say, Christoph,' I begin, looking down at my broth, 'that I see you as nothing short of an angel sent from heaven in my final week.' I glance up. 'Yes, indeed. A guardian angel.'

He glances at me askance and pushes up his spectacles – the steam from the burner is always causing them to slip. 'Heaven and now angels? And you, a non-believer ...'

I shrug it off. 'Ah, but angels are different,' I say. 'They are a different entity altogether.'

'You believe in angels?' he asks.

'I am looking at one. But yes, I think that perhaps there is something ... more out there. That does not mean to say I have changed my thoughts on the Bible.'

'Which are?'

'That it is a story written as a blueprint for living.'

'Well, some people prefer to work from a plan,' he says. 'You said Fortune gave you a new attitude to life – to death? I'd be interested to hear what that was.'

I think how to answer while enjoying the warmth of the broth slipping down my gullet. 'She felt that death was not to be feared, but rather, looked forward to. Like the ultimate adventure. And, as it happens to all of us no matter what, she felt that we should not approach life as if it is a train journey heading towards a destination we are afraid of, but something different altogether. Something to be embraced ... but that is easier said than done, especially in these circumstances. One does not want to leave the things one loves behind, you see. To be ready for death, one has to surrender to the transience of life. She did not expect us to live each day as the last, that would be impossible, but to just accept it. Just live. Be content and not expect more, and always be happy to say goodbye.'

'And are you?' asks Christoph. 'Ready?'

'No. For me, it is the prospect of leaving my life just at the point where it became wonderful that is the most painful. Without Hitler, I would have had a life with Sophie; would have held the children we might have had.'

'Without Hitler, you would not have met Sophie at all,' Christoph reminds me gently.

I smile. 'That's true enough, I suppose.' A distinct commotion begins in the courtyard. 'Are you not required up there?' I ask, my hands beginning to tremble around the cup.

'Not today,' he says, concentrating on the tea.

I glance up at the grate. 'Why?'

'They are not to receive the comfort of a chaplain.'

Again, the question has to be asked, 'Why?'

Christoph sighs while swirling the freshly made tea in the pot. 'The Allies approach at pace from the west. France is falling like a house of cards. No one says so, but everyone knows that Germany will not keep Paris. The Parisians have become excitable and High Command has begun to cover its tracks – as you know, many things have happened here that they do not wish the Allies to know about.'

'I notice that you have begun to speak of the Germans as "they" rather than "we",' I say.

'I always have. You simply haven't noticed.' He pours more soup into our cups and my spirits lighten … If the Allies approach at pace then perhaps they might liberate the prison before my turn comes for the courtyard. Christoph reads my mind. 'And as for the prisoners …' he says, 'I have to be honest with you, Sebastian. *Kill them quickly* seems to have been the order from on high.'

'But why bother to kill us now? If Paris is sure to fall, why not opt to simply leave us here to rot? Why go to the bother of … well, you know?'

'Dead men can't talk,' he says, dully.

My chest tightens and the lightness fades to black. The tyrant will fall – his minions know it – and yet they will pretend otherwise until the end. Christoph reads my mind once again and says,

'Now does he feel his title
Hang loose about him, like a
Giant's robe
Upon a dwarfish thief …'

'Macbeth,' I say.

'Macbeth,' he confirms.

I hear a man scream out. Bizarrely, Christoph chooses this moment to show a more musical side to his personality. He begins to hum a tune I remember from the '30s – 'The Sunny

Side of the Street' – but there is no drowning out the noise. Hell will not be silenced.

'Now then,' he says, interrupting his own merry tune. 'Are you finally going to tell me how that teapot of yours found its way from Sark to Paris? Or will I have to go to my grave a disappointed man?'

'I am not,' I say. 'Not just yet. Although perhaps, given the noise coming from the grate above, I had better speed this story along.'

He places a hand on my knee.

'Do not rush,' he says. 'But nor should you linger. So should be the case with all stories, I think.'

Chapter Thirty-Six

It took a week for Elijah to put word around to his old comrades that the gardening club at Godolphin was to reopen its doors two days per week, and as we approached Christmas we had increased our number to twenty. It was not difficult for me to find plenty for them to do, although quite often they wished to do nothing more than sit around the garden and talk.

For her part, Fortune scoured the countryside, harassing her neighbours while on the lookout for tree saplings. She was insistent that every person should only become a fully-fledged member of the club once they had planted a tree in the meadow, hopeful that it would eventually become a wood of remembrance, although we would rather it developed into no more than a copse; after all, the more trees we planted, the more wounded soldiers we had been required to assist. Bunny often mumbled away in the kitchen about how she was having to 'rob Peter to pay Paul' in order to scavenge enough flour to make the bread that accompanied the watery broth she supplied for the soup kitchen. Nevertheless, I saw the way she looked at Fortune, and indeed the way Fortune looked at Bunny when the garden was full with men of varying degrees of infirmity, including blind (from the gas) and deaf (from the shelling), and it was a look of pride and love, and my own heart on witnessing such emotion, swelled with good feeling too.

Opening the club also meant a return to my true profession. Many of our guests were persuaded to come along by Elijah who, it turned out, had a heart as big as a house. He promised food and pledged that they would receive 'first-class medical help from that new Polish fellow' (I knew I could trust him) which meant that a long queue had usually formed at my potting shed door by nine a.m.

Ailments were, on the whole, minor, although the lungs of two of the men troubled me. In the moments when I wracked myself with guilt that I was not fighting, I would look at the queue of men at my potting shed door and was reminded that at least, in my own way, I was providing a service. It did not remove the guilt entirely, but it helped, and when the last of the men meandered away down the lane at the end of another day, I fancied that someone – a nurse I once faced across a courtyard – was standing beside me, encouraging me on. Yet there was more to be done. The sap was rising within me. The horizon called. And from somewhere out in the ether, so did Sophie.

Chapter Thirty-Seven

I t was approaching lunchtime. Elijah and I were in our potting shed cleaning tools, and Fortune and Bunny were in the courtyard, having spent the morning foraging for greenery to make sufficient garlands and wreaths as decorations. There was to be a party at Godolphin tomorrow night, Christmas Eve, to say thank you to the members of the Veterans' Club (Fortune had agreed that perhaps the 'Walking Wounded Club' was a little inappropriate). The men built a bonfire and Fortune declared her intention to donate a little of the cider we made this year as a hot punch. There were to be carols from local school children and (as Fortune called it) 'a cornucopia of magical things!' by which she was referring to the fact that the men had whittled wooden toys for the hamlet children and Bunny had fashioned a Santa Claus outfit for Elijah.

'I think you're ready to lay that hedge up old Pendennis field on your own now, old man,' said Elijah, who was sitting on an upturned crate and sharpening a machete with great care.

I looked up from my own occupation of fashioning a wreath made of different coloured whips of willow – a special request from Bunny as a gift to Fortune.

'Really?' I was genuinely surprised. 'But you have not yet shown me your special technique for the sloe?'

'Ach, you're a natural woodsman. So long as you remember that a good hedge is about creating a habitat, not just a boundary, you're halfway there.'

I put down my tool. 'I am very grateful to have had you as my teacher, Elijah,' I said, 'but tell me, who was it that taught you such skills?'

Elijah held up the blade to inspect it before answering. 'My father,' he said, taking up the stone again to sharpen further down the edge. 'He was land agent for the St Auburn estate over Marazion way.'

'An honourable position indeed.'

'Indeed. Wonderful man … taught me all about looking after nature first and management of the business later – not that I ever put the business side of things to any use. Some of the hedgerows round here date back to the Bronze Age, you know …'

'Really?'

'Take yourself for a walk over to Zennor sometime. Walk the cliffs to St Ives and you'll see a whole patchwork of fields that look almost exactly as they did five thousand years ago.'

'Is that right?' I took up my tool again. 'Incredible.'

'The first hedgerows in England came about after the clearing of the wildwood. And then the Romans, when they came, they added to them – the Romans knew the advantage of a good hedge, you see.'

'The Romans knew the advantage of a great many things,' I agreed.

'And that's why we've ended up with a country made up of a patchwork of fields – all engineered by humans, over time. We've cleared too much of the wildwood, no question, but at least we've got the hedgerows.' He glanced up. 'Remember when you're laying a hedge just how vital they are … to birds, voles, mice … They reduce flooding, they're good for foraging – not just for berries but herbs, too. They provide shelter for the beasts, and plenty of wood to burn and to make things. The toys we've whittled for the young 'uns all came from the hazel. There's seventy miles of hedgerows at Godolphin …'

'That much?'

'Blackthorn, hawthorn, elder, sloe, hawberry rosehips, hazelnuts, blackberries – how do you think I've been managing to live, these past years?'

'From the hedgerows?'

'*From* them. *In* them. I owe the last ten years of my life to the English hedgerow …Food, shelter, bedding … There's many a fox and badger that's come across me in the night fast asleep. Remember how desperate we all were, in France? Trees reduced to nothing but black stumps, mile after mile of shell holes and mud …'

I did remember. Like it was yesterday. I nodded and returned to weaving the willow for my wreath.

'For six whole months at Passchendaele, the only wildlife we saw was rats – big, juicy, grotesque rats, fattened on the bodies of a million dead. And I said to myself, "Elijah, if you believe that you will die, then you will surely die, but if you visualise yourself back in Blighty, surrounded by the lush green fields of home with Father, picking the primroses and the cowslips and the campions from the hedgerows in the spring, then you've got a half-decent chance of getting back. If you don't, you might as well take that helmet off, climb over the top right now and let the rats eat out your eyeballs.'

'A good philosophy,' I said, remembering that my own mental attitude at the time was similar.

He smiled to himself. 'There was a time in the war when I was certain my father was beside me.'

I paused in my questioning for a moment to think of my own father, so very different, and to wonder how, twenty-five years on, the educated son of a land agent had come to be roaming as a tramp and sleeping in hedgerows.

'And when you came home? Did you spend time with your father?'

Elijah kept on with his rhythmic motion of sharpening the blade.

'He died while I was gone. Mother said he died of worry. She died too in '19, not long after. I was his pride and joy, you see, and he was hers. And then ... well, I couldn't quite pull myself together after that. First I hit the drink, then I hit the road. You know the rest from there.' He glanced up. 'What about you? Similar story?'

What about me?

I had shied away from answering this type of question for many years, not just because I would receive no benefit from reliving the past, but also because – as is the way with all wars – not long after it was over, merely a matter of months, the questions from those who were not there disappeared. Life moved on, and no one really cared about what happened in the trenches anymore, not really, except of course, for the people that it happened to. The truth was, it was a time of butchery and unspeakable murderous cruelty, and why would any man wish to relive that? But today, tending to the tools with a man I once faced across the trenches, a man that, after all, had shared part of his story with me, I felt that I could, perhaps, talk a little.

Two hours later I found that I had spoken not a little, but a lot. I began at the beginning, in the way that stories of angst often begin for grown men – with my father. I explained that in Germany my family were once regarded as nobility – nobility with a history of military prowess – and that my father expected his two sons to enter into the army. Politically, he encouraged war mongering – and was absolutely delighted on our seventeenth birthday when we were eligible to enlist. We were taught to shoot at a young age, of course, and I was always regarded as the more gifted soldier of the two brothers. Sascha apparently lacked what my father referred to in English as 'bottle' and as a result Sascha spent his early years desperate to please him, mainly because Father would beat him mercilessly if he failed in our overtly manly country pursuits. Father broke Sasha's ribs one time when he failed to shoot the deer cleanly, and I recall a broken nose when he failed to wring the chicken's neck, or skin the rabbit. None of these things came naturally to Sascha, who much preferred to be at home with Mother.

For most of the war my father was officer in charge of the Tir national, which was a firing range and military training base in Brussels. On 12th October 1915 – a date etched into my mind like no other – I had been due to travel to join an artillery regiment at the front, but my brother was to remain at the Tir national to work with Father (Father believed that Sascha required further 'training' before he would allow him to be out in the broader army, feeling that the family name had a reputation to live up to). On one particular day, as I was putting the last pieces of my kit together, a very distressed Sascha came to my room at the Tir and begged me for help.

There was to be an execution of a British nurse that afternoon, he explained, and to please Father Sascha had put his name forward as part of the firing squadron. Sascha was shaking. 'I can't do it!' he shouted. 'I can't do it! But if I don't, Father will kill me – he'll kill me, Sebastian.' I asked what he wanted me to do, and the answer to Sascha was simple – I was to take the shot in his place. As identical twins, only our mother could tell us apart. I knew that Father would beat Sascha into unconsciousness if he failed. Family honour was everything to Father, and he had clearly been happy to put Sascha forward to display his own family's strength in such a high-profile execution.

At this time in my life I was a particularly straightforward person – smug, even. This nurse, whoever she was, was a traitor and, male or female, the lines in war were clear to my arrogant, young mind. Although I pitied Sascha, I was loyal to Father and at that time I believed his propaganda. And yet, to save Sascha's skin, I agreed to step in. Of course, I was a very young and extremely naïve man – just a boy, really – and had no idea that the doing of the thing when it actually happened would be beyond unthinkable, beyond barbaric, beyond inhumane. Nevertheless, when the dreadful deed was done, Sascha took the credit from Father, who could not have been more proud. Only mother knew which one of us really shot Edith Cavell. I left for the front afterwards and Father decided to make Sascha his right-hand man at the Tir for the remainder of the war, which meant that neither Sascha nor Father ever saw true combat. I began to resent my father. It is never the people who bully the most who ultimately fire the shot. As for my time in the trenches … I glanced at Elijah and saw that his eyes knew my pain. I had no idea how many men I killed, I said, either by grenade, rifle, gas or flame thrower. It was kill or be killed. I became a savage. We were, as they say, lions led by donkeys. When ultimately I realised it was over and I had survived, I walked away and kept on walking until I landed on Sark and could walk no more. From that point on I vowed I would only cure, never kill.

'You wouldn't fight in this one then, if they came for you?'

'After the horror of the last one – the war to end all wars – I would not.' I said this easily, feeling that, of all the people asking that question of me so far, Elijah would be the man who understood, who would act the same way. 'Would you?' I asked, certain of his answer.

Elijah didn't hesitate.

'I would,' he said, and his words floored me. He must have noticed my despondency for he added, 'which is very easy for a man who will not be called to fight to say, of course.' He pats me on the leg. 'But listen, at least we've got this place. And Fortune and Bunny.' He put down the sharpened machete.

'Indeed.'

'In fact,' he went on, 'let's hope that eventually, when all the crazed men have finished killing each other, a battalion of grey-haired women will amass on every border, and in their own special way, very gently take over the earth.'

I laughed. 'Now that would be a wonderful – if formidable – thing!'

He rested a hand on my shoulder. 'Do you ever wonder how on earth you survived?' he asked.

'Sometimes,' I answered honestly. 'Although I more often wondered *why*?'

After retiring to the courtyard for a much-overdue lunch I found a tray of 'cold eats' (as my English friends called this kind of repast) waiting on the picnic table. There were also two bottles of cider and, peculiarly, two sealed envelopes. Both envelopes were addressed to me – one to my real name and the other addressed using my Polish surname. Bearing in mind I knew no one in England outside the hamlet of Godolphin, and of those people I did know, none knew my real surname, this was more than a little disconcerting. One of the letters was very tatty indeed. I looked up to see Bunny watching me through the kitchen window. Her troubled features pictured my own.

I opened the letter addressed to the Polish Sebastian first, and sighed with relief. It was from Fabian, my Polish brother. I read the latter quickly with a broad smile, keen to learn of the brothers' ongoing adventures. Fabian wrote that he was sorry to have taken so long to be in touch, but that it had been a hectic couple of years of training and then what with other operational commitments, he had become caught up in his new life and was distressed to have failed to keep in touch. He explained that he had been trained as an aircraft technician and was now based at RAF Scampton, which was a considerable distance from Cornwall in a county called Lincolnshire. I realised as I read how little I knew of the mechanics of the war and how it was being fought. Fortune took a newspaper daily, but Bunny refused to read it, which meant that Fortune could only provide me with a well-selected precis, choosing to read out only the bits Bunny could bear to know. He had lots to tell me, he explained, including the fact that he was engaged to be married to a young English woman who drove the station ambulance, but alas, now was not the time to write of nice things because he had some distressing news concerning his brother, Alek.

Alek had been proud to be selected to train as an aircraft gunner and had gone on to be part of the crew of an aircraft called a Lancaster bomber. His aircraft was shot down over Germany in October and Alek was presumed dead. Fabian refused to believe that this was so, and was hopeful that Alek was not dead, but would rather presume him to be a prisoner of war in Germany. 'He wore a parachute, after all' he said. I paused a moment to allow the reality of the terrible news to register, and remembered something Alek said when we hit the storm after sailing from Sark – that he was beginning to wonder if their dead brother hadn't been gifted with the better option by being removed from such a traumatic and unrelenting existence. If Alek had been captured by the Germans, then he would truly know the meaning of trauma now.

I told Elijah my news.

'Sad business,' he said. 'Sad, sad business.'

I agreed that it was, and with a heavy heart turned to see Bunny's anxious eyes which were still watching me through the window. Fortune appeared from the barn wearing a white beard and a red suit while shouting Ho! Ho! Ho! Elijah nodded a nod of understanding as I raised myself up from the seat and headed towards the kitchen to deliver the news, leaving the second letter unopened on the table. Meanwhile, the sap rose further.

Chapter Thirty-Eight

I t was late afternoon by the time I turned my attention to the second letter. Despite Bunny's tears and Fortune's profanities after breaking the news of Alek, we did what everyone does after hearing terrible news during a war – we were sad, we got angry and then we got on; after all, *die show muss weitergehen*.

And what a show it was. Elijah excelled himself in the creation of the nativity scene, which was set up in a corner of the courtyard, with local children playing out the parts of the key players while wearing wonderful costumes stitched together from whatever odd bits of clothing could be spared by their mothers. Mary arrived on a real donkey and our piglets were allowed to roam free to add a touch of real-world ambience. (I'm not sure they had pigs in Bethlehem, but no one seemed to mind.) Fortune handed out presents and Bunny handed out hot milk, bread and butter and a biscuit in the shape of a star for the children. It was wonderful. Truly wonderful. And all the while Fabian's letter, which Fortune had carefully returned to its envelope, sat in the drawer of the kitchen dresser, as if by doing so the emotion of the war, like the letter, could be put aside for the evening.

It was as the first of the carols began to be sung – 'Away in a Manger' – that I gathered my courage and took the opportunity to return to the solitude of the kitchen to open the second letter. The date at the top astounded me, for it was written a whole year past. I also noted that the address of the sender was not known to me, so I turned to the last page to see from whom I was receiving this correspondence. It was Sophie.

The Grand Majestic Hotel
Rabat
Morocco

24 December, 1941

Dear Sebastian.

I hope this letter finds you safe, well and happy at Godolphin. (In truth, I will be content if it can just 'find' you there in the first place, as I have no idea if you arrived safely, and there is not one night I have not lain awake, praying to God that your little boat made it). In the belief that all is well, I begin by saying that I'm so sorry not to have been in touch sooner, but I was not as expeditious as I hoped in bringing about my departure from Sark. Although I was looked on with suspicion at the beginning, thanks to Sybil developing such a firm relationship with the Commandant and also to my American passport, last December I was able to hitch a ride on the lifeboat to Guernsey (where things were/are not at all good, I'm sad to say). From there I was able to secure passage to France. The situation when I left Sark was relatively benign, but only in the fact that the islanders were 'behaving' themselves and adhering to the German way of things, which was strange but bearable. The children are being taught to speak German in school, which is galling, and food is not at all plentiful, but thanks to Dame Sibyl's guile and diplomacy, island life on the whole was not beyond bearable when I left. I wouldn't say she has the commandant wrapped around her little finger, not at all, but the relationship between the Dame and the Devil is as good as one could possibly hope for – she was right about the occupation, after all. Nevertheless, I fear that if food supplies become scarce, or if there's a bad winter, the occupying forces may not be inclined to be quite so lenient, or lenient at all, really. Time will tell, but I look forward to the day when we can return to Sark, help tear down the barbed wire and the newly built gunning towers, and frolic in the buttercup meadows once again, and all the while the lambs and the cows will gently graze around us.

But back to the present. You will be wondering why I am in North Africa? I have been wondering the same thing myself. It turned out that it was not so easy to return to England as I had hoped. How naïve I was when I arrived in France to think that as an American citizen I would simply be allowed to cross the Channel. 'On which boat will you sail?' was the response of the bewildered American ambassador, and it soon became clear that if I was ever to return to England, or get any news to you or of you, my journey would have to be a convoluted one. And so, stranded in Calais, I took a room above a bistro and found a job serving as a waitress. Vichy France is a strange place, with German boots parading down every street and their smug mouths supping in every bar. I needed to get away before America entered the war as I was sure they eventually would, but where to go? It took a couple of months of asking around and making contacts, but eventually I befriended an American journalist – an amazing woman called Maisy Cox – who was such an inspiration and I cannot wait to tell you about her one day. It turned out that Maisy also wished to travel to England to take up a new position with a different bureau and had been told that the only way to get there was via Lisbon. If I wished to travel with her, she said, I could. So off I went.

The journey was long and dogged by setbacks, but after a month of travelling through France, across the Pyrenees and onward through Spain to Portugal, we eventually arrived in Lisbon only to discover that a whole army of other civilians had made exactly the same journey and were also desperately trying to source tickets to board a plane to England or a ship to America, all of which meant the price for a ticket, if indeed you could get one, was astronomical. It took a month to secure passage, and even then it was a passage to Africa, which must seem counter-intuitive, but Maisy discovered that it was easier to secure passage from North Africa to England on a Dakota than it was to secure a passage from Lisbon. So, we boarded a cargo ship bound for Africa, which is where I am now, in Morocco, soaking up the heat at the Grand Majestic Hotel. Maisy has changed her plans and will be heading back to America soon. She is going to post this letter for me because having wired London I suddenly find that I, too, am headed in an altogether unexpected direction. Despite my journey so far, I am to return to Paris. But this is the point in the letter where I can no longer while away my time with a travelogue of potted history because I need to tell you something that is difficult to write down – I need to tell you about some aspects of my life that I did not speak of in Sark. All that I can ask is that you read the following with as open a mind as possible and try to believe that I did not set about to deceive you, but that I simply had no choice but to play my cards very close to my chest, even with you. Sometimes we have no choice but to hold things back to protect the innocent, please see it this way rather than any attempt to purposefully deceive.

To begin with, my name is not Sophie Hathaway and Dame Sibyl is not my aunt. I am, however, a divorcee from an American, and everything I told you about my marriage is true. I was sent to Sark by the government to parcel you off to England – by force if necessary – and also to implement other policies on the island, which I'm afraid I cannot go into now. Most importantly, please do believe that it was not my intention to deceive you or even spend so much time with you, but from the moment you walked into Sibyl's living room with a tray of plants under your arm, I was … well, I was crazy about you. I will confess that it seems odd to write to you now, with all these months gone by and literally so much water having passed between us (and if I'm honest I'm worried that I may have misread our last days in Sark, which were the happiest of my life, and you may not, after all, be waiting for me), but the truth is, I am waiting for you, Sebastian, and unless you tell me otherwise, I always will be. But just in case you haven't forgotten me, I think you will agree that 'our' time is not now, or even soon, but hopefully it waits for us somewhere in the future, like a wonderful old friend that can't wait to welcome us home.

If my journey this far has made me aware of one thing, it is that there has never been such a dynamic time in the true emancipation of women. We have never had so many opportunities and we have never been more needed – more vital for the fight. You once said that this was Sophie's War, and you were right. I want to be part of that fight, Sebastian, and recently the best way for me to help with the war effort has been presented to me. You once said that you do not wish to be the main character in your life, and I understand that completely, but at the same time, I do. I want more than anything to do my bit. What kind of life can we hope to look forward to if Hitler is not defeated? It's difficult to explain but I really do feel that some kind of destiny has led me on to play out a very definite role in this war, and it seems that the final piece of the jigsaw is beginning to unravel. I feel a magnetic pull towards my future as clearly as I felt the world pulling you to Godolphin, and to the walled garden that I pictured you so clearly working within. Was I right, I wonder? All I can do is keep playing my part with the hope that one day, either you

will find your way to Paris, or I will find my way to Godolphin, and
when we meet, surely we will know heaven again.

Happy Christmas, Sebastian,
With all my love,
The woman you knew as Sophie
P.S. I am hopeful of securing a long-distance phone call to you, so
hopefully by the time you receive this letter, we will have spoken.

No wonder the envelope was tatty. The letter had taken a full year to reach me. Goodness knew what kind of convoluted route it had taken and how many palms it had crossed. A rosy-cheeked Fortune stepped into the kitchen. She was unwinding her scarf as I put down the letter having read it a second time.

'You have the look of a confused and troubled man about you, Sebastian.' She glanced at the letter on the table. 'Correspondence?' Her hand paused with the scarf half unwrapped as she saw my name on the envelope.

'Do you remember taking a telephone call for me here …' I asked. 'From a woman?'

Fortune completed the unwinding of the scarf and started on her coat buttons. 'No.'

'What about Bunny?'

'I'm sure she would have mentioned it if she had. When?'

'Christmas last year, perhaps? Or any time after that?'

'Is it important?' she asked.

'Very.'

'In that case …' She opened the door and called out into the courtyard.

'Bunny?! I say, Bunny? Pop into the kitchen a second, will you … yes, I know they're about to bring out Mary … on the donkey … yes I know, and she's very sweet, but it will only take a second or two …'

Bunny popped her head around the door. The bobble on the woollen hat took a second to stop wobbling.

'Ah, good. Quick question, old girl. Have you ever answered the old dog and bone to a woman who was asking for Sebastian?'

'What?'

'It's quite simple, Bunny. As anyone ever telephoned asking for Sebastian?'

Bunny scrunched up her ruddy face in concentration, sending her eyeballs to the roof, where they stayed for a moment.

'Yes,' she answered, finally.

'When?' asked Fortune.

More thinking followed. 'No idea, but a long while back. Terrible line. I could hardly hear her. But I did exactly what you told me to do, you know, if anyone ever asked if a Sebastian Braun lived here. And I said no, absolutely not.'

Fortune sighed. 'You didn't think to tell her to hold the line while you checked?'

'Checked? Why on earth ..? But that would give the whole bally game away, surely! As if I wouldn't know who was living in my own house! Anyhow, the woman refused to give her name or even say how she knew him. All she asked was if I knew of a German man who'd sailed from Sark and had looked for shelter in Cornwall. I thought it must be a trick or something, and I specifically remembered the conversation we'd had – that we were to deny *all* knowledge of a man called Sebastian Braun ever stepping foot in Godolphin, even if the king himself asked, you said, because we were passing him off as Sebastian Nowak – as Polish. Loose lips sink ships is what you said.'

'But why not mention it afterwards?' asked Fortune, who

was a dog with a bone now.

'I don't know … maybe I didn't want to cause any worry. And you would definitely have worried, Fortune. And then, well I suppose I just forgot. Is it important?'

Fortune glanced to me for an answer.

Was it important? How to answer that? How to explain to these two remarkable, kind, generous women that my heart had just shattered, and that Sophie's heart would most likely have been shattered too? How to explain that Sophie would have put the phone down believing that I had not survived the journey across the Channel? That I had been unnecessarily watching the driveway every day for all this time in the hope of catching glimpse of a vibrant, dark-haired, joy of a woman skipping down the lane towards me …

And yet, there was no blame to be apportioned. I went to the door to kiss Bunny on the cheek and said that it was of no matter and bid that she return to the party. Once Bunny slipped back outside, I turned to face Fortune. Unable to even begin to explain, I invited her to read the letter while pouring myself a glass of water.

'Oh, Sebastian. That is really most upsetting. Yes, most upsetting.'

I placed the letter in the envelope and made my excuses to retire to bed. Sulking suits no one, but I had no taste for a party now. My time at Godolphin had been magical. Despite being under what was effectively a self-imposed house arrest, I had learned a great deal and been treated with nothing but grace and love. But this was not my home. I was, after all, a refugee, and I accepted my displacement because I had a great ray of hope shining down on me, and that hope came in the form of Sophie, because I really did believe that one day, she would find me here. That hope was now gone. She would never come to Godolphin. And not only would she never come but, thinking I was dead, another love may come along. Sophie was young and deserved to be loved. And so I was broken. There were a great many people for whom this war had taken so much more than it had taken from me, but that was the problem with star-crossed love – the certain knowledge that the life you hadn't experienced would have been the sweetest thing you had ever known, made all the sweeter in the imagination for never having tasted it. There was only one course of action for me now, and that was the correct word to describe it too … action.

I drank my water, washed out the glass and placed it on the drainer before turning to say goodnight to Fortune, who was sitting on her chair by the range, staring into the fire. I turned to leave but she called me back.

'Will you enlist now?' she asked.

'Tomorrow,' I said. 'I shall enlist tomorrow.'

But tomorrow never came.

As I turned to leave, the kitchen door flew open and Bunny, her bobble hat in her hand and a wildness about her that would look well on a cornered stray cat, dashed in. She threw an arm towards the courtyard.

'They're here! They know! Elijah is stalling them. He's sent them round to the front door. God help us all!'

Fortune rose to her feet. She rested a hand on Bunny's arm.

'Now Bunny, remember that confusion is the enemy of wisdom. Clear your mind and start again.'

Bunny closed her eyes for a moment, jumped at the sudden loud knock echoing from the front door, took several deep breaths and eventually, once composed, was able to say, 'The police have come to arrest Sebastian. And they're going to take us away too.'

Chapter Thirty-Nine

S he was right. They did take me away, and Fortune too, but not because she was harbouring a German. The police came because they had received a tipoff that the inhabitants of Godolphin were black marketeers and that the gardening club was nothing more than a cover for a network of profiteers who were operating out of Godolphin and using the barns to store their stash.

Network of profiteers? The Veterans' Club? How soon society forgets those who have served. Yes, there were times when Elijah was able to 'find' extra supplies not marked on any ration card, but it all went to feed an army of men without hope or means who, before finding Fortune and Bunny, were nothing more than starving vagrants.

The authorities eventually saw this to be the truth. Had the case been left to the local constable I would have been free to return to Godolphin with nothing more said of the matter. But the Sergeant from Penzance sniffed the unfamiliar odour of promotion about the case. Since I had been living at Godolphin for some considerable time and having proven myself to be a valuable member of the community – I'd delivered the constable's twins just the previous week – I thought the better course of action was not to continue to pass myself off as a Polish immigrant but to tell the truth as to my background (as I told Margery that day on Sark, 'it saves a great deal of bother later on') and explain that I was German. I also explained that I wished to enlist – on the British side, of course. On this particular occasion, telling the truth was not the best course of action after all, and once I had shown my hand to the sergeant in Penzance, all hell broke loose. The questions were endless and asked directly without clever guise and in the form of an amateur sleuth novel: was I running a Fifth Column ring? Was I a spy? I shook my head over and over. I was simply Sebastian Braun, I said, looking around the room at people I knew well. I was the same old Sebastian that had delivered surplus potatoes to the hamlet folk and cured the local Lord Lieutenant of his latest bout of emotional malady.

It mattered not one bit.

My offer to enlist was met with a scathing mirth.

To the authorities I was a person of 'interest' who had arrived in England under clandestine means and had purposefully hidden my nationality to the authorities. It was decided that my behaviour had been that of a classic 'spy' or if not a spy an infiltrator who was deeply involved in the goings on of the Fifth Column. I was taken to a military base at Plymouth, thrown into a cell and interviewed for several hours, day after day. They were beginning to believe my story right up to the moment when they discovered I had a brother who was known to Hitler and held high rank in the SS. I was moved to London – to Greenwich – where, under house arrest within a military barracks, I underwent yet more questioning and although there were no thumbscrews or water torture, by the third week of my internment I felt myself transitioning into a man who had lost any notion of hope or belief that there existed any goodness or civility in the world. I was not a man anymore – a human, exhausted, innocent man – I was a German, and in being so deserved no kindness or compassion. It struck me that in Sark I had been the 'Good Doctor' and then Sophie had called me 'the Generous Gardener', but to the authorities, none of this mattered because my place of birth marked me as the enemy, and so my life was reduced to nothing. *I* was reduced to nothing.

At the beginning of February, despite having gained no insight from me as to anything concerning my brother's role in the SS and having uncovered no insights into any spy ring or Fifth Column (although the Gardening Club did come under intense scrutiny at one point) my paperwork was stamped declaring me to be a sufficient enough threat for internment. I asked for how long I would be a prisoner and received the answer of a shrug and the words, 'As long as we like, Kraut.' The plan was for me to be taken to the Isle of Man to be imprisoned at Mooragh internment camp which, one decent young Subaltern informed me, wasn't too bad a billet as most of the Germans were accommodated in old boarding houses on the seafront. 'You'll love it, old chap!' he said. 'You'll bloody love it!'

And so it seemed that like my Polish friends before me, I was yet again to be forced to move on, and all because there was no longer any trust in the world. Everyone was viewed with suspicion and all men were guilty until proven innocent, even if that innocence was impossible to prove because no one was prepared to accept a man's word anymore.

But there was to be yet another twist to the tale when one particular detail, a detail that had been initially overlooked by the authorities, proved to alter my trajectory irrevocably – the letter from Sophie, which was found within my things. The initial investigating officer (clearly a novice) had disregarded the letter from Sophie believing it to be nothing more than what it genuinely was – a letter from a friend from whom I was separated. But when a later investigating officer, Major Jacobs, went through my possessions before handing them back (I have long since accepted the fact that I am entitled to no privacy whatsoever) he read not only the letter but the details between the lines and wanted to know exactly who this 'woman I once knew as Sophie' was. I told them what I knew, which wasn't much, except for the fact that I had fallen in love with her – I took great pleasure in saying this out loud. Sophie's identity was duly investigated and after discovering that she really did exist, my captors accepted the validity of my story but I was told that the details of 'the woman I once knew as Sophie' were not to be further probed into or even discussed. Nevertheless, the fact that this woman had once decided that I was not to be regarded as any kind of threat to the nation, carried great weight, and all of a sudden, I was no longer to be interned in the Isle of Man, which led to a discussion as to what to do with me next.

'I was going to enlist,' I said. 'As a military doctor …'

'For the Allies?' I was asked.

'Of course,' I answered.

Two days later, the cheery subaltern who had been tasked to generally look after me while I remained under house arrest, said, 'Oh, you'll be enlisting all right. But not as a doctor. They've got other plans for you, old chap …'

'Other plans?'

'You're off to Scotland. The major will tell you all about it when he comes … ah, here he is now. Well, cheerio. Hope it all works out for you, you know, in the end. Nice meeting you.'

And in a flash, he was gone.

Three hours later, I was on a train that was bound not for Scotland, but for Cornwall, to pick up my things and say goodbye. As the train worked its way to Cornwall I remembered what Fortune had said when I offered her the teapot. 'That little teapot is your future, Sebastian. One day, when this chaos is over, you'll want to start again, and you'll need money to do so. Take care of that teapot and one day, it will take care of you.'

After a brief hour or two with Fortune and Bunny, which was wonderful but emotional, I found myself on the sleeper train bound for Scotland with my escort, Major Jacobs, by my side (they still did not trust me) and my teapot hidden in my suitcase. I realised within moments of being back at Godolphin that it was best I was not returning permanently, for I would no longer have a reason to watch the lane in the hope of the arrival of Sophie, and despite enjoying my time there and having learned so very much about the land, about the people, about myself, I was not sure that I would be quite so happy there now. As I watched the English countryside go by, I felt that the authorities were quite correct when they referred to me as an 'alien', for as much as I felt welcome and at home in Cornwall, as for the rest of it – this was not my home, and although my mind inhabited a body that was still breathing and still moving, the heart – the soul, the passion – had gone. Disappointment no longer slipped down my spine to linger in my gut, or if it did, I was numb to it. And yet I still carried my teapot, and a cutting of my mother's rose wrapped in a damp cloth that Fortune pressed into my hand as I left, which meant that somewhere deep within my belly – where even disappointment feared to tread – I must still carry the last vestiges of something that might be regarded as the lingering traces of hope.

Chapter Forty

La Santé prison, August 1944

'Your final journey began at this point, I think,' says Christoph, rubbing his forehead.

'It did,' I say.

'You came to find Sophie, rather than serve a foreign king and country.'

'You think correctly.'

'I seem to remember you saying that you had lived in Paris before?'

'Yes. In the twenties – which were also my twenties – when I was a wild fool and a troubled soul. The irony is that although I thought I had matured, when I returned to Paris for a second time, the wild fool in me seemed to resurrect himself!'

'It is the city, perhaps?' he said.

'The City of Light, yes, it must be. Paris is an incredible place, although not quite the same as I remembered in my youth, when there were no swastikas hanging from every building. Also, from the moment I arrived, there was no time to think, or feel, or ponder. I was no longer considered a good doctor, or a generous gardener; from that point on, all I could do was to try to exist.'

'And we shall return to that existence shortly,' he says brightly. 'But before that – tea!'

I smile. Christoph's entire existence seems to revolve around the making of tea. And he is very good at it. He opens his satchel and takes out a small muslin bag which he hands to me. 'Smell that,' he says.

I do and immediately my mother is with me. I glance up. 'The Apothecary's Rose!' I say.

He nods, and his face is alive with pleasure.

'But … how?'

'I had a hunch I would find one in a garden I know. The garden was once part of a monastery, and I asked some questions of an old retainer there and found that I was quite correct.'

'But when did you…'

'Last evening,' he says, nonchalant. 'It was a fine night and I needed the air.'

'I am … amazed – delighted!'

He begins in the preparation of the stove and is still smiling, I see.

'But you were telling me of Scotland,' he says, his hands priming the gas. 'I have jumped ahead when referring to Paris.'

'You have, but not by much. Major Jacobs deposited me at a remote country house overlooking the sea on the west coast of the Highlands. The location was like nowhere I have been before – remote, wild, beautiful – achingly so. I am glad to have seen it.'

'And why were you there?' he asks, before following on with, 'although I can probably guess.'

'Yes, I should think you can. To train as an agent. pure and simple, although there was nothing pure or simple about it. After training I began with a number of missions – you will understand, my friend, why I do not give you details of the how and the why and the where, you are still wearing the uniform of a Nazi, even if you are my friend.'

'Of course.'

'Needless to say, I have been operating throughout France since July last year. Mainly short trips, flown in and out by the British under darkness.'

He glances up from the pot. 'So, you gave up on your pledge to never kill another man after all?'

'I have killed no one since the last war,' I say. 'The purpose of those trips involved a more nuanced roll. But then came my ultimate mission – the one I knew they would ask me to undertake eventually.' I glance around and sigh. 'The one that ultimately led me here.'

'And your purpose … for being here?'

'Was quite simply, to become my brother, Sascha. As I explained at the beginning, my name is Sebastian, not Sascha.'

Christoph places a tin cup filled with water on the stove and watches as it begins to boil.

'But if you became your brother,' he says, 'then what became of him?'

I take a moment to consider my answer, but Christoph does not allow me the time to do so.

'Wait. You allowed your brother to be captured?' he asks, his voice rising.

'Allowed?' I repeat. 'I had no say in the matter, I assure you. And do remember that I have brushed over my time in

Scotland … but believe me, my friend, it changed me. I learned of things – terrible things – that I never imagined my countrymen would be part of, and from that point on, it was inevitable that I would find a way to help the war effort, with or without a gun.'

'But, just to confirm, you are a pacifist?'

I sigh once more. How many times must I explain this? 'At no point have I ever declared myself to be a pacifist. That was assumed by others. I said that I would never kill another soul again, and I have stood by that – stand by that. What I had not realised was that there are other ways to fight without killing. Looking back, perhaps my road to Paris began on the day that Elijah said that he would fight again. It humbled me. It shamed me.'

He returns to the preparation of the tea while muttering, 'Shamed you enough to throw your brother to the wolves.'

This surprises and hurts in equal measure.

'My friend, do remember that my dear brother would have happily seen me dead?'

'Dead? I do not recall him sending out such instruction?'

'Yes … remember? When the officer visited on Sark, his instructions from Sascha were to send me back to Germany. If I refused the consequences were to be severe, and with the Nazis, as you are well aware, "severe" can only mean one thing, I'm sure.'

Christoph shakes his head and stands. He picks up his stick and walks to the door. 'I will return in an hour,' he says, his knock on the cell door already ringing out.

'But Christoph,' I shout. 'Will you not drink your tea?'

By the time I have hauled my broken carcass onto my feet, the door has already closed behind him.

A little while later, Christoph returns and lowers himself onto his stool with an almost inaudible moan.

'You may carry on with your story,' he says. His tone is not curt, but it has lost a little of its expression of companionship.

I nod and busy myself boiling the water. We have silence while I perform a mini-ceremony, but there is something about his manner that draws me away from my own story and further towards his. There is a great deal that this man is not telling me, especially regarding his health. I pick up the lantern and hold it towards his face.

'Might I take a look at you, Christoph?' I ask. 'As a doctor – a friend.'

'Nein!' he says, shaking his head angrily, before adding, 'You may only continue with the story. And it might be advantageous, if you start to hurry it along.'

Chapter Forty-One

My first day in Paris while masquerading as my brother, a German officer, was bizarre. I stood in front of the long mirror in my apartment – Sascha's apartment – on the Rue de Ponthieu and tried to take it all in ... the wool tunic in field grey with shoulder boards, the iconic breast eagle, army collar tabs, belt and buckle with pistol holder (and pistol), breeches and highly polished boots, which were a little tight but not unbearable. The belt buckle held the inscription, *Gott mi tuns* – 'God is with us'.

I doubted it.

I shook my head as I took in my reflection. This was the one thing I swore I would never succumb to, and yet here I was in uniform again – a German, a soldier ... a Nazi.

I practised the salute with a click of the heels.

'Heil Hitler,' I said.

No. Too weak. Again.

'Heil Hitler.'

A little better, but ...

'Heil Hitler!' I shouted.

The last one was believable, but only just.

Despite the meagre salute, there was no doubting it. Sebastian Braun was living in Paris as a Nazi. I wouldn't believe it myself if I hadn't known it to be true. And it was true because somewhere in Britain an operative decoding German messages had noticed that Sascha was being dispatched to Paris for an urgent appointment. Shortly after, somewhere between Berlin and Paris, the resistance had kidnapped Sascha, stripped him of his uniform and all the possessions he was travelling with, which consisted of just two trunks, and bundled him, blindfolded and gagged, into a waiting truck. At the outset I had agreed to the fiasco on the understanding that my brother be allowed to live, because although Sascha was now a stranger to me – a stranger who had been prepared to throw me to the wolves – I could not help but love him still.

I was told that Sascha would be bundled into the same Lysander aircraft that would drop me in France. He would then be taken back to England for questioning and imprisonment. It had all been a tremendous risk, of course, and any number of things could have gone wrong, but as I had discovered in Scotland, everything the men and women of the Special Operation Executive did was a tremendous risk. Some risks paid off, some didn't, but the ones that did were the key to the winning of the war.

And yet here in Paris, standing in my brother's apartment, I could not help but feel a sense of deep regret – of what might have been, if circumstances had been different between us. Identical twins were supposed to share an unbreakable bond – a psychic connection – where each understood and felt the emotions of the other without being present. I had once thought this the case for Sascha and me, when we were young, but after the First War it seemed that somehow that invisible connection had been severed and I decided that this was because Father had contorted my brother into a gargoyle of himself, preventing Sascha for being able to feel any form of emotional attachment. And yet, wasn't it I, after all, that had been the one to walk away from emotional attachment? Tucked inside a nightshirt deep within one of his trunks was a photograph of the two of us standing in the garden, I with my arm around my mother. I stared at the photo for quite some time, lost in melancholy, before placing it upside down in the bottom of the trunk, beneath summer uniform. My training in Scotland taught me to avoid melancholy. It would not pay to look back on things with rose-coloured spectacles. My brother was not dead, but captured. He was captured but safe. I, on the other hand, was not.

My mission in Paris was two-fold:

As far as the British were concerned, I was to feed intelligence back to my resistance contact regarding the mood and plans of the Wehrmacht. This was very straightforward, but then I have discovered that the most daring of operations often are. When the Allies discovered that Sascha was being re-commissioned to Paris as the 'cultural attaché' to the military governor (after spending most of the war in Berlin) not only did they know that the job title must be a cover for something else, but they also knew that there would never be a better time to do the switch. Intercepted messages hinted towards Sascha being sent to Paris without an aide to carry out contingency planning for the Führer, but no detail was given. I was to bluff it out until I discovered the plan.

The second part of my mission was entirely self-appointed: I was looking for Sophie. The letter she wrote from North Africa said she was headed to Paris. Of course, she might not be there still, but if anyone could seek her out, I could, or rather, Brigadier Sascha Braun, cultural attaché to the General, could.

Inside Sascha's trunk I found a tatty, much-thumbed pamphlet called, *Der Deutsche Wegleiter fur Paris: Wohin in Paris?* – The German Guide to Paris. The Nazis really had thought of everything at the start of the occupation, hadn't they? I used the guide as a starting point, although the last intelligence briefing I was given before leaving England gave a stark precis of the current political climate in Paris, and it was this:

Hitler had been nervous since the Russians retook Stalingrad and this nervousness had filtered

to the troops and was especially felt in Paris. The Allies had made good ground in North Africa, and when Corsica fell in October last year, those who previously supported the Vichy Regime saw that a different way forward might be emerging and began to hedge their bets and turn their support to the resistance. German troops sent to Paris these days were not the superior troops dispatched at the beginning of the war, quite the reverse. They were either older reservists or the inexperienced very young, the fittest and most highly trained soldiers being required for the Eastern Front. The question of when the Allies would land in France was on every German's lips, because land they most surely would, and Hitler and the whole of his Command knew it too. Although the troops of the Wehrmacht were not the elite force they once were in Paris, the Gestapo had taken over the role of enforcing security measures, which led to an upsurge in the arrest of political prisoners and even more of a feeling of unease amongst the French, who were hungry, tired and depressed. Many Parisians were riddled with tuberculosis. The lines for food, bought with rationed coupons, were long. There was a nightly curfew and blackout. The streets were empty of French vehicles except bicycles, most of which were no longer road worthy due to a lack of rubber and oil. The French could no longer generate enough power to provide electricity to Paris for the whole day and the Nazis routinely sent most of the crops farmed in France back home to Germany, along with hundreds of thousands of Frenchmen who they enlisted to work in German factories – there were simply not enough men in Germany anymore to keep the place going.

And then came the details of the extent of the barbarism directed towards the Jews. Jewish

round-ups in Paris were commonplace. Most had lost their houses and all of their possessions and had been quite simply sent 'away'. My briefing did not state where the Jews were taken to, but there had been some intelligence recently regarding the establishment of so-called 'camps' further east. Then there was *Operation Furniture* – I could hardly believe the name of it, but it was absolutely true. The Nazis had been robbing the Jews of their belongings from the moment they took occupation. Warehouses had been established near train stations to ship it all off to the Fatherland, and it was women from the Jewish community that were forced to organise the dispatch of the items, which meant that these women saw all of their own belongings being shipped away. The Vichy government and French Police were complicit – they had been complicit with lots of things, especially regarding the Jews.

This was the limit of my knowledge on my first day in uniform. 'You'll just have to bluff your way through, old chap,' was the advice from my commanding officer at the SOE, which did not fill me with optimism. The day after my arrival I was to report to Wehrmacht headquarters to discuss my new role. British intelligence had been unable to confirm exactly what kind of character Sascha had portrayed himself to be. I was blind. The boy I knew could surely not have remained inside the man Sascha must have become. In my heart, I did not believe I could do it, and yet I must. It was odd, this switching of characters – almost a role reversal from our youth. Who was Sascha Braun, that was the question? Truth was, I had no idea.

By late afternoon on the first day I was beginning to feel that I was making no inroads into figuring out how to play my brother. He had never stepped foot in the Paris apartment and so it held no clues as to his lifestyle or work pattern. Other than the trunks he travelled with, Sascha had brought only an attaché case that had been left by my resistance contact – Magician – leaning against a reproduction Louis XVI chair in the hallway (at least, I thought it was a reproduction). I found the key in the pocket of Sascha's uniform. Inside were mainly ledgers of some kind, accounting for more money than any man could ever possibly need. There was also a great deal of cash money, some dollars, some German marks, stashed inside one of the case pockets. Some ledgers carried the insignia of the Reich, and some were coded and did not. Looking in a small notebook listing items of furniture and objets d'art of varying age and value, I saw that he had annotated some items with 'C' and some with 'G' and began to wonder if Sascha had decided to run a dangerous game of parallel lives. Deeper inside the attaché case was Sascha's appointment notice, ordering him to report to General Wölf at the Hotel Lutetia on the left bank of the Seine on the Boulevard Raspail the next day. The Lutetia Hotel was the location of the headquarters of the Wehrmacht intelligence service – the Abwehr – which was an indication, Magician said, towards the true nature of my new role.

I put down the appointment notice, sat on the chair and

looked around at the soulless apartment. Was I really here? Could I really do this? I glanced at myself in the mirror again, and there I was, Sebastian in uniform. Only I wasn't Sebastian, I was Sascha. I was a Nazi. And if I was to survive this thing, I had to remember that.

Chapter Forty-Two

The Hotel Lutetia was not quite the same as I remembered it, back in its heyday in the twenties, before the Nazis replaced its Gaelic charm with German utilitarianism. As I pushed my way through the revolving door I thought of Joseph, when he had lifted his carrots to see if they were prize winners. As the fork went in he had said, 'No going back, now!' I straightened and began to take on the imagined arrogant persona of my brother, but then I stopped myself. I had no idea how Sascha as a man rather than a boy walked or how he portrayed himself to the world in general. I might overdo the arrogance? The old Sascha had such a gentle way about him. But was he arrogant, now? Overbearing? Aloof? This was not the man I remembered; I was imagining my father, not Sascha. Exiting the door and stepping into the foyer I decided that my face and uniform alone would be sufficient to fool the world – I needn't add to the act and spoil it. Also, his new colleagues would be strangers to him. They would have no prior knowledge regarding Sascha's manner, would they?

'Willkommen in Paris, Sascha!' exclaimed General Wölf as he rushed towards me like an old friend and held out his hand in greeting. I attempted to deliver the practised salute but the handshake was vigorous and two-handed, his left hand overlaying mine.

Like an old friend …

'Hello, Sir. It's very good to see you.' I omitted the obvious 'again' at the end of the sentence, just in case.

He gestured towards a chair and was still smiling as he sat down. Nothing seemed amiss. There was a knock on the door as I took to my chair. I took in the fabulous view of the Seine and waited.

'Ah, Freda,' said Wölf. 'Champagne, bitte!' He turned to me. 'Or is it perhaps a little early for champagne?'

'It is, perhaps, a little early for me, Sir,' I said.

He glanced at me, genuinely confused. 'Really? I didn't think I would ever see the day when Sascha Braun would refuse champagne, whatever the hour?'

I smiled my agreement while wondering why on earth I hadn't accepted the offer. I must stick to my guns now, however. 'Nevertheless,' I said.

Freda nodded and departed, and as the door closed behind her, General Wölf said, 'I brought my own administrative staff with me from Berlin. You simply cannot trust the French!'

Half an hour of polite conversation passed by and I have no idea how I survived it. My brother remained a mystery to me as Wölf clearly thought of him as a socialite and a man of particularly strong right-wing views, even for a Nazi. But then, all these men were men of strong right-wing opinions; they had to be, or be shot. But Sascha, a ladies' man? Given the way Wölf hinted towards conquests with ladies in Berlin, I could only presume this to be the truth. Eventually, after much cajoling in the right direction, he began to talk about my new role as Cultural Attaché.

'Regarding your new assignment,' he said. 'I hope you agree, it is one that is perhaps suited to your particular talents.'

I took a gamble that the intelligence I had been given was correct. 'I understand that I am to carry out contingency planning … for the Führer.'

'That is correct … although no one really believes that it will come to it – the need for the plan to be implemented. Nevertheless, he has ordered plans to be drawn up, just in case … well, in case the unthinkable happens.'

'Quite a plan,' I said, fishing (and hoping).

'The destruction of Paris? Yes, you could say that. The Führer is adamant that we should flatten the place as we retreat – *if* we retreat, of course, should the Allies get this far. But like I said …'

'It shouldn't come to that,' I concluded for him, trying to appear nonchalant but all the time wondering what on earth Hitler was thinking of. I always thought that Hitler must be insane and there were rumours that he had become quite unhinged, but this?

'No, it shouldn't,' agreed Wölf, 'but with our troops required to fight on two fronts, well, it may be that the Allies are lucky and break through, and if they are successful – which they won't be – but if they are, then it is assumed that they will head for Paris.'

'Paris? Why?' The question was out before I could reel it in, and so was the rest of the sentence. 'If I were an Allied General I would bypass Paris completely and head straight for Berlin,' I said. 'Surely invading a city such as Paris would bring nothing but trouble in logistics and lead to guerrilla-type warfare, and they simply don't need to take Paris.'

He looked at me as if I were mad. 'My dear man! All major road and rail links lead out from here, and also, they would see it as a trophy, would they not?'

I didn't think that they would. Taking a place just for the look of things – as a trophy – was Nazi thinking. That was what had happened with my beautiful Channel Islands. There had been no strategic reason whatsoever to take them, and yet Hitler had invaded and given himself a logistical headache, just so he could say that he had taken British soil. Also, I didn't think the British gave 'two figs' as they would say, about liberating Paris. The Allies would enter France purely as a means to end the war, not to free Parisians.

I said none of this. My self-censorship as a German soldier had begun.

'You are correct, of course,' I said. 'And when you say, destroy Paris …'

'I mean every last brick of it.' He turned to look out of the window. 'Which is a terrible shame, I know. All that history. All that … beauty. But the Führer has ordered that Paris burn – no landmarks, no theatres, no museums are to be left standing. He even quipped that the Eiffel Tower could be crashed down across the streets to act as a barricade – the Parisians do love their barricades.' Wölf turned to face me and scratched his head. 'I think the Fuhrer appreciates a certain wild irony to it all. I think he has become a little …'

He paused.

'Go on …'

'Nothing,' he said. 'Forgive me. I think nothing.'

'Well. Sir,' my tone was enthusiastic, 'if the Führer wants Paris to burn, then I shall make him a bonfire to end all bonfires. I have no sentimentality with the place. Perhaps I shall start by destroying the bridges.'

He returned to his seat.

'I knew you were the man for the job. It needed someone with …' He paused, thinking. 'A certain clarity of thought. No offence, I assure you.' I shrugged my acquiescence. 'But the most important thing is not to take the whole thing too …' He pondered a moment.

'Expeditiously?'

'Almost. Although, I was going to say, vigorously. I have every confidence that our boys will not let the Allies through. Paris is a wonderful city, even during these times. Enjoy it! I cannot recollect if you have been here before?'

Have I been here before?

I hedged my bets and said, 'Yes,' and offered no more. 'Do I have men under me?'

'No. For this particular assignment you work alone … as you prefer, I recollect.'

I stood. The longer I stayed the more likely I was to make a mistake. 'In that case, if Freda could show me to my office, I can begin to plan.'

'Of course, of course.' He rose as a portly man will slowly push himself up from the table after dinner, and yet he was not portly, simply tired. He headed for the door and paused with his hand on the handle. 'There is … one other thing.'

'Yes?'

'There are works of art dotted around the place … in the Louvre, and so on. They would need to be … let's say … removed, beforehand, if the unthinkable were to actually happen, you understand.' He slapped me on the back. 'But do not be too precipitous with your planning. As I said, enjoy yourself.'

I nodded and went to leave.

'And Sascha … remember that we are the only two people

in Paris who know of the Führer's plans. It would not do for the soldiers – or the Parisians, especially – to learn that he had even begun to think that ...'

I cut him short. I was playing up to my part already, just as I was taught in Scotland. 'And we are not thinking of it,' I said. 'This is merely a plan that will never come to fruition.'

'Nevertheless, if you could let me have the dossier by, let's say, the end of July?'

'Very good, General.'

He opened the door and I threw up a salute.

'Heil Hitler,' I said, with gusto.

'Heil Hitler,' he repeated, and I was surprised to see that his reply was less than robust and his saluting arm was less than straight.

As I walked out of the hotel, passing soldiers going about their business, it seemed to me that I alone had the smartest uniform, the smartest demeanour, and possibly, the smartest outlook. These men had had enough, the act was wearing thin. And that was exactly what this war had been for every single soldier – an act. Some believed it, some didn't. To put on the uniform of a Nazi was to begin a charade of power and arrogance – even I could not help but adopt an arrogant gait as a Nazi. I wanted to stand in the foyer, strip down to my underwear and implore my German comrades to do the same – to shed the uniform of aggression, shake away the shackles of pretence and finally be themselves, raise the white flag and go home to their farms and their families. I wanted them to say to Hitler and Rommel and to all of the monsters in Berlin, monsters who sat in safety, as they always do, 'We will not do this! We are human and you have dehumanised us – all of us! How can so few people dictate the lives of so many?'

But of course, I did not strip down to my underwear; no

one ever does. Not since *The Emperor's New Clothes* when the boy shouted out 'The king is in the altogether,' has anyone had the courage to denounce the stupidity of a despot. I put on my cap, pushed my way through the revolving door and took out my 'guide to Paris'. I needed coffee. Despite shortages, there were still cafés to be found and drinks to be had – Paris would always have its cafés. I doubted even the devil himself could close them.

I walked a while before turning down a road I knew well – a road everyone knew well: the Champs-Élysées – the boulevard of my youth. My boots seemed to have instinctively taken me there, although perhaps it was my feet rather than my boots, as they were Sascha's boots after all and a little tight. I once lived above a charcutier on the Champs-Élysées during my days in Paris, and as I turned the corner and saw the Arc de Triomphe in the distance, I remembered how once, for a short time, I fell in love with Paris. It was odd to see the Champs-Élysées so quiet now and so lacking in vibrancy.

A little further on I saw a café across the street that I remembered frequenting in my youth. The café was called Café des Fleurs and taking a quick look in the soldier's guide, I saw that it was not listed as being particularly recommended for Germans. This pleased me. I did not want to drink where Nazis drank. There were a handful of customers sitting at bistro tables on the street outside. Half of the seating area was bathed in sunshine, the other in shade. It was a warm afternoon by now and most sat in the shade, drinking and smoking. I was about to cross the road when a woman wearing a black apron over a scarlet skirt swished out carrying a tray. She had a manner about her walking that conveyed a confidence I hadn't seen in a while. I smiled. She reminded me of Sophie. Even the hair was the same – dark, shoulder-length, perhaps a little less shiny. I was halfway across the road when Sascha's noisy boots stopped echoing because it is difficult to walk when your heart has stopped. The woman looked like Sophie because she *was* Sophie – older, thinner, more tired perhaps, but Sophie all the same, who had come to my boulevard after all. She delivered a coffee to an older gentleman before taking a seat herself.

Chapter Forty-Three

I set out early the following morning. It was a cool morning for June as rain had come in the night and there was damp in the air. My walk was an aimless one, and yet I knew exactly where all the streets I walked would lead to in the end. I received odd glances as I walked along; after all, it was not often the early risers of Paris would see a high-ranking German officer walking down the road, his pistol on his holster, his cap pulled low over his eyes. But sleep had alluded me and I needed to be outside. The café would open at ten, I surmised, which meant that I had three hours to figure out how to say 'hello' to Sophie, because after several hours of night time deliberation, that was exactly what I intended to do, say hello. It was madness, and yet I had no control over my emotions. No control whatsoever – Fortune's fool once more.

And yet I did not intend to give away my true identity to Sophie, not because I wanted to play games or trick her in any way, but because my part in the war was too important now (I was the man who would burn or save Paris, after all). However, I wanted to see if I could discover more of what she was doing Paris, because one thing was for certain, Sophie Hathaway was not merely idling away the war as a waitress. She had hinted in her letter that she had an important job to do, but what was that job? Was she in danger? Were the Gestapo, who were becoming more and more active in the city now that the war was headed in a direction the Fuhrer had not expected, aware of her? All such things I was certain I would be able to find out, and in doing so perhaps keep her safe. Not for the first time I pondered over the fact that the woman I was desperately in love with was nothing more than a slippery mirage to me – maybe the ultimate illusion – and always had been. I had no idea who Sark's Sophie Hathaway was. I pressed such doubts from my mind once again and did what any man desperately in love chooses to do when common sense leads him to question his trust of a woman – ignore instinct and push on blindly.

As I walked the empty streets I fooled myself that it would be perfectly reasonable for me to simply arrive at the café, order coffee, exchange pleasantries and then bid her adieu. There was the undeniable fact that she would recognise me, believing me to be Sascha, of course. It would be a surprise, no doubt, but Sophie was made of grit and iron. She would not falter even if her heart and mind were racing with questions and surprise. To while away some time, I spent an hour talking with a young German soldier I found fishing on the banks of the Seine. My heart broke for him. Despite the uniform, he really was just an ordinary young boy – not more than a child, really – who wanted nothing more than to be at home on the banks of the Rheine with his mother. He was shocked to be talking to a senior officer, of course, but he offered me a go with a spare rod and I was grateful of the mindfulness of the action as we whiled away the time until the café opened. I should not have been fishing on the Seine, and I should not have been meandering my way to a café to catch a glimpse of Sophie. I should have been in Sascha's apartment, planning the destruction of Paris (or fake planning the destruction of Paris). I had become distracted already persuading myself that General Wölf was quite correct when he said that I should not act too precipitously in my planning, and if I could only see her, only be close to her – just make sure that she was all right – then I would be more able – more determined – to cope with whatever horror lie ahead. This was what I told myself, the fool that I was, the arrogance of the uniform having already seeped into my soul. If I had known as I set out on my journey that morning that not too far away, on the beaches of Southern England, thousands of Allied troops were massing to begin a perilous journey of their own, I might not, having handed the rod back to the young man, subsequently turned onto the Champs-Élysées and headed towards the Café Des Fleurs at a slow but steady pace. Then again, I probably would. I was, after all, just an ordinary man, desperately in love with an extraordinary woman and nothing, not war, not famine, not tempests, not volcanoes and hurricanes, would ever stand in the way of that.

Chapter Forty-Four

La Santé Prison, August 1944

'So you found her, your Juliet,' says Christoph, staring into his tea.

He surprises me by referring to Sophie as Juliet.

'How do you know that?' I say, my voice betraying a suspiciousness of Christoph that I have not experienced since our liaison began.

'Know what?' he asks.

'Her name, man?' I shout, suddenly frightened that I have spoken – revealed – far too much. 'You called her Juliet!'

He leans away and gestures with his hands to show his surprise at my aggressive stance. 'I merely referred to her as Juliet because that is how you have often referred to her – the Juliet to your Romeo. Come, settle yourself.'

I release a sigh. 'Of course,' I say. 'Of course. I am sorry for my tone, but you see, that is what she is called in Paris.'

'Juliet?' he asks.

'Juliette.' I confirm. 'It is an alias, of course.' A thought hits me. It is a thought that should have hit me some time ago. 'Our conversations,' I begin, 'they are listened to in the manner of …'

'A confessional,' he concludes for me. 'Yes.'

'But I am not a Catholic,' I say. 'So will you honour me in the same way? Will you keep my secrets?'

He leans forward and places a hand on mine. 'I am only here to help you through a difficult time,' he says. 'Do not see intrigue where none exists. I will take your words to the grave, I assure you.' He pauses. 'I am still amazed that you found her so quickly. It seems almost *too* miraculous.' He removes his hand, shakes his head and smiles. 'But then, the Lord works in mysterious ways. I, of all people, know this.'

I glance around the cell and wish that the all-benevolent Lord would throw another miracle in my direction.

'Perhaps,' I say. 'But I am more inclined to see it as an incredibly lucky coincidence, rather than direct intervention by God. And also, Sophie was drawn to the place where I had lived during my time in Paris, I think. To feel close to me. There is no miracle in that.'

'You still do not believe,' he says, putting down his cup.

'In God? In miracles? I do not. But believe me, padre, I truly wish that I did, given my circumstances.'

He nods and we let the space in.

After a while a thought hits me. 'It's rather like knowing you have an examination to sit, isn't it?'

'What is?'

'Death – or rather, our preparation for the end of it, I mean.'

'In what sense?'

How to explain. 'When studying medicine, there were many examinations to be done, but there always seemed such a long time to prepare for them, and so I would push the thought of any serious study from my mind, telling myself that I'd prepare nearer to the time. And then, before you knew it, the exam was scheduled for next week, and you hadn't prepared yourself a bit, and you knew that it was too late to prepare now, and you were going to be lucky to scrape a pass ...'

'I see.'

So did I, finally. 'That's how I feel about death, how I think most of us feel about death. We all know that it's coming, but we put off thinking about it to the very last moment, and then we panic and it becomes a horrible, upsetting mess, rather than something that we have prepared ourselves for – an exam we pass with flying colours. But how to prepare, that's the thing? How to genuinely reach the moment when you say to yourself that you are content for this thing to happen now, for surely that is the better way to go. I seem to have forgotten all that I was taught by Fortune. During my many years as a doctor, I attended to a number of my neighbours in their final days, and many of them said exactly the same thing to me ... "I'm not ready".

'And is that what you are saying to me now, Sebastian? That you are not ready?'

I look down, afraid that he will see my tears. 'I am, my friend,' I say as my voice catches. 'I am.'

Christoph did not allow the space in.

'Then let us have more tea and talk of Sophie, for your story is not over yet, and you have still not told me about the teapot!'

I cannot help but smile.

'You are right,' I say. 'Although I feel you will not believe my story when I tell it.'

'Try me,' he says, patting my knee. 'Try me.'

Chapter Forty-Five

I saw Sophie from some distance down the road. She wore a red shawl wrapped around her shoulders and was preparing the outside tables for the day ahead. I slowed my step, suddenly unsure and yet desperate with excitement. She was here and I would see her, speak to her, my Sophie. I had dreamt of this moment every day since the summer of 1940. How utterly ridiculous life was that I could not simply rush up to her and say, 'Sophie, my love. I'm here. I've found you!' I slowed my step further. What if Sophie, thinking me dead, or even worse, *not* thinking me dead, had fallen in love again? She rushed back inside as I neared the café, having only glanced at me briefly as I approached. What a difference a uniform can make. In Sark, wearing my gardening clothes and sauntering down the lane, I was as threatening as a mouse, but here, as a Brigadier, my walk was brisker, my posture straighter, and my persona that of a powerful official. Didn't this prove my point of how ridiculous it all was, really? Was I not the same man?

No, I wasn't. I was Brigadier Sascha Braun, a Nazi officer, plain and simple. No wonder Sophie dashed away quickly.

I took a seat at table seven facing outwards towards the boulevard. Unsure suddenly, I began to fiddle with my left boot, which was even tighter than the right. This was when the absolute folly of my decision to come to the café hit me like a train. I was about to jump up and dash away, but felt a presence at my right shoulder and it was all too late.

'Bonjour, monsieur.'

I began to straighten. 'Pardon. Bonjour.' I glanced up, finally. Sophie's gaze was fixed on her notebook.

'Coffee and a pastry, perhaps?' she asked, retrieving a pencil from behind an ear. 'Although, I should tell you that we have no cream today ...'

'No cream? Why?'

She sighed. 'There is a war on, Monsieur.' She answered me while still looking at the notebook. I wondered if she behaved this way with all the soldiers, refusing to make eye contact? Knowing Sophie, probably, yes, but she was running a great risk in displaying notes of sarcasm to a very senior officer. I waited and eventually she had no choice but to look at me, and when she finally saw my face, I knew for certain that I had done quite the wrong thing in coming here. I was a foolhardy, selfish, irresponsible buffoon.

'Sebastian!' she said, her hand flying to her mouth.

'Sophie,' was the only reply I could muster as she fell to the floor.

The fainting episode lasted only a few moments. I shouted towards the open café door – 'Water! Bring water!' I knelt to take her pulse, which was racing, and gently pulled back her eyelids to check the response of the eye. Once happy she would not faint again, I helped her to her feet and noticed that she was nothing but bones under loose clothing – clothing that would have fit her quite snuggly during our halcyon days on Sark. The hollows under her eyes were dark, too. No wonder she fainted. This woman hadn't known a decent meal for years.

'Pardon, Monsieur.' Sophie glanced away, embarrassed. An older man appeared with a glass of water. He handed the glass to Sophie with a concerned smile before nodding towards me anxiously.

'Thank you, Sir,' he said. 'I'm so sorry your coffee is delayed. I shall help Juliette inside and be with you as quickly as possible. Perhaps you would like a croissant? On the house! They are fresh?'

'I would, thank you,' I said. 'And also, bring the same for the lady …'

'For Juliette?' he said, confused.

I glanced at Sophie whose head was cowed staring at her feet. She was wearing threadbare canvas shoes with wooden soles.

Juliette?

A pseudonym, perhaps? And the name she had taken … I smiled.

'Yes, for Juliette,' I said, before realising that this man would not have sufficient coupons to make fresh croissants for both his staff *and* his customers. 'I shall pay, of course. She is weak and requires sustenance.'

The man glanced up and down the street. Sophie began to recoil. 'I am grateful,' she said, her voice shaking a little while still refusing to look at me. 'But as you see, I am quite well. It was nothing and I have work to do. I will bring your coffee in a moment.' She turned to the man. 'Come, Louis. We must get on.'

I sat at table seven for two hours. This was the seat where Sophie had also sat, just yesterday, and countless times before, no doubt. This was the table on which she had also rested her elbow, and her view particular of the Arc de Triomphe, was my view now, too. Taking out my notebook, I began to make notes on my plan for the destruction of Paris while Sophie worked around me. The destruction of Paris … mein Got! It was a bizarre, frankly crazy situation. The café did not receive many customers while I was there, I noticed, and those who came sat inside. I should not have stayed there, but a moment's selfishness for a man who had been lost in a wilderness of longing for the duration of the war was, if not acceptable, then understandable. Just to know that she was there, near me, carrying on with her day, was enough to make the unthinkable situation I had found myself in, suddenly, well … bearable. Occasionally I felt her eyes fall on me and I would turn and smile as if to say, 'Yes, you are not mistaken, it is me. It is Sebastian, and I still love you'. But she would glance away quickly, leaving me ridiculous.

Ultimately, I could justify lingering no longer. More and more soldiers had begun to walk past, saluting suddenly on noticing my rank. I batted each of them off in the manner I expected Sascha would have behaved – disdainfully, and with arrogance – until I realised that Sophie was once again watching me through the window in the café. I stood to leave and she came to the door. The colour had returned to her cheeks, as had a sense of pride and determination I knew from the Sophie of old.

'Goodbye, Juliette,' I said, settling my bill with Louis while nodding courteously in her direction. 'I'm glad to see you are looking much improved. I will see you again, perhaps, but in the meantime, look after yourself.' I was only a few paces down the road when I heard footsteps – wooden soles – racing after me.

'Monsieur!' she shouted. 'You did not take your change.' She held out her hand to offer me the money.

I shook my head. 'Keep it.'

'But … it's too much.'

'On the contrary,' I said, quietly. 'It can never be enough.'

I turned to leave.

'When I fell,' she said. 'You called me Sophie. Why?'

I closed my eyes to think. 'You reminded me of someone,' I said.

Sophie turned away anxiously to see Louis step out of the café. He was looking down the street while running a bar cloth though his hands, watching us.

'It was a good coffee,' I said. 'Perhaps I shall return tomorrow.'

She nodded, turned in her worn-out plimsolls and ran back down the street.

And I did return – the very next day, and the day after that, too, and in my mind I saw myself returning to the Café Des Fleurs every day just to catch a moment with Sophie ad infinitum, or until the end of the war, at least. I sat at the same table, not only because it was the furthest away from the door, but also because it was situated behind three potted trees, all of which needed attention in the form of a little light pruning, which I began to do, but nonetheless acted as the perfect screen. She would lower the coffee cup to the table silently. I would glance up and smile, and then she would be gone. It was selfish of me – allowing her to think that she was serving Sascha. But she was here. I could see her. It was enough.

When I wasn't at the café I was either at my desk at the Hotel Lutetia or at my apartment, all the while planning a campaign – a campaign for the destruction of the most strategic and historically important places in Paris, should the Allies come. The plan was barbaric – insane. There were hushed murmurings of Hitler's diminished mental health – I thought his mental health had always been questionable, but kept that to myself. If the time came to activate the plan (*when* the time came to activate the plan) I would, of course, sabotage the scheme, being the man best placed to do so, which meant that I required one plan to present to General Wölf and one to hand to my resistance contact – my head saboteur, Magician. It struck me that I would also have to devise a way to prevent the Nazis from stealing the most significant pieces of art from the Louvre as they retreated, which they would undoubtedly attempt to do, but as I said to Magician, I am, after all, just a country doctor, and despite my training in Scotland as a so-called 'spy' I had no idea if my plans would be sufficient. Magician reminded me that I was in my youth – lest I forget – a trained soldier. Training like mine during the last war was buried into the soul, he said. Nevertheless, he would help; secrecy and urgency were vital.

And then there was the question of Sophie. I returned constantly to the question, who was Sophie Hathaway? Who, for that matter, was Juliette Vernier? Who on earth was the woman I adored, that I had risked my life just to see, the woman with the wild hair, Romani looks and vibrant Yankee ways? Not that Juliette had Sophie's bright-eyed vibrancy. Juliette Vernier seemed rather more hollow-eyed and war-weary. It was not that I felt I could not trust her – not for one second did I consider this – but who was Sophie involved with? What was her true purpose for being in Paris? Was she in danger?

Despite my misgivings, that first week passed like a dream – this espionage business seemed to be almost too easy. When you reach the rank of senior officer very few people exist that are prepared to question your actions or motives. Then the 6th of June arrived – the date of the Normandy landings, and everything, absolutely everything, changed. It was happening. They were here. The Allies had actually landed and what might be the beginning of the end had begun. My colleagues in the Wehrmacht ... well, they were beginning to itch. To make plans. And most importantly ... they were taking great pains to cover their tracks.

Chapter Forty-Six

I did not tell Magician about Sophie. She served me coffee once, sometimes twice per day, which made everything else bearable.

I had placed my life in grave danger by travelling to Paris and impersonating a Nazi officer. I had a challenging – impossible – job to do, and yet I was happier in those brief weeks in June than I had been for years, and all because I could be close to Sophie every day. But as my old friend Romeo said: *Come what sorrow can, it cannot countervail the exchange of joy that one short minute gives me in her sight.*

How very true, and how very irresponsible.

The inability to have an open conversation with Sophie meant that I remained blind as to her true activity in Paris – she was not merely a waitress, that was for sure. The Gestapo were doubling up on efforts to crack down on resistance work, and it would be so like Sophie to operate on the limits of safety. And yet, was I not a senior officer in the Wehrmacht? Did I not have encyclopaedic amounts of intelligence at my disposal, if I simply asked the right officer to research it for me?

And so I researched Juliette Vernier, not by liaising with the Gestapo – that would have been disastrous – rather, I asked the intelligence agency within the Wehrmacht to do a little digging. I hinted that she was a lady that I might like to get to know a little better. They understood perfectly, they said, and two days later a report appeared on my desk: Juliette Vernier was born and raised in Paris in the fourteenth arrondissement, the daughter of a school teacher father and an academic mother. She followed her father's footsteps and became a school teacher in her own right after which she married Victor Vernier, also an academic, but he died shortly before the war began of tuberculosis. She had never remarried or been known to be involved with another man. There were no children. She now worked in the Café de Fleurs with an uncle on her husband's side, Louis Vernier. They both lived in an apartment above the café. Louis was being monitored by the Gestapo due to the political leanings of the customers that regularly frequented the café, including the existentialist John-Paul Sartre and other outspoken academics.

I read the report and wondered what Sophie's real name was. She had confessed to not being Dame Sibyl's niece, but instinct told me that the account of her American husband and upbringing in Paris were true. I also doubted very much that anything written in the intelligence report was true, including the name, except for the fact that the café was being monitored by the Gestapo, *that* I believed. There must be more to Sophie's story than anything the Wehrmacht had uncovered, and to her credit, whatever it was that she and her café friends were involved in, their ventures remained uncovered, which was no mean feat.

Nevertheless, I made up my mind to try to find a way to warn her of the Gestapo's interest in the café and that they were on their 'watched' list. I did not have to devise a Machiavellian scheme to achieve this aim. At seven p.m. that evening, after spending the afternoon with General Wölf running over initial plans for both the retreat from and the destruction of Paris, I turned the key to my apartment, walked into the sitting room and found a woman sitting on the sofa.

'Hello, Sebastian,' said Sophie, smiling up at me softly.

She had left the sofa and fallen into my arms before I could even begin to deny it. And once her hands had tenderly touched my face and her lips met mine, I didn't even try to.

That was the moment.

That was when our love affair truly began – in Paris, in an apartment rented for my brother while the Allies, with tiny, agonising steps, edged ever closer.

In Sark, we had been childlike lovers, playing in the pastures and the meadows on a make-believe island, tiptoeing around each other – playing out less than convincing performances of our roles. Neither had wanted to be the first to confess to love, not until the end, when the bombs had begun to fall and it was all too late. I wouldn't make that mistake again, because we were not Sebastian and Sophie any longer, we were playing out new roles now – we were grown-ups, Sascha and Juliette – who were different characters altogether. The past four years had changed us to a point almost beyond recognition. The woman standing in front of me was not the woman I had said goodbye to or who had written the letter from Morocco. This woman had experienced a very different war to the one she had expected it to be. I knew that look of despair, for it was the same look of loss and grief that echoed on my face in 1918. She was wrung out with the insanity and the cruelty of it all.

'I understand now,' she said as she kissed me. 'I understand everything.'

For my part, I was no longer a reclusive man, hidden from the wider world on an island. The past four years had cured me of that. Each person, each new experience I met along the way had brought about a change in me ... my Polish friends, Bunny and Fortune, Elijah and his gang of gardening veterans, my spy masters in Scotland and even General Wölf, they had all, in their own way, worked a little magic on me, as if working collectively to help me to become the man that perhaps I always should have been had the last war not taken its toll, which was the man who could stand here now, take Sophie in his arms and finally do what he had wanted to do from the moment he saw her at La Seigneurie – kiss her properly. Kiss her passionately, the way she had always deserved to be kissed. Of course, the kissing was nothing more than a precursor for the true intimacy to come, that we had both longed for so very much. When I swept her into my arms and paused to ask if she would like to take our love further, she smiled and said, 'Did I not always hope for a wild Parisian affair? To be swept off my feet? And you did promise, Sebastian Braun, to kiss me the next time we met like no woman had ever been kissed before ...'

And so I swept her off her feet, and stray tears of love, regret and happiness fell as I carried her to the bedroom, where we held each other and loved each other until dawn. Despite everything that has happened since that moment, I would not have missed Paris for the world.

Chapter Forty-Seven

Sophie said she knew at our first meeting that I was Sebastian Braun, not Sascha. Not only had I referred to her as Sophie – an amateur mistake, she said – but I have a black spot to the left of the pupil on my right eye, and it was unlikely Sascha had exactly the same marking. My examination of her on fainting had merely sealed the conviction – it was such a Sebastian thing to do, she said, and my bedside manner was unmistakable. I was, she concluded, an appalling spy. She also knew that the plan by the British intelligence service had always been to find a way for me to impersonate my brother and infiltrate the Reich, but she had never thought they would persuade me to do it. Then, when I had returned the next day, and then the next, to a café that no Nazi soldiers would ever frequent, she knew, without doubt, that it was me and had had me followed to discover my address. The notion of her trailing me – a Nazi senior officer – seemed to show just how utterly ridiculous the whole thing had become, and how well-connected and truly courageous the woman I loved was.

Courageous or not, Sophie's decision to come to the apartment that evening had been reckless and had I been a wiser man or less desperately in love (the two are perhaps not compatible) I would have ordered her out for her own protection. Parisians were either collaborators or non-collaborators and the two camps did not see eye to eye. Sophie (Juliette) had played with a straight, non-collaborator, bat since her arrival in Paris. When I asked why she had risked coming to my home she had said, quite simply, 'Because you were right; war is a fool's game, and I'm so very tired of it all, and I love you.'

I told her nothing of my task in Paris and she knew better than to ask, but when she returned on the next evening before curfew and we lay in bed, she told me of the seventeen Jewish children presently hidden in secret room inside a children's home where, on some afternoons, under the guise of being a teacher, she went into the school, into a secret room, and taught and fed them. Everyone who cared about the welfare of the few remaining Parisian Jews had prayed for the Allies to land in France, she said, expecting that the Nazis would shift their focus away from the persecution of the weak. But this had not happened. Ever since the Allies had landed, the Gestapo in particular had increased the raids in the city, increased the arrests and increased the torturing of the innocent. Why, we wondered, before concluding that the answer was simple. To show strength. To invoke fear. To quell any possible notion of uprising, before it could begin.

'I've spent the past two years working to help Jewish children escape to neutral countries, mainly to Switzerland.' She lay on her side, naked beneath a sheet covering her frame, resting on an elbow.

'Was that the reason you were sent here?'

'No. My first assignment was as a secretary to a German officer, but he brought in a German woman and that was the end of that.'

There was a slight crack in the curtains. It provided just enough light for the moon to shine a soft line across her delicate shoulders. I reached out a hand to run a finger across her collar bone and down her arm. She took my hand and intertwined her fingers in mine. 'When I couldn't get out of Paris, I started teaching in order to earn a little money – and it matched my cover story – and then I found out about Drancy.'

'Drancy?'

'Haven't you heard it spoken of?' she asked, amazed. 'Not even within the Wehrmacht?'

I shook my head. 'Remember, I am still in a whirlwind. I have been in Paris only a short time and I work alone, on the whole.'

She squeezed my hand.

'I still can't believe you are here,' she said.

'And nor can I,' I confessed. 'But tell me, what is this "Drancy"?'

And what she told me over the next hour broke my soul in two. Drancy was a detention camp where throughout the occupation, the Gestapo and the SS in collaboration with the French police had corralled French Jews and kept them prisoner. Families were separated, their homes raided, emptied and re-possessed. Drancy was designed to hold hundreds of people but Jews had been crushed inside in their thousands, left without much food or water, before being transported to these so called death camps that the resistance were hearing word of. So far, working alongside an incredible mime artist called Marceau, Sophie had helped to prevent over four hundred Jewish children from being sent to Drancy, before further assisting them to cross the border to safety.

'I've always done the Swiss border crossing,' she explained, resting her head on the pillow and lying back while staring at the ornate plasterwork of the ceiling rose. 'The trick is to keep the children quiet while making it all seem like a game. We've managed it so far, but we've been lucky, I know that.'

'And to think, I have been in England, in safety,' I said, 'while you were here, doing all of this. I am ashamed, Sophie. Heartily ashamed.'

She rolled over to face me.

'Don't be,' she said. 'Truly. When this war is finally over, if then, just twenty years later, I was told that I had to go through it all again ... I wouldn't. I couldn't.' She touches my face tenderly. 'Honestly, my darling. What you experienced in the trenches was even worse than this, not that you can really set a scale for such misery and depravity. Had more men behaved as you behaved, we would have had no war and there would be no suffering.'

'And yet, I am here,' I said with a sigh. 'My Nazi uniform hangs on the rail and my boots are polished and waiting by the door.'

She snuggled in and rested her head on my chest. 'Tell me what happened,' she said. 'From the moment you left Sark, tell me it all.'

I wrapped my arms around her.

'Let me see ... well, there was this little boat, three Polish prisoners and a woman called Sophie Hathaway ...' I sat up lightly to glance down at her. 'Have you met her?'

She laughed. 'No ... but she sounds like one of those terrible Americans you hear about!'

'Oh, she is ... she is.' With my story forgotten before it had begun, I took Sophie's face in my hands and kissed her very gently. 'She is absolutely terrible,' I whispered before sliding a hand under the sheet. I began to pleasure her.

'I hear she's an absolute vixen in the bedroom,' she murmured, her voice hoarse as her body moved with me.

'Oh, she is,' I said.

'Show me,' she murmured, her face a flash of intoxicating excitement.

And so I did.

Chapter Forty-Eight

La Santé Prison, August 1944

Christoph has a hand to his chest, holding his cross as I finish talking.

'You disapprove of our affair, I think?'

Christoph sighs and once again his spectacles fall forward on his nose.

'Then you think incorrectly. But still, you were both incredibly foolish.' He removes his spectacles completely and shakes his head. 'Were you not seen? Did no one notice Sophie entering your apartment?'

'They did, and we were seen,' I say, bluntly.

Christoph shakes his head again. 'I think that despite everything, if I have understood you correctly,' he gestures with his spectacles around the cell, 'you would do it all again, just to have your Romeo moment with Sophie – with Juliette?'

My first reaction is to say that yes, I would, but I take a moment to think about it. Christoph deserves an honest answer. 'No,' I say eventually. 'I would not place Sophie in such a vulnerable situation again, not if I was of my right mind. But you have not quite heard the whole story yet. I will come to it but there is something I must do first.'

I pick up the stove and struggle with my twisted hands to unscrew the lid from a small cannister hidden inside the stove. The cannister houses a couple of tiny tools included for the repair of the stove. I take out a tiny screwdriver and am pleased to see that the fingers on my right hand have healed sufficiently for me to hold it – just.

'Hand me your spectacles,' I say.

Christoph hands them over without comment and I hold them to the lantern, which is showing the flickering signs of fading out. I gently bend the metal frame in the hope that they will sit tighter on his face, but my hands are awkward and I shout out with frustration.

'You don't have to do that, Sebastian,' he says.

I don't look up but continue to tighten the frame.

'Listen,' I begin, 'about my friends at Godolphin … when the war is over, will you write to them? They would want to know what became of me, and I would like … I would so very much like you to tell them about the light in my eyes when I spoke of them. And tell them … tell them that I loved them, as a son loves his family.'

Christoph nods his understanding.

'Life can swing from ecstasy to agony in a heartbeat,' he says.

I hand the spectacles back.

'Indeed,' I agree. 'Which is why we must … what was it Geothe wrote? *Enjoy when you can and endure when you must?*'

The lantern flickers to blackness. I am now in a period of enduring while knowing that there will never be another time of enjoyment. Except, is not Christoph's companionship enjoyable, in its own way?

Reading my mind, Christoph says, 'Have you enjoyed, when you could?'

I think back to my life on Sark, and all the wonderful people I knew there and all the incredible beauty I saw and created, and then I think of Cornwall, and although it was a brief moment in my life, it was a truly enlightening time. And then I think of Sophie …

'I have,' I say, feeling considerably lighter suddenly. 'I really do think that I have.'

Chapter Forty-Nine

June, then, was a month of extremes. We met often, too often, either at my apartment or to walk along the Seine in the evening before curfew. It was everything that a love affair in a beautiful city ought to be … passionate, daring, risky, intense. And yet all of the risk lay at Sophie's door. If a German soldier such as I was seen courting a Parisian woman, no German would bat an eyelid, but Sophie's fellow Parisians would not view her behaviour so lightly. I did express my concern on this, eventually, but she refused to stop meeting, arguing that, as soon as the Allies arrived in Paris, she would move far away and resume her old identity of Sophie – Juliette Vernier would no longer exist. Also, being seen to be a fornicator (I winced at her word) with a Nazi officer might lead the Gestapo off her trail.

And she needed them off her trail.

By mid-July she was at short notice to move the next tranche of children across the border. Another orphanage had been raided and searched. The children hidden there had been sent to Drancy and the teachers imprisoned awaiting execution. Someone had informed against the teachers. Mistrust ruled in Paris. Mistrust ruled the whole world.

As for myself? As the Allies forged eastwards towards Paris, my colleagues at headquarters became increasingly frazzled, which was excessively enjoyable to watch. General Wölf, to his credit, was unflappable, but then he had seen a great deal worse than the destruction of Paris during his time on the Eastern Front – not forgetting his experience of the last war, of which he was a veteran, like me. Our memories of the trenches (I awarded Sascha my record from that particular war) drew us closer, like true brothers in arms, and bit by bit, as June merged into July, we began to trust each other. On one beautiful afternoon, after sipping on champagne in his office, we took a walk down the Champs-Élysées and suddenly he stopped walking and said, 'You are not the man I expected you to be, Sascha.'

I glanced at him amusedly but my heart was racing. I decided to be as honest as I could within the limits of the game.

'I admit,' I said, 'that I am a changed man of late. That my priorities are somewhat … changed.'

He patted me firmly on the arm and nodded towards the Arc de Triomphe.

'In that case, I feel that I can confess that I do not believe we can destroy all of this … this beauty, this history. Even if the Führer wishes it.'

And somehow I knew that he was not trying to trick me and that the tide was turning on Hitler – that perhaps all across Europe, officers of the Reich were beginning to say, 'I do not believe we should do this' – and together, Wölf and I, could save Paris. We simply had to make it look as though we were not intending to, just until the Allies arrived. *Please, God*, I thought, *let them get here soon*.

'We need another plan – a parallel one. A plan to save Paris and all the artwork in the Louvre and so on – and not for us, but for the French.'

I looked at him straight. 'I have already made a parallel plan, the beginnings of one at least.'

'Show me,' he said, turning briskly on his heels.

I made many plans in July – was it really only last month? – one of which I made with Sophie and it was our eventual plan of escape. Sophie was waiting for a signal to move the children, and when she made her move, she would be gone for two weeks. On return, if the Allies were approaching the city, she would hold fast working at the café, support any final children that had been placed into hiding at the children's home, and wait for the rumble of Allied tanks to hit the Champs-Élysées. But what of me, she asked. How would I persuade the Allies when they rounded up the Nazis, as they surely would, that I was not Sascha Braun at all, but Sebastian, an Allied spy? I told her not to worry. This possible eventuality had been considered during the planning phase in Scotland. When my job was complete and I had exhausted all relevant information and the Allies were pounding on the doors, I would slip into civilian clothes provided for me by Magician, assume a French identity – the paperwork for which was already secured – and simply walk away from the city. And I would walk west, I said, in the direction of home.

'And will you walk away with me?' I asked one evening. We were in the apartment, dancing. It was a muggy night. The windows were cracked slightly and the blinds were closed but the slow, soulful music being played in the club two buildings away filtered into the room, and we swayed along. Despite everything, we were so incredibly happy.

'I'll walk anywhere with you,' she said, swaying seductively, her hips against mine, her head tucked into my shoulder. 'Where would you like to go?'

I stopped dancing and looked down at her. 'Home,' I said. 'To Sark.'

'Then that's where we will walk to,' she said. 'Or even better, gallop! If only I could find a damn horse!'

We laughed like teenagers who had not one care in the world, and I surprised her by quickly throwing her over my shoulder and heading off to the bedroom, while she screamed out in happiness. But as I gently lay her down on the bed and she began to unbutton my shirt, there came a pounding on the main door. Her hands stopped.

'Only the Gestapo knocks that way,' she whispered.

'They wouldn't have bothered knocking,' I said, standing and buttoning my shirt. I kissed her on the nose. 'Hide.'

There were two men at the door, one tall and blonde, one short and dark with a gap between his upper front teeth. Sophie was right: Gestapo. They did not wait for an invitation to come inside and yet greeted me with the warmth of acquaintances. Had my journey to Paris been satisfactory? They had not seen me in a while … not since Munich. Did I miss Berlin?

I offered them coffee or wine. One took coffee, the other wine.

My teapot was sitting in its box on a side table. One of the men removed it from its box.

'I see you've begun collecting already, Sascha!' he said.

I took the teapot from him and thought it best to play down the piece by using it to make the coffee.

'A cheap reproduction,' I said. 'I was fooled into purchasing it some years ago. But I liked it so I kept it.'

The conversation was bizarre. Had I prepared a list of new items, they asked? What was the date of the next drop?

It was difficult to appear completely composed and in full understanding of the facts when I hadn't an idea of the true topic, and then I remembered the attaché case and the lists of items in the ledger, and the obscene amount of money handed over for most transactions, and then the mist began to clear. It was as I suspected: Sascha had developed a side line in the selling of antiquities – antiquities twice stolen, first from the Jewish community, and then from the Reich. And these men, although certainly Gestapo, had their fingers in the till too. The only way out, as one of my SEO colleagues had said, was to bluff my way through it and to speak as little as possible. I thought of the Louvre and how I was working with General Wölf to secure the artwork, and so I told them that I would soon have greater treasures than any that had gone before, but they needed to give me time.

'How much time?' the blonde one asked.

'A month,' I said.

He scoffed.

'You have two weeks, our contact leaves for Vienna then and the goods will go with him.'

'Two weeks is not enough,' I said. 'And the Allies will not be here inside the month. We have time, surely it is better to …'

But I did not have the chance to explain. He took out his pistol and pushed it into my throat.

'All right. You have three weeks,' he sneered, 'or else that new General of yours will soon find out all about your dirty little secret. And don't think the fact that you've been parading that whore of yours around town will make any difference. You will understand that our colleagues take immense pleasure in dealing with your kind, let us say, in the most appropriate manner …'

And then he spat in my face. 'Three weeks,' he repeated, leaving as suddenly as they arrived, ridiculous in their melodrama, and all I could think was, *thank God they didn't find Sophie*.

That was on the fifteenth of July, the day I woke up to the reality of my situation. Yes, I had always known that impersonating my brother was a crazy, almost suicidal undertaking, and despite my pacifist leanings, had come to believe that it really was the obligation of every person in the free world to find a way to do their bit. But this … Sascha was crooked, and the fool had somehow found the nerve to double-cross even the Nazis. But Sascha wasn't here anymore, I was. The man who always seems to dodge any kind of danger had done it again. *I* had fired the bullet for him at the Tir national, then Father had kept him safe during the last war, and Hitler had kept him safe in Berlin during this one, and while other men fought and died, he had not only hidden away in the safety of Berlin but had been running a racketeering business on the side, selling off the possessions of Jews to line his own pocket. I felt sick at the thought of his depravation. I told Magician of the encounter and he had only one word to say: 'Fuck!'

Two days later my life deteriorated further, and on two counts.

On arrival at the Hotel Lutetia I was summoned directly to General Wölf's office. The glance he threw me was furtive and when Freda entered the room behind me he told her to leave and suggested she return to her apartment and finalise the packing of her case ready for her departure. She closed the door behind her.

'Freda is leaving you?' I asked.

He gestured to the chair opposite his desk.

'I'm sending all my administrative staff back to Germany tomorrow.'

'Really? But won't that look as though …?'

'We've lost? Yes. You've seen the quality of my troops here – the very young, the very old, the reservists. All the decent men are in the east. We don't stand a chance.' He sat back in his chair and closed his eyes, before asking, 'How are the plans coming along?'

'I've begun the removal of the major art works to safe houses.'

'Who is helping you?'

I hesitated, but with the Allies approaching ever faster, it seemed ridiculous to lie to a man equally as implicit.

'I have a French contact.'

'Collaborator?'

'Let's just say it's someone in the art world who is sympathetic to the cause.' (It was Magician, the most elusive and sought after spy in France).

'Good. When the Allies come they will hear that you and I were the saviours of antiquity. That should stand us in good stead afterwards, don't you think? They will reward us with benevolence for disobeying the Führer and having the honour of doing the right thing by Paris, will they not?'

Ah. So that was his ruse?

'I should think so,' I said. 'Although I doubt the Fuhrer will see things quite the same way, should you leave before the Allies arrive.'

Wölf took a deep breath. 'I shall not return to Germany just yet, I think. But there was something else I wanted to speak to you about …'

'Oh?'

'I was paid a visit by a couple of our friends in the Gestapo …' He paused as if encouraging me to interject, but I waited. 'They wanted information on someone they refer to as the woman at table seven.'

My pulse quickened.

'Go on.'

'They showed me these photographs …' He handed an envelope to me. In the first photograph I am sitting at my usual table at the Café des Fleurs, looking up at Sophie as she serves me at our table, the next she is sitting there by herself. Another photograph shows Sophie entering my apartment, while the fourth shows Sophie sitting inside the café with a number of men.

'Two of those men are now dead,' he said. 'Shot this morning as enemies of the Reich.'

Should I shrug it off or be angry, I wonder. I opt for brusque.

'I do not know the men and the woman is no one special, just a very pretty face I could not resist. She gave me the impression she was interested and I followed up on it … I thought it better than frequenting the brothels. I shall not see her again if you would prefer, but I am certain she's of no risk.'

'There was a suggestion …' He put his elbows on the desk and rested his chin on crossed fingers. 'A suggestion that, your liaison with this woman might be a smoke screen.'

I absolutely did not follow his line on this and my expression must have shown that.

'That your sexual activities in the past … well, let us say, they might have led you to find yourself compromised.'

What on earth had Sascha been up to?

I stood. 'I assure you, General, I have done nothing by which my position could be compromised. These men from the Gestapo … I am guessing that one was blonde and my height and the other short with a gap between his front teeth?'

'Well … yes, but?'

It was time to turn the tables. It is often said that fear of a thing can be greater than the thing itself. That was not the case with the Gestapo. They were an evil tribe. Nevertheless, the end was coming, and it was time to remember my training with the SOE, turn the tables and fight back.

'They have already paid me a visit, suggesting I supply them with art, presumably for their own purposes to sell after the war, or before, depending upon their contacts. I was to receive a generous cut, apparently.'

'But how can they possibly have known to come to you … how would they know of your role here?'

Despite having the name and rank of someone who should be as wily as a cat, General Wölf was, on occasion, somewhat naïve. He was old-school German, of that I had no doubt, which could only play in my favour.

'Come, General!' I said. 'Isn't it obvious? You have a mole … Freda perhaps?'

He glanced towards the closed door, confused.

'Freda? But surely?'

'It must be someone. All I know is that I was in bed with a beautiful woman one minute and had a revolver to my throat the next.'

Wölf ran anxious fingers through his silver hair. 'Good God! What did you say to that?'

'Say? What could I say? I bluffed it out. They've given me three weeks to supply adequate loot, or else…'

'Or else, what?'

I was so far into the roleplay I was almost believing it myself, and it wasn't all a lie as my story was partly true.

'I have no idea.'

He shook his head. 'It will be the woman they will punish – to punish you. They suggested that there was more to tell about her, but didn't say what and I didn't push it. They must have something on her – or are framing her – poor bitch. I doubt she'll live the week out.'

'What?'

He glanced at me, annoyed by my tone.

I must be careful. I must be careful.

'I thought she was nothing more than a whore to you?' he said.

I wafted my hand to dismiss it. 'You are right, General. I apologise for my tone. It just seems somewhat unfair on the girl, that is all.'

'Unfair?' he repeated with a snort. 'I sometimes wonder who you really are, Sascha? The woman at table seven was mysterious enough, but you, perhaps, are even more so. Your reputation suggested a personality belonging to a different man altogether. Do not mistake me, I am pleased – for the sake of Paris – that you are not a brute. But be careful, Sascha. If you are starting to make friends with the enemy – even to save Paris – then remember that the Allies are a month away still, and it is not too late to find yourself drowning in high water, and I will not be able to act as a float.'

I was dismissed and walked to the door.

'Do we understand each other?' he said as I turned the handle.

'Perfectly,' I answered, before opening the door. Neither one of us saluted.

I left for the café but called first at the apartment to change my shirt which was drenched from nervous sweat beneath my tunic. As I sought the key from a pocket, I noticed Sophie hidden inside the doorway. She was wearing her familiar yellow silk scarf worn as a turban around her head. Her eyes were tearstained. She lowered her head when she saw me.

'I can't stay,' she whispered, her tone urgent as she pressed a letter into my hands. 'And I can't see you again, not here, not like this. I've written some things down.' She nodded towards the letter. 'Read this straight away, and then burn it.' She turned away. The street was empty so I grabbed her arm.

'Please, Sophie. Just come inside and tell me what on earth has happened.'

Tears appeared, a shower running over her lips. Her eyes reached out, pleading for me to understand. I touched her face but again she turned away to leave. My hand caught the scarf, which fell away, and what I saw acted as the awakening I had needed from the moment our affair began.

Sophie's head had been shaved, and not carefully. Whoever held the blade had cut her scalp in several places.

'Who did this?' I asked, my temper almost uncontrollable.

'Just some friends,' she answered, looking at her feet.

'Friends!? But what kind of friends would do such a thing?'

'Resistance friends.'

'Why?'

She glanced up. 'It's what they do to women these days … women who cavort with Nazis. They shave their heads so that everyone can know that they have … been corrupted. I'm so ashamed, Sebastian. What will the children think of me now?'

With shaking hands she retied the scarf around her head. It was not a good time for more bad news, but it had to be said. 'The Gestapo are watching you,' I whispered. 'Is there anywhere you can hide? With the children, perhaps?'

She nodded.

'I know about the Gestapo. And there is a place. I've already arranged to go there.'

'When?'

'Tomorrow.'

'Then stay here tonight,' I said. 'Don't be forced to walk the streets feeling as you do. We will huddle on the sofa and keep watch, and you can go directly to your safe place in the morning.'

She pulled away and ran the back of her hand across her eyes and nose.

'I can't,' she said. 'Louis will wonder where I am.'

I looked at her then, as if for the first time, and realised how utterly perfect she was, more so now than ever, and how terribly unfair it was in life that women must always suffer for the inhumanity of men. Would a man who had 'cavorted' with a German woman have been treated in such a way? He would not. Such was the persecution of women. And for my part, I had enabled it.

'This is all my fault,' I said. 'When I saw you across the street I should have stayed away, but I couldn't … I just couldn't. I've been so selfish, Sophie. So ridiculously, terribly selfish.'

She rested a hand on my arm briefly. 'We have both been

foolish,' she said, 'but not selfish. Never selfish.' She held my gaze through her tears. 'I must go. I need to think. But please, read the letter, and never give up, Sebastian. Whatever happens now. Never give up.'

'Please, just wait,' I said, grabbing her arm. 'I have something for you … please, Sophie.'

I ran up the stairs and ripped the cushions off the sofa. I had sewn Sascha's money into the lining. I ripped out great handfuls, stuffed them into a pillowcase and ran back down the stairs. Thank God, she was waiting for me.

'Take this!' I said.

She glanced inside the pillowcase.

'But I can't possibly …'

'You can. It was Sascha's and I suspect it was not earned but stolen – from the Jewish community. I beg you to take it. Use it to help the children. Bribe if you have to. Paris is about to explode. You just need to find a way to make it through the coming weeks – or even days – until the Allies arrive. Please, Sophie. Take it.'

She stood on her toes to brush my cheek with hers, and I heard the echoes of her sobs as she ran down the road.

Darling, Sebastian

I write this note in haste to say that we cannot see each other for the remainder of our time in Paris. We must wake up to our situation. You are Sascha Braun, a Nazi senior officer, and I am a French woman. It was only a matter of time until I was watched, by my own people as well as the Gestapo. I must take what has happened as a stark reminder to return to my duty. But please do know one thing: I love you with every ounce of my body and soul and I do not regret the days we were gifted in Paris. If I am not to survive this war, then I will die knowing that I have experienced something truly incredible – magical – because for the first time in my life I have known the absolute pleasure of passionate and everlasting love. You once said that you didn't believe in Romeo and Juliet, that the lovers should have found another way – to live, not to die. You and I will not end our days with some hare-brained scheme, where you think I've swallowed my cyanide pill, but really, I haven't and then you swallow yours and it all goes horribly wrong. No. That is not the way for us. We are both far too clever for that.

So here is a plan – a promise.

On the day the liberation forces arrive, as I am certain they will, take off your uniform, dress in your peasant's clothes and find a way to meet me at Le Jardin du Sénat, at the fountain of the observatory at one p.m. and as the American tanks roll in, you and I will walk away to the west together as planned. If I am not there, then try the next day and then the next, but only for a week, after which time, don't hesitate to walk away alone. Remember Occam's Razor? The most obvious answer is the correct one? If I am not there, then I am most likely dead. Whatever happens now, never give in, not until the very last moment, but keep planning, hoping, scheming and there is always a chance, as slight as it may be, on changing the outcome.

We both have things to do now, but please, please take the greatest of care and God willing, we will meet again.

With all of my love, for always,

S

Chapter Fifty

The following three weeks were a blur. With the help of Magician, artwork was hidden around the city and plans to secure Paris were made. The hardest part was not knowing what had happened to Sophie. If I were to make enquiries then I would only arouse even greater suspicion and lead the Gestapo directly to her door. General Wölf was agitated and fatalistic in equal measure. He was trying to control a city that was quickly turning into a melting pot – evacuating some of the troops while leaving sufficient on guard to prove that the occupying force did not think Paris would soon fall. A sense of order needed to be maintained amongst the Parisians who were prone, historically, to revolt. The city was a tinderbox, primed and ready to ignite at a moment's notice, leading the Gestapo to become more suspicious and even more vicious, if that was possible. The thinly disguised chaos of the Wehrmacht meant that it was straightforward for me to pick up snippets of information, which I readily handed over to Magician. Yes, I was telling tales on my countrymen, but they were Nazis; some were reluctant ones, but they had all carried out the wishes of the Führer, and the war had to end. It was as simple as that.

When my three weeks' grace from the Gestapo came to an end there was the inevitable knock on the door and when it came I was ready for them, thanks to Merlin, who had gathered together several small crates of worthless objets d'art. So long as they were not experts – and I doubted that they were – the crates could be taken away and I would be gone before they realised they had been tricked. I hid my teapot, of course. There was no way I would gift them my teapot. I was also ready for them in a way I had not anticipated. Magician decided that it was time to turn the tables on the cowards who hid behind the reputation of the Gestapo in order to manipulate life to suit their needs. It was time to take them down at the knees, he said, and we would use the teapot to poison the evil bastards. I was not pleased that he had used the word 'we'. Despite everything, the words of Edith Cavell would always echo in my ears, and I still believed that killing any man was not only never the answer, but that with each further death, more pieces of my own soul would be destroyed. I had been responsible for so many deaths in the last war – countless – that I felt I had very little soul left to give, which was why I refused to be a part of it.

'Then we shall drug them,' he said. 'I shall arrange for them to be taken away … for questioning. You need to know no more than that.' He slapped me on the back and laughed. 'There will be a wonderful irony to it – using an assassin's teapot to drug two assassins, because make no mistake, Sebastian, the only reason they have not killed you yet is because they need you. That brother of yours must have had quite the racket going.'

I knew better than to refuse Magician completely – he was

dangerous in his own right – and so when the knock came to the door, I greeted them as friends, showed them crates full of priceless items awaiting their collection, told them I had only coffee, took out my assassin's teapot, and poisoned them.

It was all so unbelievably simple.

Which was why I was surprised the following day when I entered General Wölf's office, ready to hand in the two final sets of plans he requested for the salvation of Paris, only to find two further members of the Gestapo standing behind him as he sat at his desk.

Wölf's expression as I entered was impossible to read, except that it was a display of extreme discomfort. Were those piercing eyes telling me to run, or was he showing his anger? I could not say, but I did not have to wait long to find out.

He rubbed his forehead. 'These men have come to question you, Braun.' His voice was steady if tinged with fatalism.

'Oh?' I placed the file I was carrying on Wölf's desk. He glanced at it nervously. 'How may I help you, gentlemen?'

They could be here for three reasons, I deduced: they had either discovered my true identity, arrested Sophie, or uncovered our plan to save Paris.

It was none of them.

Wölf stood, navigated his way around the desk and offered me yet another envelope.

'Open it,' he said.

Inside were more photographs, which were enlightening in that a great many issues regarding my brother and my family suddenly made complete sense. Sascha was homosexual – the photographs were explicit and his preference was perfectly clear. I felt both sorry for him at having to hide for all those years and angry that it was I, once again, that would shoulder the consequences. So this was what the men in my apartment meant by having evidence of my 'ways'. How the photographs had arrived on the desks of the new men, I had no idea except to assume that it had all been part of an elaborate plan, no doubt, with Sascha set up the whole time to be discovered. He had been such a fool to dance with the devil in this way.

'Do you deny that one of the men in the photograph is you?' asked Wölf. His glance suggested I had tricked him in the most underhand manner.

Did I deny it? What an impossible situation to find myself in. In order to deny it I would have to declare that I was not, after all, Sascha, but his twin brother, working for the British SOE. To do so would find me shot in the head where I stood.

'I do not deny it.' I gestured towards the file on his desk. 'The plans you asked for are there.'

He nodded curtly.

'Everyone warned me that you could not be trusted,' he said, 'but I thought I knew you better than that. They were right to watch you, the man hanging around at table seven, because Lord alone knows who you really are.'

At this point I had nothing to lose.

'Shall I tell you who the man at table seven is?' I asked. 'He is the same man that sits at table two, or five or nine. He is every single man who is sick of political games. Countries all over the world are run by the wrong people. No one who *wants* to be in power should be allowed to be there. I'm sick of alliances and stand-offs and trade-offs and greed and self-interest. I'm outraged beyond comprehension that in 1914 a small bust-up between two insignificant territories led to a pile-on of countries taking one side or the other when truly, all they had in mind was self-interest, leading to the deaths of millions of men. And after that, I was outraged that one small insignificant but insane man was allowed to pray on the embarrassment of an unnecessarily humiliated nation to create a monster of a country I no longer wish to call my own. The man at table seven has only ever wanted to live a small life in peace while pottering in his garden and tending to the sick, but the wants and needs of others prevented him from doing so. But you know what, Wölf? Above all, the man at table seven feels like a failure, because he knows that he should live by the maxim that patriotism is not enough, and that he should feel no hatred or bitterness towards anyone. And yet, I cannot. I have failed in my principles. That is all you really need to know.'

Wölf pulled the file towards him and turned to the two men.

'Take him away.'

Chapter Fifty-One

La Sante Prison, August 1944

'And they brought you here,' says Christoph.

'Not at first. I went elsewhere for interrogation and a beating, and then more followed. I made out that I was left-handed – something I was taught by the SOE.' I raise my left hand and turn it while assessing the form. 'It is healing in a deformed shape, I'm afraid, but my right?' I lift it up. 'As you see, it's slightly better. I manipulated the bones into place and bandaged it with strips of my clothing. I knew that I could still attend to my patients one day if it was mended, you see ... but that is irrelevant now.'

'I noticed it before,' he says. 'I'm sorry. But tell me, what happened after the beating?'

'The Gestapo handed me to the SS who were no more lenient. They wanted to know who the other man from the photograph was and who else in Paris was involved in my activities. But I could not tell them what I did not know. And so they beat me more for protecting him.'

'Him?'

'The man in the photograph. His face was obscured due to the nature of the act – I'm sorry if that shocks you.'

'It does not.'

'I thought they would beat me until my last breath came, but they must have moved onto a more interesting catch as I was thrown into this cell, and after several days of waiting to die, of listening to others die in the courtyard above me, you came …'

'I'm so very sorry,' he says, tipping his head forward and rubbing his brow. I was pleased to see that his spectacles did not slip down his nose.

'Don't be. You have helped me through the worst days of my life, and for what it is worth, during the limited time that I have left, I will be forever grateful.'

He stands but does not begin to collect his things. Instead, he steps towards me and takes my face in his hands and I see that silent tears have begun to ebb down his face. 'Nevertheless,' he says. 'I am truly sorry that this has happened to you. More than you can ever know.' He picks up his cap and steps towards the door. 'I will return tomorrow.'

'How long do I have?' I ask it in barely more than a whisper, as if asking quietly makes it more bearable somehow. With only the thin, splintered light of the grate lighting the cell, we hold each other's gaze. 'I'm ready to know now,' I say.

'They are working down a list, and your crime is less severe than some others, but I heard that a Nazi commander in Caen executed all of his prisoners in one session yesterday – a last show of aggression. He wanted to hide all traces of his work before the Allies move in. Tracks are being covered.'

'Give me a date, Christoph.'

'Day after tomorrow.'

I thought of Sophie's letter – *do not give in until the very end*. The end? I was surely there now.

'In that case, dry your eyes, my friend as I have two tasks for you, and I would swear my allegiance to Christ forever if you would only carry them out for me.'

He smiles and wipes a hand across his face. 'I can hardly refuse that. What are they?'

'I need to know what happened to Sophie. Go for me to the Café des Fleurs, it's on the Champs-Élysées, and ask after her. They will speak with a chaplain, I'm sure.'

He raises his brows. 'A German one?'

'If she is dead they have nothing to lose. I would like to pass over knowing that she is going to survive this thing.'

'Very well. And the second?'

'I wonder if you might accept a little generosity – a thank you, for all that you have done for me?'

'It is unlikely, but …'

'You remember I told you about my teapot …'

'The assassin's teapot? Of course. I should like to have seen it.'

'Hear me out and you shall. I know it will be difficult for you to cross town, what with your breathlessness – which must be examined properly, Christoph – especially as you will have already been to the café, but I need you to go to my apartment. There is a key that I hid for Sophie behind a broken tile above the door. Once inside …'

'But I couldn't—'

'No, please, let me finish. The teapot is in a box inside an antique dresser in the lounge. You will also find a tea caddy in the kitchen, inside are some dried rose petals. When you come tomorrow, bring the teapot and the caddy and bring spare fuel for the stove. The petals are from my mother's favourite rose, you remember – the Apothecary's Rose?'

'I do. I sought out some petals myself you may remember.'

'Ah, of course. You did. But the point is, if you do this, the teapot is yours thereafter – it is worth a great deal of money. You could sell it and help the poor, or do whatever you religious types choose to do after the war to cleanse your souls. Bring me the teapot, Christoph. I am ready to go now.'

'Are you? It would soothe me greatly if I thought that that were true, that you felt you had had a good life.'

I shake my head and smile.

'My life? Let me tell you about my life. In my teenage years I shot a defenceless woman at short range and was then pushed into the most terrible war the world had ever known, where the levels of suffering and inhumane depravity would make hell look like a holiday. Having survived physically if not mentally, I began to travel, to search, to wander, to find peace, to serve my countrymen as a doctor, and then, having finally found peace and having eventually known what it is to love, to truly love, I was moved on. I went to England, to a place of safety, but again I was told, you cannot stay here, you have the wrong blood, the wrong passport, the wrong accent. My life, looked at in such a way, has been hell. But speaking with you, I have found that if I write my story in another way, if I spin the yarn with a lighter thread, I can only conclude that I have been blessed. Five years ago I was happy. I was living a simple life tending to people and to the natural world around me. I knew what it was to enjoy birdsong, to grow my own food and raise a little livestock. It was enough. My dear friend,' I conclude, 'how can I not be ready for death, when I have known life – I saw this planet – *this* planet! I've known passion. I know what it is to see a dog's face welcome me at a cottage door. I have made the sick well. I have felt the cold sea on my warm skin. Yes, I have known disappointment, but I have also known joy. So let us conclude that yes, I have had a good life, and I am ready.'

He smiles. 'Then I shall carry out your wishes,' he says, heading to the door. 'But regarding your story, one final detail is unfinished. Did Sophie ever tell you her real name? Her nationality? Her true motivation for being here?'

'She did not,' I say.

'Do you know why?'

'I presume it was because, in the end, I did not ask.'

Christoph knocks on the door for the guard to come. 'Heil Hüttler, Sebastian,' he says, the tinkle in his voice unmistakable. The door opens and I know that never in my life was there such a friend – such a kindred spirit – as this.

Chapter Fifty-Two

La Sante Prison, August 1944

'And if you look inside, you will see the teapot has two chambers,' I say. 'If you were wishing to poison me, for example, then my tea would go in one chamber, and yours in the other. I will demonstrate with water first.' I attempt a laugh. 'And if you ever use this in anger, my friend, it would not be a good idea for you to do it the wrong way around!' Christoph does not smile at my joke, so I move on to demonstrate which hole to place a finger over to allow water to pour out of which chamber. He concentrates intensely and then practises with plain water.

'What news of Sophie?' I ask. Christoph has barely spoken since his arrival. In fact, he seems to be in a monastic trance. His breath is especially laboured today. If only there were more light and I had my doctor's bag with me, I would be able to assess him properly – a final gift.

He takes as deep a breath as his body will allow. 'The café was raided two days ago,' he says.

'It was burned to the ground. I asked the neighbours and they said that Louis Vernier was shot dead in the street by the Gestapo. I saw the mark of his blood on the pavement. I am sorry, Sebastian.'

'What about the children's home? Any news of that?'

'That also was raided.'

I braced myself to ask the final question.

'And Sophie … Juliette?'

'No one knew. She has not been seen since her head was shaved. Some thought her dead, others that she had fled. I did my best, Sebastian, but I'm afraid that is all I know. But forgive me – and I know how greatly you love her – but perhaps it is time to focus on this moment and carry out our final tea ceremony together, if we are both truly ready. I'm afraid I will not see you again after today.'

'You will not be with me, when they come for me?' I ask.

He does not look up from his task. 'That will not be possible,' he says as the water begins to boil on the stove. 'Come then!' he adds, his manner suddenly joyful. 'Let us not think of such things now, let us enjoy this very moment, let us eat the food I have prepared and drink the tea that is infused with your mother's love.'

I nod, and for a final time feel disappointment slide down my spine.

And so we eat, and somehow, we laugh. Christoph asks of my childhood with Sascha, encouraging me to remember the happy times, of which, now that I remember, there were many. Ultimately the conversation lulls and we sober our thoughts. It is time for tea and all that has begun to be associated with it between the two of us within this little cell of mine. Christoph takes longer over the ceremony today. He has removed his boots and coat and has draped them carefully across the stool he brought on his second visit. The whisk turns methodically, first in one chamber, then in the other. His purpose, I know, is to bring me to the moment.

'Close your eyes,' he whispers. 'Feel the presence of your body – every muscle, every bone, every fibre. Know what it is to be a soul within a body. Be present.'

I do as I am bid, but no matter how often I practised this ritual with Fortune, no matter how expertly she guided me through life and towards death, here, today, knowing what tomorrow will bring, all I can think of, all I can see, is the love I have known and all of the people that have blessed it. When I open my eyes Christoph is smiling at me. After we bow to each other he hands me a steaming cup infused with rose petals, and the steam, when I hold it to my face, is my mother's love rising up to me.

Christoph removes his spectacles and holds his own cup to his face for several moments, also taking in the scent, before closing his eyes and drinking back the tea in one long thirsty motion, as if all the tea in the teapot would not be enough to quell his thirst, then he leans his back against the damp cell wall and finally, closing his eyes, he relaxes.

'What will you think of, when they come for you?' he asks me.

The question surprises me. I take a sip of my tea and think of a letter I once wrote to another padre, in another time. I had said that I would think of Sark, of its beauty, of home.

'I will try to think of all the things I have loved,' I say, 'and try to swaddle myself in that love, which I do see now, is eternal.'

'Tell me about it again,' he says, his eyes still closed, his breath calm and slow.

And so I tell him. I tell him of Germany and of my mother's

garden and how her eyes were always full of love and yes, I speak even of Sascha, for I hold no bitterness towards my brother now, there really is no point. And I tell him once again of my great luck at meeting Fortune and Bunny, and the raw beauty of Cornwall, and Elijah, and the hedgerows – I linger a long while on the hedgerows. And then, of course, I turn for home. To Sark and my cottage and my garden, every path and verge and wild flower, and eventually, ultimately, I turn to Sophie, and her smile, and her vibrance and her life.

'It's odd,' I say, a thought coming to me, 'that the memories I wish to remember are mainly ones created since the war began. Sophie, Cornwall, and you too, Christoph, you have all seeped into my existence and nourished it. And Sophie, you know, went so far as to succeed where Juliet failed: she kissed life back into her Romeo. I can only conclude that while the last war took my life away from me, somehow, this one gave it back … for a little while, at least.'

I chatter on for a while, reminiscing, talking of anything rather than let the space in, and when at last I have told him of all the love I have ever known, I notice that he has fallen to sleep. I should leave him to rest, I think, but the damp wall against his weak chest will not award him comfort later. I touch his leg.

'I'm afraid I have bored you, my friend.' I feign laughter and shake harder. 'Christoph … my good friend.'

I crawl to him and touch his face. His head falls forward.

'Christoph.' I shake him. 'Christoph!'

But this cannot be.

Taking a moment to think, to process, I take him by the shoulders and lay him down. I feel his

neck for a pulse. There is none. I grab the lantern and lift his eyelids – nothing. I try and try to resuscitate, before ultimately having to accept what I knew when I first grabbed his leg – my friend, my brother, has gone.

Struggling to understand, I hold him in my arms and rock him. After some moments, confused and desperate, I rest my friend against the wall and notice a piece of paper clutched in his left hand. I gently unfold his warm fingers and hold the note to the lantern.

My final gift to you is the gift of life. Do not waste it with grief and do not tarry. I gave the guard a bottle of cognac as I entered the cell. He is French and I think without any particular loyalty to the Reich. He will be drunk by now. Swap our clothes, put on my spectacles, pull down the cap, grab your teapot and go. In the left breast pocket of my jacket there are two letters. One is for you and one for Sascha. The price for your freedom is for you to deliver the letter to him one day, that is all. My letter to you explains everything, but do not read it now. Right now you must put any sorrow you have for me in your pocket with the letters, make the most of this opportunity and go. Goodbye, dear Sebastian, and good luck!

I look at the teapot and the realisation seeps in that Christoph has used it – my own trick – to take his own life.

Minutes later, I step out into the Parisian sunshine while trying to disguise my difficulty in walking, push Christoph's spectacles up the brow of my nose, and slowly, regretfully, I walk away.

Chapter Fifty-Three

To Sebastian, my friend.

There is a great deal to explain, but this is a better way to do it, I think.

You may recall that on my first visit I referred to you as Sascha when I entered the cell. That was because I believed, very briefly, that you were him. I knew Sascha very well, you see, because I am afraid to say that I am the man in the photograph; Sascha was my partner, my lover, my life, and you can't know what a relief it is to finally say it out loud, or if not out loud, on paper at least. Sascha and I were based at the same barracks in Berlin for much of the war. I'm sorry I let you believe that I was the prison chaplain when I was not. I am a chaplain, that much is true, but I gained entry each day because the guards were corruptible and I wore a cross. As you said, with rank comes privilege; it was that straightforward.

As soon as you declared yourself to be Sebastian I knew that it was true – I know my Sascha, and although the similarity is uncanny, he is not you and you are not him. You once said that only your mother could tell you apart, well now you can add two more names to the list – myself, and Sophie. It is ironic that I am writing this note while sitting in the apartment that would have been Sascha's had you not come along and saved his life. You did not intend to, of course, but he is alive today because of you. The least I could do, I decided, was to keep you alive too, and my plan, if it works, will produce an outcome that is fortuitous for both of us. I am ill – as you know – and the reason I would not allow you to examine me is because I have already been examined and my malady is of such a severity that I have six months to live at the most. When you told me about the teapot it seemed to provide the perfect solution – I cannot think of a better way to say goodbye to this world than to take tea with a man I have grown to love like a brother one final time, before passing quietly away. Knowing that I am giving a life to someone while helping my own to drift away awards me great peace and comfort – the method is a tad melodramatic, I grant you, but if you only knew of all the other ways I have imagined to break you out of La Santé then you would be grateful that I chose this one! Some might say that I am flying in the face of God by doing this, but I have searched my soul and conscience and I do not believe this to be true. Please do not feel one ounce of guilt or regret once I am gone, the alternative was to stand by as you were executed while knowing that I would die a miserable death alone before the year was out. This way, I will not be alone, I will be with you and in you, I will have my God with me.

I must not tarry, but it is vital before I go that I tell you about Sascha because he is not the man you think him to be. You think him to be an unpleasant brute of a man, but he is not. You were right to say that your father twisted him into a grotesque image of himself, and I'm certain that you are correct in saying that he did this because he suspected that Sascha was the type of man of which he did not approve or understand. The most important thing for you to know is that during this war, during his time in Berlin, Sascha worked covertly with me to improve the lives of many by stealing from the

Nazis (who first stole from the Jews) and every single penny he earned in his highly dangerous business came to me – the money was thereafter spent on those who needed it most. In your story you said that Sascha had ordered you shot if you did not return to Germany. This was not correct. He would never have done that. Nevertheless, he knew that you would not be allowed to stay on your island and so made it clear that you were to be brought back to Germany by any means. Once home he intended to keep you safe for the duration of the war. He loves you dearly Sebastian, much more than you can ever know. He is an exceptional man who I am proud to have loved and I am not ashamed of that love. It was God given, I am sure of that now.

So now it is my turn to make demands, and here is what I want you to do:

Firstly, if you are at the apartment reading this, when you leave please take the attaché case with you. I will explain why momentarily. Secondly, when the Allies arrive do go to your fountain and wait for Sophie, but please, Sebastian, do not wait forever. Do as Sophie said, and if she is not there during the first days of liberation, move on. If she is alive she will find you one day, of that I am certain. And this leads me on to a most important point: in the years to come, if you do not after all find Sophie, you might feel desperately lost and lonely and wonder what might have been – I feel this now about Sascha. You may also experience some guilt because you feel that you ought to be very happy. After all, you will tell yourself, Christoph gave his life so that I might live! But do remember that I was a dying man, and so what I am trying to say very simply is, whatever comes, give it time, my friend. Give it time.

Thirdly, once the situation with Sophie is resolved, seek out your contact, Magician, and arrange passage to London – not Sark. The SOE will wish to debrief you on your experience with the Wehrmacht and General Wölf and you will not be safe in Paris. Yes, your French is good, but someone may recognise you as a disguised German *officer, and if they do they will shoot you, I have no doubt about that. Also, you must insist that the British send you for medical help for your hands and for a general health check. Yes, I know that you are the doctor, but I ask that you do this for your own good, your own future. And finally, I want you to promise to seek out Sascha in London. Inside the attaché case you will find proof of our activities and how he was not faithful to the Reich. Further evidence can be gained from other sources to prove his actions. It would be tragic for Sascha to be imprisoned as a war criminal, when the absolute truth of the matter is that he is not.*

My last request is to ask you to hand Sascha my letter, and make peace with him. He loves you so dearly. He has never forgotten your kindness or your sacrifice at the Tir national that day. The sad reality is that he was always on the brink of coming to Sark to see you, but at the last moment he would always change his mind, frightened of rejection perhaps? Who knows with families? It is a most unnecessarily complex business, and one always assumes there to be more time. I ask also that you gift the teapot to Sascha, so that he can begin his life again. You gifted it to me, after all, and I would now like to pass it on to him. I suspect, when this is all over, you will return to your cottage on Sark and carry on from where you left off, a changed man, yes, but a secure one, nonetheless. The sale of the teapot would offer Sascha a new beginning, and by God, he is going to need one.

Well, that is all, my friend. It is time to begin the last day of my life, and truly, if I cannot spend it with Sascha, then it gives me great comfort to spend it with you. As I wandered away from the prison today, I walked past a school. I do not think the school has been open for some time but in the yard some children were playing, and it struck me that we really should carry on playing through life because after all, for our entire lives we are nothing more than children in a schoolyard, waiting ultimately for the bell to ring. I think the key to it all is to not worry about the bell, but to just keep playing – *die show muss weitergehen*, after all.

I am ready.

'You have made my life no longer than the width of my hand. My entire lifetime is just a moment to you; at best, each of us is but a breath'. Psalms 39:5

With God's love, my dear, dear friend.

Christoph.

Chapter Fifty-Four

Sark, October 1945

I have done – or tried to do – all that Christoph requested, and I have succeeded in the most part, except to find Sophie. A year on, and I still have not found Sophie.

The Allies rolled into Paris three days after my escape. Christoph returned the apartment key to its hiding place and on leaving the prison, knowing that I had just enough time before Christoph was found, I returned to my apartment, changed into civilian clothes and grabbed the fake documents Magician had provided for this very eventuality. Within a large satchel I placed the attaché case and the remainder of the money I had hidden, and the teapot in its box. I was ready to go.

Walking to the door of the apartment for the final time, I saw poor Christoph's clothes draped across a chair where I had quickly thrown them off. His large silver cross – Christian rather than Nazi – sat next to his boots. I grabbed the cross and his spectacles and placed them carefully into the satchel. I had known the man for less than a week, and yet I mourned him as any man would mourn a beloved brother.

For the first two days, before the Allies arrived, I hid in the park at night and roamed the streets during the day. Paris was a melting pot of confusion and dissent. Those last few German soldiers who remained were frightened – edgy. Small pockets of visible resistance began – as General Wölf had known would happen – but it was too late for Wölf and the Wehrmacht now. As word spread that the Allies were approaching the city, barricades were built across the streets and bit by bit, the faded and ripped swastikas began to disappear from the buildings, only to be replaced by homemade French flags. The tricolor was returning to Paris once more and I couldn't have been happier.

I kept to the shadows while chaos broke out on the streets as the Germans fought back with a last blast of vigour. I was proud, nonetheless, that Paris had not begun to burn at the hands of the German army. Wölf had taken my plan to save Paris and had run with it. Rather than set up incendiaries at every railway station, bridge, museum and historic landmark (as the Führer had demanded), he had slowly edged his troops out of the city, leaving only enough as a show of force. Those left were lambs to the slaughter, of course, and Wölf and his last band of men could only hope that they would be lucky to be taken as prisoners by the Allies; if not, they would be shot without hesitation by the French. Despite everything, I hoped Wölf was safe. He may not have saved me, but he had saved Paris, and that was enough to wish him well.

Three days after I left my cell the Allies rolled in, led by the Free French, and Paris, true to its history, became both a party city and a barbaric hunting ground. Collaborators found themselves in desperate need to change allegiances, but for many it was too late. Parisians who had remained loyal to free France were not a forgiving tribe. But for me, the arrival of the Allies meant renewed hope that Sophie would be able to fulfil her part of the promise. I waited by the fountain of the observatory as she requested, only leaving briefly to find food and water, before returning to watch from my makeshift camp within the shrubs. Day and night, I waited. For three long weeks I waited and I searched and then I waited some more. But with the September nights growing colder I remembered Christoph's words and accepted that even I could wait no longer. I sought out Magician and with passage secured to England, the rest of my life slowly began to take shape.

I was given a spell in a British hospital for recuperation before being granted money and accommodation in London and interviewed at length by the SOE. Then, just as Christoph said, I asked for further medical help for my hands and returned to hospital to have the left one dislocated and reset. It is not perfect, but it is an improvement. With my hand in bandages I was even given a new job. I lived in London and found myself dodging the V-bombs the Germans still threw across the Channel in their last-ditch attempt to fight back. Paris may have been liberated, but London was still at war. I stayed on until Christmas.

Tracking Sascha was not so straightforward. During my debriefing by the SOE I handed the paperwork from the attaché case to the authorities and told them Christoph's story, but they did not believe it. I tried to explain that liaising with the British would not have been Sascha and Christoph's way. Christoph was a man of the cloth, a man I owed my life to. Together, they did what they could in their own place and in their own time, but that did not make them any less deserving of recognition. Sascha had taken incredible risks, I said. But the

British saw him only as a Nazi with a deadly reputation and felt that the tale told by Christoph was the convenient story of a man attempting to save his lover. Sascha remained in prison in the north of England and I was not allowed to see him or communicate with him. Nevertheless, I believed Christoph's story, and I still do.

During those months, I found the time to cross the Channel once more and return to Paris in a desperate attempt to find Sophie. I met up with my old contact, Magician, but the news was not good. He believed that Sophie had escaped the raid on the café and the school, but heard that the last tranche of evacuee children had been captured at the Swiss border. My anger knew no bounds because I simply could not understand why the Gestapo had insisted on continuing with the barbarism of rounding up the Jewish community quite literally until the very last day of the occupation. With each passing day I moved further and further away from the ethos I had sworn by since the last war – that I must have no prejudice towards anyone.

The department I was working for wound down eventually and I found myself without employment. All I had was a teapot and a few clothes and my papers. Where would I go, they asked as I cleared my desk. With Sark still under occupation, I could only think of one place in the world I wanted to go – the only place I could feel even remotely at home – Cornwall. The scream emitted by Bunny when she opened the door to me would have shattered glass in Moscow!

I remained in Cornwall until June 1945. I laid hedges with Elijah, made bread with Bunny, and eventually, when I was ready, drank tea in the garden hut with Fortune. We carried out the ceremony as we always had, and I told Fortune about Christoph and his ultimate sacrifice and his humanity, and I told her how despite the circumstances, and despite the fear, the quiet man with the spectacles halfway down his nose had taught me not only how to live, but more importantly how to die, and then (and only then) for the first time since the whole thing began, I wept.

Sark was liberated on the 10th of May. Later, when Fortune rushed into the kitchen to announce the news that the whole of the Channel Islands were finally free, Bunny and I danced around the kitchen like wild children. We waited anxiously for further news– any news – jumping at the sound of the telephone, rushing to the postman to snatch up the post, desperate that Dame Sibyl might get in touch. It seemed utter madness that Paris had been liberated the previous August and yet the Channel Islands remained occupied in a last bloody-minded act of defiance – the Allies had thought them too strategically insignificant to bother liberating. News began to filter through of maltreatment and starvation of the islanders on Jersey and Guernsey. We could only hope that Sark had fared better, but we doubted it. The phone call we hoped for came a week after their liberation. It was Dame Sibyl. Her telephone had only recently been reconnected and she was desperate for news – had Sebastian made it to Cornwall all those years before? Was everyone safe? What had happened to the Polish prisoners? Of course, there was good news and bad, but when Dame Sibyl heard my voice down the line she began to weep. I hadn't the heart to tell her about Sophie's disappearance; she needed to enjoy liberation first, then I would tell her. I would tell her everything.

'When are you coming home?' she said, through laughter and tears. 'I have a great deal to tell you … and also, we want our doctor back!'

'As soon as I can,' I replied, shouting down the crackling line. 'I'm coming home!'

And so I have come home, to my island, to Sark.

But nothing is quite the same. The islanders have set about clearing miles of barbed wire, but the concrete gunning escarpments will prove more difficult to remove and I doubt we will ever be rid of them. My cottage is much as I had left it thanks to the efforts of Dame Sibyl and her clean-up party, and yet something about living there now does not feel quite the same. It is almost as though I am, too, an interloper. Perhaps I will feel differently one day, or perhaps I need a fresh start altogether? No, I fool myself. The truth is, I simply want Sophie to be here with me. Nothing will ever be the same unless she comes home too. Christoph was right about that. He was right about everything.

As for my garden … it is an overgrown jungle of bramble and weeds. It is incredible how quickly nature will assert itself once the hand of man retreats. Little by little, and with Joseph and Peter's help, I am persuading it back into shape, although maybe this time I will allow the wilderness in a little more – Fortune taught me that. (My mother's roses, I am pleased to say, are as strong as ever.)

It is incredible just how isolated my old neighbours have been. For the past five years they have known nothing of the war beyond their own boundaries. Abandoned in the dark, towards the end they were practically starved to death. Once France fell, it became impossible for the Germans to re-supply, leaving them to manage on practically nothing, and never had Dame Sibyl's vow that the island should be self-sufficient been more proven. With my doctor's bag in hand I have visited each of my patients in turn to offer a health check. I am not as nimble with my instruments as I once was, nor am I able to cycle around the island quite as quickly as I could, but with each day, I am improving. My rounds also take longer than usual because everyone has a story to tell and I let them tell it. It has been a bad war, they say, but not as bad as it might have been if Dame Sibyl hadn't shown those 'bloody Germans' what's what! It seems that she has been a rock and a leader to the end – dear Sibyl. As far as my own story goes, I have told it to only two people – Peter, the major (we are becoming good friends and I knew he would understand) and Dame Sibyl. I have told Dame Sibyl about Sophie, too. About her work in Paris and how she failed to meet me at the fountain.

'I have searched and searched,' I pleaded when I arrived. 'And just as soon as I can I shall return and search some more.' Dame Sibyl patted my hand.

'I know you have,' she said. 'But for now you must rest and leave the searching to me. We need you here, and honestly, Sebastian, you may have had rest and recuperation in England, but you look dreadful. Your time in prison has not served you well and you must rest. I tell you what … I'll make sure Joseph puts up a new sign dictating your surgery hours.' She winked at me. 'And the hours will be every bit as limited as before!'

That was three months ago. And I have rested and I have roamed and I have pondered, and bit by bit I am coming to settle into my old life again, but sometimes I do wonder … do I really want to?

Nevertheless, we are to have a party tonight, on my birthday of all days, at La Seigneurie. It is the autumn equinox and the whole of the island will be in attendance to celebrate the end of the occupation. Of course, the occupation ended five months ago, but Dame Sibyl felt it would be in bad taste to celebrate our freedom before the war was completely over and everyone, the world over, was free. And now it is over and we are all relieved but wondering what on earth was the point of it all, which is exactly how I felt after the last one. Joseph has built a bonfire but I am not in the mood to party. I would much rather light a fire in my own garden to burn away some of the weeded detritus, grab a chair and a glass of elderflower wine (Joseph hid a couple of bottles for me – good man) and raise a glass to my dear friend, Christoph. But I cannot let Dame Sibyl down, so I shall paint on a smile and go to La Seigneurie. But every room, every window, every part of the garden reminds me of Sophie and disappointment no longer slips down my spine, but has embedded itself permanently in my gut. I despise myself for such despondency. A man gave away the final months of his life to award me my freedom, and I owe it to him to be happy. But as Christoph said, *Give it time, my friend. Give it time.*

I arrive at La Seigneurie later than I should, grasping a tray of seedlings to give to my neighbours. The fire is already lit and it is a roarer. Everyone looks happy, even the dogs. Poppy finally had her pups who are all older dogs now. Dame Sibyl kept them, but goodness knows how she fed them. In Jersey, the Nazis ate dogs just to stay alive. This is how my mind thinks now.

It is my birthday so I am certain that there will be a surprise and it will be a cake. After coupons and shortages, a cake is exactly what we all need, but I have no appetite for it. Nevertheless, despite my misgivings, it is a wonderful party. There is even wine, brought over from St Malo this morning. I have spent most of the evening talking to Peter about roses. I feel most relaxed when talking to Peter about roses – or anything horticultural come to that. He understands that I do not wish to speak about the war.

At eight-fifteen Dame Sibyl begs for silence, or Joseph does (why have a dog and bark yourself?) and before we know where we are, I am standing on the terrace and the whole of the island is singing happy birthday. A cake appears and I suddenly feel overwhelmed with gratitude and yet all I can think about is Christoph, and how he enabled this, and if he is watching down on us from heaven like an angel, although not 'like' an angel, because surely, he is one.

The birthday gifts and surprises do not end there. The islanders take turns to queue on the terrace to offer me handmade gifts. I cannot speak. It is all simply too much. And then Dame Sibyl bids for silence again in order to bring in my main present. Main? Has what I have received so far not been enough? Clearly not, for I am told to look to the patio doors for my next gift, and my heart lifts when I see it – her – because from behind the swag curtain an old friend appears. It is Fortune, come especially at Dame Sibyl's invitation, and two steps behind her out pops Bunny. I am overwhelmed.

But still, Dame Sibyl explains once I have sought out wine and cake for my guests, the surprises are not over yet. My next surprise, however, is particularly special and is waiting for me in the privacy of the study. I can only pray that it is the gift I have been waiting for, and for a very long time.

It is not. And yet the sight of my gift is a miracle all the same. I have no idea how she has done it, but then, Dame Sibyl's talents for making the impossible happen seem to know no bounds – for my gift, the best of the evening, is my brother, Sascha.

Chapter Fifty-Five

Sark, Christmas Eve, 1945

I invited Sascha to live with me and he gratefully accepted. The house is not as lonely to me now that he is here, although there is one downside to the plan: I have shown him the garden and I do believe it is lost to me, but then, as I once told Christoph, Sascha was really the true gardener of the family, not I.

Dame Sibyl had already explained to Sascha that Christoph had died, but his reaction on reading Christoph's letter was extreme emotion. I will never know what was written in that letter, but somehow Christoph found the words to award my brother a degree of peace and happiness, and only a truly wonderful soul would ever have the ability to do that. I worried before handing over the letter that Sascha would resent me – that he would think my life had been traded for Christoph's, but he did not. He was not surprised to learn that Christoph had taken such action.

'He knew nothing but kindness and a true capacity for

love,' said Sascha, a day or so after reading the letter. 'We were so lucky to have known him.'

'We were,' I agreed. 'And remember, the teapot is yours whenever you need it.'

'It is ours,' he said. 'And I don't need it.'

And so, we have decorated the cottage for Christmas. Never before have I added much more than a sprig of holly to the door, but Sascha insisted that we do – 'Think of Prince Albert,' he pleaded two days ago, his arms full of greenery collected from the garden. 'Is it not in our German heritage?'

I couldn't help but agree that it was, and that is why we have spent this evening drinking elderberry wine (this season's and all the worse for having not yet matured) and draping garlands of holly and ivy around the place. We sit at the kitchen table making paperchains for the Christmas tree. Despite this bonhomie, Sascha has seemed distracted all night.

'You keep watching the door,' I say, adding the finishing touches to a paper angel. 'You haven't arranged a surprise party, have you? Because there is barely enough wine left for the two of us, let alone Joseph and his friends.'

'I thought I heard a noise,' he says, pushing his chair backwards.

'It will be bats,' I say. 'They were the only thing our brethren did not eat!'

'You will be right, of course. But I shall take a quick look.'

'The war has left you jumpy!' I say as he heads out of the door. He appears not ten seconds later.

'Bats,' he says, smiling. 'I am tired though, and my mind is full of thoughts of bygone years tonight. They are memories I would not wish to forget, just yet. Would you mind if I retire early with a hot drink and my thoughts?'

I shake my head and smile. 'But perhaps we should raise a

glass first,' I say, raising my glass. My eyes brighten at the thought of the words.

'To Christoph!' I search Sascha's face, hoping to have done the right thing.

Sascha raises his glass. 'To Christoph,' he repeats. 'The most wonderful man in the world.'

I carry my lantern to bed not ten minutes later having picked up a book Sascha suggested I read having taken it from Dame Sibyl's library. It is a biography of a Buddhist monk who spent twenty years alone in meditation. I wonder what on earth the monk has to say that facilitates the book being so thick … I shall no doubt be fast asleep before page six.

The book falls to the floor at just before eleven p.m. with the bookmark positioned at page thirty. Sascha was quite correct – it is a surprisingly riveting read. I have just turned over for the second time in an attempt to get myself settled when I hear a noise – a scratch of some sort – on the window outside. I turn over and ignore it – it will be the bats again. But no, it cannot be bats, for there are surely stones of some sort hitting the window pane. I pull back the covers and head to the window. There is a moon, not full but sufficient to glance around the garden. I open the window, look outside, and notice that Sascha has opened his window too.

'What is it?' he whispers.

'Those bats again,' I answer. 'And why are you whispering?'

'In case it's intruders!' he says, and I can't help but laugh. My brother, the so-called terror of the Reich, worried about intruders! Then I hear a voice.

'*What light through yonder window breaks*,' it says – *she* says. '*It is the east and Romeo is the sun. Arise, fair sun, and …*'

But Juliet is not allowed to finish her line, for I have flown down the stairs and sprinted out into the garden before she can even think of 'killing the envious moon'.

'My love, my love, my love,' I say, taking my Juliet – my Sophie – into my arms. I kiss her head, her nose, her eyes, her ears, and finally, her mouth. 'I waited and I searched,' I say, holding her at arm's length now, searching her face in the limited light. 'Have you been safe? Have you been free? Where have you been?'

'Oh, everywhere and nowhere,' she says. 'A prisoner for a time. But let's not think of that

now. It's over. My hair has grown back, you see.'

'I do see, my love. I do see.'

We embrace again, and then hear another voice from yonder window break. It is Sascha. I

had forgotten all about Sascha.

'Who is it, Sebastian?' he says. 'Shall I fetch the poker?!'

I look at Sophie and shout towards to the window, '*No need. It is only Juliet. She doth teach the torches to burn bright. It seems she hangs upon the cheeks of night …*'

'Ah, right. Shall I go back to bed then?' he says.

'I think you probably should,' I shout up, laughing.

I turn to lead Sophie inside the house, but she doesn't want to come in.

'I thought we might take a walk across La Coupée,' she says. 'We said we would walk home together, remember? I'd like to do that. And also, suddenly, everything, all that we have seen and done, it seems a little … overwhelming.'

'I know, my love,' I say, pulling her in close. 'I know.'

She nods into my chest and I feel her tears come.

And then I remember our promise, and even though I am wearing only my nightshirt, I take Sophie's hand in mine and we wander out of the garden and into the moonlight. She needs to fulfil the dream of coming home, the dream that must have endured her through whatever horror she has experienced since we said goodbye. One day she might tell me, she might tell me everything, but until then, like Christoph said, we are all just children in the playground, playing games until the bell rings.

Afterword

Please indulge me with a quick note on historical content, particularly with regards to Dame Sibyl Hathaway, who really did exist, and was every bit the force of nature in real life as she was in the novel. During my research I soon realised that it would be impossible to write a story set on Sark during this time period and not include her – and why would you not? Her sheer force of character was an absolute gift. I shan't go into detail about her here – hopefully I characterised her well enough in the novel – but I'd like to take this opportunity to recommend her autobiography as further reading which is titled, quite simply, *Dame of Sark, an autobiography*. I do believe that Dame Sibyl is my all time favourite real life character and an absolute icon. Her dynamism, bravery, leadership and sheer determination during the war years was astounding.

And when it comes to the discussion of incredible real life women, I should also mention Nurse Edith Cavell. Although Edith was alive during the First rather than the Second World War, she was the starting block for the whole novel. As discussed in the story, Edith was executed by the Germans in

Belgium in 1915, which was seen at the time internationally as an unnecessary and extremely controversial action – that being, the execution of a woman and a medic. There is much written about her story and her ethos for life, and during my research I began to wonder what it must have been like to have been a member of the firing squadron that took her life and how traumatic that might have been … this is how Sebastian was formed. Edith's final thoughts, beliefs and feelings are not imagined by me but taken directly from the notes written by the two pastors who attended her, one of them being Pastor Le Seur, also mentioned in the story.

My final note on historical content is to say that although General Wölf is a fictional character, he was inspired by an account I read regarding General Dietrich von Choltitz, who was the last commander of Nazi-occupied Paris. After the war he asserted that he disobeyed Hitler's orders to destroy Paris and (according to Wikipedia) chose to surrender it to the Free French instead due to his affection for the city's history and culture and his belief that Hitler had become insane. This account is disputed in some sources but nevertheless provided me with the idea behind the thoughts and actions of my own fictional German General.

Finally, I'd like to thank you from the bottom of my heart for reading. I do so hope that you enjoyed it.

Acknowledgments

As ever, a very special thank you to my editor, Charlotte Ledger, for her unswerving guidance, encouragement, and friendship. Thank you to my sparkly new agent, Hannah Todd; to Adrian and Emily Clark; my sister, Julia, for slogging down to London with me; and also my fab authorly friend, Mandy James. And finally, to my husband, son, and dog, I offer the biggest thank you of all.

ONE MORE CHAPTER

One More Chapter is an
award-winning global
division of HarperCollins.

Sign up to our newsletter to get our
latest eBook deals and stay up to date
with our weekly Book Club!
<u>Subscribe here.</u>

Meet the team at
<u>www.onemorechapter.com</u>

Follow us!

 <u>@OneMoreChapter_</u>
 <u>@OneMoreChapter</u>
 <u>@onemorechapterhc</u>

Do you write unputdownable fiction?
We love to hear from new voices.
Find out how to submit your novel at
<u>www.onemorechapter.com/submissions</u>